W9-CLI-653

THE
HOUSE
OF
CRAY

THE HOUSE OF CRAY

Pamela Hill

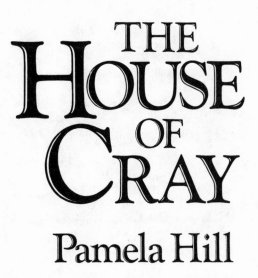

OLD CHARLES TOWN LIBRARY
200 E. WASHINGTON ST.
CHARLES TOWN, W.VA. 25414

St. Martin's Press • New York

82002691
OLD CHARLES TOWN LIBRARY

Copyright © 1982 by Pamela Hill
For information, write: St. Martin's Press
175 Fifth Avenue, New York, N.Y. 10010
Manufactured in the United States of America

Library of Congress Cataloging in Publication Data
Hill, Pamela.
The house of Cray.

I. Title.
PR6058.I446H6   1982   823'.914   81-21533
ISBN 0-312-39260-5   AACR2

First published in Great Britain by Robert Hale Ltd.

For Ursula, Edna,
David and John

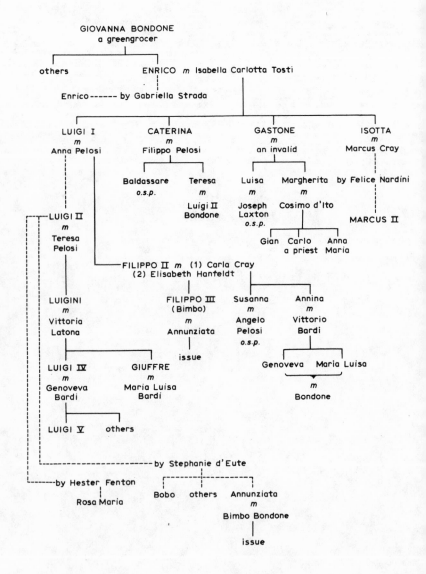

BONDONE FAMILIES

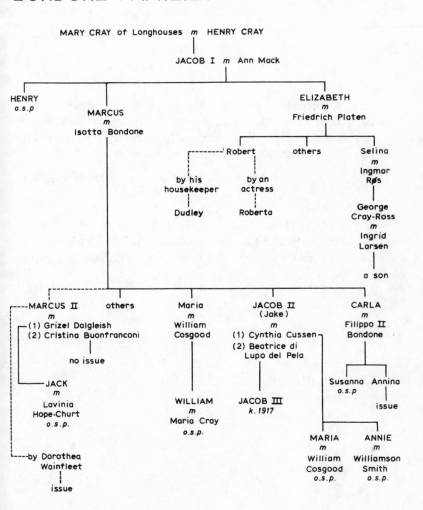

I have a (probably crackpot) theory that though Charles I was clearly the father of James II, he was *not* the father of Charles II. They were totally unlike in mind and body. And Henrietta Maria . . . was certainly not bred for fidelity.

Phrase from a private letter to the author.

The paternity of Louis XIV was openly ascribed to Richelieu at the time of his birth and the King's brother, Gaston d'Orléans, was exiled for publicly saying that the baby Dauphin was a bastard.

Evelyn Anthony, *Anne of Austria*.

PART ONE

1

The convent slumbered on its hill in the autumn sunshine, its honey-coloured bulk screened by olive trees already turning dull. Beyond, criss-crossed by the dusty white road, were other hills, climbing slope upon steep slope until at last, with an elusive colour like black grapes seen through mist, the Apennines hung. Behind them again the sky was metallic blue, and beneath that sky, still clad in light summer dresses and wide straw hats, the young lady boarders were taking their twice-weekly lesson in the use of watercolours from the visiting drawing-master, Signor Ercole Cerulla.

Signor Ercole was middle-aged, with a wife in the town and four children to rear; so there was no romance evident about him, except in his mind's eye, which appraised the day, the heat, and the young ladies favourably enough to cause him to flick at the tip of his carefully dyed moustache with elegant fingers. He then gazed at the trees with their ultramarine shadows, lastly at the sketch-blocks whereon his pupils worked; and frowned a little. Above in the hill field pumpkins were lying in bright rows ready for lifting, and between them the nuns, hooded like mules, walked backwards before the Mother Superior. It was the daily recreation and nobody gave it any thought; nobody, that is, except Lucy Nardini, whose cruel brush had already sketched the portly figure of Donna Maria della Misericordia herself with a swashbuckling curve of the robes that suggested caricature. "Gently, gently, my child," murmured Signor Ercole, who was a kind man. "If the good mother sees that it will hurt her."

"Well, she is too fat, and it is as well if she is reminded of it. She should fast more often. How can they walk backwards like that without tripping over their habits, especially as they cannot turn their heads?" Lucy's tongue, narrow as a snake's, flickered over her thin pink lips; she gave her enigmatic smile and tossed her head. The rest giggled undutifully. There were not many senior girls to teach; by this age, thankfully, most had been taken away by their papas and mammas to attend finishing-schools in

11

Arezzo, in Florence, or even in Paris. Isotta Bondone was to go there after Christmas, late because she had been ill last year. She was now recovered, and painted quietly and without talent, her pretty head bent so that an expanse of white neck showed between cotton lace collar and straw hat. Signor Ercole's gaze rested on it for some moments before he recalled himself. The little Isotta was a parlour-boarder and her parents paid the convent more money than anyone else's. For this reason Isotta was accorded many privileges. The good gentleman did not see, for he was behind her, her dark eyes, redeemed from stupidity by a gleam of toffee-gold in their depths, wander from her painting to the exquisite small watch which hung on a fine gold chain about her neck. The hands, moving across an enamelled face of flower-posies on a turquoise ground, travelled too slowly. Isotta gave a sigh, and turned her gaze to meet the sardonic blue-green one of her bosom friend, Lucy. Nobody but Lucy would dare caricature the nuns so; by now she had done with them and was painting pumpkins in green, chrome yellow and orange, with vivid stripes. Isotta breathed her name, softly.

"It is almost time," she said in a low voice, and looked at her watch and then at her painting, which showed scrabbles of nothing at all. Then a notable thing happened, very quietly. Lucy held out her narrow palm and Isotta pressed two gold coins into it. Lucy slipped one coin into her bodice and then rose, went to where Signor Ercole was, and slid the other into that elegant hand. Nobody said anything, saw anything, or if they did reflected that certain temptations might well assail a father of four whose salary, like most things at the convent, was frugal. Signor Ercole strolled, like a figure in ballet, to Isotta's abandoned painting, took up her brush and began to fill the paper with masterly strokes portraying olive-branches. Lucy returned to her stool and her work. Isotta had already gone.

She walked at first sedately, so as not to be remarked by any sharp eye cast from the pumpkin-field above; then having gained their shelter started to run swiftly between the trees, her pale dress flitting in and out of the dappled shadows, her hat flying back on its chin-ribbon to reveal dark hair, fine as silk, clustered in little curls about the face and neck; her lips, parted, were the colour of ripe strawberries, and the haste made her cheeks pink. Fool, she was telling herself already, he will not be there waiting for me; he hardly ever is waiting for me; I must always do so for him. It is understood.

But today he was there, by some miracle, tall, nonchalant and green-eyed, with a skin swarthy as a Moor's which showed off his harsh attractive features; the young Count himself, Felice Nardini, Lucy's cousin, all six feet of him enveloping at last Isotta's small form; they melted into one another like two snow-flakes, and there came the sound of kissing; hot, demanding, still unsatisfied, enough perhaps to alarm and shock the nuns on the hill; then the sound changed and became a murmuring, a demand and an eager, muffled response, then soon a moaning. Isotta moaned, softly and still half in fear, although this was the ninth time she had given herself to him. It was as though they were married, the rough thrusting part of him soon within her, deliciously, incomparably; soon now would come the climax, when she would cry out and bite his shoulder like a mad thing, a beast, a little beast for the time sated, but with her hot blood surging still.

Count Felix—he had English Jacobite blood, and he preferred his intimates to use that version of his name—spared a glance for the exposed, white satin thigh, above the cotton stocking with its blue silk garter; and thumbed all three. It had taken him, during the summer holiday they had all three spent together at Lucy's uncle's place in the mountains, a whole fortnight to seduce Isotta. At the time when she was unattainable he had been mad for her, but by now she was only one more little bourgeoise; her father, although rich, was nobody. Count Felix slaked his immediate desire, and waited a little before taking Isotta again. One had always to keep an eye out for those damned nuns, for one could not rely on the water-colour lessons not being more closely supervised, especially if, after her walk in the field, as sometimes happened, the Superior herself came down. The Count smiled a little; the prospect of being found in this particular situation by Donna Maria della Misericordia amused him. There was no risk to him personally; his family had owned lands in the region for centuries, and were closely related to the dead Countess Ildefonsa di Lupo del Pela, who had endowed the convent.

Isotta raised her small hand, and stroked his face. "Why are you smiling?" she asked softly. Her body was agreeably on fire, as though the sun coursed in her veins. Presently, if they might, they would make love again, and then she must go. If only there could be a time once more like it had been in the mountains, when they had lain and lain together in the shadow of the pines, and had secretly bathed naked in the lake! It was fortunate, if one might put it so, that Lucy's parents were dead and that her uncle, the old Count, had not troubled to provide a duenna for the holiday.

Felice prevaricated and would not tell her why he had smiled. "*Cara mia,*" he said, softly and predictably, "little white flower, white rose, *carissima mia*. Why, you are as white as if you were an Englishwoman; my fingers are brown as walnuts against your flesh. Again, little flower, again for us, quickly, quickly; then I must go."

The second time was less sweet; they were tired and he withdrew early from her. Isotta began to arrange her clothes, discontent still surging; always it ended thus! "When will you come to me again, Felix?" she asked him. It was like a suppliant whining for crumbs; already she had the fear that there would come a time when he would not return to her, would come no more to the olive groves, and she would die, a nymph forsaken. The prospect of Paris had seemed such wonder once, when Papa first suggested it, but now—

Felix had turned away to button himself. "I must go back to Padua on Monday," he lied; there was still another week's vacation, which he would spend in town. He found his law studies dull, and constantly sought to enliven them; well, this had not been a bad interlude. He felt tenderness for Isotta suddenly and was distressed to see tears on her long dark lashes, a fringe of silk against her cheeks bearing silver beads, or perhaps crystal. If she went on crying, weariness would no doubt claim him; and her tears would spoil his coat. But now, for their last moments with one another, he was tender.

"I will write, and address the letters to Lucy," he promised. He took Isotta in his arms and began to kiss her mouth, her throat, her eyes; she was gasping again and her hat, which she had replaced, was awry; as well to straighten it, for through the trees at last came Lucy, seeking them, amusement in her face; what fools they were!

"The Superior is on her way down," she said. "We'd better run, Isotta; old tin-whiskers is upset and might lose his job."

She giggled as they ran off together, hands already clasped in one another's; they twisted to blow a kiss to Cousin Felice, that

14

doughty lover, as they rounded the corner. He did not see it; he had already turned away and would walk the few yards to where his horse waited, hidden and patient, its reins tied loosely to a tree. By the time he did turn, at the crumbling wall, there was no sign of either girl. He was thankful to get away; he disliked unpleasantness, and now, if questions were ever asked, one could deny everything, or blame the drawing-master. He vaulted the wall in one leap, and was gone.

"Your painting is much improved, Isotta," said the Superior heavily, regarding the brush-strokes on the paper. Then she lifted her myopic gaze to the girl. "Mercy, child, how flushed you are! The sun is not good. Go back inside, to the cool parlour. Why, the child's torn her dress; a pity, such fine embroidery!" She plucked at the snagged threads, removing a leaf that had lodged against Isotta's shoulder. Lucy came to the rescue, her sang-froid unabated; the Superior had not even noticed the caricature.

"It is the trees, Reverend Mother. Their branches need pruning."

The Superior ignored her, in fact only half heard her; a poor relation of the Nardini, and pert besides! Isotta Bondone, on the other hand, meant money; a pity she had to go soon; it would not do to have to tell Enrico Bondone his daughter was out of sorts next time he came up the hill. This time in particular, Donna Maria had reason for wanting to be on good terms with the art-dealer; there was something she hoped to sell him. "Take off the gown and give it to Sister Chiara, and she will mend it like new," she told Isotta, fussing over her like a mother hen. Isotta, borne away, desperately sought out Lucy's gaze with her own. The other's eye closed in a wink.

Some days later, the heat had not abated; the road was white with dust even in the early morning, when it should have been laid by the dew. At such an hour, to get the best of the day, a young man was riding towards the hills. Seen in the saddle he was a graceful and almost regal figure, slender and composed, with a high round forehead, chestnut hair, well-marked brows and magnificent whiskers in the style of Signor Ercole, except that Marcus Cray did not use dye. He wore a small trimmed beard which made him look older than his age, which was twenty-four. His

15

eyes, his best feature, large, dark, hooded, and for no present reason mournful, were fixed on the near distance; accordingly he was unprepared when the horse stumbled, and, narrowly regaining his balance, dismounted with lithe ease. Seen on the ground it was evident that he was of small build, short-legged, of no compelling presence. But the hands which examined the hired beast's lame hoof were beautiful, slender, shapely, and with long sensitive fingers like a woman's. The horse, which had been got in Arezzo, stayed quiet under this stranger's touch; there was a loose shoe. Marcus frowned, the vertical creases extending up over the high forehead like an expression of personal pain. There would be nothing for it but to walk with the lame animal to the nearest inn or cottage, where he could hope to get word to a smith. He led the horse gently, talking to it in a low voice. "Easy, good one, easy; none will hurry you, tread lightly, take it slow." But in fact to arrive late did not suit him at all; he had hoped to be received before anyone else at the Convent of the Perpetual Adoration, and now, if they had an inkling of the news he had himself received, dealers would be out ere long. But perhaps they had not yet heard; his own old father, left behind at home, had a knack of earmarking such news before other men.

"The Frankish Crucifix, Markie. They say—" and his loose mouth had slobbered a trifle with eagerness, inflicting on Marcus the dual feelings he always had for the old man, half disgust and half affection. Old Jacob Cray was both scholar and dilettante and clung to his only remaining son after the elder boy's death. He would treat Marcus with whimsical extravagance nowadays, as witness the late matter of the Featherstone heiress which had only made a fool of them both. It would never have served to marry that overbred young woman; she had disliked him, and had aroused no spark of feeling in himself. "But an heiress, Markie! Take yourself to market; you have all the accomplishments to please a woman; a rich wife would repair our fortunes here at Longhouses, and it is your duty, boy—ay, your duty—to wed one." But then, after it had been made clearly evident that this particular heiress was not for him, old Jacob had uttered no single word in reproach for the tailor's bills incurred in fitting Marcus out as a suitor and his close friend George Massingbird as companion, and had instead told his son to travel alone into Italy to buy, at the lowest price possible, this Frankish Crucifix, said to be the same brought south long ago by Charlemagne when he rode to Italy to receive the Lombard Crown.

Walking alongside his liability of a beast, without George Massingbird's irresponsible gay chatter to cheer him and make the time pass, Marcus let his conscientious, somewhat slow mind assess the matter. He had been happy enough to escape from England for a while, to forget his rejection by Alethea Featherstone and, still more, her family, who had shown him stiff courtesy but had not encouraged his suit. It was pleasant to see new places, and he had taken a shy delight in trying out his Italian, a smattering of which he had been taught, together with French and Latin, as a boy. That had been while his elder brother Harry was still alive, handsome confident Harry who excelled at all sports, leaving Marcus, then the least important member of the family, alone in the spartan schoolroom. He had been a delicate child and it had not at first been expected that he would live. His mother, a blonde neurotic Scotswoman, had taken little heed of him. Harry and the girl, Elizabeth, had filled their parents' days when there was no bickering; old Jacob had been pleased enough, their mother fiercely resentful, when beautiful gay Betty had married a young German lecturer in semantics at Edinburgh University. "They will never have any money, and who are his family? their mother had fretted; and she had been right, for Friedrich Platen had died of pneumonia at thirty-eight, leaving an attractive widow (but Betty would never marry again) with three strapping sons and a small plain clever daughter, Selina. Come to think of it, it was a long time since Marcus had seen his sister; the distance was inconvenient, and at Harry's death she had not come to the funeral. Harry dead! It would have seemed an impossible thought; all that animal strength stilled, fevered, drained, gone. Marcus himself had also caught typhoid fever but he, the weakling, recovered; after that there had been much to do in the comforting of his parents. His mother had never recovered; she had died soon, no doubt of grief, and now there was only old Jacob left alone in his firelit room, with the portrait on the wall of his unknown, beautiful, disgraced mother, whose name was never spoken at Longhouses and whom Betty was said to resemble. There it was; a lot of water had run under bridges, and now he, Marcus, was the Cray heir with all that it meant, and must no doubt look about him for another rich wife. The prospect daunted him.

17

He had walked on with the horse for some miles before he saw an inn, half hidden against the slope of the hill, of the kind met with in this country, half *albergo* and half shop, with cheese for sale and three or four pumpkins lying, one cut open to show the ripe flesh. Nearby, a thin goat grazed. Outside was a table and a bench, with a fig tree shading them, and Marcus went to the place thankfully when he had made arrangements for the horse. He would sit for a while and drink wine and refresh himself, giving up the notion of an early arrival by now; the walk had been hot.

He had knocked at the open door, and a middle-aged woman in a black apron came out. Marcus stumbled through the Italian phrases he needed, and the woman yelled "Agostino!" and a young man like a god sidled round from the back of the shop, took the reins and led the limping horse away. On Marcus' query the woman tried to reassure him; yes, yes, there was a place where it could be free of the sun and the flies; there was a smith in the region; Agostino would fetch him as soon as it might be done.

I must walk to the convent, that is evident, thought Marcus. Aloud he said, "Is it far?" They had brought him rough wine in a flask; he sat by the table and raised it to his lips again and again, glad of the cool draught. His limbs had begun to stiffen and he was not anxious for the further walk. But that would not be necessary, the *padrona* told him; today was the day Signor Enrico Bondone came by custom to visit his daughter who was at the convent school; one need only wait to be taken in his carriage.

Marcus' frown showed; he would have preferred to arrive alone. Then an echo of recognition came to him. "Signor Bondone," he repeated. "Tell me of him."

The *padrona* replied that Signor Bondone was famous, and almost as though a bottle had been rubbed her small thin spouse, wizened as a monkey behind huge greying moustaches, came out, a finger scratching at his shaven head, and added that yes, everyone knew Signor Enrico Bondone, he had a great shop in Florence full of pictures which brought him much money, though he did not paint the pictures, and his brother-in-law, Filippo Pelosi, had a prosperous photographic studio in Milan. In fact, the *padrone* erred; Filippo Pelosi was no relation and his tie with the Bondone clan was tenuous and complicated.

So it was indeed Bondone, the art-dealer, who was to come to visit his daughter. Marcus' hopes sank; certainly he could not stay in the field against such a bidder, but perhaps, although it was unlikely, Bondone had not yet heard of the impending sale of the crucifix. One could only hope, and meantime trudge on; it was five miles to the convent, he had elicited, and he would sooner walk than wait for the dealer and his carriage, which after all might not be here for some hours; these people had no notion of haste. He had already written to the Superior to expect him, and preferred not to keep the lady waiting. However his expectations of being able to purchase the rare crucifix were now very low; perhaps it had always been a chimera, another of old Jacob's enthusiastic whimsies. There was not enough money to rival such as Bondone.

He had downed his wine, and had risen to pay what he owed and to make his excuses for not waiting longer, when the carriage in fact came in sight. It was an expensive equipage, well cared for and polished to a degree, although the road-dust clung by now to its sides and its elegant yellow-painted wheels. A good pair of matched greys drew it, and a footman in livery stood behind. The carriage having stopped, he jumped down and opened the rear door.

A middle-aged gentleman emerged who resembled Mephistopheles. He wore a caped coat, despite the heat, and his tall hat was set on his head at a flamboyant angle. He removed it to speak to the *padrona*, revealing a helmet of thick iron-grey hair and eyebrows in ·twin defiant peaks. His hook-nosed face was smiling, the words spilling from the full red lips before Signor Bondone was inside the inn. It was evident that he was persuasive and well liked. In instants everyone crowded out to greet him, and he chucked the *padrona* under the chin as though she had been a young serving-maid and the greatest beauty in Italy, which pleased her greatly.

"Make one of your good grape tarts for the *signorina* today, Emilia, and perhaps before that a bacon stew. At the convent they eat nothing but cabbage soup and their own pumpkins. After our little drive I will bring her here to you and we will eat."

His instructions once taken, he listened to the tale about Marcus' horse. "But the English gentleman must of course travel with me," he said, surveying Marcus with the light, hypnotic gaze which had successfully seduced many a young woman. It was evident that the art-dealer liked what he saw, for he bowed a little, and came over to where Marcus stood. "I am Enrico Bondone, of Florence," he said simply. "Will you not join me in a glass of wine? My footman Pablo will be glad of the rest, for he is like myself and loves the rough Chianti they serve here. We will travel to the convent afterwards together; it is a pleasure to me to have company."

Marcus replied with his own name and was about to offer to pay for Bondone's wine and also that of Pablo, for he was keenly sensible of favours. But the art-dealer's eyebrows had already disappeared into his peaked hairline, and he spread out his gloved hands.

"Your name is Cray, *signore*? I have an old acquaintance of that name, who like myself admires and collects beautiful objects and who lives in the north of England. He and I, in our youth—"

"Jacob Cray is my father." Mark had withdrawn into shyness at first meeting with such ebullience, but he was aware of reluctant pleasure when Bondone now advanced upon him, opened his embrace and kissed the Englishman on both cheeks. "The son of an old friend!" he cried. "It is the providence of God that we meet here in these hills. You must come to my showroom, Signore Cray; I have a fine Tintoretto which needs cleaning, that I want you to see and tell your father of when you return. But you will not return quite yet? Having so fortunately met it would be a pleasure to prolong the meeting. You must also behold my daughter. Will you not dine with us here later today? Emilia, a still larger tart and more stew; the English gentleman will remain with us."

They drank the wine together, shy Marcus saying very little, even finding an old half-forgotten hesitation in his speech which had afflicted him as a boy. It would sometimes return although he had largely conquered it. To oblige Bondone suited him well enough; he had no immediate plans after seeing the Superior and her crucifix, and it would be pleasant to continue for a while in the company of this forthcoming and, evidently, well-found gentleman. As for the schoolgirl daughter, that must be endured; the father would talk so much that he himself would not, perhaps, be called upon to contribute much to the conversation.

But the talk in the carriage was mostly in the form of questioning, and Enrico Bondone seemed genuinely concerned with news of Jacob Cray's health, which had never been good; he told one or two cautious stories embodying remarks made in the old man's youth; he probed with knowledge into the details of the *objets d'art* Jacob had acquired over the years, and seemed keenly interested in the architecture of Longhouses. Had the Romans indeed built a pavement there? A unique possession. Now, today—

The elfish face surveyed the controlled, courteous young man who was the son of so famous a connoisseur. In Bondone's light eyes was a touch of as much wistfulness as he ever allowed himself to display. He preferred young men of bravura, flaunting the insolence of their youth, ready to show enterprise and perpetrate rash deeds, such as he had permitted himself twenty or thirty years ago, before marriage to his Isabella. He had little time for the two spineless sons of the marriage, Luigi and Gastone; it was as though God punished him for having married his wife for her money, to set the business on a secure footing; his own mother had kept a greengrocer's. His elder daughter, Caterina, had been married while still very young to the enterprising young photographer in Milan, and only the other day had sent home a stiff family group with herself, Filippo—the man was sandy-haired and unattractive—and in front of a potted plant the engaging dark-eyed baby Baldassare, whose eyes looked out of the picture beyond one, like a little angel. But Isotta! His younger daughter, almost an afterthought, was worth all the rest, he was convinced. Bondone adored her, and was determined that she should make a good marriage. His questioning had already made plain to him the fact that this young heir of his old friend Jacob Cray was neither wedded nor affianced. It was early days yet, but if it could be—"He has understanding of great art," the dealer told himself. He had brought into the conversation Titian, Rubens, the Dutch masters, and had been met by a quiet competence, showing that the other was not ignorant but waited to hear the older man's comments. That was as it should be. An admirable young fellow, if somewhat too grave; and the Cray blood was ancient even though there was no title, Isabella might be placated.

The carriage bowled at last into a small paved courtyard beyond which cool arched Romanesque cloisters reared. Mark followed his patron out of the carriage, gazing at the pleasing symmetry of the building; perhaps twelfth century, with later accretions. It must be pleasant to live here even at the cost of parting with the world; in such a climate, and with the beauty of the hills beyond! Yet he himself would never put down roots in a foreign country; he enjoyed the experience, but would soon be longing again for

21

England, the grey skies and the long stone dykes of his heartland, and his own fine horses between his thighs. He had made himself master horses as a small child, despite all discouragement; any stallion now would own him master, and together they would execute any figure laid down by the riding-schools. In a way horses had taken the place of playmates for Marcus, for these he never had; he had been backward and his contemporaries had scorned him. Harry and Betty had pitied him, it was true; but pity is not friendship. Then George Massingbird had come, with his wit and splendour; and laughter, so loud that Marcus had at first distrusted him, but Jacob Cray had from the first adored George as a visitation from the gods. George would be keeping the old man from fretting now, telling him bawdy stories.

Marcus recalled himself to the present and followed Bondone across the court to where there was a door with a small grille. "This, you comprehend," he said, "was once a palace. It was in the dowry of the young Countess Ildefonsa del Salle, and being devout she gave it on her marriage to the nuns, who had nowhere to go. They are fortunate to have such a place, the fields and the farm. It had belonged to the Contessa's family for centuries, since the time of the Normans. The Conte di Lupo del Pela, whom she married, may well have grudged it to them, but said nothing."

The spatulate thumb and fingers fastened themselves about the bell-rope which hung by the door, and jangled it absently. "There is a thing I wish them to show me here," he said. "You say you have an appointment with the Superior. I too await her." Marcus protested that he would not keep the other waiting. "Then let us go in together," said Bondone gaily, and Marcus knew he was very well aware their errand was the same, leaving aside the outing for Bondone's daughter. He was resigned; it had been something of a forlorn hope that he himself should ever purchase the famous crucifix with such funds as were available. But there would be much to tell Jacob on return.

A pair of eyes had appeared at the grille and Bondone beamed widely. "Let us in, Sister Josefina, it is I, with a friend," he called. A smiling nun, still clad in her linen apron, opened the door forthwith. "We would see the Superior," the dealer told her, and they were ushered down long cool corridors of patterned stone, less ancient than the pavements at Longhouses. Marcus tried to remember the impression he had of twining bands, fish, and circles as they walked by. Each symbol would have a meaning, and he was aware of his own limited knowledge and swore to amend it; he had always responded to the challenge of stored unknown beauty and never rested till he was expert. Those cloisters, with their cushion-capitals, the stone too soft for detail to survive the weather of six centuries! He gazed beyond the arches to an end door, which led to the enclosure; another was opened to the right, and they were confronted with a larger grille, large enough for a head and shoulders to be seen through it. Presently the shutters opened to reveal those of the Superior, attended by two nuns who stayed in the background. Marcus felt some curiosity at the sight of this woman, who lived out all her life enclosed behind walls. She was scarcely ethereal; as Lucy had already noted, she was too fat. Her eyes scanned Marcus and then Bondone, who was already in the midst of a burst of talk. "Greetings, good mother! You have something to show me, I believe, and it must be shown likewise to my friend here, who is an authority on mediaeval art." He winked at Marcus; he was lying and knew it, and Donna Maria knew that he knew it. She turned her head aside and murmured to her nuns. Presently a package was brought, wrapped carefully in linen.

"It will not pass through the grille," she said, and her plump fingers unwrapped the object reverently and held it up for the two men to see. Marcus Cray's eyes widened and shone. It was an ivory crucifix carved with such detail that the thin hanging figure of Christ was almost rivalled. Heads of twining beasts and fish, small men or devils supported the cross; there were arabesques reminiscent of the illuminated texts in Irish monasteries. The ivory had hardly yellowed with age, having been kept carefully. Marcus turned to Bondone, whose eyes were still intent on the figure. It came to him that despite appearances, the dealer was a religious man. Presently, without averting his gaze, he spoke.

"So this is the *croce francesca*. A thought of pagan belief still evident, I think? It is like the famous casket with Wayland the lame smith and scenes from the Gospels. And yet it is different from anything I have ever seen."

"Or I," said Marcus, adding boldly "You must greatly regret selling, *madama*." He had never before addressed a nun.

"It is the hard times. Also we are continually anxious lest it be stolen, as it is irreplaceable. Some time ago I took it out of the place in the rock where it was kept. But such a thing should be seen, not hidden. You are interested, Signore Bondone? I will give it to the little Isotta to carry out to you, and she shall also show you and your friend the place where it once rested. I expect many offers, and should wait for the best of them." She looked openly at Bondone, who bowed.

"You know I would give you a good price," he said, "and would see that it was used with dignity and care."

"I should be happy for you to have it, if it may be so; but I should wait for other offers."

"*Basta*! You should let some fat German have it? Never, never! Let it come to me, then you need not feel that the *croce* has gone from you. I will visit you often, and tell you how it fares."

"But the price, *signore*?" They haggled for moments; of course, thought Marcus, she will sell it to him in the end. There has to be this play, back and forth; she will not have received as many offers as all that. So exquisite a thing, and so old! He forgot his shyness and spoke again.

"What is its history, *madama*? How did it come to be here? I have heard the—the tale of Charlemagne's gift."

She shrugged, the black veil shifting against the sombre habit. "All I know is what others know, and what I had from my predecessor," she said. "There was a hermit who lived here in the cave, before the *castello* was built in the time of the Crusades; it was, you understand, a nobleman's dwelling then, but always with its chapel. The great king stopped here, and gave the hermit the *croce* in exchange for some favour, perhaps his prayers. That is all I can tell you. Isotta will show you the place. Signor Bondone will inform me?" She still had her mind on bargaining.

"I will inform you without delay," Bondone said. "But first I must examine the *croce*." Mephistopheles smiled agreeably, his moustache exuberant.

"Assuredly you shall do so. I need not ask you to have a care, for it is old. You know of such things."

Farewells were said, the grille shutters were closed behind the mesh, and the visitors were sent to wait in the convent parlour. Presently the door opened and a young girl came in, lashes demurely lowered, the crucifix, its linen wrappings loosened, in her hands. She gave the little bobbing curtsy the convent pupils acquired, then presented a smooth cheek for her father's kiss. Bondone, still with an arm round her, said proudly "This is my Isotta. My child, this is Marcus Cray, from England. Now practise

24

your English. Signor Cray is interested in *objets d'art*." He winked. "Let me have the package, my child; ah, how rare, how very rare! Even in Rome such a thing is seldom found. We must not abuse it; I will go with it to the light at the window, that I may see."

He moved away, and Marcus and Isotta were left in one another's company. The girl stole a glance at him, with an upward flick of her lashes; it was not in her nature not to flirt with a young man. However she found this one dull, despite his eyes, and grave. Marcus said little, for he had no small talk. He thought that Isotta was very pretty; her eyes and skin were attractive, and the gently curling hair; and she was small, as he himself was, and so did not make him feel inferior. The brash schoolgirl he had expected would have scared and alienated him; but this was different.

Isotta tried to break the silence, chattering of this and that; she had been taught that it was polite to put visitors at their ease. The light voice said "You like Italy, *signore*? You have travelled a long way; was the journey hard?"

He sought for words, as though his English were foreign. "Lately a little; I had a hired horse, which stumbled and needed a shoe; waiting for a smith, I met your father. This was a pleasure, as I had often heard of him."

"Papa is famous? But how fortunate; we must tell him. No, perhaps not; it will make him conceited, as he has a good opinion of himself already." She had dropped back into Italian, but he could follow her; he smiled. She was smiling also, revealing a delicious tiny dimple in the place between cheek and chin. He was beginning to be drawn to her; he watched the red, desirable mouth shape its words in either tongue, and noted that her teeth were white, but projected a little; it was better when she did not show them. This flaw endeared her to him. He continued to try and talk, slowly and gravely; and was in mid-phrase when Bondone turned round.

"It is almost certainly Carolingian," he said. "I could not, when I beheld it behind the grille, be sure. It might have been a twelfth-century copy, and I cannot exclude that until I have made certain tests. But meantime I am satisfied. My child, do you go to the great door and ask the Superior if I may keep the *croce* for a little. She will not refuse, I know." He is wily, Marcus thought; if other dealers come here seeking it, it will be gone.

Isotta took the package carefully and went out. Bondone came back to where Marcus stood, and the younger man could feel an almost electric vitality emanate from him. "That is an end to business for today," he said triumphantly. "Now we will have pleasure. Isotta shall show us the cave, and then we will take her for our little drive, and then we will eat together at the *albergo*. After that, my friend, you must no longer stay at inns. My wife Isabella and I will gladly offer hospitality to the son of Jacob Cray."

The cave was almost beneath the convent, reached by a round-about path. The nuns had given Isotta a little lamp burning in oil which she shaded with her hand; in the shadows of the passages the honey-coloured light flared up softly on her young flesh, showing the curves of cheek and throat. Perhaps if there had been no lamp Marcus Cray would not have fallen in love. As it was, the sensation left him silent; dazed with a kind of awe, so that he was not able immediately to see the narrow chasm of the cave entry, where Isotta held the lamp high so that they could look. There was a ledge of rock, on which had been put a wooden crucifix to replace the ivory one which had remained there for so long; and many votive offerings of the old sort, showing organs which had been healed, silver hearts, hands, legs, a liver. "They cannot come any more," said Isotta. "The nuns have closed the public way."

Enrico Bondone stood at the entry, where he had been before; he was watching his daughter and the young man. Yes, it would do very well; in this matter he would overrule Isabella.

"That lamp," he said aloud, "that you carry, is the self-same kind used twenty-one centuries ago by the Etruscans, who were foremost in the invention of such things. The need has not changed, and neither has the lamp."

"Shall we show Signor Cray the chapel?" asked Isotta, and her father nodded. When they came at last to the great door he took off his hat, and he and Isotta genuflected before the altar, which was dressed with hand-made lace. The interior of the chapel was dark except for votive candles, and one did not look towards the back where there was a grille taking up the space of the whole wall, behind which nuns prayed. Marcus stood awkwardly; he did not wish to be discourteous, but could not bring himself to genuflect to the Sacrament. Instead, he turned his eyes to the plaques on the wall. Presently Isotta joined him.

"That is the memorial to Countess Ildefonsa, whom I remember when I was a child," she said. "She was very thin and used to pray here a great deal. Then she died and the Count married again, and the new wife would come here; now she also has a memorial, just below the other. That is the pew where they would kneel; the cushions were embroidered by the two Contessas."

Her profile was towards the wall; it was young and pure. Marcus was aware of great happiness in being left here with her; Bondone seemed to have abandoned them to one another. Now, however, as they came out of the chapel, he stepped forward and sent Isotta to ask for the *croce* to take back with them, if the Superior would not mind. He knew that it was virtually his and that Donna Maria knew it also; she was no shrewder than he, and he was the shrewdest man in Florence. At the back of his mind was a slow pleasure at the attraction his daughter had for Marcus Cray. There would be no need to send the little one to Paris.

The subsequent drive was uneventful. All three passengers, and Pablo the footman, enjoyed the bright day, the skyline with its hill towns and towers, the scattered forests, vineyards where the fruit was reddening, clearings for farms, and always the road winding whitely into the distance. After perhaps two hours the horses were turned and they began the return journey, stopping for food at Emilia's *albergo*. They sat on the bench in the sunshine, the one fig tree providing welcome shade. Isotta sat between sun and shadow, looking enchanting in a silk grogram bonnet and matching pelisse, the colour of Michaelmas daisies. She knew she looked so; all through the drive she had been thinking of Felice, and how pleasing it would be if he rode out from his ancestral place, which they had passed among its pines, and had seen her in a carriage with a strange young man. But he had not come; of course, he was in Padua.

She fell silent, as though the well of her artless chatter had dried up. By now Marcus could not keep his eyes off her. Bondone was pleased at the way things were going, but he was disturbed when the bacon stew came, and Isotta merely toyed with it and did not eat.

"Finish it, *cara*, for it is good," he said. "When I was a boy I had to live on pasta my good mother made, and she would sell the rest in the shop. Never refuse good food, Isotta."

She closed her eyes; how many times had she heard that story about grandmother Giovanna! "I am not hungry," she said aloud. "It is the carriage rolling."

"The carriage is well enough sprung. No *grappa*? But it is special; try a little."

But Isotta would eat no *grappa*, which at other times was always her favourite. Bondone frowned; he disliked waste. "That colour you are wearing is too old for you," he said. "Mamma was right; it makes you look pale." He hoped that she was not going to be ill again; the anxiety drove the thought of Marcus for moments out of his mind.

They returned to the convent after the meal, restored Isotta, and collected the crucifix, Bondone handling it like a relic. He bore it in his hands all through the return drive, after Marcus left him to take the hired horse, which Agostino had meantime seen shod. Marcus and the art-dealer parted with many directions from Bondone as to where to find his Florentine house. The young man found that he was looking forward to the visit.

"Lucy, it's happened again. I feel sick again. And I haven't . . . you know . . . this time. Lucy, I'm frightened. What shall I do? I dare not tell Mamma. And nobody here can help me but you. Lucy, help me. I must get word to Felix, to Padua. Oh, Lucy, I . . ."

Lucy Nardini looked with cold eyes at her friend. "It only means," she said, "that you and Felix weren't careful enough. What do you expect me to do—or him, for that matter? It's your trouble, not ours."

Isotta stared at her, pale lips fallen open, eyes blind. "Felix must marry me," she said stubbornly. Lucy smiled, and turned away to where her own things were kept in the tower room they shared. Four towers, all for the senior pupils, named after the four archangels. Now, perhaps an angel would help Isotta. Otherwise, what was to happen? It was true that babies could be taken away, but even Lucy knew little of how this might be achieved. She firmed her lips obstinately, and turned round.

"Felix can't possibly marry you; the Nardini must marry into the aristocracy. It won't be of any use to write to him. My uncle would disinherit him if he married a commoner." This was not true, but Lucy had thought of it on the spur of the moment and it sounded well. And this little goose would know no differently.

28

Truth to tell, Lucy was glad the hurried meetings among the olive trees during painting classes had come to an end; she herself had been in danger as an accomplice, and might have been sent away from school in disgrace, thereby rendering unlikely further financial help from her uncle, the old Count.

Isotta was staring at her own hands. How changed, how strange and cold, Lucy had grown! And to have said she was a commoner was . . . mean. She suddenly clenched her fists in her skirts and willed the brimming tears not to spill from her eyes. She felt proud, cold and proud; they should not use her so. When she spoke again, it was in a light calm voice which trembled only slightly. "Send a letter from me, to let him know," she said. "Then we shall see what he may do. He must be told, at least."

Lucy shrugged. "Write by all means, if you must." There had not, she knew, been a single letter from Felix to Isotta folded into her own mail since he had left last time for Padua. No doubt other matters claimed him. She kept silence, as she was beginning to learn how to do. One's duty, after all, was to make a good marriage in gratitude for one's education, and husbands expected a virginity. Isotta must think of some tale to tell; she, Lucy, no longer had anything to do with it, and as for sending on letters . . . But she would let one be written; as well do that.

Later Isotta handed her a folded note. Surely Felix would send word when he received it, would tell her what to do, where to go for help! He could not be so cruel as to do nothing, simply not to answer! The matter was as much his fault as hers.

But no answer came.

A letter in fact arrived; the Superior would no longer open it once one had passed the third year. It was from Papa.

My dear little Isotta,

I want very much to write to my darling about a matter which concerns herself, and your mother is as pleased about it as I am. You will recall the young Englishman Marcus Cray, whom we met the day I last took you driving. (There has been much pressure of business in the shop, with both Mamma and myself greatly occupied, otherwise we would have come to you with all this.) Marcus Cray has in fact asked for your hand in marriage, and if you are not opposed to such a scheme—and from what I have seen I do not think you dislike the young man—I have given my consent. Perhaps you did not fully realise on our drive that Marcus' father Jacob Cray and I used often to meet many years ago, for we were both in pursuit of objects which were beautiful and rare. As you know I had to make of this a business venture, but Jacob Cray did so for beauty's own sake; that was when he was young. Later he was forced to curtail his activities for lack of money. They are not, accordingly, a rich family, but are very well born. When you become Marcus' wife as I hope you will, I should like to keep you both near me for a year or so, teaching Marcus such aspects of the trade as he does not yet know. (He has been helping me in the Florentine shop and shows great promise, has excellent taste and is willing to learn.) After that a great hope of mine will be realised; I intend with the help of God to open a branch in London, and Marcus shall be the manager. You will like to live in London, my Isotta. It is a rich city with much trade. There are openings for anyone in our line of affairs, for the citizens lack taste as a whole—it is as bad as their food—and need careful and tactful advice as to what makes beauty and what does not. It is perhaps less simple than I have made it sound. You and Marcus will go about among them, meet them—he has the right introductions—and, in short, encourage them to buy. There will also be an agency for English artists and sculptors.

I know that you will be a helpmate to Marcus in this way; in all ways. I would trust neither Luigi nor Gastone with so important a project, which shows what a high opinion I have already formed of this young man who is after all no son of mine. As for your dowry, it will make nobody ashamed.

Think about this letter, my Isotta, for a day or two, then write to me. I would not force you, as you know, but I should like you to consider the advantages of such a match and whether it is not, as things are at present in this country, the best that all of us may hope for. Everyone will be content with it, even Mamma.

Your loving father,
Enrico Bondone.

He had made up his mind, that was evident. Panic claimed her; where was she to turn for help? Mamma was useless, and would only be angry and perhaps beat her; Papa must never know the truth; Lucy had failed her, Felix also. There was only one person left to whom to go, her sister Caterina. Caterina had been so much older that Isotta could only dimly recall her as a bride, with a frost of white veiling over her dark curls, a bouquet with white ribbons, and sandy-haired Filippo waiting at the altar. Then there had come babies, oh, yes, Caterina would know all about having them, for she had come home, one remembered, when the first was on the way, and Mamma had fussed and had given advice. Surely Caterina would help her now; perhaps one could go to stay with her, till the child should be born; some way must be found to continue to deceive Papa, who must not be hurt. How miserable she was, and how strange and frightening not to be able to discuss everything with Lucy, no longer her friend! She was indeed alone in the world. She must write at once to Caterina in Milan.

She had hardly taken leisure to think of Marcus Cray and his proposal. Later, there would be time.

Caterina Pelosi received the letter, and in a panic did not even show it to her husband; a man would never understand. To have an illegitimate child, to think of having the child here, and to try moreover to conceal everything from the neighbours who spied behind their potted plants! Of course it could not be done, and Isotta should never have thought of it; there were many things of which Isotta should never have thought, and they believing all the time—when they had time to remember, between rearing the children, entertaining the customers who came for photographs, and dealing with the accounts—that the girl was safe in her convent! Papa and Mamma have been so greatly occupied that they let her go to that *castello* in the summer, and now look what has come of it, Caterina thought, and as the whirlpool of her thoughts increased in pace she realised that there was only one thing to do; write to Mamma, enclosing Isotta's tear-stained, blotted letter. Mamma would know what to do; one could then wash one's hands thankfully of the affair, and life in Milan could go on as before.

Isotta had waited in terror and fear for an answer. It came, in appalling guise, in the form of Mamma herself, containing a monumental rage till they were alone in the carriage going back to Florence. Isabella Bondone was a large woman, with a bosom still described by connoisseurs as fine, a vulgar face which time had turned red, and snow-white hair—she had Lombard blood, and in her youth it had been a pleasing light brown—piled high beneath her bonnet. She had already requested that Isotta's things be packed, as the girl would not be returning to the convent; a marriage had been arranged for her. The nuns had kissed Isotta goodbye and had wished her well; as for the other girls, there was too much haste about the departure for Isotta even to take leave of her friends. The honey-coloured walls receded blankly as they drove off. Now would come the storm. Isotta waited, huddled against her place on the cushions; she felt half dead with fear. But there was in fact little said; this was not one of Mamma's hot rages, when rapid words would spill from her while her bosom heaved, and her hard eyes flash fire and then it would be over. No; this was something different, cold and deadly.

"And what your father would say if he knew I leave you to guess. I have not told him."

"Please do not." Isotta spoke as if she lacked air. "Do not. I love Papa."

"You love nobody but yourself. There will however be no question of telling your father. The sooner you are married the better; it may just be contrived without arousing the suspicions of these English. I was against it at first, but it is a fortunate enough chance. You will marry this Cray and make him believe the child is his. If you are prudent it may be achieved."

"Mamma, I cannot—cannot—" Memories of Felice, treacherous, uncaring, beautiful Felice, with his tall indolent carriage and seductive ways, returned hotly, then vanished like a wave in the sea; there was no hope. He was a Nardini and had not answered. She began to weep. Isabella leaned over from her place and slapped her daughter on the cheek.

"Stop that; the coachman will gossip about the noise. There is no prospect of marriage with the father of your child; oh, I know it all. We should have kept you close in Florence instead of letting you go off gallivanting and visiting above your station. It is a mercy you wrote to Caterina and she had the good sense to write to me, or God knows what would have become of us all."

"Caterina betrayed me. I begged her to tell nobody."

"When you have a great belly to show it will tell everyone fast enough," her mother rejoined coarsely. "*Dio!* It is my misfortune that I am needed by my husband in his business, and have not sufficient time to keep an eye on my own children. I can trust none of them, except Caterina."

The thought of Caterina was becoming hateful. "Mamma, please, please do not make me marry yet. I do not . . . I do not . . . Papa said that if I were opposed to it it should not happen." To say so now was useless, no doubt; Isotta brought out her lace-edged handkerchief and dabbed at her wet face; one cheek still tingled from her mother's slap. That lady bridled. "Opposed! If this young man were the devil himself you should marry him to hide your shame. That I should have a daughter who lets herself be taken advantage of behind the first tree!"

Shaken with sobs as she was, Isotta felt a little flame of rebellion rise. It hadn't been like that. There had been a long time when Felice had wooed her, coming upon her like a young god whenever she was reading or walking or lying in the sun. When it happened at last it had been beautiful, not sordid. Mamma spoke as if everything was common and dirty. And now—

She could hardly remember the features of Marcus Cray. She recalled that he had been civil and grave. What a fate, to have to marry quickly as though she had been a servant girl in trouble! Yet according to Mamma it was like that.

She retched and said faintly, "Please let us stop the carriage for a moment, Mamma. I feel sick again." There was no escape. She would have to endure what came, and make the best of it. At least Papa would never know.

Marcus Cray and Isotta Bondone were married in the parish church four days after she had returned home. The haste was due to an unforeseen circumstance; the bridegroom's father was very ill in England and word had already come that his son must journey home at once. For Donna Isabella this had presented a difficulty; supposing the young man lingered abroad for months, and did not present himself in time to have fathered the child who—God knew what exact date it would be born, for Isotta did not—had caused all the haste, and lack of proper bride-clothes? But Marcus was much in love, and quite agreeable to the suggestion that Isotta, who in some way had grown more delightful than ever, would fret if he went away without first marrying her. At the ceremony, however, Isotta was overcome by tears; he was aghast at this, but, as her mother explained, every bride had feelings of a hysterical nature; it would be different after the wedding-night. Tomorrow Marcus could journey to England, console his father, and in due course return to claim his wife.

So it was done, and Marcus' inept knowledge of women enabled the matter of the missing virginity to pass without comment. In what was in fact his own first possession of a woman he fumbled, though always gently; that he was gentle with her brought Isotta comfort. She had given herself stiffly and grudgingly, as befitted a virgin, not because she intended deceit but because she still felt woebegone and longed for Felice, and even, despite his treatment of her, tried to pretend that it was the young Count's body which entered her own at last between the sheets of cool hand-embroidered linen. But the man who was with her now was different from Felice, as she sensed soon enough. There was no roughness; Marcus considered her always. Afterwards, he kissed her tenderly and with gratitude. The strangeness of it all would return to her once he had left; but in the morning there was Mamma, bustling and wreathed in smiles, saying that after they had seen Marcus off they would go together to the shops to buy clothes, in order that Isotta's husband might return at last to a suitably dressed young matron. There was solace, after all, in going to the shops and mantua-makers, choosing velvets for gowns and lawn for chemises, and cobwebby lace to trim everything. She would not disgrace her husband when they returned together to England. Already she was thinking more of England than Italy, of Marcus than Felice; at some point, the latter vanished from her mind.

2

"If we are not doubly careful with Papa, this Englishman will take our inheritance."

The two sons of Enrico Bondone stood at one end of the great shop, away from the large-paned windows into which passers-by might conveniently gaze. Its display-shelf held two T'ang horses Enrico had acquired some years ago and would not sell. Beyond, in the comparative gloom of the show-room, the Tintoretto stood on its great easel, partly cleaned, the packed writhing figures already showing more of the great master's brushwork than had been formerly visible. Enrico had an affinity for Il Furioso; when the time came he doubtless would not part with the painting either.

The showroom walls were upholstered in heavy red paper, for Enrico claimed it set off the varying colours and restricted palettes he aimed to show to advantage. There was some truth in this, for a pair of Cuyp cattle scenes hung amicably beside a Guido Reni with warm shadows, and a doubtful Poussin with none. Every possible space was hung with the paintings it had been Enrico Bondone's life's work to collect from unexpected places, cottages, convents, auctions, palaces. A great tarnished mirror, found long ago in Venice by the canals, reflected everything as if under water, making the show-room appear double the size it really was; unwary customers would often be brought up short by its baroque frame. Further on there was a smaller room where Bondone would show off work by current painters who showed promise. It was an accolade to be accepted by him for the sale of one's work. The brothers Luigi and Gastone, both of them slight young men with thin sallow faces, stared unseeing, too familiar with the rooms and too greatly taken up with their own troubles to notice anything except one another. Both had been too often whipped by their mother in youth; no doubt that was why they did not inspire confidence. Beyond the engraved glass door which led to the office, Donna Isabella's snowy head could be seen bent over accounts. She was rapacious and observant:

nothing at Bondone was lost, misplaced or unpaid for. She was a good business woman but a bad mother; her sons had respect for her, but no affection.

Luigi, the elder, who had made the remark, had small talent and no charm. He had an attractive wife who disliked him, and no children. Gastone, on the other hand, had charm in abundance, and some brains; he had married before his brother and his ineffectual, constantly ailing wife had presented him with two leggy tomboyish little girls. Accordingly the brothers gazed upon one another with solicitude, but no great liking.

"We will see," said Gastone. "Someone is coming in. *Dio*, it is that madman Ravallo. He must be made to stop coming here."

The doorbell had already jangled and a small balding man of about forty came into the shop. He was unshaven and carelessly dressed; his protruding eyes roved quickly round the shop in search of Enrico Bondone, who was not there but in Verona, at a sale of house-furnishings. Ravallo set down his heavy canvases, accordingly, and tried to speak to the brothers; but Luigi, with a haughty gesture, forestalled him. Luigi liked to wield power, and seldom had the opportunity.

"The *padrone* is not in today," he said. "Take these away again; we have no room."

"*Messeres*, I have not had a meal today, or yesterday. The good signor your father promised me that if I would bring him street scenes, he would consider them. Here is a view of the Lung'Arno, another of the campanile. I have painted hard for many weeks. Do not, I beg of you, ask me to take them away; if I could leave them till the *padrone* returns, and meantime—"

"By no means," said Luigi, but Gastone had taken time to stare at the canvases with their bright smeared colours; it was not what he called painting, but with Papa one never knew. Luigi was still shaking his head. Gastone took sudden pity on the little man. "Try again when my father is here," he said. "He will be here tomorrow."

"But why take them away? They are heavy and I have no strength. If you will even look, you will be convinced—"

"You do not convince us," Luigi told him. "As my brother says, come back after our father has returned." This was giving in, and he was sulky with Gastone; but the harm was done.

"But in the meantime, I beg, a little silver, enough to buy a meal—"

"That is not our concern. Good-day, *signore*." But Ravallo held his own; his eyes almost stood out from his head with emotion, and his hands shook. He was, in fact, a trifle mad.

"You know nothing, nothing," he said. "You have never worked for a starving wage. You live well and are never hungry."

"Will you go, or must the Austrian police remove you?"

He went at that, and they saw him trailing dispiritedly down the street again with his heavy paintings. Gastone turned away. "There are too many of them," he muttered. "Our father gives them money because he is sorry for them. That is not the way to run a business."

"Leave it. Now, this Englishman," began Luigi, and they returned to the topic of Marcus Cray.

Old Jacob Cray was dying. In his room the fire burned brightly because of the frost. The sick man lay on his bed propped with pillows, for his breathing had become difficult. At times he had become confused and at others clear, so that he knew Marcus was with him. Once while he could understand, Marcus had told him about his marriage, hastily adding that the bride was rich, a daughter of Bondone. The congested face worked for moments and then Jacob said "Rich . . . and bonny?"

"Yes, she is bonny, with dark eyes and hair; small, and dainty in every way. I love her dearly." He heard himself begin to stammer; he was grieved for his father and could not say as much. But Jacob smiled. The bloodshot eyes, the colour of Marcus' own, rolled beneath their hooded lids; they were the eyes of Mary Cray.

"Tell me . . . of London." He already had some idea of the Bondone venture, but liked to come back to it, like a child with a story. Marcus talked gently, saying again that they were to be set up as art-dealers in Piccadilly "and also—this was my idea, father—the sale of other beautiful or rare objects, fine furniture, hangings, things of that kind. Bondone will send them to us at first from Italy and France; he has shares in a shipping-office at Brest. He—"

But the face had changed, and Jacob had drifted off again into half sleep, half death. His breathing had grown more laboured; Marcus thought he would die soon. Opposite the bed hung a portrait of a tall woman in a dark gown. Jacob Cray's hand reached out as though to bring it nearer. He had begun to talk again.

"My . . . mother. I scarcely remember her or my father; he was not well liked, they said, but he was kind to me. When he died I was shocked, I remember, and lay awake all night, hearing the clocks chime. They said he died . . . conveniently."

"It was long ago, father. Forget it now."

But Jacob talked on, as if to lay the ghosts. "She ran off afterwards with her lover, a black-avised fellow who raced his horses, and they met their death when the carriage overturned on the black ice of the winter road. If it had not happened she . . . they . . . might have been brought to trial. My guardians tried to make me . . . frightened of her, later. They said she was a wicked woman. It may have been so, but sometimes her face, so fair and perilous, would come to me in dreams. If she had thought to take me with her I . . . would have died too."

"Yet you lived, to be my own dear father." Marcus laid his own hand over the old man's; they were similar in shape, long and white, the hands of Mary Cray. He reproached himself; all of his own boyhood he had not greatly heeded his father, being too much occupied in overcoming his own backwardness, his stammering. Now he could picture that other little boy, odd, lonely and afraid. *Her face would come to me in dreams.* Marcus looked at the painted foxy, beautiful face, with slanting dark eyes which told nothing, holding their secrets. Mary Cray's innocence or guilt would never be established now. In time, all things found their rightful place; it no longer mattered. Jacob would die and be buried, and Harry was dead; he himself, the last-born weakling, was the heir of the house of Cray.

Jacob had fallen into a fitful sleep. Presently there was a scratching at the door and a very tall young man entered, impeccably clad in peg-top trousers and a pearl-grey waistcoat with a jewelled pin. He closed the door softly, laid aside his gloves and hat and came to the bed. Marcus watched him enviously; this was George Massingbird, whom since Harry's death his father had loved almost as another son. Marcus himself had disliked and distrusted George for a long time, but the other's charm had won; by now they were friends.

"How is he?" Massingbird asked, lowering his voice. His brilliant eyes stared down at the dying man, and the long fingers felt Jacob's pulse. He shook his dark curling head, tightened his full red lips, and laid the hand back on the bed. Marcus continued to stare at it; the beautiful hand of an ugly man, who had loved

38

beauty. Jacob had always pampered his hands, using rosewater on them like a woman. He wore no rings. All of his jewels were kept in a strong-box in this very room, and after he died it would be necessary to list and value each one; they came from all over the known world, and some were curious rather than costly. Marcus' eyes sought Massingbird's. It seemed long ago that they had both ridden south finely clad for the courting of Alethea Featherstone. Massingbird had already been married, to a young heiress he had carried off despite her parents. There were two children now and a third on the way; Cathy Massingbird was a quiet little thing who left George to go his own ways. Without Jacob he would be in difficulties, for he had long ago got through his wife's money. Marcus was certain his father had lent sums to George, but the knowledge stayed in the back of his mind; now was not the time to voice it. One must think now of his father only. He became aware that someone was missing; Betty. Betty should have come from Edinburgh. Perhaps it was too far, or she had not the fare, or was busied with her family.

"Is that you, Jojo?" the old man's voice whispered. Jacob had always given them pet names; himself Markie, George Jojo from some forgotten joke. Massingbird had knelt down by the bed, leaning forward so that the failing eyes might see him. "I'm here, Dad," he said, and Marcus felt a ghost, no more, of the old jealousy rise. Yet what did anything matter if it pleased the dying man? Perhaps George had taken Harry's place. His father now was trying to say something; Marcus drew close in order to hear.

"Your venture . . . in London. Take Jojo. Promise me."

Marcus was embarrassed; after all the venture was Bondone's. But the dying ears strained to hear his answer; he could do nothing but agree.

"I promise." Tears stung his eyelids; how like children old folk were, with their obstinacies and fears! Now Massingbird would have to be watched for extravagance . . . he might take him with him when he returned to Isotta . . .

He thought of Isotta suddenly, with great tenderness. She would be waiting not for George, but for himself. It would be like going home; curious to think of another home than Longhouses, where he had spent his youth.

Jacob Cray died at four o'clock in the morning, and both Marcus and George Massingbird were by the bed. Afterwards George stood looking down at the smooth dead face. There had

39

been timely infusions of foxglove put in Jacob's ale and his sugared tea of late days. The full sum he was owed would have been inconvenient had it become known. Jacob himself had not known of it. Now, no one need ever do so. And the old man had been in pain. It had been a kindly act to help him on. Massingbird's conscience, as usual, was clear.

When the will was read there was no mention of Massingbird, however; all of the Cray inheritance, discounting a tiny annuity for Betty, was left to Marcus. He found he was not listening to the lawyers; he was too greatly filled with joy. Isotta had written to say that she was already expecting a child. It made Marcus feel tall and whole, no longer a shy stammering undersized stripling whom the Featherstones, and their world, had rejected. He had proved himself a man, and he loved his wife. He wrote back tenderly that same day, promising to be with Isotta soon.

He had written already on his arrival, and this letter reached the Bondone family at breakfast. It had been placed before Enrico and he handed it solemnly to his daughter as a recognition of her married state; previously it had been his prerogative to open her letters. Isotta glanced at her mother, who nodded permission, and then opened it. The table was littered with the remains of their food; knobbed fresh rolls, butter curled delicately upon silver, thin Greek honey in a jar. The coffee-pot still steamed. It had come from Meissen and was of white glazed porcelain, with modelled ivy leaves trailing about it in relief. It was difficult to keep clean; each week it was washed and scrubbed with a soft brush dipped in ammonia. Presently a maid would come to take it and the other things away.

Enrico had unfolded his morning paper. He had enjoyed his breakfast as always, pouring with relish the glistening red-gold honey from the spoon to his bread, wiping his moustaches finally with a thick damask napkin of snowy whiteness. Now he put on his eye-glasses, to which he had unwillingly taken lately; his sight, which had been excellent all his life, had begun to lose its keenness, and he dared not allow the fact to spoil his observation of detail. He conned the news, murmuring of it now and again to the women. Suddenly Isotta broke in.

"Excuse me, Papa, but it is bad news. Marcus says that his father is sinking and that there is no hope. He may be dead by now; the letters take so long to come." She looked at the date on which it had been written; it was some time ago. The mails were bad. She replaced the letter carefully in its envelope. Enrico had looked up.

"Old Jacob dying? That was to be expected; we all die. Isabella, you will ask Father Pietri to say masses. No doubt the funeral has already taken place. *Dio!* That Jacob was a knowing one. I remember in Lyons, once, before the abdication in France—"

He got up and folded his paper. Isabella never read it; it was not fashionable for wives to do so, but she contrived to keep herself informed of affairs. "There is in fact another death in the small columns," Enrico said. "Your friend Lucy will be sad, my pet. Young Count Felice Nardini was killed in Padua last week, in a duel. It does not give any details."

Isabella tossed her head. "It will have been about a woman, depend upon it," she said. "Too much licence is permitted these young men."

"The coffee is still hot," said Enrico. "May I have another cup, my dear?"

She poured it, and he drank it standing, while Isotta stayed still, not lifting her quivering lashes. So much life, and now—Her feelings confused her; she wished to be alone to weep, naturally, but it was for someone known long ago, in another world, another life. Another life? She had thought Felix' name branded on her heart, to be carried with her always. If only Papa would go! She dared look at no one.

Enrico was already staring curiously at her. He had suspected her pregnancy—such things happened from the wedding night—and was pleased with the fact that nevertheless she ate daintily and well, like a little bird. He had put down her silence and pallor to shock over old Jacob Cray; but Isotta had never known the old man, and it was improper that she should say nothing of regret for the young one she had known on holiday, who was so untimely dead. "Have you nothing to say, Isotta?" he asked reprovingly.

"What should she say?" burst out Isabella. "She is intent on her husband's letter."

"It is very sad, Papa," Isotta managed to answer in a low voice. He nodded, and made ready to go from the room; he was always early at the showroom. Once he had gone Isabella wasted no time at all on Felice.

"You must write today, in your reply, that you expect your husband's child," she said. "It will cheer him while he mourns his father."

"Mamma, not yet. I will write only that I am sorry for the old *signor's* illness and that I hope he is better. It—it would not be--right to tell Marcus now. Let us wait for a little."

"If you do not write it to him, then I will," said Isabella firmly.

Isotta flushed where before she had been pale. "You would not dare! Not even you—you would not!"

"There is no need for histrionics; quietly, the servant is coming. Write at once. And do not give me further impertinence. Dare, indeed! Some will dare more than others. You were not without daring yourself, my girl, when you—"

"Mamma, please, please! Very well, I will write it. Promise to say nothing. It is only that I do not want to trouble Marcus. He will be sad, and perhaps busy." She had thought constantly of her husband since he had left; she was filled with shame over the trick that had been played on him, and now despite everything there was a great lifting of the heart because he need never, never, by chance or design, meet Felice Nardini in the flesh. That she could hardly have borne, and if the baby turned out to be like its true father she would have been undone. At that instant, a resolve grew in her that Marcus should be the baby's father in truth, just as if he had himself begotten it. Never, by word or look or shadow, should he be made to doubt his son. And herself? There was only one thing to do; she would think constantly of Marcus through the pregnancy, remembering every word they had ever spoken, remembering his tenderness and love; perhaps, in such a way, something of him would enter the baby's soul.

"Do not forget that the post goes at noon," said Isabella placidly. She was satisfied.

Luigi and his discontented wife Anna, who was the sister of Caterina's husband Filippo Pelosi, lived in Fiesole, as three or four young married couples had begun to do instead of remaining a part of the family. They had breakfasted together in silence, as there was nothing to say. Luigi left for the shop in reasonable time, and after he had gone Anna idly poured herself more coffee and then thrust it away because it had grown cold. She was indolent and took no interest in the housework, leaving it to the maids, whose brooms could be heard already sweeping the adjoining rooms. Anna went to the window and stood behind the curtain, fingering its knotted fringe with hands that were the most beautiful in Italy; white and plump, with tapering fingers and burnished almond nails. She grew tired of watching the carriages drive past into town, and was careful not to be seen by them, for no woman of refinement would be caught watching at windows. She took herself presently back into the room where the breakfast things had by now been cleared, and began strumming aimlessly on the piano, a wedding-gift from her brother: it had been expensive, with quilted green silk panels below the candelabra. She left it soon, tiring of it as she tired of everything; even Luigi's half-hearted fumblings did not arouse her, and for some time now the couple had occupied separate rooms. Anna thought of that, her full lips pouting, and ventured back to her bedroom where a pier-glass stood. In it she saw her face and figure, the latter's fine bosom veiled in lace. She smoothed her gown over her hips—it was made of satin—and shifted position a little so that she could admire her white swan's neck. Her hair was dark gold, thick, fine and dressed fashionably; but who was there to admire it? They went seldom into society, and, apart from a lively woman friend who called now and again with the latest gossip, Anna was bored. She stared at the perfect oval of her face, and knew foreboding; soon she would be old, and had never taken a lover.

A sound came at the door and Anna spun round, irritated at having been caught gazing in the mirror. It was the servant who had come with her from Milan, Gianetta; the woman's face bore a half-smile, and Anna knew she had been seen preening herself in the glass. She flushed a little, and said "What is it? You know your duties."

As some do not, the woman thought; aloud she said "Signor Riccione has called. I have put him in the small parlour."

"Riccione the notary? What did he want? Did he say?

"Naturally not. He wished to speak with the *signor*."

"He has left for the office. Why did you not say I was not at home?" Anna felt panic rise; she could not explain to herself the effect the lawyer had on her, except that she disliked him and was in some way certain that he had influenced her husband against her. She ran her hands over her hair to ensure that each curl and wave was in place, and said "Put out the wine, and tell him I will come down."

"The madeira? It is too early."

"Do as I tell you. You are growing insolent. I will not endure it; I will send you home."

She flounced down the short passage and the staircase and opened the parlour door. A greenish gloom of plants met her gaze. Luigi had a passion for them and set them in pots and containers everywhere; they claimed the light like greedy children, spreading their fronds and leaves. Between them and herself the notary rose to his feet; she saw his cool grey eyes assess her, and felt her knees turn to water; this man desired her, and knew that she knew it.

She heard her own voice speaking coldly. "My husband is from home; you need not have expected to find him here at this hour. It would be best to seek him in town. What may I do for you? Is there a message?"

She heard her own voice run on, against his silence; and saw him rise and come to take her hand and felt him kiss it, the lips dry against her skin. He was a cold man, above medium height, with correct dress enhancing his well-preserved waist and slender figure. He wore the moustaches and small imperial which were fashionable this year; he moved in the best society. He had never married and there was a mystery about him which she could not fathom; perhaps it was true that he was a member of the *carbonari* as they said.

The wine came and they sat politely drinking it and making small talk, while Anna felt herself blushing hotly. At the same time she told herself that she was a fool; she was not, God knew, in love with the man; as well take a spider to bed. After all he was the family solicitor; he had come here in hope of business; she need not be alarmed. Yet alarm grew in her, together with the sensation that she was somehow in this man's power; she kept her eyes lowered, however, and answered evenly.

He stayed for a quarter-hour and then rose, bowed and left. The visit had been entirely correct. Why was she so disquieted, and why had he really come?

Down at the Bondone show-rooms everything was as usual, Donna Isabella behind her accounts-table and Gastone exercising his charm on an early client, the wife of the Austrian depty commissioner, tightly corseted and swathed in furs. She peeled

44

off her gloves and fingered the objects he showed her, gilded *putti*, a Chinese bowl, a necklace copied from the Greek, a tile, a ceramic bull in terracotta; but did not ask the price. Presently he would take her to his mother in the office and they would drink sweet Turkish coffee out of tiny cups, and perhaps admire the *croce francesca* which now at last, having passed the tests, hung in its glass case. These Austrians lived for coffee, sausages and cakes, Gastone was thinking grudgingly; no wonder most of the women were fat, though their husbands rode trimly past in white uniform. Gastone did not in fact share the general detestation of Austrians; they might have annexed his country, but they were paying customers. He parted at last from the corseted lady and went to rejoin his brother at the back of the shop. Luigi was lackadaisical, as usual. He was staring at a group of paintings, having nothing better to do. Bondone himself was nowhere to be seen. He often disappeared without explanation.

"Those will sell," pronounced Gastone, "and that and that will not." He indicated the failures with his foot. "Papa buys such things because he swears he can see further ahead than other men and knows what will be in demand next year, or else is sorry for the painter. I tell you we cannot afford to go on in such a way. We lose money on everything we do not sell, now, now! Take that Ravallo—" and he almost kicked a pile of the daubed paintings the bald man had brought back earlier in the week, when Bondone had again been present. "Everyone knows that man, he is a laughing-stock and mad, Papa has advanced him more money than he will ever be worth, and still he brings more, and more. He would be better learning a trade or being a greengrocer. I think that I have finally persuaded Papa of it. Yesterday he agreed with me that if we lumber ourselves with much more useless stuff our name will suffer. Why pretend to be *cognoscenti* and display rubbish?"

Luigi shrugged; it was all true, but Gastone talked too much. "Put them in a cupboard where they will be forgotten, and next time Ravallo comes make him take them away," he suggested.

"Mamma will find them in the cupboard and ask what they are doing there. She misses nothing."

"Well, Mamma has news to occupy her this morning, when she has said farewell to your lady friend. Our brother-in-law—" he sneered unpleasantly—"is returning, and bringing a friend with him. They are both to learn the business here, then set out for London, to found the new branch."

The brothers' swarthy faces grew gloomy; they disliked the idea of the English venture, for it would be out of their control when Enrico died. "When do they come?" asked Gastone, not greatly caring. Luigi shrugged again, listlessly; he was without hope for the future; why should a strange young Englishman suddenly supersede him, the elder son? It was always some other who aroused Papa's interest, never himself; even in his boyhood he had been left to Mamma and the birch. Had he not worked faithfully in the shop since he was eighteen years old? Had he not brought money into the firm by his marriage? Was it his fault he had no heir? And now this Englishman, two Englishmen, would come, and flatter Papa and take away the inheritance.

"Find out from Isotta when they will get here," he suggested. "She may come in this morning."

"Supposing she does, what will it matter? We are never told anything until it is too late to act. Nothing now will prevent their arrival unless there is a shipwreck, and then they will come later in a lifeboat. It is fate, whatever the Church says. We have no control over our lives."

"You had better not be overheard saying so, Gastone, or we are in trouble."

"Yes, we must be respectable; you are better at it than I."

Nothing did prevent the arrival of Marcus and Massingbird, and Isotta and her mother waited to greet them in the square, the wind tossing irreverently at their hair and skirts. As soon as Marcus' small figure emerged Isotta began to run, then checked herself; she must behave like a married woman. But her eyes shone with love as Marcus came up, embraced and kissed her. So that is that, thought Isabella.

Her critical gaze scanned the tall man who had come with her son-in-law, and such was her experience of character that she summed him up at once, and correctly; a womaniser. Nevertheless he bowed over her hand as if she were a queen, and she could find no fault with his manners. Flattered despite herself by the attention, she gave Massingbird her arm and they followed Marcus and Isotta, now deep in talk, to where the carriage waited. Bondone had not come with them.

On the drive back to the house Isotta chattered still, Marcus' eyes on her in adoration; after the gloomy nature of the past few weeks it was pleasant to be back. As for Massingbird, she gave him scant attention; there was only one man in the world for her now. The child in her womb grew quietly and she was happy; Mamma had been right, it had been better to write the news, they could not discuss it here. By now she had made herself forget the child was not her husband's. She curled her small gloved fingers into his, glorying in such a partner; kind, handsome and approved of by Papa. Once she looked across at the opposite seat and felt a trifle of discomfort; George Massingbird, of whom Marcus had so often written, was surveying her with irony on his beautiful face, and whatever the reason might be she felt shut out. A man should not be so beautiful; she would put him in his place. She deliberately excluded Massingbird from the talk and it was left to Marcus, always courteous, to include his friend. Then Isotta was jealous. Why had Massingbird left his wife? But she knew more of the world than she had done while at the convent school; it would not be wise to show envy; one must be patient. Yet her dark eyes sparkled uncontrollably with anger and the one remark she flung at the guest was so trite that he merely bowed, knowing it required no answer. So this was Markie's little Italian, the prettiest creature in the world! She did not interest George physically, and so he had no time for her; he preferred statuesque and queenly women.

It gave Marcus great pleasure to have his friend with him in Florence, for despite his love for Isotta he had felt somewhat solitary among her family. Now, the days were spent in working together at Bondone; and often, after the show-room closed, when the days lengthened, he and George would hire horses and either ride about the city, seeing the sights, or into the near hills to shoot small game. They explored painted churches, tavernas, the bell-tower, the cathedral, the shops. Once at a jeweller's Massingbird, who had received money from Bondone that day, bought garnets; Marcus thought of poor Cathy smothered beneath their dark fire at home, but they were not for her; George would not say for whom he had bought them. "For the lady of my heart," he jested. "I have not yet met her; or have I?"

Marcus did not laugh, as he usually did at George's jests; a married man should not talk so. In any case George had paid too much for the garnets, as he did with everything.

Bondone himself was less pleased with George than he might have been; he had seen through him at once as a handsome wastrel, knowing enough in a superficial way to persuade ignorant clients to buy, but otherwise dangerous because himself ignorant. He instructed his sons, therefore, that Massingbird was not to be permitted to approach favoured customers; at the same time, for Marcus' sake, he would talk to the young man and try to extend his knowledge, if only for the time when he would, inevitably, travel with Marcus to London and the new shop. However, Isotta was unhappy, and this made Bondone angrier than he would admit. She came to him one day, head high but near tears.

"Where is Marcus?" he demanded instantly. The shop had closed two hours since.

"Need you ask?" she said. "He is out with Massingbird. As soon as they may, when the work is done, or when they have eaten, off they go, leaving me alone; Marcus tells me I must rest, but how can I? Massingbird mocks me all the time, even though he does not speak of it. And Marcus will believe anything he says; and he wants Marcus all to himself. They laugh together."

Bondone drew her to him; her waist had begun to thicken a little. "Do not show what you feel," he told her. "Envy is not pretty in anyone, especially a charming young wife. Give Marcus a little time; they have been sad in England, and now he needs joy. He will tire of this friend when he finds out how worthless he is; Marcus is not a fool."

"They have been friends since they were boys," said Isotta dejectedly. A thing Massingbird had said the other day made her angry, remembering; it had concerned some heiress he said Marcus had wanted to marry, and he had done his best for Marcus, but the girl would not have him. She would never mention such a tale to Marcus himself, who had been made to look a fool even if he was not.

Bondone was regarding her with wise eyes. "I rejoice to see you happy in your marriage, *cara*; do not make it miserable. Let me think for a while, and I will see if there is any way of ridding ourselves of this young man whom we do not want."

Nevertheless he would hardly have planned what happened. It came about in spite of him.

Isabella, who liked a gay social life now and again, had suggested that, as the ceremony itself had been so hurried, they should celebrate Isotta's marriage with a dance; quiet and with a few guests only, because of the tacit mourning for Jacob Cray. Bondone was agreeable; Isotta was pleased, because it gave her something else to do than think of Marcus and Massingbird; and both women submerged themselves in dresses and invitations. Naturally, all the family would come, as well as a few business acquaintances, and Riccione, the lawyer, who knew everyone. Bondone suggested that they also ask a diva to sing during the evening; there was a famous singer from Milan in town, and it would cool the heat of the dancers to sit and listen a while; they must not forget that Isotta was pregnant. This suggestion was accepted as a novelty, and pleasing; no one else had thought of it, and it would make the evening a little different. In fact, Bondone knew the diva very well indeed; but kept his discretion.

On the night, Anna came on Luigi's arm, looking ravishing in white satin with diamond ear-drops, twinkling like stars above her bare shoulders. Gastone's ailing wife was cast into the shade, as always; nobody remembered what she wore. Isabella herself, magnificent in olive-green faille with black lace inset medallions, and an aigrette in her white hair, received the guests beside Bondone; he, quietly triumphant, savoured the names of several prominent citizens who would not have thought to know him in the days of Grandmamma Giovanna and her pasta. It amused him to think of the past, and compare the present; the violins tuned audibly, the hot-house flowers glowed, and everyone was waiting to dance; but Bondone paused a moment, surveying the important gathering, saying to himself at last that all the effort, all it had taken from the beginning, was his own; and Isabella had helped him as she did always; they had their differences, but it was a good marriage. He turned to her and, with a certain innate courtesy he possessed, raised her hand in its white glove to his lips, and kissed it.

"Well done, my dear," he told her; and she knew that he did not mean this evening alone. She flushed, and felt pleased; then said, "The dancing should begin."

Bondone looked round for Marcus and Isotta, who should have opened the ball; but they were occupied with a party of other guests, and the occasion was scarcely formal. He seized his lovely daughter-in-law about the waist, and spun with her into a waltz. At the end everyone applauded; Anna herself was rosy-cheeked and dishevelled, which added to her attraction. Suddenly she knew that she was being watched by a young man. The others began to dance, and she stood still; she knew that he would come to her.

He asked her to dance; but she would not dance any more. They stood regarding one another. His eyes travelled from her face to her breasts, then raised themselves again, slowly. She could see that he was as beautiful as a god; in all of her life she had never encountered such beauty. She could not describe the feeling that overwhelmed her, except that, as her upbringing had taught her, she must ascribe it to the heat. This man and Riccione, both in the room, both gazing at her!

She turned suddenly and made her way beyond the dancers to the conservatory, which in French fashion Enrico had had added on to his house. It was made of glass and fashioned like a half-dome, and already the palms inside had grown as high as the roof. She came to a place to stand beneath them, at the same time seeing the picure she made, a beautiful woman standing beneath palms. Must her thoughts always mock her so? It was as though she watched her body from outside itself.

Massingbird sidled in. Beyond him, through the opened door, the dancing had ceased and there was an instant's hush and a chord on the piano, then the diva's voice rose pure and clear, a thrush among English hawthorns. "They will not follow us now," he murmured. When the song ended, would he be her lover? She began to tremble; he was close to her, whispering in her ear; the diamond drops shook and sparkled, letting fall a cascade of light. The singer's voice soared in the distance: she was singing Mozart. She is my father-in-law's mistress, Anna found herself thinking; I heard it from the gossip of that woman who comes. She could not now recall the woman's name although she had known her for three years.

His fingers grasped her arms and slid upwards, caressing flesh and gloves. Anna bit her lip; she should have stayed with the others. She made a convulsive movement, and his fingers pressed; she tried to draw away. "My husband will be watching," she murmured. It was true; Luigi would miss nothing, and would taunt her afterwards. Afterwards, when *he* had gone . . .

She heard him laugh. "Your husband is not a man. You know as little of love as if you had never been married." The hands

50

stroked, soothed, explored. She felt near to fainting. What did she feel? She was no longer Anna Bondone, no longer anyone; only a weak force, surrendering to irresistible strength; Leda and Jupiter. But this was not the king of gods disguised as a swan, but Hermes, beautiful, deadly and self-seeking; his lips smiled and his eyes devoured her. "Let me love you," he whispered. "You know we both want it. When you saw me in there, you knew. It is a fire that will not die." She heard the foreign slowness of his speech and knew who he must be; the Englishman who had come to the shop with Marcus Cray.

"Have pity on me, I implore you; when may we meet? For we must meet again. I will come to you wherever you may be." She saw him shape the words and appraised their crazy fantasy; as an employee of Bondone how could he think himself free? The reality of their situation began to be clear to her and she drew away; he seized her.

"Let me go." His hands were at her breasts. She felt response rise, strong and quick; its presence surprised her; she had never before acted in such a way, the marriage bed had been dull. Now—

He kissed her throat, breathing in the scent she wore. He was adept with women and would have taken her there, hard and greedily, without shame. "I beg you to let me go," he heard her murmur, "we must not be found here. What will people think?"

He laughed; the exquisite little prude, the shy beauty! He had awakened her; he triumphed in it, but still she struggled, and against his hands her dress was pulled down, exposing more than was seemly; he kissed her nakedness. It was as though a flame burned in them both, breaking out here and there like moor-fire; soon they would blaze together, and . . .

"Release the lady, as she asks. May I remind you that we are both guests of the house?"

Anna gave a little cry and wrenched away; Riccione stood there, unmoving. He must have watched from the beginning; a little smile played on his lips. She flung a hand over her breasts, and contrived to pull at the boned bodice, raising it to a suitable height. Massingbird was scowling.

"Who the devil are you that you order me?" His Italian had failed him and he spoke in English, but the meaning was clear. For instants the two men regarded each other, while Anna crept back to the ballroom; they were alike in hatred, jaguar against

51

great cat. The air froze with their enmity. Beyond, the music had started up again; neither man heeded it. Presently the notary turned his back, saying as he left, "Have a care, Englishman; in this country we guard our women."

"She is not yours, you bastard!" But the other had already gone and Massingbird's voice, echoing among the abandoned palms, sounded ridiculous even to himself. A thought of challenging the other man came to him, then passed; he was not expert, and had never fought anyone. Sulkily, after adjusting his tied stock, he returned to the company, and spent the evening drinking indecorously. Anna did not appear again; a servant had come to say that Signora Luigi had a headache, and had driven home alone; the carriage would return to wait for her husband in an hour.

The dancing continued until three o'clock, and then was stopped owing to Isotta's delicate state. The celebration ball was over.

It might have been said that George Massingbird learnt everything Bondone could teach him about beauty through the medium of the latter's daughter-in-law. Her image was in his mind, day and night; she was Aphrodite, wrapped in her scented hair; he had known her for a thousand years, and would desire her for ever. He was not used to have such desire continue unsatisfied, and his anger surged unguessed at, for this kind of thing was not confided to Marcus. By day, working beside Luigi in the shop, he would both envy and dislike the colourless creature who had possessed Anna. Such a boor would never satisfy her. And never to have had a lover, as he could tell . . . so glorious a woman, left alone in her house at an hour when he, owing to the tyranny of work, could not go to her! But the notary could go. What had that cold fish to do with her, as though he had rights over that incomparable body? What could he himself, irresistible to women, do now? What, and when? Would he even see Anna again? Ah, this family . . .

". . . and this is a painting by one of the lesser lights of the sixteenth century, when the fluid line had almost given place to caricature. By then they had become too sure of themselves, and had lost their freshness."

Damn the sixteenth century, and all pictures in their frames, and all black-clad showmen, including himself, grouped about, conveying customers with eyes as stupid and blind as tamed oxen; damn Bondone for bringing him here, damn even Marcus for keeping him here; even Markie, chaste as a monk except for his marriage to that little fool, would not understand the nature of the consuming fire. Dreaming of Anna between waking and sleep, and in his mind possessing her, feeling the soft thighs yield, the mouth quiver open . . . before leaving here he must become her lover, or else go mad . . .

Outwardly he was the same, laughing and whispering to Marcus as he had done always, so that the latter noticed nothing wrong, not even the controlled rage of his beloved Isotta.

Massingbird tried sending flowers and other gifts to Anna, but without success; she returned them through a servant. He had kept the garnets, wanting to give them to her personally if a moment could be found; but how might this be? He saw her as if in a cloud, surrounded by her husband's relatives; on Fridays the women of the family sometimes met in Isabella's office to drink coffee and gossip, but Anna had not come since he had been here. If only she would do so!

Then, one day, she came.

Anna herself knew that it was unwise. With the passing of time, her folly on the night of the ball had abated, and she again saw reason. It was fortunate that Riccione had come in when he did, and she should be grateful to him, but was not. Otherwise she contrived to fill her mind with other things, but life had no savour. At last she conquered her dislike of her mother-in-law sufficiently to visit the shop one Friday: she would be in town in any case. She dressed carefully; she had her maid lace her into a morning-dress of narrowly striped white-and-red satin, with a bonnet garnished with small white flowers, and a veil. She looked what she was, a rich man's wife; there was no need to pay any particular attention to young Massingbird if they should meet; she knew her place, and he ought to know his.

So she had told herself, but the visit was not uneventful, though nobody could blame Anna, this time, for anything. On meeting with Massingbird—how handsome he was in his working clothes, with the long limbs set off by a frock-coat!—on meeting, he had bowed over her hand, with everyone watching, then had spoken in a somewhat familiar fashion, following her into the office where the rest waited. Just at the door, he said to her, "Signora Anna, I have been waiting for you to appear in such a dress."

"You could not know that that would happen." His Italian had improved, she was thinking; but he had no discretion at all. She persuaded herself that the feeling she had for him was motherly; a badly brought up boy! She smiled, and George was ravished; and went on talking about having bought some garnets in Florence, knowing that, one day, he could give them to her. "Do me the great honour of letting me see them on that gown," he said, and Anna stepped back in confusion. What would her mother-in-law say?

Gastone was present, and had overheard them, and laughed; if it had been Luigi, he would have been more spiteful. "Try them on, Anna," he said, "and we will get your portrait painted to hang in the shop." He thought privately that his brother's wife was a fine woman; if only he himself had had such fortune! Luigi was a fish; no wonder Anna pleased herself, with Massingbird or another. By now, George had brought out the case, which he carried always with him. Anna gasped at the shining beauty of the stones, while Massingbird whispered that he wished they were rubies, but, alas, he was too poor. Isotta, who was present, came over laughing for once, and helped hang and pin the jewels, while the coffee grew cold in its cups. By the end, Anna looked like a queen, gleaming and coruscating; the dark stones embellished her white neck, her ears, her fingers. She began to try to take them off again; as before, she was confused and trembling, and dared look at nobody. All her feeling for Massingbird had returned in a wave; pilloried thus, she could do nothing, and everyone was watching her.

"Do not take them off, I beg; they are yours." He could not resist a small, triumphant flourish; there, she had put them on, he had seen her again, and in his garnets! "Always in my heart I will carry your image so," he murmured. Poor Anna's colour rose, and she looked about wildly for succour. Fortunately Bondone, just then, had seen a client out; he came into the office, exclaimed courteously at the jewels, and shook his head when he heard the tale, but with a twinkle in his eye.

"Anna is right," he said. "She cannot accept them as a gift from you. Her husband, and propriety itself, would not permit." He fingered the necklace, admiring the well-set stones; how much had the young fool paid? He would be generous, however. "Let me buy them from you, Signor George, and present them to my daughter-in-law. An old man may be permitted to pay homage where a younger is not."

So it was ended amicably, and Massingbird got his money back. Donna Isabella was not pleased.

Nor was another. The lawyer Riccione had kept himself informed of the situation regarding the flamboyant Englishman; it was his business to know such things other than personally. As many suspected, he was high in the councils of the *carbonari*, the secret band of freedom-fighters who loathed Austrian domination, and had determined to end it when the moment came. There had been many deaths unexplained, one of a certain young Bonaparte prince who, the paper gave out, had died of fever. Most knew otherwise, but nothing was said; men went about their business quietly, waiting for the summons. Riccione could command men by lifting a finger and he did so now; no one would question it.

A small man in a broad hat came, and stood twisting the latter in his hands like the peasant he was; he would obey implicitly. His face was badly shaven and he had no notable feature; such people are useful. He listened to Riccione's instructions, then nodded silently. The lawyer frowned for a moment, and detained him.

"You are certain of this man's description? There must be no blundering."

"I already know the Englishman; he rides much about the city, and spends money."

"Soon he will take his last ride and spend his last coin. It would be better to happen out of town, perhaps in the foothills, where they go to shoot. An accident—"

"Leave it to me, *capitan*. I will see it done."

After the man had left the lawyer sat for moments inactive, regarding his own long-smouldering passion for a woman he knew was a fool. The time would come when he would be her lover; it suited him to wait, and meantime remove encumbrances. It was doubtful, at any rate, if Massingbird was by now Anna's or she his; respectability was a formidable obstacle.

Come away with me, I leave for England tomorrow by a sudden decision of the old man. How can I leave you? I have money no one knows of, and friends in England who will protect us. My life is worth nothing without you; I think of you day and night.

You must come to me. I shall be waiting tomorrow, Wednesday, in a closed carriage near the house, at ten in the evening. If only to say farewell I must see you, but if not . . . ah, the bliss! Do not fail me. Your G.M.

It was another of Massingbird's imprudent letters, brought to her by the servant who must already have become suspicious. Anna was not alone, for a neighbour's wife had called to collect a subscription for some charity. There were in fact few visitors to Luigi's house; it was said he and his wife gave themselves airs, and they were not liked in Fiesole. Anna had, therefore, been glad of the caller's company and had invited her to take a glass of negus; now, she regretted it. She schooled her face to show nothing; the white, rose-tipped fingers tore the letter to shreds and put it in the fire, which was lit today. The neighbour's observant eyes were all attention.

"An unwelcome bill, *signora*?"

She is impertinent, thought Anna coldly. Aloud she replied "No; my husband pays our bills promptly."

"How fortunate you are!"

They talked politely; the visitor sipped her negus, and Anna, the deed done, sank down in her place again and nibbled a wafer flavoured with vanilla. Food was often a solace. To behave as usual was the only thing to do; later, when she was alone, she must think about the situation and what Massingbird's going would mean to her. She suspected that her father-in-law had found it convenient to send him away; no doubt the episode of the garnets rankled; fortunately the rest had remained unnoticed. But how dull it would be when there was no longer, in Florence, the prospect of seeing his pleading eyes, long limbs and rich hair!

She gave the visitor an adequate contribution in silver, and that lady departed, starved of gossip.

There was gossip enough about what happened next, though nobody connected it with Anna.

Massingbird had arrived in a hired carriage. It was already dark, and the lamps in the coachman's seat exuded only a low light as they waited. There was a smell of horse-manure, worn leather and straw. Beyond the hood, Fiesole reared, its villas black against the lavender sky, sending out here and there a chink of yellow light behind drawn curtains. It was growing cold.

Massingbird brought out his watch, but could not see the time. Surely Anna would come! The prospect of being sent to London, ostensibly to supervise building-alterations at the new shop, dispirited him; to leave a love-affair without success was not in his nature. No doubt the old man was sending him out of the way, urged on by his virago of a wife. Poor Anna, with such a mother-in-law! Ah, she must come. It was not possible that she would let him go without at least a farewell between them; his conceit would not allow of it.

The minutes moved on; one white hand, delicate as a woman's, emerged from the shelter of Massingbird's travelling cloak. He surveyed his fingers, aware of mounting boredom; it was the waiting. His passion was at its height, but how could one continue so, banished, watched always, and in any case with so little to go upon? Even his gift of jewellery had been paid for by another man, robbing the gesture of its bravura. How could she be so cruel as to have no pity for him? In his agony it seemed impossible that she should resist, should feel nothing at all.

A shadow slid into the carriage out of the dusk; she had come! "Anna," he breathed, and turned towards her; then the shadow moved again. The dagger slid easily, almost lovingly, between Massingbird's ribs. He gave a gasp and fell forwards, blood gushing from him, unseen against the dark except as a sticky surface that caught the light of the lamps. The man who had come withdrew quickly lest blood soil his clothing; his task was done. "Drive into the city," he told the driver in a low voice, "then find him dead in the back seat and fetch the police. Remember you know nothing."

The driver shrugged his shoulders; he did not look round. He started the horse, and the carriage with its huddled burden moved off slowly into the night.

Luigi came home early next day, taking off his overcoat in the hall downstairs; it was still cold weather. He saw Anna at the turn of the staircase, and called to her, "Your *cavaliere* Massingbird will not trouble anyone again; he was found dead in a carriage this morning, somewhere near the bridges. The police are asking questions, but have found out nothing."

His closed smile was catlike. Anna had not moved from where

she stood. Her hand closed about the baluster, as if to support her from fainting: her eyes closed briefly. That was all. "It is a pity," he heard her say. "He was so young."

She turned from him and resumed her ascent of the stairs. Luigi shrugged, in much the same way as the carriage-driver. Anna was not passionate, as he had reason to know. In any case the young man had had no opportunity to become her lover.

"I loved him. He was so tall and glorious, all I could never be. While he was there I never felt alone. And my father loved him better than . . . than myself. His last words were to beg me to bring George here, and now—and now it has been his death."

Isotta stroked Marcus' hair; he was kneeling at her feet, his head in her lap, very near the child in her womb. He had been to identify Massingbird's corpse at the city mortuary, an appalling task; the body had been entirely drained of blood. "He died quickly; he would know nothing," she said softly, for her father had told her. Bondone had ordered a mass to be said; that was like him, generous to everyone. She herself had felt fierce triumph at the death, but she would never tell Marcus of that. His sobbing had eased; presently he turned a tear-stained face towards her, and they kissed one another. "I am troubling you, *cara*," he said, "and the baby is to come soon; I should not fatigue you; I will go away."

"Stay with me," she told him, but he left her and began to walk up and down the room with his short strides, talking nervously. He was concerned about Massingbird's family, about the breaking of the news. "Poor Cathy must be told. I will write to her today. The child must be born by now; she never wrote. I must look after his children."

Why should he? He will have children of his own, she thought. She raised her head to where her own portrait, newly commissioned by Bondone, hung; she had worn a grey silk dress with flame-coloured ribbons, and her face was turned back over her shoulder, showing to advantage its oval shape and the dark eyes which looked out at the beholder. Marcus had been much taken with the portrait when he first saw it and had asked to be allowed to have a copy made for London; now, he was aware of nothing but that Massingbird was dead. "The police will find the murderer," Isotta told him, and was astonished to hear her own voice so calm and cold. "Your faith does not believe in prayers for the dead," she went on. "I will pray for us both."

And so she did, faithfully saying over George Massingbird's name like a talisman, as though she had never hated him. The dead could not fight back. Meantime, there were the preparations for England, where shortly Marcus must go for himself to see to the alterations Massingbird should have supervised. Marcus would be better at it; he had sound, restrained taste and was not extravagant: Papa would be pleased. As for herself, it depended on the birth whether she would go now or later. But no one should ever again come between herself and her husband, not even this child; not any of their children. She swore it, and to this purpose would devote her life.

3

The studio of the painter Ravallo stood on the third floor of a derelict building near the Ponte Vecchio. Among the clutter of props, stools, easels and painting-material he worked with his canvas placed to receive the light from the small square window which was covered with oiled paper. Light fell on the model, a young woman of about thirty-two, with her child by her, a little boy. She was pregnant, very beautiful, and her dark hair was twisted in a knot behind her head. Dressed as she was in the simple gown of black stuff all working-class women wore, Ravallo had varied its severe lines by casting a blue scarf across her shoulders and breast. She stayed still and quiet while he painted, and so did the child; they did not talk. Once the boy, who was aged about nine and had black curly hair and aquiline features, wriggled a little; his mother bent her head to reprove him, revealing a profile like an angel's, only the slight slackening of the jawline revealing the loss of youth. "Never mind it," said Ravallo roughly. "I have finished for today."

He threw down his palette and brushes, and went to where a small oil-stove burned, supporting a steaming kettle. Without further words he made coffee and brought it to the woman, who had risen to stretch herself. She smiled. "I am thankful for that," she said. "You kept us posing a long time today."

"It was a good day. I wanted to paint."

"Well, you have done so." She bent to give the boy a sip from her cup, but he turned his head away. Gabriella walked over to where the painting stood, the painting of herself and her son. All her movements were regal, as if she had been reared in palaces; Ravallo watched her hungrily. Many years ago she had been his mistress, but was now Bondone's; the boy was Bondone's son, also the child in her womb. The thought brought the dealer himself into the room, filling it with his personality. Beside that, Ravallo had long known himself to be of no importance; even his paintings seemed dull. He drank his coffee bitterly; he was very poor.

Gabriella was tactful. "You have a good likeness there of Rico, I think," she told him. Ravallo grunted. "But not of you," he said. "You always elude me. Even in the days when I painted you constantly it was so and now it is worse. You should not have come."

She smiled softly. "I came at your invitation, Ravallo." Only the use of his surname indicated the slight degree of formality now evident between them; she would not have permitted further familiarity, nor would he have sought it. As it was, his thoughts were sour. Bondone—Bondone again!—had been generous with money for a long time now; it was part of his compensation for the taking of Gabriella. The latter he kept in comfort, whereas she had not previously had enough food. One ought to be grateful, but could not. The change in her circumstances had made her flesh sleek; he had tried in vain to portray it. There was perhaps to be one more sitting, the last; then she would go back to her owner. Ravallo had not made the success he hoped for; no doubt Bondone would buy the painting of Gabriella and give it to her to hang in her room. It was called *The Mother*. Suddenly Ravallo clenched his fists savagely and stared with his protuberant eyes at the woman and her son.

"You have ruined me between you, I say. Even the boy is his. When I am dead there will be no one to remember." He raised the clenched fists to his eye-sockets and beat uselessly at them. Gabriella said softly "Rico will remember you, though you are not his father. He likes to come here; do you not, my child?"

Rico did not answer; he stared at the jumbled paint-tubes and bric-à-brac. Ravallo sometimes erected backgrounds of his own, and this diverted Rico; otherwise, he was bored. He preferred to be active, sailing boats he had whittled for himself out of wood, or playing and fighting with boys his own age. But he adored and obeyed his mother, and when she bade him come with her he did so without trouble, and kept interminably still while Ravallo painted. He accepted, though he did not understand, the place Ravallo held in his mother's life; it was different from Bondone's. The latter, whom he knew to be his father, was always kind to him, but seldom gave him money to spend. "He must learn to live with the others in the street, or else rise by his own efforts," Rico had heard him tell Gabriella. The remark filled him with a kind of resentment, and a determination indeed to rise. One day, he would have a house of his own, with *mammina*, her hair quite grey by then, seated in a great chair covered in velvet, drinking

61

tea with lemon.

He took her hand now to go and said nothing, merely nodding goodbye to Ravallo as he had been taught. The painter's figure was dark and still against the light from the window. The pair turned away and descended the rickety stairs, and when they came out into the sunlight of the street Ravallo was forgotten; there was life, the sky, the river under the bridge, shadows, other people.

They walked towards the street where they lived, passing motionless washing in rainbow-colours, hung out inevitably to dry between the upper houses which leant towards one another narrowly, their pink or yellow plaster peeling. Rico's mother kept hold of his hand; her face had grown pale. He sensed that she was not well and looked up at her.

"You are ill?" It sometimes happened that way; when she was so, he nursed her. She smiled a little. "I do not feel very well, it is true," she said. "It was all that time sitting in the cold room for Ravallo. He cannot afford to light the stove for long enough to be warm." Always her thoughts were for other people. Rico squeezed her hand fiercely. They were almost home.

"You must lie down on your bed and I will bring you coffee," he said. He was proud of his ability to help her; other women had husbands and families; she had nobody but him, and Bondone. Gabriella's smile twisted a little "Not that," she said, "the coffee in the studio was enough for me. It was not good."

"Ravallo can perhaps not afford good coffee."

"No. Poor Ravallo."

They came to the entry; by now she was white as a sheet, and shaking. Rico gazed at her, anxiety shining in his dark eyes. "Is it the baby?" he asked, for he knew all about that. Gabriella stiffened her lips against pain.

"Go and buy food for us," she said, though she could hardly bear to think of it. "I will lie down for a little." She counted out coins and put them into his palm. He gazed at her for instants, then went. Gabriella entered the room where they lived. She felt very ill. If it did not go away of its own accord she would send Rico for the old woman, the midwife, when he returned. But perhaps it would pass. She had felt ill before.

She had always kept herself aloof from the neighbours, who knew she was a kept woman and derided her; and so she did not ask for help now, when she was in pain. Presently she lay down on the bed, having unlaced herself. The ceiling had cracks in it and she stared at them, trying to remember her rosary and to forget the pain; but it grew worse, and soon she writhed in agony. Rico returned with the food, and she was able to tell him to put it on the stove; he must eat, for he was growing. The taste of the coffee she had drunk at Ravallo's was in her mouth again, thin and sour. If she could be sick, it would be better. She tried, retching. Rico came over afterwards with a plate of carefully cooked cabbage, but she turned her head away. "Eat it," she said. "Do not waste it." She felt a great tenderness for him rise; without her, what would become of him? Why think of that?

She clenched her fists and waited till Rico had emptied his plate and then said faintly, "Go to the midwife and tell her the pains have started." It must be that. She thought she felt better. Rico ran off not too unwillingly; the old woman, who lived two streets away, had once given him an orange. He ran fast, less however because of that than because of his mother.

The pains had stopped; the sickness remained. Gabriella was aware of a heavy dead feeling in her body, as though the very blood were chilled in the veins. She got up and tried to walk up and down the room, but felt weak and dizzy. The sound of the old woman mounting the stairs came and Gabriella called, "Send Rico out to play." The black-clad figure came into the room, wrinkled face concerned and kindly beneath its wrapped shawl; Maria Felucci was more charitable than her neighbours. "Lie down again," she said to Gabriella, "and we will see what is to be done." The other's appearance shocked her. It was a miscarriage, certainly; perhaps more. Presently the dead child came, all at once with much blood. Maria cleaned up the bed and the floor, heated soup and brought it to Gabriella to drink; but she would not take it. "Which would it have been?" she asked faintly.

"A boy. A fine boy with a large head. A pity."

The tears ran weakly down Gabriella's cheeks. That would have been a playmate for Rico, who was often solitary because the other children's mothers drew them away when they could catch them. Two little bastards could have been happy together. In her weakness she began to long for Bondone, whose presence in the room brought warmth and comfort. He was both father and lover to her, and had bought her from her grasping mother when she was eighteen years old. They had finished with Ravallo

63

by then. She did not regret having gone to Bondone; he was kind.

The midwife left and said she would look in later; she had baptised the dead baby and now took it away. Gabriella tried to turn her head and go to sleep, but could not; she began to be hot and cold by turns; there was still something wrong, perhaps everything had not come away with the baby. She lay still and at some time heard Maria come in again, tread softly and come over and look at her. She heard her say, "We must tell Signor Bondone." Then there was silence. When the dying woman opened her eyes it was to see the old woman seated by the stove. She had sent word, and then had come back. She was praying. "You are good, Maria," the sick woman whispered, then closed her eyes.

It was too late when Bondone came. He stood at the bedside looking down at Gabriella's dead face. Somewhere there was sobbing; it must be Rico. He should be sent to stay with a neighbour. Where were the neighbours, why did they not come?

He turned stiffly away from the body. Gabriella had gone. He felt his heart dead within him; he was too old and too tired to take another mistress. It had been a pity about the baby. He turned to the midwife who still waited and said "If you will look after my boy, I will see that money is sent you."

She responded with a sudden outburst of words; she had used the time to discover everything; the painter Ravallo had poisoned Gabriella. "He gave her coffee which tasted bad. She told me of it. That child should have lived. She herself was well enough. Why should a man do such a thing unless he is a devil?"

Maria crossed herself. Yes, she would look after the little boy. She had none of her own, and he was welcome.

Bondone left the house and walked through the busy streets to Ravallo's studio. He saw nothing of those he met on the way. It was almost as if he had thrust Gabriella's very death to the back of his mind, to be dealt with later; and yet she would always be with him. He would question Ravallo. There rose in the layers of his mind the feeling he had always had for the painter, mostly compounded of pity, no doubt because the man had been Gabriella's early lover. In those days he had looked much as he did now, the shock of hair already balding, the eyes like a startled hare's. Gabriella had often given him money to buy food or paint.

64

Bondone had always known that.

He mounted the derelict stairs and came to where the studio door stood ajar. There was a smell of spirits first and then he saw Ravallo. The man was seated with his fists against his eyes. He had been drinking—God knew where the money had come from—and when he looked up his eyes were bloodshot. He did not rise to greet Bondone.

"So she is dead," he said. "A neighbour told me."

Bondone stood looking down at him; when he spoke his voice was stern. "There is a tale about some coffee you gave her," he said. "Is that the truth, Ravallo? I must know the truth. Did you kill Gabriella? Why, why?"

The painter laughed mirthlessly. "Why?" He raised an arm to where the painting stood, still on its easel.

"Because in that moment she was mine, not yours," he said. "She was mine as she used to be. How lovely she was then! You know nothing of youth, of the days we spent here together, poor and in love; yes, she loved me then. She never loved you, old man; yet it was not I but your lust that killed her. You got a child on her, then lately another. You thought nothing of that. Do not speak to me of poison." He swayed to his feet, and came to where the dealer stood; his breath smelt of spirits. "I will kill you," he said, "because you killed Gabriella."

His hands were suddenly about Bondone's throat. The latter brought up his knee with a sudden movement and drove it into Ravallo's private parts. The man jerked away in agony, let go his grip and fell to the floor, writhing. He made no attempt to get up.

"Have a care to yourself, and keep out of trouble for your own sake," said Bondone calmly. The other did not reply and he went out. Going downstairs he passed a hand over his stock; it was disarranged and chafed his throat, which was already swollen. The episode had banished his grief for Gabriella for as long as it lasted, but now the grief returned; it no longer seemed worth living. He made his way on foot back to his office oblivious of passers-by.

Isabella rose from behind her accounts-table, and stood facing him. He knew an unwillingness to see her, speak with her. "Where have you been?" she said. "There have been enquiries. Your stock is ruined. Are you ill? Why do you look so?" She spoke coldly; at such times there was no affection between them. Her dowry had been useful, no doubt.

"Would you like coffee?" He shook his head. He had not looked at her directly. "There was a mishap," he told her, "that is all. I will go home and change my clothes. Think no more of it; it does not concern you."

Her eyes followed him as he went out. There were few customers in today, which was fortunate. Bondone had looked very strange.

Events took their course. Friday mornings at the show-room were still set apart for informal meetings of the family, if they chose to drop in; a few favoured clients sometimes joined them. Isotta had come today though Anna had not, and was sitting in the office drinking coffee and nibbling small ratafia biscuits which her mother passed about. She was very heavy with child, her figure concealed by a filmy scarf. Marcus was in the front shop, listening to Luigi as three or four people were shown round; his Italian still needed improvement. It had been decided that he and Isotta should not go to London till after the birth. Most things there were in readiness, and the description of the building, with its Adam ceilings and staircase, had excited the Bondone parents so much that Isabella pronounced that she would like to see it, and proposed paying the young couple a visit early in the new year. This project simmered, like others not nearing fulfilment for the shop was busy; the Austrian woman who had come in the other day, having obtained the permission of her husband, had returned to buy a sentimental painting of which Bondone was glad to be rid. She drank her coffee too elegantly, with the little finger raised, and could not take part in any of the talk. Bondone himself stood nearby, charming her with his ready wit; it was a triumph to have sold that painting, and he knew a little German. How much time was taken up in talking with clients, how little in selling to them! But he was content enough, looking round his family; as much so as he had been since Gabriella died. That part of his life was closed, and he had put it behind him, aware that sadness still lurked in corners of his mind.

He was not to be allowed to forget. The outer door swung open and a figure struggled in, carrying an unframed canvas; it was Ravallo. He directed his protuberant gaze to the glass front of the office, saw Bondone with his family, and kicked the door open. He thrust the painting in front of him, and bawled so that he could be heard in the shop. His linen was dirty and his hair

66

unkempt; he was evidently drunk. The painted figure of Gabriella, her child by her, stared from the canvas; it had a strange life of its own. Isabella Bondone had risen to her feet; what kind of behaviour was this? Bondone should never have encouraged the fellow.

"This is Bondone's woman and his son; another, as you can see, was on the way."

"Be silent. You must leave here."

"But why? I have brought it to sell. If Bondone will not buy it, who will? I am only a poor painter, not a dealer in flesh and blood and bones. How much will you pay, Messer Bondone, for the portrait of your woman? She is dead; it should be worth so much, so much." He stood there mouthing obscenities; the Austrian visitor had risen as if to leave. Such encounters should not happen; it was awkward. But Bondone barred her way.

"Be seated, *signora*, and behave as if nothing had occurred," he said in a low voice. "I will speak to him alone; I can deal with him. Ravallo, listen to me."

He had taken the man's arm and had drawn him away, almost out of earshot. As she was bidden, the Austrian sat down, but stiffly, on the edge of the chair. Isabella's lips were taut; there was scarcely surprise in this kind of thing, but it was distasteful and bad for custom. Isotta had half risen, trembling; her mother pulled her down. On the table the coffee-cups grew cold unheeded. Everyone began to make desultory small-talk as if nothing had happened; beyond the door Bondone could be heard reasoning with the unseen man. Then there came the sound of a shot.

"Papa!" screamed Isotta, and was first out of the door. Bondone lay on the carpet, a smoking hole in his coat above the heart. He was dead; a faint expression of surprise remained on his face. Isotta cast herself down beside the body, oblivious of danger; above her, the madman still brandished his gun. Luigi and Gastone huddled in the shop, their faces ashen. A woman screamed; it was the Austrian. Isabella Bondone took three strides to the door, and stood over her husband's body.

"Luigi, take the gun. Gastone, you will inform the police. I must apologise," she said as she turned to the crowding customers. Only after that did she let her gaze stray to the dead man. Her eyes scanned him, impersonal as though he were a stranger. No one said anything. As if in the distance, sobbing

67

could be heard; it was Isotta. Marcus had already run to her, taking her up in his arms; she leant her head against him, crying like a child. "Take her home," Isabella ordered. "I can tell the police what they want to know. Will nobody disarm that madman?" For Ravallo still stood, gun in hand, but as though he did not know how to use it any longer; the canvas of Gabriella lay on the floor and someone had trampled on it, tearing the corner. Tears were running down Ravallo's face. Presently Gastone came to him, and took the gun away.

When the police arrived, in contrast to his former behaviour Luigi tried to assume command of the situation. After all he was the elder son, and would inherit. Someone had flung a handkerchief over Bondone's face.

Isotta's son was born that night. Everyone agreed that the distress had been enough to bring on a premature birth. Isabella, still in command, had seen to everything, and now was sent for to view the baby. She stood calm-faced, holding him for moments, then gave him back to the nurse. A glance had told her all she needed to know; this was no premature child, his hair and nails were present and perfect. As well that nobody would dwell on it; the other matter occupied all minds. And there was consolation; every prominent citizen of Florence would come to the funeral.

The will was read afterwards. All of the relatives had come; a susurration of sable, silks and feathers sounded as the women entered with their husbands, in prosperous black to a man. Only one old woman, a child with her, wore a head-shawl and was ignored by the company.

The hush of talk stilled as Riccione came in, followed by a clerk. He took out the document and began reading it at once; his eyes did not stray to the audience. In it, Marcus Cray waited beside Isotta's sister Caterina and her husband Filippo; the big sandy-haired man had prominent foggy eyes like those of a prawn. Caterina's pretty dark curls clustered beneath her mourning-veil. Marcus had tried, in his halting Italian, to speak to them of the baby and they had listened with downcast eyes; at the first opportunity they began to talk of their own Baldassare, who was tall, strong, clever, and desired one day to enter the business. They had not brought him to the funeral; his schoolwork was important.

Luigi, in the front row as befitted his position, and Anna sat nearest the lawyer, with Gastone by them; his wife had not come. Anna's head was bent to show an expanse of white neck beneath her bonnet, resplendent as the latter was with curled black feathers. She was the best-dressed woman in the room, and knew it. Now and again she allowed her glance to stray to the lawyer, but he did not meet it. He had dispensed with the preliminaries and came to the main bequest. The relatives stiffened with expectation; Marcus Cray looked down at the floor.

". . . all my assets to my eldest son, Luigi Bondone, with the wish that the business remain in the family. To my wife Isabella Bondone, an annuity for life from the Treviro shares, at her death the capital to revert to the business. To my daughter Isotta Cray, the choice of any one article in the show-rooms, to be given to her outright."

Riccione had closed his folio and sat down. A buzz of talk broke out in the room; Isabella, seated alone, bristled with affront; an annuity only, as if she had been nothing but a hindrance! No doubt Luigi would be glad of her help in the office, however. Her mind turned over what she had learnt; nothing for Gastone, nothing for Marcus Cray. That last was surprising after all the talk there had been about the London branch. One would have expected a little help there; no matter. Bondone had been a hard man in his own way. As for his women . . . but there, there was nothing.

Marcus had excused himself to the Pelosi couple and to Isabella, and blundered out. The world had turned dark; no doubt others fared as hardly as he. As for the old woman in the shawl, she rose, and laid a hand on the little boy's shoulder. He wore a black armband and everyone could tell from his features that he was the son of Enrico Bondone.

"There is nothing for us here, my child," she said. "Let us go home."

Isotta was sitting up against the pillows, the baby in a cradle nearby. When she heard Marcus' step she passed a hand over her hair and smoothed the ruffles of her nightgown. She looked forward to hearing the results of the will; Papa would have treated Marcus fairly, she was certain. Already he had grown much fonder of her husband than of Luigi or Gastone, but of course an inheritance—

But a glance at Marcus' face told her; something was badly wrong. He was pale-faced; he came silently to the bed. She flung her arms out to him, crying, "What has gone wrong? Tell me of it."

He slipped down on his knees by the bedside, and laid his head against her. She cradled it in her arms, loving the soft richness of the chestnut hair. In his cradle, the baby slept through it all; he was placid and nothing as a rule seemed to wake him. A mercy, she thought; a child's screaming now would have stretched their taut nerves unbearably. "Tell me," she said again.

"It is not as we had been led to expect." He raised a haggard face to her; at that moment she could see him as he might be when an old man. "Bondone has left me nothing, it is all to go to your brother; not a word about the London branch, nothing—except that you are to have the choice of any one item from the show-room. It's like a bad fairy tale." He laughed mirthlessly. "I have entered into debts concerning the London house which it will take me years to pay off unaided. Bondone told me to go ahead and order what I wished, and it is too late now to withdraw." He got to his feet and turned about the room, not even looking at the baby. "He is dead and one cannot blame him," he said at last. "No doubt he thought first of his family."

Her eyes had narrowed; they must think what best to do. "Papa cared nothing for Luigi or Gastone," she said. "Perhaps he made a later will which has not been found. I am certain he would not have seen you go without money for the London shop. It was what he wanted, his own suggestion, almost his own child. He would not have left you to bear it all alone. I will consult Mamma."

"No, my heart; the thing is done. All the relatives heard it and no one said anything, not your sister or her husband, or Gastone. You at least have the choice of one thing, which may be very valuable. He loved you, Isotta, best of all his children. In the short time I knew him I grew certain of it."

She brushed that aside. "Papa knew there was no need to provide further for Caterina," she said, "Filippo is making a great deal of money with his society photographs. And Gastone made a rich marriage. No, there is something wrong, I am certain."

"He did not expect to die. Perhaps, like many men, he intended to make a new will, and delayed it."

Isotta spread out her white hands on the coverlet; she stared at

70

the wedding-ring she wore, looking suddenly old and wise. "I know what I shall choose, and I believe Papa meant me to choose it," she said. "I shall take the *croce francesca*. Then if we are short of money we may sell it later on. For now, we will do everything as cheaply as we can; I will help you in your office, as Mamma helped Papa."

His eyes had grown tender, but he spoke stiffly. "Not in London, Isotta; it is not the fashion there for wives to work. You will stay at home and look after our little rascal. See how he grows!" He smiled. "It does not seem only the other day that he was born; he might have been with us always, he is so much a part of us. I swear he knows me already."

He bent over the baby's cradle, and hearing her sob suddenly said to her, "Never fear, darling; we will make something out of this coil. We are young, and have hope and strength, and our son."

After he had gone Isotta cast the covers aside and got up and went to where the cradle lay. The baby was in every part the son of Felice Nardini; the swarthy skin, the hooded eyes, the muscular long body. She would be glad to leave Italy with Marcus. London was a challenge, after all; as he had said, they would meet it together. She lifted the baby and strained him to her.

"You are Marcus Cray," she whispered, "the second Marcus Cray. You will have a great inheritance, and grow rich, and make us proud."

She began to feel dizzy; it was the first time she had left her bed unaided, and she soon set the baby down and sank into a chair. Marcus the younger crowed a little, not protesting at having been wakened from his sleep. He put his fat fists in his mouth and nuzzled them. He was good-natured and healthy, despite his hurried birth.

The following day was a holiday of obligation, and, except for Marcus and Isotta, the family went to Mass. Early next morning, a letter was handed to Luigi Bondone at the show-room, which had opened again after its mourning, though black crepe bows still decorated the doors. Luigi had been trying to suppress, for propriety's sake, the surge of pleasure his new position gave him; as the eldest son of Papa, he had at last achieved recognition. No more subservience to Mamma in the shop; he was her employer now, and one of the richest men in Florence. As for Isotta and her

71

husband, they must arrange matters for themselves; it was no longer his affair.

He took the letter which had come, and slit it open with an ivory knife Bondone had always used. More than anything these small gestures made Luigi feel himself master. He had already looked round the show-room to decide what he would keep and what remove. There would be much rearrangement; he had not always agreed with Papa.

He stared at the sheet of paper he now held. *I would be grateful if you would call to see me urgently. There is a private matter to discuss.* It was signed by Riccione. Why could the lawyer not have spoken to him two days ago? Luigi frowned; his day was upset. Best get it done, no doubt; but in future the notary need not think that he, Bondone, was at anyone's beck and call. He called for his hat, gloves and cane to be brought; and went out into the bright day.

Riccione was in his office, at a desk cluttered with briefs and deeds relating to property. Against the walls, each one piled in its place, reposed painted black boxes with white initials; in its way, the room was like a cemetery. The seeming disorder had method, however; Riccione could have put his hand on any named document at once. By the time Luigi was shown in the lawyer had a paper in his hand and was reading it carefully.

"You wished to speak with me. It was inconvenient, but I came, as you see." Best adopt a blustering manner, now he was head of the firm; otherwise this man might overreach himself. Both men seated themselves; Luigi sat with legs crossed, surveying his expensive tailor-made trousers and well-polished shoes. Riccione was smiling a little.

"Forgive me, but it would have been more inconvenient had you failed to come," he told the other.

"Why? You saw me two days ago, after the funeral."

"Let me apprise you of the contents of what I did not read after the funeral. Tell me your thoughts on the matter then, if you will."

He began without delay in seeming parody of what had been formerly read: this time, the business was divided equally between Luigi and Marcus Cray. Cray was to be permitted to use two-thirds of the available capital to launch the new business in London. As before, Isabella was given an annuity; likewise a woman named Maria Felucci, whom no one knew.

Luigi blanched. "When was this signed?" he asked. Bondone's

scrawl was clear at the bottom of the paper, also that of two witnesses.

Riccione looked across at him. "It was signed last month in this office."

"Then—the other, which you read out—"

"Is invalid; that is if I choose to reveal it. You will appreciate now why I had to see you in private, Signor Bondone."

"Then—then I—but why, if so, did you read the other? Why? It is a felony; it—I may not—" He was stammering, stupefied; the face of the notary remained expressionless.

"Do not mistake me," Riccione said, "you can prove no felony. If you want this later document, let us say, discovered, I can say that it was found during a search of the house in the course of my duty as executor. In fact, I have carried out this duty already as you know. But I can cover my part in the affair, and you will be the loser of a large sum of money to Marcus Cray. If you prefer this, say so."

"Of course I do not prefer it." Luigi's voice had grown squeaky. That Englishman, that stranger, who had captivated his father, to inherit more than himself, the heir! "One could claim," he said, "that my father was of unsound mind in making such a will. I—"

Riccione's lips twisted. "No one who knew Enrico Bondone would say that he was of unsound mind. One has to be down-to-earth in such matters. In any case, the expenses of such a suit would be large; they would swallow up a great deal of the capital if Cray chooses to fight."

"Give me—" said Luigi, and held out his hand for the later will. Riccione twitched it away, his eyes like steel. "No," he said, "it will remain with me." He placed the paper in a drawer in the table, locked it and replaced the key among his near effects. Luigi had begun to pound his fist on the table-top; like most weak men he gave way quickly to temper, even hysteria. "It is against the law," he kept saying, "it is against the law."

"Then we will fulfil the law, and have this will read. You need only say the word, for no one knows of its existence except yourself, myself, and two clerks for whom I will be responsible."

He clasped his hands and laid them on the table. Luigi stopped his antics and stared at them. They were long, shapely hands, with scrupulously kept nails, and a crested signet.

"What do you want?" he heard himself say, and at the same

time was afraid. It was known that this man was a leader among the *carbonari*; Massingbird, after all, had died. Why? Questions, seemingly irrelevant, chased themselves across the blank expanse of Luigi's mind, and he waited open-mouthed for the answer. It came.

"I will tell you what I want. I desire to possess your wife. Those are my terms. One occasion will be enough. I am not greatly interested in women, but she gives my mind no peace."

"You would . . . you . . ."

"Think of it; if you prefer, you may have a little time, and come back here and let me know your answer. If it is negative, this second will favouring Cray must be read. On the other hand, if you will grant what I ask no one will know of its existence, as I have said, except ourselves. On that you have my firm promise, and I am a man of my word."

He sat still, and Luigi found himself staring at the man like a rabbit confronted by a snake. To desire Anna, Anna! And for that, no more, he himself would be a rich man, unless . . .

It came to him that he had never greatly cared for Anna; the marriage had been arranged by their families. There remained the unspoken taunt between them that she was his superior in looks, wit, breeding, the rest. She despised him and showed it. Now—

His mouth was dry. "How, if I say so . . . how will you . . . she is a virtuous woman. She may raise the alarm."

Riccione's narrow smile widened; he had been confident from the beginning. "Leave it to me," he said. "Admit me into your house one night we shall arrange, and see and hear nothing. That is all."

"Give me that paper," said Luigi hoarsely. The notary shook his head. He seemed to be fashioned of metal, unyielding; even his hair was the colour of iron, smoothed back from his forehead. The filtered sunlight through the dusty office window shone on it. He lowered his head towards his clasped hands, as though he were praying.

"No," he said aloud. "The paper will in any case remain in my care. You need have no fear that it will be seen by anyone interested. I have as much to lose in this matter as yourself."

Anna lay in bed in a lawn nightgown trimmed with point lace. She had lately had the house redecorated to bring it more in fashion with the neighbours'; the style everywhere was ornate and heavy, the turned legs of mahogany bulging with curves solid as a man's arm. The curtains were of ball-fringed chenille and on this night she had had them drawn close, so that the room was in total darkness after she turned out the lamps. There was no moon outside, and only a sliver of diffused light crept between the curtains from another house still lit nearby. Anna lay awake for some moments, then slept.

She wakened again after a time, she did not know how long. It seemed to her that Luigi was in the room, moving stealthily as he always did on his rare visits. She shrugged to herself, bored; it was long enough since he had come to her. She listened to his soft footfall and then sensed his coming near the bed. A strengthening of dislike came to her, and she called out sharply "Is that you, Luigi?", but the sound seemed muffled by the curtains.

"Who else?" came the answer, softly; she felt him slide into bed. He reached out to her, with a smooth accustomed motion; gently, he eased the nightgown up. Anna closed her eyes and endured his handling of her; she had taken the marriage vows and this was her duty. But he used her differently tonight, caressing and exploring her body with a sure avid touch, as if he were a lover. She felt him enter her presently with a sensation in herself that was like an indrawn breath, a gasp; gradually she was becoming aware of him. The bed shook and trembled with his riding of her; the questing hands had not grown still; they had sought out the secret places of her body, soothing, separating, stroking, fondling. Her mouth had fallen open and he laid his lips on hers; it was like no other kiss she had ever known. Massingbird was dead. Yet she would rather a dead lover than a living husband were with her now; and with that waning memory came the certainty, horrifying and elating her at the same time; *the man who lay within her was not Luigi.*

She could not cry out; his mouth was still on hers, muffling the sounds. Anna took the only refuge open to her and fainted. In that lost awareness he might do as he would with her; she would feel nothing, know nothing more.

When she came to herself he had gone, and daylight was in the room. There seemed nothing to show that he had been. Had she dreamed it? No; her body warred between outrage and contentment, and the lace-trimmed nightgown lay on the floor.

Next night there was a moon, and shuddering she allowed its light into the room, not drawing the curtains. The clouds chased before it in the night; she turned away from them, willing herself not to recall Luigi's smug face at breakfast. Whoever her lover had been, Luigi knew it all. She shivered; they should not steal a march on her again. She did not admit to herself that she hoped whoever it had been would come back. But he did not; she was alone.

Shortly the wind died and there commenced a heavy calm, frequent after heat such as had been in the day. Later in the night thunder pealed, the rain fell in torrents and there were flashes of lightning, illuminating the flat roofs of the old part of town. Anna woke and sat up in bed, terrified; she dared not go to the window to draw the curtains, which would have protected her; such a night! She cast wildly about her, looking for her silk négligée to put it round her; but it lay on a chair, out of reach. She cowered in bed, aware of nothing but the storm, its flashes lighting up the room. She screamed, for the door-handle had turned. Who was coming in?

But it was Luigi, holding a small lamp which cast flickering upward shadows on his face. She was irritated; he could have found his way without it. She lowered her eyes as he came and stood by the bed; he had set down the lamp on her dressing-table. His dark eyes scanned her; he passed his tongue over his lips.

"Are you afraid of the storm?" he said, and she thought that it was strange that he showed no fear. He was a coward in most things. "Yes," she said, "I am afraid," and she watched him get into bed beside her by the light of the spluttering lamp. It had come to her that this must be done; on such and such a night, her husband had slept with her. Yet she loathed his prurience; he took her, furtively; aided by a kind of spiteful eagerness like that of an unpleasant child. He knew about the other, that was certain; she would ask him nothing: he should not have that satisfaction. Her body made no response to him, any more than it ever had; a disagreeable duty was fulfilled, no more. He left her in the end and turned over on his back to fall into hunched sleep. The maid would find him there in the morning. Riccione should not boast that he had cuckolded him, he had determined before drifting off; if anything came of it, Anna had been his lately also.

In such ways Anna never knew for certain who was the father of the child she conceived, though she had her suspicions. She went through a bad time, queasy and ill in the mornings; then told Isabella, who told Luigi. Bondone's widow was pleased; at least now the name would continue. And a birth would settle Anna, who had always been flighty; a child made a tie. That was all, and nobody expected that the baby would be less than healthy or other than a boy. A boy was required, and in due course he came, forcing his predestined way out from Anna's pampered flesh, perhaps hearing her cries, showing himself at last to a world of lace and perfumed satin, plump pillows, anxious women. Women were to be anxious all of young Luigi's life; now, however, they washed his strong little body, laid the dark head against a cosseting shawl, and placed him in his frilled peach-coloured cradle before hastening back to his mother, who had screamed aloud so many times in course of the labour that it might have been thought it would kill her; but she did not die.

After the birth of her son fate somewhat abandoned Anna, and she divided her thoughts between her son and her food. She was overtaken soon by a pervasive fat, invading especially her arms and bosom and her chin. She was still handsome after the fashion of many an overfed matron, but no longer took trouble with her dress, favouring black as a rule. Nothing, then or later, was ever whispered against Signora Anna's reputation; she had become very devout, abandoning her prayers chiefly for meals or, for instance, to choose a fresh *gouvernante* from the list of available Englishwomen repeatedly sent by Isotta from London. There was, indeed, enough to occupy a governess in the Bondone household soon; Anna gave birth to a second son two years after the first. He was small and puny, and was called Filippo after his uncle in Milan. Shortly after that, the elder Luigi was to die of pneumonia, having enjoyed the directorship of the Bondone interests for a very brief time.

One thing Bondone had been able to do before his death was to write a letter of introduction to a merchant banker in London. Marcus presented this soon after his arrival, and was shown into the inner office, warm with its red Turkey carpet and redolent of cigars. He stated his case. The banker frowned, leaning back in his swivel chair and watching his own fumes ascend to the ceiling. He had already offered Marcus a cigar with his whisky; but the latter did not smoke and disliked the habit. He sat modestly waiting for the verdict, feeling a despair that had now become familiar. It was going to be impossible to launch the venture without financial help.

"The thing to do is float a company," the banker said presently, "put shares on the market and allow buyers to come in."

"Provided the discretion is left with me, that should be possible." Marcus raised his arched eyebrows. He had thought of such a course himself, but was uncertain how to go about it. "Can you advise me regarding procedure?" he asked, staring likewise at the blue ascending smoke. After the clear air of Florence, London seemed unbearably foggy and dull; had the whole enterprise been a mistake from the start? Only time would tell.

"You yourself would have to keep a majority of shares, and that is where the Bank could come in and, perhaps, hold them." The suggestion was gently made, as such suggestions are, but Marcus chafed at the prospect of supervision, delayed choice; bargains could be lost by such means. He frowned a little. "I would prefer that my share be independently held," he said. "There are other assets, though not many." He thought of Long-houses, still unsold; he had not had the heart to put it on the market, remembering the days when he had been a boy there, at last able to ride and scramble over rocks and heather with the best; and George, his curly hair tossed by the wind from the moors, steady with a gun at his shoulder, laughing with the sun in his eyes. Why did his thoughts roam so? He should be attending to what this knowledgeable, worldly man was saying. The Bondone brothers had been no help; Luigi when approached had made it clear that, though he would trade with the London office, he wanted no responsibility.

"—and he has put his money largely into railroads, which as you will know are giving a good price for land. He might be interested in this company; he has capital to spare, and is honest." The banker went on smiling a little. "I will not say that he is what one thinks of as being knowledgeable over art. But he would learn."

"I had thought of having other avenues than paintings, which of course would be the main interest of Bondone and Cray, as it was in Italy. I had in mind Chinese silks, Indian muslin of limited design, perhaps pottery, silver, glassware, all of a high standard."

The banker nodded. "And you have the premises, centrally placed. Provided there are buyers, you should do well."

"If I can start at all."

There was no offer of facilities. "You must meet this man Youngchild," the banker said. "If he is interested, he will have his own views, naturally. It is for you to decide, after meeting with him."

Marcus eventually invited the banker and his friend Youngchild to meet him at the Piccadilly shop. It was as well to give the man, if he came in, an idea of what he was about to buy, in part. The part itself caused Marcus much unwillingness. He had looked forward to being in sole control, as Enrico Bondone had intended.

They met in what was to be the boardroom, seated at a superb refectory table Jacob Cray had found in a Sienese monastery long ago in his youth. On the walls, newly painted a light mint green, hung the portrait of Jacob himself, sad-eyed and bearded, and at the other end the painting of Isotta. Marcus looked at it as he made his halting speech; at such times his stammer came back to him. And he disliked Youngchild; rich as the man might be, he might as well have asked a grocer to join the company. Youngchild was not tall, but gave the impression of great height because of his stance, like a bull about to charge; his hair was scraped over a balding forehead, his green eyes were watchful, and his face discoloured with eczema. He had his hands on the table in front of him and they were not clean. Marcus averted his gaze, and went on with what he had been trying to say. Youngchild chimed in, with his Yorkshire accent; he had owned much land up there, and still held the coalfields which had been found on his estate.

"See, lad, I'm pleased with the premises; they're central, as our good friend here says, and you've done them up a bit newfangled, but it'll serve. I doan't like all these light colours myself, but no doubt they're the coming thing. Thing is, if I put brass in aught, I like to control my money. I'd settle for a major share that'd have some effect if we fell out, say." He smiled with closed lips; Marcus raised his eyes and met the green gaze. "I myself would prefer to keep the controlling interest, naturally," he said. The banker joined in, tactfully.

"If it were a company with, as we hope, several shareholders,

79

there need be no hard and fast decisions without the vote of the majority. I think we know that Mr Cray has the expert knowledge needed to keep up standards. But in this kind of business there must necessarily be much money bound up in stock which may not sell quickly."

"A quick return's what I'm accustomed to expect," put in Youngchild. "How if, as well as these high-falutin lines Mr Cray suggests, we have some down-to-earth goods that'll make a quick turnover, say imported teas and brasswork and the like? I have interests in shipping, as y'know, and I'd—"

He went on about what he would do; and Marcus blenched at the prospect of his show-rooms being made to contain painted tin trays and Birmingham ware. He stiffened a little in his seat. "We don't want," he said, keeping his voice low and courteous, "to make this just no more than any other store, Mr Youngchild. Bondone and Cray are names which are known internationally for fine taste and discernment. It will, I grant you, take a little longer to become established, but I personally am not in favour of lowering our standards in the interests of quick sales. In Florence—"

"Ay, but in Florence they'll not put their brass into't, from what ye say," announced Youngchild, and blew the smoke from his cigar straight towards Marcus' face. The young man fought off a feeling of distaste. "I think," said the banker, "that we'd better give it time."

They parted, amicably.

Youngchild became a major shareholder in the business of Bondone and Cray, foreign merchants, on the condition that if Marcus' plans for the running of the business failed after two years to produce a valid return, the emphasis should change and the store be run according to Youngchild's pattern. In the event of failure then, the business was to be thrown open to public purchase. As from the present, Youngchild would share the costs on an equal basis.

Marcus took the whole depressing business to Isotta, who had helped him choose the colours and style of the furnishings in the show-room; he was glad to find that she had taste in such matters. Young Marcus was learning to walk, and staggered in petticoats between one parent and the other; his nurse was within call beyond the door. The bright, dark eyes surveyed each

80

parent sleepily. "I think he has my father's eyes," Marcus said, holding out his arms. The warm, living bundle ran into them, and he set his lips against the little boy's dark hair. "Why do I complain?" he asked. "I have you, my son, and my health; we will beat this man Youngchild somehow. How I wish I could raise the money to buy him out!"

"There is one thing we could sell; the *croce*."

"Never. I think of it as having brought you to me. It is our talisman."

"Nevertheless, it may be necessary," said Isotta. She smiled a little. "You see, young Marco may not—will not—be the only one."

"Isotta, you—?"

"Yes. Probably in April. It is as well that you have forbidden me to help you in the office. I shall spend the time on my sofa, with my feet up, like the ladies of fashion here. How extraordinary they are about expecting their children! They will not mention it, and blush when I do. Where I come from we are more natural, less coy. I find the English strange."

"You are my beautiful love, and whatever you do is perfect. But do not alienate the English ladies."

"Oh, no." Her eyes twinkled. "We need their custom, is it not so?"

He kissed her, and worry was forgotten for the time; but would return later, especially in the night, to gnaw at him. Not least of it was that he had had to jettison the Bondone name when the money was put in; the firm was Cray and Youngchild now. Well, he must accustom himself; at least the venture was at last begun.

4

Isotta was walking in Hyde Park. A little way ahead were the children and their nurse; she liked to watch them. Marco, dark, chubby and strong, already made it evident that he thought the pace too slow; he leapt back and forth, disdaining the hoop and stick which had been given him. Maria, the baby, stared at him with golden eyes, safely held by the nurse's hand; she was a quiet child, very observant. Isotta expected a third, and again, as last time, hoped that on this occasion it would be a son, a true heir for her husband.

Otherwise, she was content. It was pleasant that Mamma's promised visit, which had endured far too long, was ended; and that they had successfully postponed that of Aunt Betty Platen from Edinburgh, who had written suggesting herself and her daughter Selina but said they could not afford the fare. Isotta had dealt with that matter ruthlessly; she did not want Marcus' sister in the house, taking in everything and gossiping about it afterwards; she had fobbed off Betty with some excuse. There was enough to think of without relatives.

She passed a distinguished acquaintance, and nodded gracefully, pleased to be acknowledged. People of taste and discernment flocked to Marcus nowadays, and as matters progressed he would often invite the men, and later their wives, to the house in Piccadilly where he and she now lived. Subsequently they would be asked to pay return visits, and in such a way one's social position was strengthened, one's new gowns and hairdressing noted; it was all very pleasant. With her increasing knowledge of English—she could speak it now without an accent—Isotta would be able to follow the talk, and appreciate the witty sayings of some *bon viveur* who had perhaps bought a painting or even a figurine whose value lay in its age. Isotta never put herself forward, though as Enrico Bondone's daughter she knew as much about the business as these men; instead, she watched Marcus happily. He was already spoken of as the foremost authority in England about certain periods of art. His championship, about two years ago, of an almost unknown painter whose work fetched much money now that he was dead had been fortunate; nobody but Marcus had housed and shown the paintings at the time. And not long ago he had journeyed abroad, leaving her with the children, and had brought back much of interest including what was almost certainly a Claude Lorraine. Yes, the firm was doing well; it had not even been necessary to let that odious man Youngchild have his way in too much, though he constantly struggled for it.

Marcus' advice was much sought. She wondered how he fared at this moment; an important client, a Wiltshire land-owner, wanted the portraits in his country-house restored, and Marcus had travelled there to give his advice and stay for a day or two; he should be home tomorrow. That would be more work for the shop; altogether, matters were flourishing and Bondone himself would have been pleased with the way the London branch had come up to his expectations. It had not been needful to sell the *croce*, even at the beginning when the future was less certain than now. Yes, they had arrived.

"I think that they are tired now," she called to the nurse, who caused Marco to pivot round, once again bowling his hoop. The fringed baby-carriage rocked on its leaf-springs; Maria was lifted back into it and sat chubbily, her red-gold curls glistening under her hat.

They made their way home past the riders and carriages in Piccadilly—until lately it had been possible to meet the Queen out riding—and Isotta knew satisfaction at the sight of her own front door. The outer steps were scrubbed daily with milk to keep them white, and the brass of the handle and finger-plates shone. Round the further corner, as everyone now knew, was the handsome building with the Cray and Youngchild sign painted in gilt on a black ground, and the leaded glass windows showing fine wares discreetly. But the house itself was a gentleman's private residence, its convenience making it easy for Marcus to visit the store at all hours. He would be there now, and would come home in time for luncheon. That event took place at four o'clock, with the children upstairs in their nursery. There was time, accordingly, for callers between now and then, and Isotta was not surprised when the parlour-maid informed her—they did not keep a manservant—that a lady had come, and had waited this past half-hour. "Take my furs," said Isotta, and removed her bonnet and smoothed her hair in front of the great mirror edged with *putti* which she and Marcus had brought with them from Florence. Then she went into the smaller drawing-room, where callers were put to wait if she were out; and made ready a little speech of apology. She had not asked the visitor's name; everyone who was anyone might call.

But the speech was never made, and a well-dressed woman rose composedly from the couch; the last person in Isotta's mind, and the least welcome there.

It was Lucy Nardini.

The blue-green eyes scanned her, mockingly; their sly oblique glance had not altered. Otherwise Lucy seemed prosperous; she wore clothes which were timeless, expensive enough, but without jewellery. Isotta kept her own face stiff with the smile of welcome, giving nothing of her fear away. Lucy began by talking of her marriage to an old nobleman who had lately died, leaving her free but almost penniless. Here it is, thought Isotta. Lucy was still mocking the world and herself. "What we will do, my dear, for a name! His was ancient, but we could cut no figure in Rome, where one needs a great deal of money to live suitably. So I bethought myself of my friends at last, and came here to you."

"It is a long time since we were friends, Lucy."

"Ah, time passes. And I have . . . as you know . . . a certain letter you once wrote. You will remember it."

"I do not."

"Then I will refresh your memory; I have it by heart. *Felice, I am going to have a child; it is yours. Will you help me? Would you marry me? I dare not write more, but you know I love you always. Your Isotta Bondone.* You were a confiding little creature, my dear; such things should never be put on paper."

Isotta heard her own voice, icy with disgust. "How did you obtain it from Felice?" The shadow of the past lengthened; how long was it since she had thought of her dead lover, who had once been all the world?

"Felice never saw it," Lucy told her. "I did not send it; I knew it would be of no interest to him, and one day, very possibly, useful to me."

"Then he never saw . . . never knew . . ."

The room whirled about her, then was still. A stirring of pride

84

rose in Isotta; if Felice had seen the note, he might not have abandoned her. As things had turned out, it had all been for the best; but something deep within her, a shamed and crying child, was comforted. Yet Lucy had not come to bring consolation.

"Never," said she. She shrugged her slender shoulders. "As I told you at the time, it would have made no difference. He would not have married you, a commoner. You have done much better for yourself, that is evident." She looked round the graceful, restrained furnishings of the room. "Your reputation soars, my Isotta; oh, yes, I have been in London for some weeks."

"Lower your voice; the servants will overhear."

"And that would never do, would it? And your husband? If he were to be shown such a letter, what would happen? Your pretty edifice would tumble like a house of cards. It is perhaps worth a little compromise; I will not be too demanding." She began to fan herself slowly with her gloves; the movement was graceful, mocking, deriding. Isotta's face was white; the eyes burned in it.

"What do you want of me?" she said. Lucy smiled amiably, and patted the couch where she sat; it was upholstered in narrow stripes, and was the *dernier cri*.

"That is better," she said. "I knew you were practical, my dear. A little money for pleasure, regularly paid, will suit me very well; and my dressmaker's bills. It is several months since I have had a new gown. I have never, you see, been able to enjoy life as freely as you do, with your accommodating conscience; always there have been obstacles, burdens. First I was the poor relation of Felice's family, then the unwilling bride of the first old lecher who happened to offer for me in the marriage-market. They were glad enough to be rid of me; I have had my miseries; now I want to enjoy myself. I have no children, no ties. It might be worse, might it not, Isotta *mia*?"

From Florence came the news of the death of Luigi, who had failed to change his clothes after a heavy shower of rain. The past year had not been happy for him; he had fallen in love, unsuitably, with a very young lady, the niece of a woman friend of Isabella's who had come to look after the Bondone accounts, during the latter's absence in England. Signorina Angelica was fair-haired, blue-eyed and gentle; she did not return Luigi's passion or that of any man. She entered a convent, as she had always intended to do; Luigi's heart, and such spirit as he had ever had, broke. Afterwards he did not care what became of him, and no doubt died because he had not the will to live; his going caused no particular gap in the family.

One surprising fact emerged at the reading of the will. Luigi had left Anna an annuity, as his father had done for Isabella. Gastone—the two men had not been on good terms lately—was to continue in charge of the shop on behalf of the boy Luigi. But neither to Anna nor to Gastone was the guardianship of the two boys given, but to the lawyer Riccione. Gastone regarded this as an insult, and was hard put to it to swallow his pride and remain. Of Anna's opinion nothing was recorded. Riccione would do his duty by the boys, as might have been expected of him.

After Luigi's funeral, Anna had waited in her widow's weeds, with young Luigi by her still in petticoats, his long dark hair hanging in rich curls to his shoulders. The notary was announced and came in, bowing; there was nothing but respect in his manner. Anna inclined her black-veiled head graciously; beneath it the hair's assisted gilding showed a trifle dimmed. It occurred to her that Riccione had put on less flesh than she; he was as lean as ever, perhaps too much so; his face seemed gaunt and stretched over the cheekbones, with a yellow look. The glance he had given her on entering had been impersonal; he had penetrated her mystery long ago; by now they were lawyer and client, no more. He sat down and spread his papers in front of him, assiduously helped by the young clerk who had come, and whose name was Massini. The latter gave an admiring glance at Anna; a handsome woman, perhaps on the fleshy side, but he liked them so. Anna returned the glance equably; she knew where she was with such a person.

Riccione had begun reading in his dry light voice, assuring Anna of a comfortable income, as might have been expected. Young Luigi surveyed everyone in the room with his oblique honey-coloured gaze; he was bored, but realised that the occasion was one of importance. Filippo had been left behind in the nursery, playing with his toys. He liked dolls, like a little girl. Luigi, staring at the two men's intent faces, wriggled away from his mother's plump white grasp and turned his head to meet what he knew would be there; the ever-present plants with their green underwater shadows, one of them like the spread fingers of a man's hand. He knew his mother disliked the plants, but would not part with them. His father, on the other hand, had liked them. Otherwise there was not much to remember about the undistinguished shade which had already passed on.

Riccione had finished reading the will and rose. He came to where the boy was and laid his thin fingers on that dark head. "May God bless and preserve you, my son," he said; an odd phrase for one who claimed to be an agnostic. Otherwise there was nothing remarkable about the meeting, or, of course, any need to worry whence the money was to come. It would continue in the male line of the elder branch of Bondone; everything was satisfactory.

Isotta's time drew near again, but without the peace of mind she had had at Maria's birth; now, everywhere was quicksand. She and Marcus even quarrelled, a happening which could never have been dreamt of and which left her in misery. It concerned a pair of drop pearl ear-rings Isotta seldom wore, but she cherished them because they had been a gift from her husband after their daughter's birth. Desperate for money now that Lucy's demands must be constantly met, she had taken the ear-rings to a jeweller and had pawned them, meaning to retrieve them somehow when things improved or Lucy went away. The latter was constantly at the house nowadays, frequently for meals, which irritated Marcus for he did not like the Marchesa di Lara. He was unable to understand Isotta's evident thirst for the woman's company and would rather they dined alone. But Isotta seemed devoted to her friend and he did not wish to make his wife unhappy. One day, however, when Isotta was by herself, he came in, his face stern; in his hand reposed the ear-rings.

"I noticed these in a certain shop," he told her. "They have an unusual colour, almost pink. Why did you part with them? Do I keep you so short of money?" He was puzzled as well as hurt; Isotta had seemed extravagant lately and the housekeeping bills were huge.

She began to cry. "No, no, dearest Marcus, you are generosity itself, but I—I wanted to give to a certain charity, and did not like to ask you." She could think of nothing better than the lame pretext; she sat with her hands before her eyes and he could see her thickened body. Pity for her state overcame his anger; no doubt she was not herself. He came over and kissed her and she flung her arms about his neck, weeping.

"Love me always. Promise me that, whatever happens. I am

wretched when we quarrel." The sobs grew in her throat; gently, he took each ear and replaced the pearls. "That is better," he told her. "Now you must wear them every day to convince me that you are not giving to charities in such a foolish way again." He was smiling, but despite his forgiveness she continued in fear; as before, the thought nagged at her that this child should be, must be, a son. If Marcus had an heir of his own he might forgive even what Lucy held concealed. She must pray for that, and thank God for Marcus' love. He renewed it now, his voice grown deep.

"Love you always? Certainly; you need not ask. You are my wife and the mother of my son. I have never known such happiness as now, Isotta. Only do not act like a little fool any more; you know you only have to ask me for money."

She went into labour in November, with the fog making her cough. She had not been feeling as well as before the births of the other children. Lucy still pestered her, deft and determined; the sick-room at least was free of her presence. Isotta grew restless, feeling the pains come and then stop; outside, it grew dark early, and the lamps showed through a coloured ring of fog. If only the air were clear enough to breathe! For almost the first time since coming to England, she longed for the crisp days and constant sunshine of her own land, then remembered poor dead Luigi, and felt melancholy; it was sad to have been so unloved.

The pains began again, and she strained hard, obeying the instructions of the nurse. "Holy Mother of God, let it be a son," she prayed. All of her body yearned to give birth. Why was the child so slow in coming? The pains had begun this morning, and now it was night.

The child was born at last; a boy, and dead. She was blind with weeping by the time Marcus came in. He tried to comfort her.

"Never fret, my heart. We have our little rascal, who thank God is strong. And Maria will be a beauty one day, like her mother. What more can we desire? Come, drink this milk they have warmed for you; it will give you strength." But she turned her head away, and said she wanted nothing. He stayed by her through the night, disturbed because she did not sleep. It is all to do again, she was thinking, it is all to do again; I must give Marcus a true son.

"We must have another child," she told him soon. "Let us wait a

88

little," he said gently. "You are not yet strong." The physicians, in fact, had advised no more babies meantime. But Isotta insisted, and as usual had her way because he could refuse her nothing. Once pregnant again she seemed happier, with a kind of wild uncaring joy; the Marchesa still pervaded the household. She was like a vampire, Marcus thought, sucking her victim's blood; why must they endure her? Had he his way he would show her the door. He treated her coldly, and did not relish the tacit contempt in her manner. Isotta seemed to rely on her still, driving out with her during the day, chattering to her over the teacups, playing pianoforte duets with her in the evening as they had used to do at school. And, through Isotta, the Marchesa was making useful friends. One night she met Youngchild and his wife, a quiet plain ladylike woman, at dinner; thereafter she would visit the Youngchilds also. She was assured, svelte, fascinating in her snake's way; few women liked her, but when Youngchild was in her company his eyes began to follow her. And Lucy saw to it that she called when he was at home.

Isotta bore a daughter that year and the baby lived ten months. Her looks were fading; the kittenish beauty she had once had was gone, yet she would still dress elegantly, and use paint discreetly so that no suspicion of its presence was whispered abroad; polite women did not employ it. In fact, her teacher in the use of cosmetics was Lucy; that minx had several talents at her finger-tips.

That winter, the balance sheets of Cray and Youngchild were less favourable than of recent years. The secret was the coming of aniline dyes, with their garish colours that set everything else out of focus; ladies of fashion now wore criss-cross plaids in un-abashed blue and red and green. Marcus refused to have the new dyes in his shop, lost custom, and angered Youngchild. "We must show what folk want to buy," he drawled. "Move with the times, that's what to do; no sense in dragging t'feet."

But Marcus was obstinate; it was his duty, he said, to lead the public in taste, not pander to it. The new bright stuffs made his stored vegetable-dyed satins and velvets pale and anaemic in appearance; the pretty mint-green paint wilted before them, the gilded furniture grew spindly. Marcus detested mahogany and chenille, and both were everywhere nowadays; fashions had changed more radically than for fifty years, and not for the better.

89

Marcus maintained that to keep up standards would pay in the long run; but he had reckoned without his customers' wives, who must be in the forefront of fashion however hideous.

So the books did not balance; and still Isotta had not borne his son.

Little Marco—he was called so to distinguish him from his father—would have been happy to love both his parents, for his was an easy-going and generous nature. But he had always known that his mother did not love him; she tolerated him. With his father it was different. The finest time of the day was when Marcus Cray took his son by the hand and showed him the treasures in the shop, forever changing; the little boy had an eye already formed for beauty. He knew the *croce francesca* well and that it had brought his father and mother together; and he would always remember being shown for the first time the great Han dynasty bowl.

It was dull tawny in colour, the colour of very old thrown clay. It had been made before men knew about glazes. It would not hold water for more than a few hours, but what it held would grow ice-cold with evaporation through the pores. All this his father told him, caressing the rough clay with long slender fingers; and Marco would raise his own brown starfish of a hand carefully upwards to trace the wheelmarks, oh, so old, made before men here in the west had learned to cook what they ate. Papa had many such stories, all true and wonderful, delivered in his pleasing voice from behind the soft beard that was already beginning to show threads of white. Everything about Papa was exquisite, careful, and clean; his stocks snowy and meticulously tied, his kid gloves immaculate. On Sundays after church— which Marco found a bore—they would all go together to the Park, he and Papa and Mamma and Maria, and would walk up and down the tree-lined paths, watching the people and the pigeons and the changing colour of the leaves; then again it might be winter, when the snow came, and Marco and Papa would build a snowman, or Marco would try to pelt Maria with snow-balls; but Papa forbade it and said that one must not be rough and frighten little girls. Papa had exquisite manners, addressing Maria as if she were a lady grown, and Marco, except when he erred, as though he were a man. He tried hard, accordingly, not to grieve Papa. As for the shop, he had always known everything in it would one day belong to him. He began to take an interest in the things that were bought and stored, delighting his father by his shrewd opinions about wild silk, jewels, porcelain and pottery.

But Mamma was a different matter. If Marco were playing near her she would ask the nurse, or Manners, to take him away. "He is too noisy, little blackamoor that he is," she would say, which hurt Marco; he might indeed be noisy when he forgot to be silent, but he was not a Moor or anything but an Englishman. It was useless to protest about it as he would only be told not to be impertinent; so he learned to keep his counsel.

Youngchild in his vest and drawers was not an edifying sight, and Lucy, on the bed, lowered her gaze to her own slim pale body as it lay. She had got what she wanted from him, given him what he wanted from her—in that order, naturally—and was prepared to continue the game, but for high stakes only. She smiled a little, veiling her eyes with her lids. She was like a nymph, she thought, no Venus, but good enough for this boor; he had desired her and still did. She would feather her nest, never fear. She put up a hand and yawned delicately.

"Tired, eh?" The man was fastening his trousers, physically satisfied. But his mind still asked questions. Why the devil should a shrewd woman—he had summed up the Marchesa well enough—demand for her price not money, which he could and would have given her, but a block of Cray and Youngchild shares which were worth, God knew, little enough these days because of the antics of Cray? The transfer had been made yesterday, and today she'd paid in kind, as promised. He'd made her pay, no question. But why hadn't she wanted brass?

Anyhow—he was tying his cravat, which was not clean—the thing was done, and need trouble him no further. Women took queer fancies into their heads. He'd always wondered if Isotta Cray were the innocent little thing she seemed, devoted wife and mother; no sense in making a proposition to *her*. But this school friend, or acquaintance, had learned a thing or two. He winked. "Convent bred, eh?" he said aloud. Lucy widened her smile.

She had triumphed; she was sure of it. In a few weeks, perhaps less, there was going to be an upheaval in Italy. She'd had a letter from a Nardini connection who lived in Rome. The *carbonari* were out in force, and this man Garibaldi sweeping all before him to get the hated Austrians out. In that event, in the event of looming civil war, what would any prudent art-dealer do with his stock? Send it, no doubt with certain funds, to his brother-in-law. Isotta would tell her of it, soon enough.

"Haven't so much to say for y'self now, eh?" ventured Youngchild, laying a broad hand on her thigh. Lucy made herself speak to him in a soft, beguiling voice.

"No. You are very masterful." The great fool couldn't see a yard in front of his bulbous nose; nobody with an ounce of foresight would have parted with those shares, but Youngchild only thought and saw in terms of garish taffeta and tin trays. Now, she was secure, a shareholder in her own right; soon, in any case, Isotta would have failed her, it was pointless to try to obtain money which was no longer there. She'd keep the disputed letter, nevertheless; in any case, all one needed to do was to go to Nardini and look at the portrait of Felice which hung there. So now—

She let the soiled hands paw her again. One could always remove one's mind from the immediate present. Why didn't Youngchild wash? It would make the situation just that little bit more bearable; not that she hadn't endured worse things.

Youngchild was thinking of Frances, his wife. He hoped she'd never learn of this little adventure. He was fond of Frances, fond in a way that could never apply to this slim naked greyhound bitch on the bed. She'd riled him, the Marchesa, that was all; riled him into wanting her, bargaining for her. Now he'd had what he wanted it would have to stop; a man could go too far, make a fool of himself. And Lucy had her shares. Had he been wrong to part with them? Sometimes a sixth sense told him he should have behaved otherwise; sometimes he almost saw himself clearly.

They parted soon.

Bondone Figli, 7th February, 1849.

My dear Marcus,

I trust that the paintings and the Torrigiani sculpture have reached you safely in the care of young Enrico Strada, Papa's son. I have found the lad trustworthy and shrewd and have made use of him on several occasions. You will especially like the Dutch interiors and, I hope, the market for such work is great in England. We here tend to demand our own still, despite affairs. But with the French in arms now as well as the Austrians nobody can foresee the future. I myself am growing old; it is difficult for me to rouse myself to any feeling except that of fatality.

We have had our family troubles, despite the fact that my Margherita—the younger girl, if you remember—is now safely betrothed. The bridegroom has worldly goods enough although he seems a strange, nervous fellow. She is not attracted to him and I have had to use my utmost persuasion to detach her from a young man who seems quite penniless. I tell her that devotion comes after marriage, not before. By rights the first betrothal should have been that of Luisa, who is older and her mother's heiress. But I can say to you, who are not intimately concerned, that her waywardness and boisterous manners—she should have been a man—have frightened off any suitors who might have been available. I do not know what will become of her; during the late troubles I had great difficulty in preventing her from rushing off to join the redshirts, fired by the fact that Garibaldi had his woman with him. However all that is over. The wedding will be in three weeks. I understand that you and Isotta will not want to travel so far, especially as she (as I am delighted to learn) is once again in an interesting situation. I hope that on this occasion everything will go off well.

I had a noteworthy visitor the other day, the Marchesa di Lara. I understand she saw a good deal of both of you in London. Very well dressed! very dashing! but I did not take to her. She said the climate of England had defeated her and she was glad to return; there is probably more to it. She tried to persuade me to buy a block of shares which she says she owns in Cray and Youngchild. I must confess that I was tempted, but decided to wait for news on the open market. I sent her to our friend Riccione with her shares; if he is interested he may buy them on behalf of young Luigi. It is their affair.

Mamma has retired from the office, at my suggestion. It is difficult for her to keep up with the times. At present she is having her portrait painted by a young foreigner who is in Florence, and this occupies her attention. We are all well here, and trust you are likewise. Give my best love to my dear sister Isotta and say that I pray for her health.

Your affectionate brother-in-law,

Gastone.

London, 18th February.

My dear Gastone,

I hasten to reply to your letter. I do beg you, if the shares are not already disposed of, to allow me the first option. It would give me great satisfaction to be in a position to outvote Youngchild, who thwarts me at every turn. Only the other day he allowed one of your paintings (the doubtful Cuyp) to be undersold, whereas it should have been reserved and kept until the market recovers. With our commission I fear that you will not obtain more than two-thirds of the present value. I was in the north at the time or it would not have happened. I am reluctantly trying to negotiate the sale of Longhouses, which we never use, to the tenant who has rented it for the past few years for the shooting. This means, again, selling at a loss, and I grieve at parting with my boyhood home.

Isotta is well, and in better spirits than when the Marchesa was here. I share your doubts about the latter lady. We await the child's birth with joyful hope. Isotta is convinced that it will be a son. I will write again to give you the news then.

Mamma writes with great enthusiasm about the young artist who is painting her. It would almost seem that she has fallen in love.

Do not force Margherita to marry against her will. Much unhappiness can come from such arrangements.

Your devoted brother-in-law,

Marcus Cray.

Bondone Figli, 8th March

My dear Marcus,

I was somewhat surprised by the ending of your letter, but am aware that such matters are viewed differently in England. I believe myself to know what is best for my daughters.

As regards the shares, I regret that Riccione has forestalled us. He purchased them for a sum which he will not disclose, for young Luigi, who may or may not write to you. He is growing into a fine boy, if spoilt. Anna is indolent nowadays and takes little interest in anything.

The artist, Pietroni, has painted Mamma in widow's weeds. There is no impropriety.

Your affectionate brother-in-law,

Gastone.

Isotta's baby was born in July after a short and easy labour. He was a boy, perfectly formed, with hair which would dry out to a fair colour. An hour after the birth Marcus was able to bring in the elder children, quietly; Isotta lay smiling on the bed, her face turned towards the cradle. Young Marco stole towards it, staring down at the small, delicate ear which showed above the covers; how tiny he was! Yet Papa had come and said, "You have a playmate, a little brother." He would have to grow very fast. Marco was excited, and began to jump up and down; Papa put a finger to his lips; one must not behave noisily in Mamma's bedroom. "What is he to be called?" enquired Maria, who was already practical.

"Jacob, after my own dear father; we had discussed it, had we not, my heart?"

Marcus leant over the bed and kissed his wife's forehead. He had fretted greatly during the labour, fearful that she might again be disappointed. But now, all was contentment; he was chiefly anxious that young Marco should not feel ousted, who for so long had been the only son.

PART TWO

5

When Marco Cray was sixteen years old his father decided that he should be sent abroad on a tour of the Italian cities. His taste was already well developed and should be enhanced. Isotta was not in favour of it; as she said, money was not as plentiful as it had been, and why not wait till Jake could accompany his brother?

Marcus smiled, the gesture lighting up the melancholy eyes above his short pointed beard, which had grown white although his hair had not. "It will be four or five years before Jake is free of his schoolbooks," he said. "Marco will be a help to me in the shop, and is eager to start. I would have him armed against the Philistines. After all, everything will be his one day."

He began to talk of other matters, to which Isotta listened in silence: it was useless to try to change her husband's mind once it was made up. She knew, and broke her heart for him, that he was finding it increasingly difficult to work with Youngchild, now in a position to be more demanding than ever and supported always by an objectionable little salesman with a red pointed nose whom he had introduced, whose name was Laxton. Even in details too small to mention they would thwart Marcus' plans, for Young-child still held a majority of shares; and it was hard to state the other major holder's preferences, for young Luigi had nobody to put them forward. Riccione had died five years ago of cancer, which he had endured valiantly; and his successor, Massini, was prudently conserving Luigi's inheritance now that the wars were over and Italy had a king. One day, no doubt, when he was of age, Luigi might visit England and state his views, if he had any. But meantime Marcus battled on alone.

Marco set out for Italy joyfully. He had grown very tall, seeming by that and other attributes to be older than he was; he had the rich dark curling hair of the Bondone family and his swarthy skin belied the light green gaze which greeted strangers. He did not look like an Englishman and the name of Cray came as a surprise. He was quiet, with an ironic sense of humour which would burst out suddenly and sometimes coarsely, displeasing his father. For this reason Marco frequently kept silent at home. He still worshipped his father, who seemed to him the pattern of a great gentleman. He was enchanted at the prospect of the Italian tour, even though it meant visiting cousins who might bore him; Luigi was younger than he, by all accounts a pampered brat, and Gastone's unmarried daughter Luisa was thirty. Nevertheless Isotta nourished hopes to herself concerning the Bondone old maid; her inheritance was sizeable and would surely compensate for her lack of appeal. Marco had received instructions from his mother that he was to make himself particularly agreeable to Luisa. One understood that she had become more impossible than ever after Gastone's death, three years back. It all seemed a great waste.

Isotta was in any case nervous at the thought of Marco alone in Italy. Apart from the fact that he was almost certain to become involved with women—he was nothing if not precocious—she had a cold fear of his meeting, and being recognised by, any of the Nardini. His resemblance to Felice was almost uncanny, but here in England nobody but herself knew that. Supposing he should meet with Lucy, now notorious for her love affairs in a liberated Italy? Supposing he met old Count Nardini himself? The result might well be disastrous, and she could do nothing to prevent it. This chafed her; she liked to meddle in her children's affairs. Maria was already being courted though she was very young; Isotta approved of young William Cosgood. Lately, though, there had been sadness in the Cray household; with the outbreak of cholera last year a girl, Betty, and the youngest boy, Henry, had died. How could a child know death when it had known hardly anything of life? Marcus had been as heartbroken as she. He loved all his children, and missed in particular the confiding little boy who had used to climb on his knee after dessert, when the younger children were brought down from the nursery.

A board meeting was taking place, held at the familiar refectory table. Marcus sat at the head, beneath the portrait of his father, the first Jacob Cray. Youngchild, grown greyer and no cleanlier with the years, sat halfway down. Beside him was Laxton, always obsequious, except when he was being impertinent; swift to hand the blotter and quill and to light paraffin matches for Youngchild's cigar. This was the more unendurable because

Marcus had received complaints that Laxton was harsh with subordinates, for whom he had a tongue like vitriol. But he was useful to Youngchild and backed all his decisions, so could not be got rid of. The question today involved a change of policy, perhaps building a new wing on to the shop.

"There's this mauve," Youngchild said. "It'll be everywhere next year, and if we don't stock up now it'll be too late."

Marcus was heard to murmur that that would be a good thing. "No," said the other, "it isn't good enough to turn away folk who come with money to spend. We should extend the department, have everything they want displayed; charge extra for the name by all means, but have the goods they ask for. I say we should take Crump's estimate for enlargin'. He's the cheapest by far, and will do a good enough job."

Marcus closed his eyes for instants, then opened them to look down the table's length at the bent heads of departmental managers and other senior staff. There was no doubt Youngchild's methods meant commercial success, but he himself was not a haberdasher. He detested the very name of mauve, the new colour which had been evolved by chemists during this past year; it was a hideous colour and became nobody. "I loathe Crump," he said suddenly, aloud. "He is a cheapjack builder who has no notion at all of colour or design. If we must have enlargement—and I myself do not consider it necessary at present—then let us employ an architect who will see that the character of the original building is adhered to and the colours employed are tasteful enough not to offend customers who come here for quality, not run-of-the-mill goods which can be bought elsewhere."

"Hard words. I'd stick to a good safe cream, like other folk," said Youngchild. "We don't need an architect; they only cost money. I can tell Crump myself what he needs to do."

Marcus' colour rose a trifle. "I have no doubt you think you can," he said with ice in his voice. "But this firm has—or had—a reputation for selling fine things and for keeping up the standards of the enlightened few."

"The enlightened few can't raise the brass. We have to be practical in this day and age, same as any other."

"This is not a draper's store."

"Then it ought to be. Sales in the haberdashery last quarter accounted for four times the amount changin' hands in the picture department. Ain't that so, Laxton?"

101

Laxton said it was, his small marmot's eyes gleaming malevolently. He liked nobody and served only himself. It suited him meantime to support Youngchild, who had recently negotiated an increase in salary. If matters changed it would be different, but Laxton would always feather his nest. The world was a hard place, and if one took that for granted it was an advantage over the next man. Cray was a fool, full of high-flown notions; with the disturbances abroad, if it hadn't been for Mr Youngchild the firm would have been bankrupt long ago. People here weren't ready for pictures, unless it was a stag at bay or the like, that they could understand. As for all them bowls and jade and that, they cost a packet that could have been spent on whalebone corsets and the kind of thing women had always needed. Women were the spenders. Laxton had a contempt for the whole sex and had no wife; he looked after himself in a rented room in Bayswater.

The meeting continued on uncharitable lines and twice Marcus had risen in his seat to leave. His head was spinning; he knew he soon had to travel north, for the sale of Longhouses still dragged and he must go there personally. To leave Youngchild in charge here at present, however, was tantamount to suicide. For moments he thought of Marco, wondering if he should have delayed the boy's departure, then recalled his son's age; he would be wax in the hands of Youngchild and Laxton.

"I suggest that we leave the matter of extension till alternative estimates can be considered," he said. "Whatever is done now will be evidence for fifty years for or against us. Let us take a little time to reflect, and meet again on the matter when other facts are available."

"Crump's estimate won't wait, and that's one fact for you," said Youngchild sourly.

Marco had plunged himself into enjoyment of Italy, the land, the cities; Venice, the green canals, the dark palaces, the fabled Canalettos and Tintorettos; Rome with its ruined columns to be discovered down every narrow alley, the water dripping from ancient fountains, with the late Pope's new thoroughfares in a different dimension, foreign; Siena and the places of the north, with their steep streets and proud skyline; Naples at last, with its sweep of bay and candy-coloured houses and Norman remains and filth; and, in the end, Padua. Here he saw the Giotto panels in the Chapel of the Arena and, afterwards, glutted with beauty, took his first girl, a young prostitute with the solid contented quality of the master's Madonnas. Her hair was braided round her head tightly, in the same way. She had been loitering in the square when he came out, and spoke to him; it was already growing dark, and one or two lamps were lit in the houses. They walked together for a little while and then she took him home. Her name was Paola. Later, lying on the box-bed with its clean linen—Paola was meticulous—they talked, made love, and talked again. She answered the questions he asked about her life, while he gazed at her big naked breasts and felt a kind of triumph. He began to talk of himself, of why he had come, what he had seen. She nodded calmly, fingering her plait of hair. "There is much to see," she said, "if one is rich. I go into the Arena Chapel sometimes to light a candle to the Holy Virgin. I am not like you, I know very little; but I like to look at the paintings. He was a friendly man, they say, always ready with a joke." She spoke as if Giotto had lived yesterday.

"I am proud because my mother had his name, Bondone," Marco told her. "Soon I am going to Florence, to see his campanile, and also my relations." He made a little grimace about the latter, and she laughed, showing strong white teeth.

"You will not like that, I can see. But it is good to have a family. When I have saved enough I hope to marry and have children. I have my father and mother, who live upstairs. There was my brother, but he was killed fighting for Italy. He was tall, like you, but not so dark. How dark you are!"

She laid her broad palm, in a kind of blessing, on his thigh; he turned to her and they made love again. When he left dawn was showing above the houses and he found the door bolted at his inn. Instead of going to bed, therefore, he walked the streets till day came, letting the rich varied shapes of the buildings sink into his mind. He felt himself a man, new, strongly made and experienced; it had come naturally, without difficulty, to make love. He would do so often, he promised himself, with many women; but he was glad Paola had been first.

He arrived at last in Florence, and took his time strolling about, seeing the Duomo, the campanile, the bridges. Then he made himself visit the Bondone house. His new-won independence manifested itself in a wish not to have to meet his grandmother and cousins. At any rate, he was safe from the charms of the thirty-year-old Luisa. She must be a termagant not to have attracted an offer with all her money. Marco thought wistfully of the money for a moment or two; it had been short on his journeyings, for Papa was no longer rich. In Naples—why should he remember that now?—it had been necessary to sleep at a dirty inn with fleas in the beds. He shrugged, and hired a *carozza* to take him to the Bondone house; the driver knew it at once.

He was shown into a room with patterned tiles on the floor, and a bare window looking out on to the street; no plants remained. The furniture was still ugly, and he was examining it incredulously when a boy came in. He was perhaps twelve or thirteen years of age, haughty and handsome, with a proud mouth and dark curls fashionably cut. "I am Luigi," he said coldly, while the golden eyes surveyed this tall rakish stranger who was neither handsome nor of importance. "I am to take you to my grandmother." He turned to the door.

Marco raised an eyebrow, and followed; Luigi had a good opinion of himself, and much poise for one so young. Upstairs a room door stood open, and from inside he saw the boy Filippo detach himself from whatever he was doing and run to Luigi, following him with the devotion of a dog; a poodle, Marco decided; the little boy had fuzzy hair. He was led into what was now the bosom of the family; it was some years since Anna and Isabella had moved into the same house. The two ageing women, both stout, extended cool perfumed cheeks for his kiss. Isabella's white hair was veiled by a film of black lace; she looked like a queen. She asked him probing questions while her hard eyes regarded him calmly; she talked mostly of his mother. How was her dear Isotta? It had been sad about the dead children. "I would like to see her again before I die," said the old woman. "My health, alas, will no longer permit that I visit England. She must come here to me."

He had been about to reply with truth that his mother would not leave his father, who was too greatly occupied with affairs to come; but now the young lady, as one could still call Luisa, was brought forward. Gastone's daughter had the same haughty manners as her cousins, but her hair was red-gold. In her youth, despite her beak of a Bondone nose, she must have been handsome, but almost at once she gave away the secret of why no one had married her; she talked incessantly, in the high harsh voice

104

which was her least pleasing attribute. Marco listened courteously, reminded all the time of a peacock; Luisa's gown was unsuitably ornate for morning wear. She was talking now about the Pelosi family in Milan, whom he had not met.

"You must go to see them, though my aunt Caterina is not well. She gave birth to an ugly little daughter last year. Teresa will be very plain, no doubt; not like poor Baldassare who was so handsome and clever. It was a tragedy about his death. They were inconsolable, and now the doctors say aunt Caterina can have no more children, and possibly will not live long. The things that happen! My own sister Margherita is unhappy in her marriage, though there are already two boys and a girl; her husband is very odd and orders his manservant to lift him away after—you know." She laughed loudly, and he was left in amazement that a single woman should be permitted to talk so to a young man; but no one attempted to check the flow; no doubt it was impossible. Marco found her so unattractive that he deliberately curbed his charm; it would be disastrous, he had already decided, if she were to fall in love with him. He looked away; the two older women were talking in low voices, no longer watching. The boys had gone off. Soon there would, hopefully, be luncheon; Marco was hungry. He would be glad when this visit was over. But he had been invited for some days; they would be slow to pass.

They passed, not too slowly as it happened: he was resilient enough. However he was less than enthusiastic about a proposed carriage-drive into the hills with his cousin Luisa. Anna was too indolent to join them and the boys were with their tutor. Isabella said she had no time for driving, the housekeeping took all her strength; this was a dig at Anna, who left it to her mother-in-law *faute de mieux*. In the end, Luisa's maid was placed in the carriage for propriety, and the coachman started the horses with Marco facing them, sitting next to Luisa and contemplating the maid. She was not noteworthy.

He grew more interested in the country they passed through, and found his cousin well enough informed. She pointed out several farms and country-houses, then said "We will stop at my sister Margherita's to see if she cares to drive out. It is a fine day and perhaps she will exert herself to come."

Margherita's house proved to be impressive, set in its own

grounds in the direction of Arezzo, with a fine view of the hills. The carriage drew up at a flight of stone steps at the top of which was a terrace, with bougainvillaea growing in urns. Inside, it was gloomy, like a museum; everything seemed baroque, gilded and carved, and Marco thought that if he had to live here he would run mad. Perhaps this explained the oddity of Margherita's husband, who was never produced. Margherita herself came down, however, and he was expected to kiss her two solemn little boys; the girl, who was younger, had remained in the nursery. "He will be a priest, this one," said his mother proudly, smoothing the dark straight hair of what Marco considered to be a very plain child, thin-faced and with the beak of the Bondone. The elder boy, who had been called after his grandfather Gastone, had no such distinction and was pudding-faced and as pale as if he never saw the sun. To Marco's relief neither child was brought on the drive with them; no doubt the sisters wanted to chat. Margherita entered the carriage presently, dressed in a grey satin driving-coat with a veil hiding her thin neurotic face. Marco had already decided that she was a most unhappy woman. He thought of women in general as the sisters talked together and the carriage bowled along: it was well enough sprung to survive the pot-holed roads. The scenery altered and deepened as they drove further into the hills; great clear distances, cypress and olive trees, and at last far peaks could be seen, with an occasional gate or lodge leading to an unseen house among the trees, with the forest hiding it. They passed the convent of old memory, but no one told Marco his mother had been a pupil there; Luisa had forgotten about it and Margherita had never known.

"Let us stop at Nardini," said Luisa. "Perhaps the old Count will give us refreshment. It depends on his health."

"Ought we to go?" asked Margherita. "It might be improper. It is true that my husband has met the Count, but I have not."

"A fig for that; Marco ought to see the house," said Luisa, who always got her own way. "Parts of it are very old. If the Count will not receive us we can always drive on, but we will have seen the roses, and the lake."

They drove on for a few miles, with the sun high in the heavens; Marco began to hope profoundly for the Count's refreshment. He would gladly have quenched his thirst at the lake, which showed blue beyond the Aleppo pines, with a little boathouse half ruined and in need of repair. Suddenly, round the weed-grown drive, they came on the house, set squarely. The entrance was at the side, and having assisted the ladies down he glanced about him at what must once have been a magnificent rose-garden. The roses now clambered and thrust everywhere unpruned, their blossoms budding, blown or withering, the scent faintly lingering in the heat of the day. It made one sad.

An old woman received them and said the Count was not at home, but would the ladies and the gentleman not come in, and rest awhile? She shuffled off and presently reappeared with a silver tray on which were glasses and a bottle of Marsala. Luisa and Margherita availed themselves of it, but Marco had meantime found something which made him forget his thirst.

It was a portrait of himself, hanging in an alcove. The likeness was so uncanny that it was some instants before he saw that the young man, painted full-length and carrying a crop in his brown fingers, was dressed in the fashion of a generation ago. Son stared at father, one pair of hooded green eyes gazing into the other. Marco had paled.

"Who is that?" he asked aloud. He would not say more; an elementary prudence forbade it in face of such a gossip as Luisa. The likeness was there for all to see, not a trick of paint. Luisa had come up, having gulped her Marsala.

"What are you looking at, cousin?" She had adopted a proprietary air towards Marco, which irritated him; now she linked her arm in his and he was hard put to it not to draw away. "Why, it is a likeness of you," she told him. She stepped back and her eyes narrowed. She surveyed Marco as if seeing him for the first time.

"That is the Count's heir," she said. "Felice Nardini."

"Is he here?" He had to say something; anything but this silence, and those narrowed knowing eyes.

Luisa laughed. "He is dead," she said. "He was killed in a duel long ago. There were scandals about him, I believe. He was fond of women." She was still regarding the portrait, then Marco's face. He felt it grow stiff as a mask; would this fool spread the news through every drawing-room in Florence? To beg her not to do so would only be to arouse her opposition, make her more outrageous. Best say nothing.

They drove home.

The discovery, if it were such, was soon superseded; at the house they were met by an agitated Anna. "Thank God you have come," she said. "After luncheon Mamma took a seizure, and is very ill. I had the doctor and he says all we can do is let her rest, but she keeps crying out and murmuring. I do not know what to do. She talks often of Isotta. Do you think it would be wise to send a telegram and ask her to come here from England? If she would do so it would greatly comfort Mamma."

Marco drove into town and sent off the telegram. He had already visited Isabella on her mountainous sick-bed. Her face was congested and her unaffected hand had clutched at him while the other lay still. Between stertorous breaths she had asked for his mother, always for Isotta. He came back, the message sent, hesitantly. Should he wait on here to help the women, or take himself off? As it was, he waited till a reply came next day; he watched Anna open it with trembling fingers.

"They have improved the efficiency of telegraphy lately," said young Luigi. He spoke seldom and when he did, it was with the air of knowing more than other people about the subject. In the ordinary way his mother would have watched him proudly, but she was preoccupied with the telegram's contents. "It is from Isotta," she said needlessly. "She says she will come with Jake. Who is Jake?"

"My brother," said Marco. He reached for the telegram as Anna handed it. There was nothing in its contents to tell him whether to go or stay. He decided that it would be more courteous to wait. Within his mind a sardonic certainty lurked; Mamma had been determined to get Jake to Italy, and now he was coming to escort her. It would leave Papa very much alone.

Papa, whom he so loved. Was he in truth his son?

Jake seemed unimpressed by the journey, and kept his grey eyes fixed ahead; he was not imaginative and had nothing to say about the beauty of Florence or the countryside. He was, on the other hand, well stored with facts, and related accurately the details of Maria's wedding, which had taken place quietly in London before Isotta set off; the young couple were to use Longhouses, still unsold, for the honeymoon. "Do you like the bridegroom?" Marco asked; he himself had found William Cosgood lightweight, and slow to see a joke; but Maria was in love with him, and presumably he with her. "There is not very much money,

Mamma says," Jake replied in answer to the question. Marco grinned; the remark was like Mamma. If William had been rich, like Margherita's odd husband, no fault would have been found in him by anyone. Was he himself the only member of the family who looked at folk for themselves? Perhaps Papa did so.

Isotta was haggard-faced and tired with the journey; on arrival she went at once up to Isabella's room and did not come down for an hour; when she appeared, her eyelids were red. Later she drew Marco aside and asked him to walk with her a little in the garden. Once there she looked up at his great height and said, "Do not tell anyone of this. Before I left London I knew that I was to have another child. I have not told Papa, for had I done so he would not have permitted me to leave, and I wanted to see Mamma before she died. Oh, yes, she will die; another seizure would be the end of her. She cannot use one arm and her speech is slurred, as you know. But she recognised me."

He walked in silence with her, guessing rightly that this was what she wanted. He had not the heart to raise the question of Nardini now. It was curious to think of having a small brother or sister at his age; he wondered when the child was due, but did not like to ask. Finally he asked after Papa, left alone in the London house. "He is very much busied with this building on of new premises which Youngchild wanted, and I do not think he is pleased with the way they are doing it," said Isotta. "Poor Papa has been short of money all his life; when he married me we hoped there would be some, but your grandfather Bondone's will was made too early to include either Papa or myself. Then your uncle Gastone wanted nothing to do with the London business, after Papa had committed himself to it, so we had to struggle on alone. That is why men like Youngchild have to be listened to and, sometimes, humoured. It hurts Papa very much to have to deal with such a person, without taste or tact." Isotta's cheeks burned crimson with anger and she tightened her little claw of a hand on his sleeve. He said gently, to cheer her, "Luigi seems interested in the London business. His guardian left him shares in it as you will know. It would not surprise me if he should come in on Papa's side later on. He is conceited, but has knowledge; he can tell you all about the workings of the telegraph, and anything else in which he chooses to be interested."

"That is good," said Isotta, and presently they returned to the house.

6

Isabella's condition did not change, and after some time Isotta began to talk of returning to London. "I can do no good to Mamma, and Marcus needs me," she said. She looked about her at all those who were present to listen, seeing how changed they were from the days of her youth. Papa had gone and Luigi and Gastone, and Caterina's Baldassare was dead. There were only women, and young Luigi; strangely he already counted as a personality, while his brother Filippo did not. The room was full of waiting sadness. Nowadays there was little news from the show-rooms, where a manager had been put in charge on Gastone's death. There is nothing to do here but wait for the funeral, she thought, and shivered a little; it was like a goose walking over one's own grave.

"Here is a messenger," said Luigi.

He had been standing at the window looking out, as if to rid his mind of all the sad women. On seeing the boy come, he went out of the room with his quick, eager stride; Filippo looked up from his toys as if to follow him, but Anna restrained him with a movement of her hand. She was thinking not of her mother-in-law upstairs, but of Massini the lawyer; since Riccione's death he had helped her greatly concerning the business, and in other ways. She smiled a little, her full underlip thrusting out, her eyes secret.

Luigi returned. "It is a telegram for you, aunt." He gave it to Isotta.

She opened it; and turned as pale as ashes. For instants there was only the waiting, beating silence, the women still and intent, no longer seeing anything but the piece of paper, held in Isotta's hand. Then Luisa said harshly, "What is it, aunt? Is it bad news?" as if it could be any other. There was ill luck about telegrams, she thought; everyone sent them after a calamity.

Anna had risen and gone to Isotta. "Child, what is it? Is it from London, the news?" She put her arms about Isotta, who jerked herself away; in this moment she had no need of any other except one. She said, in tones as harsh as Luisa's own, "Marcus is dead. He fell, they say, from the scaffolding of the new building when he had gone to inspect it. I do not believe that. I do not know how it happened, but that man killed him. Youngchild killed him."

She turned away; presently they heard the dragging of her dress as she went upstairs. She would go to Isabella, Anna thought; the sick women would comfort one another.

The talk had broken out all round her. Soon someone suggested sending for Marco and Jake; they had ridden into Florence, and might not return till late at night. "I will go," said Luigi. "I know where I may find them."

How did he know? thought Anna. She had long given up trying to follow her son's rapid thoughts. Let him go, then; he was the swiftest means of bringing the dead man's sons to their mother.

It had happened suddenly. The building was nearing completion but lacked a floor; the brick foundations showed from above like a Chinese maze, with space yawning between them and the eyes' level; above, the scaffolding reared everywhere. Youngchild and the salesman Laxton had waited for Marcus to come in; he arrived, in a silent mood, and listened to Youngchild for moments, eyes cast down; then he said "I will go and see what they have done; they are working too quickly." The two men watched the resolute, short-legged figure for instants, then as if with one thought closed in, and followed. They found Marcus staring down through an aperture that reached to the feet; in time it would be a doorway.

Youngchild never himself understood why he acted as he did, or why he looked first at Laxton, who began to examine his nails, and the other in the instant's freedom created remembered all the wearing counsel of the past months; how they had never agreed on anything, how the policy he himself had advocated, the only way to save the firm from bankruptcy in his view, was constantly denied or eroded. Without Cray they could go ahead, he thought; at least that was how the thought afterwards appeared to him. Had he thought so? What he did now was proof, if anything, that he had made a swift decision; he took a step forward, and thrust at Cray in the small of the back, and the man went over silently, down to the inhospitable foundations three floors beneath. He lay there twisted, without moving; his neck must have been

111

broken. The two men looked at one another; on Laxton's face was the vestige of a smile.

"You were always impulsive, Mr Youngchild," he said. He made no threat of going to the police.

The papers reported it, and for a time notoriety brought increased sales to the business; it became fashionable to have a picture, or an object of art, a figurine or carved ball of soapstone or ivory, from poor Mr Cray's collection. Later the aspect changed, and shoppers, mainly women, came for routine purchases, elastic and bodices, material by the yard, flannel for men's shirts; there was a vogue in striped flannel. Youngchild sat in his office, seeing few; he had answered questions about the death in a calm manner, saying Cray had missed his footing in the wall; Mr Laxton had been with them, and would vouch for all he said. It was accepted, by everyone except Cray's widow. She did not return from Italy for the funeral; there was hardly time, and the dead man's daughter Maria, her bright hair dulled beneath a black veil, sat in the mourning carriage beside her new young husband, sober in black; black was everywhere, on the trappings of the horses drawing the hearse, on crape bows draped by order of Laxton—he was always practical—over the shop doors; and of course the shop itself was closed for the day. Everything had been done, the public was assured, to provide a seemly funeral. If there were complaints Youngchild was seldom faced with them; they came to Laxton, who with unusual swiftness had progressed from senior salesman to departmental manager, and thence on to the board of directors. However Youngchild soon decided, for his own reasons, to send Laxton to Italy to see the parent business there. It turned out that Laxton had been in Italy before; he had—appearances were often deceptive—fought under Garibaldi at San Antonio. It was fitting, therefore, that he should make the visit abroad. Once he had gone, Youngchild settled into his office routine with some relief. It had been safe enough to send Laxton with condolences to the widow.

"Try to take some broth, dearest. Think of the child who is coming; you must save your strength."

Marco was a tender nurse, and would let no one else succour her; but it was of no help; she had passed the days in ugly, useless weeping, speaking to no one. She turned her head now into the pillow and said, "I want to die. He is dead and I want to die too. Leave me; I should never have left *him*. Had I been there with him it would not have happened. I am one of them, one of his murderers. He never harmed a soul and now they have killed him. The blame is mine, mine." He listened, helplessly, the spoon in his hand: he could say nothing to comfort her, his poor little mother. He would not now, or at any other time, ask her about Nardini; her grief for his father was too genuine, too searing. His own grief he had schooled quietly, by night when he sat here by her; the man he had loved might be his father or might not. It did not signify. Marcus Cray was dead, and his children mourned him.

Jake stood about in the sickroom, taking no practical part in nursing Isotta. He always found his feelings difficult of expression and resolved them by silence. He admired Marco for his attentions to their mother. Poor soul, what grief she suffered! And he himself remembered Papa; gentle, liking to play with his younger children, living a life given up to beauty and knowledge of fine things. And it had come to this. "Let me help," Jake murmured privately, still shy of the God to whom he spoke. "Let me help . . . in some way. Let justice be done. She may be right when she said he was killed; they hated him. Let justice be done."

Anna came drifting into the sickroom sometimes, to report on the state of Isabella, but otherwise, like the rest of them, remained wordless in sight of so much grief. Luisa had been asked not to come; her strident voice disturbed the grieving woman. One day Margherita had come in, sat for a time in silence, and then departed with a kiss on Isotta's cheek and drove off. No one could help greatly.

What were they to do? Soon, Marco knew, he must go back to London to find out the situation there; there was no prospect of work for him here and he must not outstay his welcome. Jake he had not consulted; that young man loved the sea and ships, and might join Grandpapa's bastard, Enrico Bondone, by enrolling in the navy. It was a time of change for everyone.

Youngchild had written with stiff and formal regrets. He said he was sending the salesman, Laxton, to Florence to see the show-rooms there with the manager's permission. Let them come, thought Marco; they can do neither good nor harm now. Let them come.

He himself, after taking much thought, had written to Youngchild to enquire about his own position. He could not lightly relinquish Papa's rights. A stiff reply had come, with condolences properly expressed. Youngchild regretted that he himself must now occupy the house in Piccadilly, as it had become a prerequisite of the business; he hoped the widow would be able to make other arrangements. That apart, he offered Marco a place in the new store. There was no promise of preferment. Marco knew that he must go soon if even this offer were to be kept open; but he would have liked to stay for the birth of the new child, if only to comfort his mother.

In the event, he had to leave before the child was born. She came into the world quietly, a tiny elfin thing with great eyes which would darken, and with a fine down of light-brown hair over her skull. Isotta had hoped she herself would die at the birth, but did not. When asked, she said listlessly that the child should be called Isabella Carlotta. Afterwards she was always known as Carla. Marcus—he could use his own name freely now—received news of it all by letter and could not get the baby out of his mind; so little a creature, and with so much against her! She would not lead the sheltered life she would have done before Papa had died.

7

"I have had a letter from your mother's lawyer, Massini. However there is no documentary evidence for the claim she asserts. The ivory crucifix is part of the firm's assets."

Like the house, Marcus thought; like everything Papa put into the business, love, time, knowledge. And could not some mercy be shown to Papa's widow by allowing her an income, however small?

He broached that, almost speaking between his teeth; he had to keep his fists clenched also, to prevent him from leaning over the desk to take this man by the thick throat, shaking the truth from him. He had never before felt hatred. It was against his own wish to be here today; Jake, who had joined the navy, had begged him to accompany him. He had half thought of the idea, then decided that his duty, now that Papa was dead, lay with the firm.

Youngchild sat there impervious, his eyes lowered; it was impossible to tell what he was thinking.

"My father's will," stammered Marcus, loathing his own weakness; he could never be uncivil. This man should be smitten as if with iron, and he could only stand here before him, stammering.

Youngchild looked up; his gaze was clear. "Your father's will left everything he possessed to your mother. At the present time the business is in debt. He had taken on considerable overheads. There would be the option of selling out, but I believe, as do the shareholders, that it is possible to bring the firm out of the difficulties created by Marcus Cray's prodigality and lack of foresight. He was warned time and again."

"You will not criticise my father in my presence. He is dead and cannot answer you, but I can."

Youngchild looked at the tall young man before him, and a shade of regret passed behind his eyes; his own two sons were unsatisfactory, one a bully and the other a fool. He had found them places in the firm, but kept a sharp eye on them. Now he must do the same for young Cray; justice no doubt demanded that the dead man's son be given a chance. Atonement? Perhaps. He said aloud, "Let it be. I will send your mother a dividend as soon as I can: otherwise, it is as well that she is with her family. To you I can offer a place in the store, but only a junior place. For what it is worth, I offer it."

The colour came up hotly under Marcus' dark skin. "My father sent me on a tour of Italy in order that I might fill a senior position. No doubt that was part of his prodigality. I know more now than when I left London, far more than Laxton whom you have made manager."

Youngchild held up a hand. "There is no room for more staff on the *objets d'art* side; we are narrowing it down. I would remind you that you are no longer the son of the director."

"No, by God! How did my father die? That is what we are all asking, and it may come to more than questions."

Youngchild rose. "Your attitude is regrettable. I have offered you a fair place which you evidently despise. There is another position available, but it may be of more interest to you than a junior place in the London company." They both knew he had evaded the direct question. "I propose," he went on, "setting up a branch—initially small—in Glasgow for foreign imports. It will be under the management of my brother-in-law, John Dalgleish. There is much money to be spent there and the citizens are rapidly acquiring social values." He smiled a little. "To raise oneself in the estimation of one's neighbours is a lifetime's preoccupation. They will spend hundreds, sometimes even thousands, on their houses and their women; they had the taste from the tobacco-lords of last century, who lived like nabobs in their day. There should be profit, accordingly."

He cleared his throat. "John Dalgleish will accept you as his assistant." He has already asked him, Marcus thought. "There will be a clerk junior to you," Youngchild said. "The staff will not be enlarged yet beyond that; we have found modest premises near the Merchants' House, the Mecca of wealthy citizens. If you choose to go there it would, perhaps, bring you new interests and new faces. London is no doubt sad for you at present."

Marcus grew sullen; he did not want this man's compassion. To travel north to the Clyde fogs and cut yards of satin for corseted Scots matrons would not be diverting. But it was better than staying here as a nobody. He had almost no money left and must take such chances as came; they might not come again. So he nodded, briefly and ungraciously. "When," he asked, "do I start?"

"At once. There has already been too much delay while you lingered in Italy."

"My mother was ill. And there was much business to see to." He kept control of the anger in his voice. This brute to complain because he had stayed to comfort poor bereaved, pregnant Mamma for a little while! And for Mamma to have to exist on what Youngchild chose to spare her! Why had Papa not made a different will, more explicit, more readily usable as a weapon against such chicanery as he had endured this half-hour? And yet, he thought, Youngchild was not altogether a villain; there was a streak of mercy in him.

He bowed stiffly, received his instructions about the journey to Scotland, and went out.

He strode through the dingy street, jostling the half-seen charcoal-coloured shapes which in clear daylight would be the folk of Glasgow, shopping or going about their cautious business. It was his hour for luncheon, but rather than wait with the company he must keep at the chop-house he had forgone it, preferring to waste his angry energy in walking, walking. He hardly knew where he was going and almost hoped to lose himself; it would shorten an afternoon at the warehouse, with the sight of Dalgleish thrown in.

He bitterly regretted letting Youngchild, as he now saw it, decoy him here; the life was almost unendurable. Nor was he paid adequately; a letter had come from Papa's sister in Edinburgh begging him to visit her, but he had not the fare. The way they spoke here was in itself objectionable, with long gargling vowels and swallowed word-endings; he found it difficult to understand and to make himself understood. Only yesterday he had made a fool of himself under the hissing gas-jets of the brash new store, cutting the wrong length for some woman who had then refused to buy it, and he would have to pay for the difference out of his meagre weekly wage. And even that was already docked to pay for his board and lodging with Dalgleish. He should never have agreed to go there, but he did not know the town or where to find respectable lodgings. Many of them, he had been told by the jocose clerk at the shop, were bug-ridden and their owners had the pox, or clap as they called it here, got with whoring. He had not as yet seen a whore he would have lain with if she paid him. He loathed them all, the bow-legged black-toothed saddle-nosed shawled throng, and worse than that the respectable of town who came with fine feathers and patronage to look more often than to buy. They were canny, the merchants' wives. He thought he would forever see in nightmares the long new mahogany counters set with their polished brass yard-marks (thank God, the clerk did the polishing) and Dalgleish bowing and rubbing his hands behind. Oh, yes, Dalgleish was pleasant to customers, but otherwise at home. There was Grizel, certainly; she beguiled the time when her father would let her. It was in fact difficult to speak to her alone.

He had found his way by some means to the Green, where fog lay thickly about the river narrows. On a fine day the women would put their washing out nearby, sitting with babies and baskets on the grass, calling to one another in their strange throttled tongue or maybe in the Gaelic. It would have been pleasant to see them, a reminder of normality; but they were not here on such a day.

Sundays were the worst. Granted the week was weary, but Sundays were the worst, with two compulsory attendances at church, black clothes and unending sermons. Dalgleish was an elder, of course. He is saved and I am damned, and God be thanked for it, thought Marcus. He had committed the heinous sin of falling asleep during the sermon, had been prodded into wakefulness and had later had to endure a talking-to from his master as long as the divine's recollecting. Ay, Dalgleish was his master, and by now he had not the funds to escape him, though Mamma would send him money if he asked; but he would not. Fiesole of the sparkling mountain air seemed far away, in another universe. How lucky Jake was, sailing somewhere or other on a clear sea, or even in a storm; not bedevilled with still, yellow fog that fouled the nostrils and one's linen. The Highland servant Phemie would wash his shirts, it was true; afterwards they smelt of harsh soap and chafed him. There was no pleasure, none, and grace even before porridge; then work from eight in the morning until six at night, work he loathed and to which he was in no way suited. It would have made no difference had he never taken the Italian journey; an ignoramus could have done his work. Birmingham brass, chenille tablecloths, mahogany whatnots, Berlin woolwork, aniline stuff by the yard! Papa would have thrown all of it out of doors. It was an insult to the name of Cray.

Papa. Somehow, by dint of work and perseverance, he must come to a position from which he could succeed Papa, avenge Papa. The fog and the misery had made him forget. He felt tears rise to his eyes and hastily brushed them away with his hand. He stared at the fog-bound willows, the tops of the reeds thrusting up through the fog. He must endure eveything; thole it, as the Glaswegians said. Grizel had explained that word. He did not find it as ugly as some.

Grizel. If her father were only out of the way! But old Dalgleish had no wife (she was dead) and liked to sit at his chimney-corner of an evening, where Phemie would have lit the fire, and read from his everlasting Bible, sometimes aloud. One could do naught but be glad of the warmth and try to forget the rest. Sometimes he and Grizel would steal a glance at one another, while the old man sat with his iron-rimmed spectacles sliding down his nose. Grizel had dark eyes, unlike a Scot. Most of the women here were sandy-haired with scrubbed complexions and eyes of a watery blue; but Grizel had clear olive skin, and her teeth were good. He thought of her plump little breasts and thighs, and longed physically for her as a woman.

The fog was lifting. It was time he got back to the warehouse. He realised that he was hungry, now that it was too late to eat, and his stomach felt as if it clapped against his spine. Clemmed, Grizel would have called it.

Grizel.

It was a month before she could show him her room. She slept on the upper floor. He wondered if she had had other lovers and if so, how they had slipped past her father. At last, he contrived it; the old man was asleep, snoring resonantly, and Marcus crept along the ice-cold flags and lifted the latch on Grizel's door. She was standing by the bed ready to blow out the candle; on seeing him her red lips formed an O, and he kissed it. In bed he found that she was not a virgin; in fact, she was a little minx. He stole back, in the grey dawn, to his own narrow bed; and so it continued for many nights. It made the days sweeter, though he was tired and sleepy at work; they mocked his lack of wit in handling change. He did not care; he only waited for supper to be over, or tea as they called it here, and the Bible readings, and their cosy mutual glances; and then, later, the warm shared bed, and her pliant body. That made his day worth while, even the servitude.

It was more than a month later that the door flew open, and there was Dalgleish with a gun, an old fowling-piece with a trumpet mouth, pointing at them where they lay. "Get up, ye whore, ye Jezebel," bawled the old man. "Sir, I'll lay about yer backside till ye canna sit. Get up, son of Belial. I'll send my good-brother word o' this and he'll turn ye off without a shillin', ye whoreson; get up, and answer for yoursel'." The blunderbuss pointed steadily, and no one knew whether or not it was loaded; they scrambled out of bed, Grizel pulling on her flannel night-gown, and he himself, for shame, flinging his shirt about him. In that state they were made to marry. It was a Scots wedding, called a handfasting. Grizel had begun to blubber, and could not get the words out. "I will not let him hurt you, never fear," he contrived to whisper, and Dalgleish roared at him to give over his cozening and say the words, or by God he was a dead man; so he said them, and Grizel said them too, with Phemie for the second witness, straining behind the door. How legal it was Marcus never knew. But Grizel told him, when they were at last alone— how had it happened that they were alone again?—that it was maybe as well, because there was to be a bairn.

He stared at her for instants. Was it true? Evidently; he kissed her. He had told Dalgleish already that if she were beaten, he would not answer for the consequences; it would be some pleasure to wring the old fellow's scraggy neck. The elder of the kirk had muttered of repentance-stools and how, in his own young days, they should have been put to stand one on each before all the congregation, for fornicating. Marcus could laugh by then. He was allowed to be with Grizel at any time now, took advantage of it, and was fond of the thought of the coming child. Perhaps it would be a son.

It was so. When they first showed him the handsome baby he could not believe he had fathered it; its flesh was made of roses, its eyes, blue at first, would grow large, heavy-lidded and dark; the mouth vigorously sucking at Grizel's breast was like a red flower. Now the days were all too long, the evenings delicious; Dalgleish had banished them from the downstairs room and read his Bible alone. During the bitter cold they sought one another's arms for warmth, the child between them; Marcus had called him Jacob. Jacob should have a future; soon, by whatever means, he himself would be master, no longer paid slave and dog's-body. Already he commanded a trifle of respect as Dalgleish's son-in-law, though the whole town guessed how it had come about, and prim mouths and averted eyes were the rule among the Christian congregation. They did not care; they were happy, and they had their son. At some time it would be necessary to tell Mamma in Florence.

In Florence, the lawyer Massini was dying; everyone was surprised that he had lived through the night. He had had a sudden attack of pain in the abdomen, had undergone a crisis of heavy sweating, and now lay grey and weak, unable to swallow food or drink. Nevertheless he had been coherent enough to insist on an interview with young Luigi Bondone, to whom he had acted as guardian since Riccione died; it seemed that without this, Massini could not die in peace. The boy came, and sat quietly hat in hand by the bed, while the servant who had admitted him went quietly out.

"You have come," whispered the sick man. "There is a thing I must show you. I promised Riccione—" his breathing was laboured—"to give it to you when you came of age; but I shall not live to see that. I will give it to you now; you are of sufficient judgment . . . to act as you think fit. Do nothing . . . hastily."

Luigi sat easily, elegantly, in that room of death; his curls were carefully cut, his cravat a miracle. He was not quite eighteen years old, and knew his world very well. He already had a mistress, who happened to be a niece of Massini. Women loved him, but he himself as yet loved nobody. He had a cold common sense, and high ambition. It gave him satisfaction that, through the years of his minority, when he had schooled himself to awareness of everything that happened in the Bondone business, sales were booming. He would be rich and, what was more, influential. The war had ended at the right time; now, everyone wanted a return to beauty and peace, with a young Italian princess already sent to Paris and the country held no longer by white-coated Austrians, or red-shirted invaders, but by black-coated civil servants and their wives.

He inclined his head to show that he understood Massini, whose voice was failing. Shortly the servant returned, with a long envelope on a tray. He must have been instructed beforehand, Luigi thought. He closed his fingers over the envelope.

121

Massini gazed at him pleadingly, his eyes glazing over like the eyes of a fish on a slab. "Open it," he whispered. "It was . . . not my doing. By the time I knew . . . the thing was done, it was too late."

Luigi had torn open the envelope impatiently, and was reading the contents, a light frown between his symmetrical brows. Presently the golden eyes flashed a glance at the man in the bed. "But you knew," he said accusingly, "and did nothing."

"Riccione made me swear . . . it was for your good . . . always he thought of that."

"There was a reason. What was it?"

"I may not . . . tell you. I . . . am not certain."

"I see."

Luigi stared at his grandfather's last will. By its terms most of his assets belonged to Marcus Cray. His mind worked swiftly; the thing was impossible; he would compensate Marcus, but in his own fashion. "I will attend to it," he said coldly. The dying man's eyes closed.

"Do not . . . ruin all. All these years . . ."

"I will ruin nothing. Trust me."

"You are . . . wise. I will leave it in your hands."

"Do so," said Luigi. A kind of compassion came to him as he gazed at the man who had tried to replace his father and Riccione. "Is there anything you need?" he asked softly. He was used to pampering his mother in her fainting-fits and attacks of ill-health. Massini's lips moved. "Nothing," he said, "but your prayers."

"You shall have them. Farewell."

Massini did not die till next day. In the meantime Luigi had gone to see the priest and had also visited the offices. This was usual and he was allowed, as always, to inspect the accounts and otherwise make himself familiar with everything. What he saw satisfied him for the time; there was enough money. Presently he went to the stove which always burned in cold weather, tore the paper Massini had given him into pieces and burnt it, watching the black fragments curl unrecognisably. He stirred at them with his foot till they were ash. Then he turned away, his face inscrutable, and left the office after sending word to Anna that he would not be home that night. He let her know nothing more.

Next day he sat with Filippo Pelosi in the photographic studio in Milan, drinking the strong black coffee which had been brought, staring with cold interest at the camera on its stand with black velvet hood and drapery. There were framed photographs round the walls and on a whatnot stood a plant, an aspidistra, which was used as a background piece for society sitters; one in a feather boa had just left. Dominating everything on the wall was an enlarged print of the dead heir Baldassare, seated on a music-stool, one crossed leg held by the ankle. His dark eyes brooded beyond them, as though he saw death. Nearby was a smaller print of a thick-set little girl holding a doll; this was Teresa, the child of consolation. Caterina had died shortly after her birth and Filippo Pelosi now was married again, to a kinswoman of his father's side who as yet had borne only dead children. All this stayed in Luigi's mind as he talked, compellingly, of the need to buy Cray and Youngchild shares while they remained at par. "They say Youngchild is ill, which is why the shares have dropped. Nobody knows what will become of the business." Luigi talked, using his hands expressively, while the thick-set older man listened. "My mother learns it all from Aunt Isotta," lied Luigi. "Neither of Youngchild's sons are fitted to succeed their father. The business will wind up unless measures are taken in time. I am under age and cannot buy the shares myself; it would take too long to convince my mother and the shop manager has no powers now that Uncle Gastone is dead. Massini, who might have arranged it, is dead too; you will not have heard. I am convinced that to buy now will make our fortune; we could expand both here and in England, selling the Scottish business which is no more than a draper's, and bringing Marcus Cray back as manager to London. He has the knowledge and I should like to help him." Luigi looked at the floor for instants, the long lashes sweeping his cheeks; there must be no suspicion by anyone of why he wanted to help his cousin. He looked up at the photograph of the plain little girl, staring out into a world she did not know. "I will contract to marry Teresa when she is old enough, if you will do this for me," he said, smiling. "And of course I will repay you at the current rate. Will you consider it? But there is little time."

"Time," echoed Filippo Pelosi. His heavy pale jaw had dropped a little as he listened; he felt a stirring of interest for the first time in many years. For the first time also, now, when both had thickened, there was a resemblance between Filippo and his sister Anna. He had grown vague, without heart since the loss of his son. Here was a young heir indeed, primed for action, full of promises; and the Bondone business was in good heart. Teresa could do worse when the time came. As for the shares, why not buy them? He had Luigi's promise of repayment.

Marcus sat on the box bed holding out his arms to Jacky, who was learning to run. The sight of the strong staggering little body gave him pleasure. He loved his son more than anything or anyone in the world, and could not understand Jake's anger at any mention of him in letters. Jacky's rich hair was already shoulder-length, curling over his pinafore. He was tall and bigly made, with bright sleepy hazel eyes under heavy lids. His face was a boy's undoubtedly, with blunt handsome features which would later distinguish him wherever he went. He was a prince in disguise, a great king's heir. Marcus smiled wryly to himself at his own fantasies; here was no court, and with the late news of Youngchild's illness and subsequent lack of control it was probable Dalgleish would sack him. His mind baulked at contemplation of what would happen then; all his instincts drove him back to Italy, to Isotta and the little unknown sister Carla who would be a playmate for Jacky despite the fact that she was his aunt. His mother's letters said that the child was adorable, and consoled her for much. She had not had the heart to be angry with Marcus at news of his marriage and his son. They were still very poor, she wrote, and did not want to accept too much generosity from Anna and Luigi. "Your father would not have wished that," Isotta had ended. She and the child were living now in a rented apartment in Florence. Marcus could send them nothing; lately he had stretched his means to the utmost and had taken a cold single tenement room in order that he, Grizel and Jacky should be away from Dalgleish in the evenings. They could buy food and pay the rent; that was all, and his own clothes had grown so shabby that Dalgleish had told him lately that he would have to smarten himself up if he intended to stay; the store did not need down-at-heel salesmen. The old man seemed to savour every means of revenge on them both; he made the days intolerable for Marcus, who wished him to the devil.

He frowned now a little and thought of Grizel; it was a Saturday and she was at the shops. Her personal odour, feminine and compelling, hung about the room, but with it was another which he had noticed more than once; the acrid smell of male sweat, not his own. He was almost certain that Grizel was unfaithful, left alone as she was all day; once he had found a man's cheap cuff-link on the floor. His dislike of scenes made him endure the situation; in any case she meant less to him now than Jacky, and he would have liked to take the boy away from her. To afford a nurse was out of the question, so meantime he kept silence; their relations with one another continued as they had always been, easy and lusty enough. But he had been careful to beget no more children on her; this one, this jewel, was to be everything, without peer. In any case they could not afford any more.

A knock came at the door, and he tossed the little boy up in his arms and went, carrying him, to answer it; it was the postman, wet with Glasgow rain. "The wee fellow's comin' on fine," he said. "A terrible day," and handed Marcus a letter with a foreign postmark. He watched the man grope his way down the darkened stone stairs of the common entry, shut the door and put Jacky down. The letter was from Italy, with the new king, like a monkey in whiskers, portrayed on the stamp. Marcus tore the letter open and noted the handwriting with surprise; it was from young Luigi. Memories raced through his mind; Isotta had written lately that Luigi now controlled the shop, especially since last month he had come of age. There had been a dance, only for the family and a few friends; she and Carla had been invited, but the little girl had cried afterwards because Luigi would not waltz with her. "He was more taken up with Massini's three nieces, all as bold as brass," Isotta had written. Marcus accordingly began to read with no great sympathy for the writer; but this feeling was soon banished in a rush of elation.

My dear Marcus, it read (how patronising the boy was!)

I have acquired a controlling block of shares in Youngchild and Cray, and I understand from what I hear that Youngchild himself is at death's door. What I want to do is arrange matters in a way that will prevent any confusion or delay at his death, with everything ready. In plain words, I want to ask you if you will accept the place of managing director, with full discretion to buy and sell as you will. From time to time it will perhaps be necessary for you to report to me here in Florence and, also, I may visit you in London to keep a personal eye on matters there. However I know your competence, for Aunt Isotta has told me. If you will accept my proposal, please get in touch with me at the earliest possible date after receiving this.

Your devoted cousin,
Luigi Bondone.

Now what in the world, Marcus wondered, had induced that young cockerel to accord him such a favour, forgotten as he had thought himself to be in this city of cold, rain and fog? No matter; it had happened, and Marcus took hold of Jacky again and whirled him round his head, to the little boy's ecstatic delight, and as they were engaged in all this the door opened and Grizel came in. Her cheeks were flushed and her bonnet had been tied in haste; perhaps, he thought, her clothes also. He set Jacky down and dropped his gaze, pretending to admire the vegetables she had bought. If they had been paid for by whoring, he wanted nothing more to do with her; but he must keep Jacky. Less and less did he see, the more he thought of it, Grizel's suitability for the position they would shortly hold in London. She would be far better left here in the north.

He said nothing of Luigi's letter, and when she remarked on his cheerful spirits—he had been gloomy lately—merely said "Jacky and I consoled one another while you were out," and gave the little boy a wink. Jacky laughed; life was good and had always been so for him, especially while his father was at home, and could play.

Youngchild was dying of an infection, an internal festering; its stench filled the room. Nevertheless his wife sat by his bedside, gently ministering to him. She had never faltered in her love for this strange, unkempt man. Her face was worn and grieving beneath the lace cap she wore. It was as though she were already a widow.

Yet he still talked, fitfully and feverishly, tossing himself from side to side, then growing flaccid as the evil gained control; at last he lay gasping, like a great fish on a bank. His hand held hers in a spasmodic clutch. They were like lovers.

"Frances," he said. "Frances."

"I am here, my darling. I will not leave you."

"I have a thing to tell you before I die." He turned his eyes towards where she sat, quiet in her sober gown. She had never

126

preened herself, like other women. What was that bitch called he had once slept with? He regretted being unfaithful to Frances, even though it had been long ago. He had forgotten Lucy's name and her face, remembering only her greyhound's body, stretched slim on the covers. He had paid for that; ay, paid. He smiled, with lips that had grown bloated and dry. His wife would sponge his face and hands from time to time, but to no avail.

"You must not talk of dying," said Frances softly. Nevertheless she knew that he would die. Their stern Calvinist religion forbade any deathbed comfort; during life one had been either saved or damned. He himself was damned, Youngchild was thinking; he had always known it.

"I killed Marcus Cray." The words came out of him singly, each like the tap of a great drum. The touch of her hand did not falter or pull itself away. "Do not speak of it," she said quietly. He stared at her, as though he had not known her before.

"You knew, Frances? You—"

"I was sure of it. Your mind was troubled then. You do things on impulse. You would not have killed him coldly."

"You are too good for me, too good," he muttered, and his head turned from side to side, seeking to escape guilt, reason, remembrance. Suddenly he began to talk rapidly, not all of it audible; he spoke to himself rather than her.

"I saw him fall. I went down to where he lay with his neck broken and I knew he was dead. If he had not been I would have finished him. I felt the bones, then was certain of it. I can feel them yet, grating beneath my touch. There was no need to call for help. I did nothing, and I felt a kind of triumph. He had been impossible to deal with, a stubborn man, thwarting me at every turn. He would pay thousands for some useless thing that would never sell in any of our lifetimes, and put it on a shelf. I have got rid of much of that for less than its value; it's scattered all over Europe. But the money . . . the money was the thing . . . sold shares abroad . . ."

"You have done as you thought fit. Do not fret over it. You are my dear husband. Rest now."

"Ay, till the trump sounds."

He died next day.

His two sons came to the funeral. They had respected their father and, at heart, loved him. The service was short and bleak, the grave left without the flowers that were beginning to be fashionable. On the way back from the cemetery they conferred together. Neither wanted the responsibility of the firm; one was a lawyer, the other a schoolmaster. They agreed to sell out their shares as soon as it might reasonably be done. There was a son of Marcus Cray in Scotland; should he be given the chance to buy?

"Possibly he is too poor; he is employed as a clerk," said one.

"A salesman," stated the schoolmaster precisely.

A thin foreigner in a black serge suit called on Marcus shortly in Glasgow, bringing a folder of photographs. Signor Luigi Bondone, he said, had recently undertaken to merge with the firm of Pelosi in Milan; he himself had suggested that there might be enough interest to justify the opening of a photography department in the rearranged Youngchild and Cray when it was in any case under new management. Marcus examined the photographs, which were in the visiting-card style with round corners, and admired their technique; they were sharply taken and properly exposed, ranging in subject from Rome and Ferrara under fire to peaceful portraits of the great Mazzini, with his long aristocratic features, and of the great Garibaldi himself in a smoking-cap at Caprera. One that touched Marcus greatly was of the young Princess Clotilde at seventeen, in carefully tied bonnet and watered satin crinoline, on her way to her wedding in Paris with the princely roué, old Plon-Plon. He returned the prints carefully. An idea had come to him; was it feasible in so short a time?

"I will gladly welcome you in London when I take charge there, but that will not be for some weeks." He had in fact to work out his hated notice to his father-in-law, who would not abate a jot or a tittle. "Meantime would you and your wife—" the woman was by chance a Scot, visiting relatives—"do me a favour which will be greatly appreciated?"

The man goggled at this tall, swarthy manager-designate in the shabby clothes. "Gladly, *signore*, gladly."

"Would you take my son here to his grandmother in Florence? I have for some time wanted to send him to her, but I myself cannot go and there was nobody suitable with whom to send him." The words came out, smooth and deadly. He would quiet Grizel somehow. Jacky must not be left with her; and it would be difficult to have him alone in London. To his relief, the Italian nodded. Marcus rose from where they had been sitting and began to stride up and down the small room, thankfulness flooding him. The photographic representative stared a little; this dingy room was not a place in which one would have expected to find the future managing director of the House of Cray. "The fare, *signore*, for a child will be less, but—"

"My cousin, Signor Bondone, will reimburse you when you reach Florence safely." He was beginning to acquire the easy excuse, the ready lie, to avoid down payment. He had scarcely enough money to get himself to London, and as for a new suit! Luigi could not contemplate such difficulties, no doubt, having been reared in comfort.

Two days later the Italian came with his wife, a motherly soul, and Jacky was given to them, warmly wrapped, excited at having been told he was to make a journey on a train, and that it was a secret. Marcus had already told Grizel that the child was to go to have his photograph taken. When the shadows deepened into evening and Jacky was not returned, she began to worry and, later, to cry.

"Where is he? I should have gone with him. What have you done with him? You tell me nothing now."

He told her, averting his eyes from her swollen face. Grizel screamed and came at him, fingers clawing, and he slapped her. They had had quarrels before, but in course of this one he told her several things, including the certainty he had that she was unfaithful. She responded like a virago; she was no longer the little brown obliging wretch of Dalgleish's house, when they had crept into bed with one another. Later she flung out of doors with her clothes in a bundle and, he surmised, went to a lover. He was wrong; in fact she hunted the streets for news of her son, and in the end, shivering, went back to her father. Meantime the party with Jacky had successfully caught their train, and were well across the Border.

Marcus himself caught a train, some weeks later, for London. He was still shocked by what had happened. Grizel was dead. The irony was that it had nothing to do with the boy's going, though to be sure the distress that had caused her might have left her the more ready to fall ill. It had been a fever that carried her off; the city itself, with its stinking drains, had caused it. On receiving the news he had blamed himself, then faced himself honestly and decided that he would have acted in the same way again, except that, had he known she was so soon to die, they might not have quarrelled, he might have kept the boy for a little longer for her comfort. She could never have brought Jacky up in the way he, his father, wished; that she had died might in fact be thought of as a blessing, but it was too soon for him to feel this coldly and clearly. The remembrance of the coffin—he had not seen her body, it had been closed when he came—weighed on him; Dalgleish would say, no doubt, that death was the Lord's punishment for Grizel's many sins. He himself was as great a sinner.

There was sadness elsewhere; Maria's young husband was dead. Marcus had had a letter from her on black-edged paper, telling him how her one solace was her little son, and he could feel for her; they had once been close, but by now he would not know Maria if he met her in the street. He was, in an especial way, alone; no doubt that was why he cherished Jacky, as a piece of himself. Well, they would not meet again yet; and there would soon be other matters to fill his mind.

He found himself in his compartment on the train, staring down at his gloved hands and at the trousers of his new, dark ready-made suit of clothes. They had given him credit in Glasgow on the strength of his expectations. When he reached London he would visit a bespoke tailor, but meantime he was presentable enough. The engine started and the steam flooded back, obscuring the carriage window; by the time they were out in open country smuts were flying. The regular chug-chug of the engine soothed him; he was going to a new life, would perhaps persuade Isotta to bring the boy to England—Jacky had reached Italy safely—and was master of his fate for the first time. Poor Grizel; as the Catholics would say, let her soul rest in peace. He reflected on his own hazy notions of heaven and hell; the latter was an embarrassing term, better not to be thought of; it would come to one soon enough, maybe.

At a station in the north of England the train stopped, and a few passengers boarded. Among them he noted the flash of a modish crinoline; presently, to his interest, the owner of it entered his carriage, with the door held open for her by a young man in a tall hat who was no doubt her husband. A pair of green eyes took Marcus in at a glance, and the curved lips smiled. He felt his sad heart lift; here was a raving beauty. If only the husband were not with her! But such a woman would not go about unescorted.

She must be about thirty. That was an age women were ashamed of, yet in her it meant fruition and fullness of ripe glory, like Ceres. Her hair was red-gold, coiled at the nape of her neck below an alluring bonnet, and her figure, such of it as he could see for the crinoline, was voluptuous. He felt desire stirring in him, and smiled at himself; he should have lived in an earlier age. Yet once the lady was settled in her corner seat, with her great skirts spread about her, and the young man, all solicitude, seated at last with his back to the engine, she herself smiled; radiantly, fully, dangerously. Deliberately she peeled off one irreproachable kid glove, lifted a little watch which hung from a chain against her breast, pretended to look at the time, and put on the glove again. Marcus reflected, correctly, that she had done it on purpose to let him see, on one small white hand, a wedding ring. She knew the game, that was evident. The young man stared ahead of him, oblivious; a fool like that deserved to lose her, at least for the time.

Marcus leaned forward. "Madam, is your seat to your liking? Would you care to exchange it for mine? Smuts fly in at the window, as you will know, and on this side . . ." He was preparing some inanity about the direction of the wind, but she stopped him with a little gesture of the gloved hand. Her smile had broadened, revealing exquisite teeth. What a creature! She was of the stuff of Cleopatra, Ninon de Lanclos, the courtesans of history. Yet she was not quite a courtesan. The husband's protection was too obvious.

"I thank you, but I am of sterner stuff than the Queen, sir. They tell me she orders that the coals be whitewashed when she travels by train. And, from this side, there is an exquisite view." She sat back, tapping a little foot and smiling at him. He could have capped the saying about the view with ease, but one had to be careful in the presence of the fellow. What a bore he was! He took no part in their talk: but of course he was less anxious to further the acquaintance than either Marcus or the lady.

They exchanged polite nothings for a few minutes; then she said, when it came naturally into the conversation, "My name is Dorothea Wainfleet and this is my husband, Roger." The young man bowed stiffly, his expression not unpleasant. "Do you live in this part?" Marcus asked. It was no doubt thrusting of him to enquire, but she would parry his thrust, no doubt. She smiled again. "My mother's people live here, at a house called Longhouses; we have been visiting them."

Longhouses! The coincidence took him by storm; how often had he heard Papa speak of Longhouses, his boyhood home, and of old Jacob Cray there! Marcus' own smile widened; he knew it was an attractive one, with splendid white teeth breaking the swarthy colour of the skin. "Mrs Wainfleet, that is my old home," he said. "It pleases me greatly that so fair an occupant has taken my place there."

"You . . . you are . . ."

"I am the son of Marcus Cray."

She clapped her hands. "Then we must be friends. I have heard of you, of course. My name before I was married was Massingbird, was it not, Roger? And an uncle of mine was a great friend of your father and grandfather. He was killed in Italy."

"I know that he had great charm, and was handsome. He seems to have bequeathed both attributes to his kin. I am very happy to make your acquaintance, madam."

"Dorothea."

Roger Wainfleet leaned forward, a trifle disturbed. "My dear—"

"Yes, Roger?"

"It—it is not quite proper—"

"But I am so often improper, am I not, Roger darling? And with friends one may use one's Christian name or . . . any diminutive one chooses. I shall call this gentleman Marcus."

"Of course," he replied. He was filled with triumph and delight. How quickly the journey was passing! And in London he would not lose track of her, no, indeed . . .

He began by inviting the couple to luncheon on an agreed date. Later it would be possible to do without the presence of Roger Wainfleet. How glorious it was to have money to do as he would, and more glorious to look upon so beautiful a woman! Clad she was magnificent; naked she would be . . . a goddess.

So early in their acquaintance, he was thinking of it; and so was she.

Marcus stood in the boardroom, empty and deserted, with dust on the refectory table; to his anger, it also bore scars of recent date as if somebody had scratched, even carved at the wood. The pale green walls of the room were drab and dirty with tobacco smoke; here and there were paler patches where paintings had been taken down. He put his head out of the door and shouted for Cussen, the old clerk, who came; on being asked he answered, trembling, that Mr Youngchild hadn't held with them and they had been put away, perhaps sold. "Where would they have been put?" demanded Marcus. Eventually a deep cupboard was discovered, and he gave orders that it was to be cleaned out thoroughly and its contents set out for him to see. This took time, but was worth while; by the end, the stacked portraits of Jacob Cray and Isotta with the flame-coloured bows on her gown were unearthed, darkened likewise with smoke and dulled with cobwebs. "There was another, sir," said old Cussen, metal-rimmed spectacles slipping down his nose; he was in fact only in his fifties and with good promise of ten years' work yet, but he looked seventy and behaved like it. He brought the other portrait; that of a woman in a timeless dark dress with a blue scarf, and a small boy, whom Marcus, peering with narrowed eyes, perceived to be like old Enrico Bondone from early photographs. The canvas had been mended at one corner. He ordered them to be cleaned, the walls to be repainted and the portraits hung; then wrote of it all to Isotta.

A reply came, crossed and illegible like all her writing; he searched avidly for news of Jacky. About the painting Isotta was unhelpful; she thought she recalled it, and it might be one that Grandmamma had wanted destroyed and Gastone had taken away, to save it. She wandered off then into news of the children, and how Carla was looking after Jacky like a little nurse; and Marcus himself forgot the other matter. Soon, he must have Mamma bring the children over. He longed to see his little sister and, even more, his son again.

Thus it was that the portrait of long-dead Gabriella Strada and her son were mistakenly claimed to be those of Enrico Bondone as a child, with his mother Giovanna. Generations of directors and management subscribed to the myth, which hurt nobody and enhanced the hereditary quality of the great store.

Edinburgh, March 15th.

My dear nephew,

I am delighted to learn that you are in London and that the family business is being set on its feet. Truth to tell I was a little offended that you never did contrive to visit me in Edinburgh; it is bracing here and the change of air would have done you good after so long in that dreadful city.

I would have liked you to meet the boys and Selina. You will know of course that my dearest John was killed at Sebastopol and that Robert was nearly so, but was invalided home with a bad head wound which has not yet healed and perhaps never will. His greatest trouble is that he is no longer fit for employment in the Army, for he adored the life. He walks up and down the drawing-room with nothing to do; it is like having a thunderstorm in the house, I wish he could find some gainful employment. Would it be asking too much for you to give him a trial in some capacity? He will certainly work for his living, as he has always had to, and is so full of energy that his old mother feels weary at sight of him. He is used to keeping records and the like, and is very intelligent and has good taste; he chose the material for the drawing-room curtains and although it was expensive, it has lasted well and everyone compliments me. I would offer to come myself and keep house for the pair of you, but am busied at this moment over Selina's engagement, at last, to a very surly kind of man, a Swedish timber merchant; but thank goodness he is not a pauper. I am thankful to have got dear Selina off my hands, as I told her she would never catch a husband with her sharp tongue, and all of her friends are married long ago. The wedding is to be next month and of course, if you can spare the time to come, we should be delighted; I will send an engraved polite invitation. I do believe the man does not know enough English to understand half Selina is saying, so it will answer very well. I do wish your poor dear Papa could have come to the wedding to give her away; as it is, Robert will do it, but he is very bad at speeches and growls when I speak of anything to do with it all. Such trials a mother has, how is my dear Isotta? Be sure to send her kindest remembrances from me when you write. Robert will come as soon as you send for him, once the wedding is over. They are going for the trip to the west coast, taking the steamer from here to Stirling, and later will go abroad.

Once again, my dear nephew, kindest remembrances from us all.

Your ever loving aunt,
Elizabeth Platen.

Robert came, and so in due course did Selina and her wordless bridegroom, a personage of the middle height who looked like a bear. Selina wore a new bonnet and chatted gaily; no, it would *not* be a good idea for dear Mamma to come to housekeep for Cousin Marcus. "She has no notion of economy, and you would be immediately in debt: and she would miss her cronies in Edinburgh. When *I* have my establishment set up it will be very different." She turned a satisfied glance on Ingmar Røs, who had evidently fulfilled his duties in a sane manner. Marcus thankfully shelved the question of Aunt Elizabeth, which he had never seriously entertained in the first place; he was not too well off for money, and the house Youngchild's widow had vacated cost a good deal to keep, as Isotta had no doubt found in her day. He had discovered a reasonable housekeeper, a Scot, who increased his dislike for that nation but carried out her tasks without troubling him, and was clean and efficient. He was at the store all day and most of the night, going into the books and other business, and had not hitherto looked forward to the advent of Robert. But when that officer arrived, very erect, with a splendid moustache spreading over the place where his head had the wound, and sparse of words so as to get on with the business in hand, Marcus felt relief. It was the first time he had had help from a kindred soul, and despite Robert's fiery temper, which the shop hands felt more than Marcus did, he was an acquisition. He had mourned for his dead brother for they had been inseparable; it was an anodyne to have an occupation. He had never married, and his interests were those of a solitary, sometimes creative man; he had carved a little, engraved a little, dabbled in chemistry and physics. Now, he bent his considerable intellect to help matters for what, at its take-over, had been an ailing firm. It was Robert Platen who was the first to introduce the distinctive window-displays, using indoor plants, dried grasses, pottery, drapery; no one else had thought of it, and the combination attracted curious clients who lingered in the store and seldom left without buying.

It was also Robert who, with military foresight, thought of installing a coffee-room long before anyone else did; but that project had to be shelved for the moment owing to lack of funds.

Providence soon disposed of Aunt Betty Platen. Marcus invited her to London for Christmas, paid her fare and met her at the station; he found a stoutening old lady manfully struggling with her own baggage, as she had not enough change to tip the porter. He rescued her and brought her home to Piccadilly, where she soon recovered and was observed to drink five cups of tea in quick succession ("I drink it all day in Edinburgh; the neighbours come in, knowing the kettle's never off the boil.") Marcus did his best; he gave orders that tea was to be served whenever it was asked for by the visitor; he himself looked in often to drink a cup with her, and to listen to the most amazing store of gossip he had ever encountered. The daughter of old Jacob Cray could be witty and entertaining about everything under the sun, whether she understood it or not, and sometimes it was better when she did not understand. It did not matter; the vestiges of what had once been great beauty still showed in her face, and she was proud of her white hands and used a thousand gestures to show them off, though she wore no jewels but her wedding-ring. Her hair was grey, cut in a skittish fashion which did not really become her; a sparse fringe decorated her forehead. She had few clothes and those all black; when Marcus invited her to visit the London shops at his expense he could have predicted neither her delight nor, in the event, the bill. In two or three hours she spent a small fortune on silk Chinese jackets, blue and green Paisley shawls, faille for a gown and yards of point lace for its trimming, two bonnets, a fur tippet, and scarlet Morocco slippers. Marcus hastily thought of some other way of entertaining his aunt, and suggested a visit to the theatre. It was a bitterly cold evening, and Aunt Betty wore the Chinese jacket, which nothing would persuade her to cover up warmly. She drove between Marcus and Robert, happy, triumphant, and frozen; sat through the performance entranced, and on the way home related all the stories she knew about the cast, who had once visited Edinburgh on tour. Marcus listened to the stories, already beginning to feel a trifle cautious; so greatly was Papa's sister enjoying London that she was capable of staying indefinitely, and neither he nor Robert, now comfortably lodged with a young Irish housekeeper, wanted this to happen. But it would be difficult to say so tactfully, and Marcus put off the unpleasant duty of asking his aunt to move on.

Next day she felt unwell, and was advised to stay in bed. She never left it. The chill she had caught turned to pneumonia, the physician looked grave, and the sick woman's difficult breathing filled the room; there would be no more stories. She died, in Robert's arms, a little more than a fortnight after coming south; and as it was not easy to take the body back to lie beside that of her husband, she was buried in a plot Robert bought in a local cemetery. After a little time nobody remembered to visit the grave; the old lady was quickly forgotten, not least by her daughter Selina, now in Sweden in an interesting situation; shortly she would give birth to a boy, and name him George.

Another birth occurred, about which very little was said then or later. At some time during that year, Robert's Irish housekeeper also bore a son. She had left her husband, who drank, and the child bore a distinct resemblance to Robert himself. He was not, in any case, discovered for some years, his father's conversation being too laconic; but it was Marcus' wife Cristina who by then noticed, one day in the Park, a little boy with fuzzy fair hair and Robert's undoubted features. She came in and when Marcus returned from the shop, told him; he said he already knew. "They call him Dudley," he told her, "and Robert says he is to go into the Army." He smiled, and they talked of other things, but Cristina, who had a sympathetic heart, was glad that lonely difficult Robert had found solace, and had a son.

8

Luigi was being magnanimous. He had offered to send across a selection of modern paintings, with twenty per cent commission to the London branch if they sold. Marcus revised his opinion of his cousin, not for the first time. He had originally thought Luigi self-satisfied and selfish, but he seemed ready to help in every way except one. For Marcus was still pressed for money, which was partly his own fault; he had made the mistake of setting up Dorothea Wainfleet in a little house in Clarges Street that had taken her fancy. The hours he spent there were delightful and sated him physically, but the house cost more to run than his own and Dorothea constantly demanded new gowns, furs, jewels, a carriage. Her husband had gone abroad. Marcus hoped that they would not come across one another when, as Luigi had invited him to do, he went over to help select the paintings to be shipped from Florence. There was less hanging space at Bondone Figli than in the London showroom, and now that he might confidently leave Robert in charge for the time being Marcus could travel with a clear mind, albeit made a trifle wary by Isotta's latest letter; in it, she said she had found a wife for him.

He stood staring at his own naked reflection in the gilt-framed pier-glass which stood in Dorothea's bedroom in Clarges Street. Everywhere else was roses; they blossomed and climbed on the bed-curtains, the wallpaper, and the great quilt of the double bed on which he had lately lain. Outside, beyond the rose-hung windows, a horse and rider cantered by; he could sense the disappearing clop-clop without being aware of anything except, beyond his lean dark figure in reflection, the woman on the bed. Her attitude, with one arm behind her head, reminded him of the Giorgione Venus, but it would be like Dorothea to assume such a pose deliberately. He had already found out her greed, her vanity, her refusal to compromise or economise for his convenience. But all went for nothing in the practised violence of her embraces, which stimulated him as no woman's had ever done before. His shoulder already, after they had made love, was raw with the marks of her teeth and would show a bruise tomorrow. He heard her laughter.

"Isn't he a handsome boy, and doesn't he like to look at himself in the mirror showing all he's got? My love, you are very tall and ugly and dark; there must be some other reason why I stay." He heard the vital, pagan laughter, bubbling up as if from a secret spring; he turned, and slapped her turned hip lightly. "If you would know, I was looking beyond my reflection at your own," he told her; it was partly true. She drew him down to her. "Why look at a reflection when you have the real presence?" she quipped, but the oblique reference to Catholic belief offended him. He drew away, and with his head turned from her said carefully, "They say the truth shows in mirrors. We only know ourselves from them."

"And see ourselves the wrong way round. Was I uglier there than I am? Is that why you turn from me?"

She sat up; she didn't give a damn, he thought. He fingered her perfect breast, a globe of translucent alabaster lit with rose from within. If she had only continued silent he would have loved her for her body's perfection. "No," he said, "you are symmetrical as a pearl," and began to make love again. Presently, as a jest but ashamed of himself for betraying it, he told her of the projected marriage. Dorothea gave a whoop of laughter.

"A little Italian, growing fat before she's thirty-five with living on macaroni! I daresay they always arrange marriages out there, like the princess and Plon-Plon. He says now that she ought to have been a nun. Has this bride of yours any money? That might be a good reason; you are always whining that there isn't enough."

He disliked her speech, but they lay in surcease and he could not trouble himself to comment. He did not tell her in fact that the Italian girl had a great deal of money, which was promised as dowry, and that that had attracted Isotta and might well attract him also, provided the girl were presentable and did not smell of garlic.

"There will always be enough for you," he murmured; despite everything he knew he was still as infatuated as he had been that day on the train.

"My son should arrive next week."

Isotta was not looking her best; lately she had cut off her hair, in despair at its ageing, grey threads and lack of resilience. The result was unfortunate, and her face had grown very thin, showing the bones beneath. She exerted herself now to pour tea for her visitors, in the English style. They had moved to a better flat since the London firm had come under Marcus' direction and the sunlight, filtered between lace curtains, shone down on the two children who were playing with soldiers. Carla had black hair, like her mother's; the sun picked out rich chestnut lights in Jacky's, still long like a girl's and curling richly; his grandmother would not have it cut.

The two visitors, one old, one young, sipped their tea. It was kind of Signora Cray to have asked them, for the second or third time; one day, after the marriage settlement was signed, they would ask her in return to Buonfranconi, half ruined behind its ivy and Aleppo pines. The elder, the mother, sharply aware of her daughter beside her, noted the furnishings of the room; they were elegant, and an enlarged photograph of the late Marcus Cray showed him to have been a handsome man; it was a tragic story about the death. Less than ever did the Signora understand Isotta's glossing over of Cristina's known afflictions; such a family would surely want heirs. Cristina herself sat unaware, drinking English tea, her beautiful eyes—they were her only beauty—soft under her bonnet as she watched the two children. Carla had grown slim and gentle; she was an adorable child. Jacky had his father's height and was masterful with the toy soldiers which Marcus had sent him lately from London. Carla was obedient about their formation and placing; she herself would rather have had a little toy farm, with cows and other animals, but Jacky must be pleased. She had succumbed to his charm on the day he arrived, and was seldom separated from him. A tutor gave them both lessons, but this was Saturday; and Carla had been told by her mother that she must be especially polite to Signorina Buonfranconi, as it was probable that her brother Marcus would be married to the young woman when he came to Florence.

Carla had looked, therefore, with perspicacity at the shy young lady; and liked what she saw. Afterwards she complained to her mother that the *signorina* never had a chance to speak; her mother did it all for her. The *signora* herself sat now, thin, rigid and garbed in black, and held forth on the questions of the day. A mercy they had a united Italy at last, in spite of the Pope (the

140

signora was a devout Catholic, but nevertheless held her own views) and Cavour was an able minister, no doubt of that. "I have had to interest myself in such questions, you understand, Signora Cray, because my husband dreamed always; always, I have had to be the man in our family. Fortunately Cristina is obedient; are you not, my chick?"

Cristina did not answer, for she knew no answer was expected of her and would not be heard if it were uttered. She heard her mother's voice going on as usual, for it had always, as far back as she could remember, been a background to her life; it was however possible to think one's own thoughts to oneself, quite separately. Papa she had loved greatly, but he was dead; and there had been a long time when she herself was ill, during which all her girlish acquaintances—the *signora* had prevented friendship—had been married off, and Cristina had been left on the shelf, with doctors attending her. Now she was twenty-six and it had not been expected, till lately, that anyone would offer for her despite the money. But this Marcus Cray, who lived in England, needed a wife; so she had been told. Mamma had said nothing about the dowry, but Cristina had always been brought up to suppose that there was enough. She did not interest herself greatly in such things, being often ill. Today was a treat, to come to Signora Cray's flat for tea. The *signora* was different; so small and intent and fierce, and yet one felt sorry for her. She had loved her husband very much, Mamma said, and he had been killed at forty-three. That was not old to die. Cristina had felt herself near to death more than once, and knew all about it. What she did not know about was the world, and men; Mamma had reared her as strictly as if she were in a convent. She nibbled a sweet biscuit now with her small irregular teeth; the older women were talking and the children playing, and she was left alone.

Marcus was obliged to postpone his departure for Italy for a few days on the eve of leaving London. He had a visitor, tall, fair and bronzed, in naval uniform. He hurled himself out of his chair in pleasure.

"Jake!" They had not met since before his own departure for Scotland, in another life. He was delighted to welcome his brother. They sat talking far into the night, and he was regaled with stories of the places Jake had visited; listening, he felt some envy, for he himself loved sailing, the sea, and strange new places. As a kind of retort he began to talk about Jacky, now safe with Mamma in Florence; and at once Jake's mouth tightened.

"From what we have learned of the mother, how can you be certain that he is your son? You are not cautious enough, Marco."

The childhood name tugged at him, even while he felt angry at Jacky's rejection. Of course the boy was his son! Could he not feel, even now, a pulling at his heart, as though a silver cord stretched between them? Jake did not understand yet; when he met the boy, it would be different.

Dawn had come and they took themselves to bed, and next day there was the shop to show Jake, with its refurbished board-room—Marcus had had it painted in eggshell blue and gold—and Robert's dressed windows. Cussen's daughter, who managed the books at the accounts-desk, rose and welcomed them; she was a plain, determined young woman with blonde hair, competent at her job. The customers had not yet started to come in; it was early. "I will leave Mr Jacob to you, Cynthia," Marcus said, with a wink at the tall motionless figure of his brother; he would be safe with such a plain young woman. "You must show him all the new departments, and ask him what he thinks of the notion we had of a coffee-shop." They had again broached, at the last informal meeting of senior staff, Robert's suggestion of a place on the upper floor where well-heeled customers could meet for coffee and talk: possibly the germ of the idea had been the Bondone Friday mornings in Florence, long ago. Cynthia Cussen knew all about it and nodded vigorously; she had none of her father's trembling airs and looked the age she was, twenty-seven.

Marcus took his brother's arm and showed him the picture-gallery, with places already marked for the paintings which would come back with him on his return, from Luigi's collection. There was nothing notable from modern English painters; he himself had not been able either to buy or sell any of Turner's, the coming man's, though he admired his admixture of paint and light. From his own experience he thought that a new movement would break, perhaps in five years, perhaps in ten; something that had not before been seen; and our conservative English will take their time to get used to it, he thought. It was always wise to buy before the rising market; he flattered himself he had an eye for developments. Jake said nothing; he had small wit and no humour, and was content to let his sparkling elder brother convey him along between the rows of paintings, then on to the Oriental department, the jewellery department, the glowing materials rich with India prints and Paisley patterns. He knew what he liked, but could not have said why. The face of the young woman in accounts remained with him; she had been predictable, which so few women were; you would know where you were with a young woman like that. He prodded at the upholstery displayed, feeling its sprung softness; Marco had made a difference here, there would be no more question of the shop's being closed down. He looked at his brother in admiration. "I am glad to see you," Marcus said, "because, also, I wanted to ask you—as I shall of course ask Luigi—about changing the name of the firm. Youngchild, thank God, has nothing more to do with it; it would have been an emporium by now. I want to call the store the House of Cray, with a gilded sign hanging out as Papa had at the beginning. It would be more personal to us, to the family; it pleases me better."

Jake did not demur. Presently Robert joined them and they went together to a nearby steak-house to eat. During the meal Jake was silent, for he had nothing more to say; he chewed with dedication, using his strong white teeth. Talk was in fact not his best point and he preferred to listen, especially where others had wit. Marcus had, and he loved him for it; together with the saturnine Robert the talk glinted like live coals.

He spent that short leave in the company of Marcus, and the last sight the latter had of him was of a gold-braided sleeve waving as the train drew out for Southampton. Marcus slumped in his seat, staring at the slats on the opposite wall of the carriage. It was empty except for himself; no crinolined beauty came to beguile him on this journey, and for almost the first time he had leisure to think of Isotta's proposal of a wife. God knew the money would be of use, one way and the other; he almost looked forward to meeting the young woman.

143

9

Isotta had not slept well, and felt unable to deal with the problems that confronted her with the chaperonage of a large picnic party of young people. As it was, Luigi's carriage, which he had agreed to lend, was so full of passengers that Marcus had offered to ride beside it, which he preferred to do in any case; his tall figure on horseback broke the light from the glaring sky. Everybody was in summer garb, and the determined black of Signora Buonfraconi was not to be seen, for Isotta had invited Cristina to stay with her for a few days alone; the girl's quiet personality was overshadowed by her mother, and Isotta had wanted Marcus to meet Cristina by herself. He had done so, with courtesy, but no one yet knew what he thought; as for Cristina, she had fallen in love. The beautiful many-coloured eyes dwelt on him even now, beneath the rim of her summer hat. She always dressed rather dowdily, Isotta thought; that could be remedied. As for the rest, she had it on her conscience; she knew it was said to be unlikely that Cristina could ever bear a child. But Marcus had Jacky, vociferous on the floor of the carriage, teasing Carla who sat on the step; nobody could want more than that handsome boy, and it left the way clear for Jacob to have the inheritance. Luigi had not come; he was too busy. His little fiancée-elect, Teresa Pelosi from Milan, who was staying at Anna's, sat primly on the seat facing the horses; she was not a taking child, having nothing at all to say and showing no interest in what others said. She was plump, and had pretty honey-coloured hair, but this was tortured into a fuzz of ringlets on either side of her face, which made it look broader, and her eyes were like her father Filippo's, the eyes of a prawn. The younger Filippo, Luigi's brother, had come with them; he was a smallish dark lad with sharp wit, who still thought girls were silly. Then there was the strident Luisa, whose chatter was for once welcome to relieve the silences of Cristina and Teresa; otherwise, Isotta was thinking, nobody in the carriage would have found anything to remark upon, except perhaps the beauty of the countryside through which they passed.

They stopped at a pinewood, and the coachman unloaded the picnic fare. Marcus had contributed wine, which waited ready in flasks of ice; and Anna's cook had done well, making pastries and providing a cold chicken, a ham, and some fruit. Marcus dismounted and tied his horse's reins to a tree, thereafter helping the ladies down. Filippo jumped early out of the carriage, and went to inspect the food. It was presently laid out in the grateful shade of the Aleppo pines, with the noise of chirping cicadas everywhere; now and again one of the small green creatures would land on the tablecloth, to be rescued and set free by Carla. She could never bear to kill or hurt anything, even an insect. Filippo jeered at her.

Isotta hoped greatly that this picnic, which had been arranged to give Marcus an opportunity to propose to Cristina, would be a success. She tried to forget the taut feeling inside her head and made herself segregate the children and Luisa, no easy task; the great creature had gazed up at Marcus as he lent her his arm out of the carriage, and no doubt she regretted not having encouraged him sooner; she was old enough now to have chaperoned the party on her own account, except that it was not proper for a single woman to do so. Isotta said a word in her ear and immediately, for she was good-natured enough, she helped to keep the children and Teresa and Filippo by them, while Marcus and Cristina walked off together into the shade of the trees. There was a Roman bridge known to be found nearby, with a little fountain; Isotta had suggested that he show it to Cristina. The young girl's cheeks were crimson with confusion; she had an idea of what was to happen, and could have done without the searching eyes on her back. She walked badly, Luisa thought; she was a scarecrow, with no style. The old maid examined her own expensive gown with self-satisfaction; then put out a hand to restrain Jacky, who said he was going after Papa.

"Papa has something private to say to the young lady," croaked Luisa, and her aunt frowned. "Jacky, sit down when you are bidden, and help with the plates." She hoped the proposal would not take too long; the ice in which the wine was kept was melting with the heat of the journey. The coachman ate his sandwiches placidly a little way off, and the cicadas chirped on.

The Roman bridge was in ruins, but one could still see the arch;

145

near it there was the little fountain, still ejecting water from the nearby stream, which had lowered itself to a trickle for summer. He pointed it out to Cristina and she bent to examine it, putting out her hand to feel the coolness of the water as it dropped. The hand was beautiful, white and slender. He found her pleasant, and restful in her silences; they were different from the silences of little Teresa, which arose from a total lack of ideas. This girl was not stupid, as he had already noted. She would make him a pleasant, undemanding wife; at that moment, he resolved to try to be faithful to her; she was not a person to be hurt. He helped her up from the fountain and said gently, "You know why we have come."

Her flush deepened, bringing vitality to her plain little oval face; her skin was good, he thought. "I—I think I know, Signor Cray." The words were spoken in so low a tone he could hardly hear them; by contrast, his own voice seemed loud. He smiled, with the smile which always lightened his face. He was not so very many years older than she was, but felt he was dealing with a child; the sensation was not unpleasant. "Come, if you will marry me you may call me Marcus, and I need no longer say Signorina Buonfranconi, which is a long title. Will you marry me, Cristina? It would make me very happy." And the money, he thought, will be useful. He was well aware that he would not have proposed had she been poor.

The long, shy glance raised itself. "Yes," said Cristina. Instead of taking her in his arms—he had a notion such abrupt tactics would frighten her—he took her wrist, and delicately kissed the place above her palm, which showed small violet veins. "Now we can be happy, and you must not be afraid any more," he said to her. "As my wife you may do as you choose. I will never be a terrifying husband, Cristina."

"I am not afraid of you," she said gently. He had let her wrist go and, instead, tucked her hand in his arm. "But you are afraid of many things, are you not?"

"Of Mamma, a little. And of becoming ill. Will it matter to you that I am often ill? You may find it tedious."

"I will sit by your bed, and feed you cold chicken and wine, and you will grow better. Let us go and receive our share for today, and we can tell them the news." He raised his head from her happy face and breathed the scent of the Aleppo pines. He was content; and it would be a blessed relief to pay some of the bills.

146

From now on, naturally, as a staid married man, he would not live extravagantly. Somewhere at the back of his mind, uncomfortably, lay Dorothea. He would have to get rid of her, and that would not be easy.

It was even less easy than he had thought. On return to the house there was a letter waiting. She must have written as soon as he had gone off. *Marcus darling, we haven't been careful enough; I'm pregnant. Come home as soon as you can.*

He wrote to her, a courteous letter, almost tender; but he held to his resolve not to go to her again. Some provision would have to be made for the child, in whom he did not, now or later, feel a jot of the consuming interest that had preceded Jacky's birth. He married Cristina within two weeks, hardly time for the bride to have clothes fitted; but he would see her gowned in London. Luigi, handsomer than ever in his suave correct clothes, gave the bride away; Signora Buonfranconi wanted the wedding-night to take place at her house in the country, but Marcus drove his new wife away into the hills, and they stopped at an inn; if they had known, it was the same where Enrico Bondone had first encountered Marcus Cray. Emilia was long gone, but the cook they had in the enlarged premises was reasonable. After supper they took a short stroll together to admire the hills in the evening light. He thought Cristina looked subdued and pale, and tried to draw her out to talk; she needed gentleness, he had decided, after that dragon of a mother. He went to their room, in the end, prepared accordingly; but found her in tears, her long hair loose on the pillow. Going to her and taking her in his arms, he tried to comfort her; no doubt she was still frightened.

"No, oh, no," she said. "It is not that. But—I do not know how to say it—the affliction that troubles women has come on. With me it is not a regular thing, it comes at odd times, always when I do not want it." She tried to laugh. "I am so very sorry; it will disappoint you, and I wanted to please you very much."

He kissed her, and stroked the long hair. "Never fret, sweetheart; we must catch our pleasure between such times. You do please me; believe me when I say it. I love my wife. Any troubles from now on, we will share." He tried to believe himself. Afterwards he would know wry laughter about his wedding-night; it was like nature to defeat him in such a way, when he had decided to be a virtuous husband.

They dallied in Florence after their return; surprisingly, Luisa announced that she wished to take Cristina in hand and dress her suitably. She had no notion of economy, having never lacked money, but her taste was good if a trifle heavy. So she and Cristina spent many days shopping, while Marcus spent his time at the Bondone shop inspecting the paintings Luigi wanted to have sent to London for possible sale. They had several differences; Luigi's choice was more florid on the whole than that of Marcus, but generally the latter was allowed to prevail; indeed, he thought, Luigi's obliging nature would never be suspected by the majority; his manner being haughty, one imagined on first meeting him that he was selfish and self-centred. But he evidently grudged nothing, and even offered to ship the pictures at his own cost. "It is worth it if you can sell them," he said. That settled, Marcus called in to visit his mother, who had sent for him to come to her alone when he could.

Isotta was also alone, seated with her back to the lace-drawn window; it was not for some moments that he perceived she had been crying. "I have a thing to tell you," she began, and without preamble launched into the tale of his parentage. He was appalled; though the half-suspicion had already come to him at the time of seeing Nardini's portrait, that day at the castello, it had been thrust down in his mind by the pressure of events. He got up out of his chair and began to walk up and down the room. "Why do you tell me this only now, Mamma? Why?"

"Because now that you have married a rich wife, it does not so greatly matter to you that the London inheritance belongs to Jacob, not to yourself."

The House of Cray for Jacob, who cared nothing for it? "But . . . I have worked for the store, spent money on it." He would not say that he loved it; he was too greatly filled with anger for so gentle a word.

"You have spent Luigi's money; that is immaterial, and matters can be straightened out. I have already written to Jacob, telling him of his rights."

"You should not have done so before consulting me."

"Why not? You are not the elder son of Marcus Cray. In his will he left everything to me, and I must leave it to his heir."

"Mamma . . . can nothing be arranged? Jake is happy in the

148

Navy, and I have given up my whole life." Remembrance of the dreary Glasgow years came to him; it had all been for nothing, he might as well have done as Jake had done, and followed his bent. Yet his heart had always been with the business, and still was so. "Will not Jake agree to some arrangement?" he asked, knowing that he was yielding ground. The shock of the news had been like a blow in the stomach; he was not yet in full control of his wits.

"Some arrangement may be made; that is Jacob's concern, and it depends what he wishes to do," she said coldly. He stared at her, suddenly seeing her with the harsh eyes of a stranger; an intriguing woman growing old, who could do much harm. Yet she had loved the elder Marcus Cray, if never himself.

He stormed out of the room and out of the house, unable to calm his anger. When Cristina returned, happy with her new gowns, he could hardly listen to her talk of them. She noticed his mood, and fell silent. Always she would do what she could to show that she loved him; they were fully man and wife now, and she reminded herself that she ought to be happy with such a kind husband, and free of Mamma. They were in fact to visit Mamma in a few days' time; she would be glad when the visit was over, and they could sail for England, which she had never seen.

The interview with Signora Buonfranconi was worse, in its way, than that with Isotta. Far from launching into the matter at once, she kept him waiting; he had come to talk about the dowry and how soon it was to be drafted to the London bank. She put off the subject time and again, talking of other matters, changing direction so often that finally, when Cristina was elsewhere, he pinned the old woman down and said clearly, "Signora, I want to know about the money. This is for Cristina's sake as well as my own. When will you send it? We would like to leave Italy as soon as we may, and I want matters settled in such ways before I leave." He fell silent, smiling determinedly; he had her now, he thought. She made a little movement with her ageing hands, as though to fan away unpleasantness. Then she said, "I regret that it is not possible to send money. All is tied up in this house and the property at Arezzo, which according to my late husband's will cannot be sold. It is yours outright, but I have the life-rent here till my death. Cristina is a good daughter and will not grudge her mother a roof. Afterwards, it may come to you; the matter is at my discretion. I regret that I can do no more."

He was white about the mouth. "You let me understand that there were considerable sums in cash to be made available when Cristina and I should marry. Do you now tell me that no such money exists?"

"I regret—"

"Your regrets are immaterial. I have been duped, and you—"

"Cristina is a good girl. You have not been entirely unfortunate."

"We will not bring Cristina into this; nothing is her fault."

"Nothing; nor is the fact that she may have no children. It is for this reason that I permitted you, a foreigner, to marry her. Otherwise—"

A barren wife; and no money with her. He was filled with rage and resentment; he had indeed been duped, made a fool of by everyone including his mother. "Did my mother know of this?" he asked in a thick voice. The Signora nodded, anxious to evade the unpleasant subject of the money. "Indeed, the Signora Cray and I discussed it often. She said that for certain reasons it was better for you to have no heir."

She smiled suddenly and dreadfully, exposing scant yellow teeth. "We must think of dear Cristina," she said glibly. "She knows nothing of all this, naturally; I have kept it from her, but the doctors gave their verdict some years ago. Otherwise she would have married sooner. Signore, please excuse me; I have to see the cook. Ah, here is Cristina. Do not distress her with what we have been saying. There is no need, and it can make no difference."

He would not distress Cristina; but a kind of impatience came to him regarding her. To have known nothing, suspected nothing! She was not a young girl, to be kept in ignorance any longer. He spoke to her, telling her of the situation regarding the money. At the end he made himself smile. "So, my dear, there must be no more shopping in Florence. As your mother would say, I regret."

10

If Marcus had examined his state of mind on returning home, it might have been that he thought he had had enough trouble for a long time; luckily, he was not given to such self-musings. In fact there was more trouble waiting; a letter from Maria, saying that she proposed to come and bring her small son for a visit, was the least of it. He gave the letter to Cristina, having introduced her to the housekeeper, and went out to the shop. But even there was strife; Cynthia Cussen sat at her desk with red eyes, dabbing at them with a handkerchief. Jake by now was back on his ship; and Marcus would not have connected him with events had not the clerk, spectacles sliding as always, come to him in trembling wrath—not, as might have been expected, against Jake himself, but against his own daughter, with Laxton the salesman maliciously attentive in the background, aware of all that went on.

"Says he'll marry her, and with any ordinary person I'd say it was about time, for she says she's in the family way. I didn't write to you, sir, as I knowed you had enough to do with one thing and another. But she's a hussy, and not fit to marry into the manager's family—set her up! I would just ask, if you was in touch with Mr Jake, sir, that you'd write and explain about the baby." His voice dropped a note. "Wouldn't have still kept her on here, sir, save that good book-keepers is hard to find, and I've been meaning to ask you about it and thought maybe, as it don't show yet, we could keep her until someone else is found. I wouldn't have had this happen, sir, for the world. Young men is an easy prey. Ashamed of her, I am, but her mother didn't have no sense, and it's her she takes after, looks like."

Marcus received this diatribe with enough control not to laugh in the little man's face, at the same time cursing Laxton for his pricked ears and Jake for his untimely intimacy. He himself had been a fool to think that nothing would happen, or rather not to consider it at all. The Bondone blood was lively, and Jake had been a long time at sea before coming home. There it was, at any rate, and nobody could put the clock back. He murmured something of the kind to Cussen, trying to put it to him that the matter was Jake's and Cynthia's affair, and that he must not punish the girl further. "I thought I might lock her up, sir, but the harm's done," concluded Cussen logically. Marcus took time to speak kindly to Cynthia, not mentioning the dire occurrence; pointless to make it a scandal all through the store: he would say a word to Laxton. The young woman kept her head down like a penitent, and sniffed; Marcus hastily left her to her books. Any other employer, perhaps even Luigi, he knew, would have sacked her on the spot; he himself did not readily act in such ways. Deep in his mind was the knowledge that a young girl named Isotta Bondone had once been in the same state herself, which made him the more tolerant of Cynthia. Ironically, Isotta now would have been the first to send her packing.

He was restless over the next few days, and Cristina watched him fearfully; she knew how upset he had been over the dowry, and felt that she had failed him, though he had continued courteous to her. She must make up for it all by being an excellent wife; she set herself to win the housekeeper's respect, and took trouble with her own toilet, having herself laced into the elaborate gowns Luisa had chosen for her in Florence, and finding a maid who could dress her hair as they did here in England, brushed down over the ears and polished with silk; it suited her, making her small face notable and emphasising her eyes and long young neck. Soon after her arrival Marcus had taken her to meet the staff at the House of Cray, and she had made a good impression there; she knew, for he told her, pleased with her gentle dignity. "Did you notice Cynthia?" he asked, for he had told her of Jake's lapse. She nodded. "She is very unhappy," she said softly. "If your brother will marry her, he should be allowed to do so, do you not think?"

He had not thought; he was tired of the affair and it embarrassed him. He was also troubled about Dorothea, who continued to write him persistent letters and notes, begging him to come to her. But he put off such a visit; he was afraid of being drawn under again, and told himself he intended to remain faithful to Cristina. Truthfully, he could tell Dorothea that he was expecting his sister and her boy and that his time would be fully taken up.

Maria arrived, matronly in a black bonnet and bombazine

gown; her pretty features had sharpened and lengthened, and she looked like a shrew. The boy, Willie, was quiet and dark-eyed; he watched everyone, then stored the impressions away in his mind; he was, Marcus decided, what is called a deep one. There was still no word from Jake, but Isotta wrote in anger on hearing of the state of affairs with a clerk's daughter, and announced that she and the children would come to London forthwith, evidently to try to prevent the match. Marcus was happy at the thought of having Jacky with him—perhaps the boy could stay on, as Cristina had loved him for himself and would have no objections. Marcus would also be glad to see Carla, whom he had found sympathetic, amusing and charming. It would be a houseful, and he could truly write to Dorothea that his time was fully taken up in preparing for the arrivals.

Two happenings occurred to mar the even tenor of the way still further. The first was the letter from Jake which Marcus had been expecting and dreading. Its tone, however, was mild if a trifle pompous.

Trinidad, 3rd August.

My dear Marcus,

Mamma tells me that she has herself informed you of the contents of the letter she lately sent to me. I have had small opportunity to reply till now, when we are laid up for some days to take on stores and water. It is very hot here and little inducement to go ashore.

As you know, circumstances now are vastly altered for us both; but I do not intend that you should suffer, or that Mamma's secret should become known to anybody except ourselves. Firstly, I suggest that we make no difference at present except that I should prefer to come home and have some say in the control of what is after all my inheritance. I have accordingly written to Luigi—nothing out of the way has been told him—informing him of my decision to leave the Navy and to come to London with the prospect, surely, of a place in the business. You will find me precise and careful with accounts, at which I have had some experience on shipboard. I do not think Luigi will refuse my suggestion, but if he should, may I rely on yourself? I mean, in fact, that you should make me your heir; this would redress the balance fully. There would then be no necessity for the unfortunate state of affairs regarding Mamma to become public knowledge. I would not like it known even after her death; we owe it to her to suppress it. If you will not do this—but I am persuaded

153

you will—then I must reconsider my line of conduct. I hope profoundly that this will not be necessary.

We are both grandsons of Enrico Bondone and I believe that we have inherited a certain discrimination from him. We should deal together very well; you will not find me difficult provided the true state of affairs is remembered.

There is another reason for my coming to London. You may know by now of my affair—I say this deliberately—with Cynthia Cussen. She is expecting a child which I had assumed to be mine, but her father, who knows her best, assures me that she is flighty. I can deal with the situation better when I am in town.

To yourself, and to your new wife, I do of course send hopes for the utmost felicity. I much look forward to meeting you both as soon as my arrangements are made final.

Your devoted brother,
Jacob Cray.

He stared at the letter, sullen and resentful. His heir!—and Jacky to be disinherited, of course; Mamma would certainly have told Jake that it was unlikely Cristina would have children. For the first time it was welcome to him that she might be barren. What a coil! And two pregnant women, Cynthia and Dorothea, to be placated and, no doubt, paid! How could it be managed without further recourse to Luigi, whose patience might understandably fail?

He went home to Cristina, and found her in tears.

That afternoon, while he was still at the shop, a beautiful and brilliantly dressed lady had called on her, saying that she was Mrs Wainfleet. Maria and her son had already driven out. The maid, who was new, had admitted Dorothea to the parlour, and Cristina had gone down alone. At first sight it had been like beholding a bright foreign bird, with bright feathers and jewelled claws. Dorothea had chatted amiably for half an hour, describing the various sights of town and inviting Cristina to take the air in her carriage on Thursday. They had parted company courteously, but immediately the caller had gone Mrs Sim, the housekeeper, had come in, her face grimly set.

"That one is no better than she should be. She should not have been received; I knew nothing of it; the master will have something to say." And she went on to inform Cristina, in forthright tones, of the true status of Dorothea Wainfleet; and even though Cristina's English was still halting and Mrs Sim was a Scot, enough had been made clear. Cristina had returned to her room and had dissolved in tears, remaining in this state all afternoon; she had not taken tea. Now, Marcus attempted to comfort her, but only made everything worse. He suspected that Dorothea had some ulterior motive for her call, although it was just possible that it had been made out of friendliness. He told himself that he preferred not to judge anyone; perhaps Dorothea herself meant their relationship to subside into acquaintance, now that he was married, and had begun in this way. That was almost too good to be true. He found himself uttering platitudes to Cristina, unable to convince her; after all what she had learned was nothing but the truth, and perhaps by now in her eyes he had feet of clay. The sensation was not pleasant. He tried to correct himself and rebuke her; but it had not been her fault. Though why had she not suspected that he must have kept a mistress before his marriage? It was the habit of most men, unless they were monks. Cristina must learn the ways of the world, he told himself.

He thought of the child that was coming. He could hardly abandon Dorothea. Would it not be for the best if the two women did in fact become friends? Typically, he seized on it; and murmured something about the proposed carriage-drive. Cristina sat bolt upright, her cheeks two patches of crimson, the tears still wet upon her face.

"I will not drive out with her. How can you even suggest it?"

"I did not; it was yourself who informed me of the invitation."

"I will not go. I shall send a note to say that I am unwell. It is true enough," and she began to weep again. Marcus left the room in a temper; and was almost immediately sorry. It was true that it would be improper for his wife and his mistress to drive out together; he would not refer to it again. As for Jake, whom he must answer tonight, he was smug, no doubt, with his discovery of his own importance. One could not however refuse the suggestion he had made, as there had been the smallest possible hint, among the phrases of the letter, that if Jake did not obtain satisfaction he would inform Luigi of everything; and there was no predicting how that young man would act in the circumstances. There was no predicting anyone or anything; thank God Jacky was coming over with the party of women, and he would see his son again!

155

Another thought had already occurred to him. If Cristina were willing--surely this time she would make no difficulty—he would like the boy to make his home with them. But the present moment was hardly propitious for speaking of the matter.

To his dismay, Cristina, taking Maria and Will, did go out on the carriage drive, abjectly thinking to please him. The party returned full of artificial chatter; it was unlikely that Maria's sharp eyes had missed the true state of affairs. They had driven into the country, Cristina told him; it had been pleasant to breathe the clear air. He was displeased, and showed it; she should not have gone. He went out of the house, leaving the women to console themselves, and, determined to force an issue at last, walked straight round to Clarges Street.

Dorothea welcomed him as he should have expected, beautiful, warm and almost purring; she had seen the little Italian wife now and knew that here was no rival. She soon disarmed Marcus' scowl; he could never keep out of temper for long, and her seductive ways were irresistible after the weeks with poor Cristina. He found himself in bed with her, his hand lingering above the place where the child lay: he was always to have tenderness for his children. When he returned he did one favour to Cynthia Cussen. He wrote to Jake, saying that Cynthia's character was irreproachable and that Jake ought to marry her. It was the only straightforward statement he permitted himself in what was, by and large, a diplomatic letter. It was alarming to think of the whole Cray clan settled in London in the autumn. Perhaps Mamma would go away again soon; her health was better in Italy; she did not sleep well.

11

"The crossing was terrible." Isotta lay on a chaise-longue with a Paisley shawl in red and grey patterned colours drawn up to her knees. Her face had thinned and pared itself into that of a prematurely old woman; a woman with large dark eyes. Her hands, bare except for Marcus Cray's wedding ring, showed their small bones through the skin. The room was full of new arrivals; to Marcus' faint displeasure, a young man named Beverley Mayne, who had accompanied them on the voyage, remained to hang about the invalid, arranging her shawl and cushions and settling her comfortably. No doubt he would soon take himself off.

"I wasn't sick," said Jacky, who had grown taller than either his grandmother or his aunt. His hair had been cut short and clustered thickly about his white pillar of a neck; he looked like a young god. "No," said Carla, "you spent all your time on deck, talking to the sailors. I had to stay below with Mamma." She looked at Jacky with her dark shining eyes, as if seeing the valiant figure he must have made above the lurching sea, his capes blowing about him. He and she were almost inseparable and it was one of the problems with which Isotta intended to confront her son; a nephew and aunt had best not grow up together if they were too near of an age. If she had known, the problem was already solved; but Marcus had had no time to tell her yet of his intention to take the boy.

Other problems were less easily solved. Jake was to arrive in a few days' time, and Marcus knew that the question of Cynthia Cussen loomed large and implacably. He put off the necessity of trouble by asking in detail for Isotta's health and for that of Anna, who as usual spent the time between bed, table and church. Luigi was to be married to Teresa Pelosi next year; it would perhaps divert Anna to have her niece in Florence. As for the cousins, Gastone's daughters, they had proposed a visit to England shortly now that Margherita's husband was finally confined in an asylum. "They will stay at an hotel," said Isotta consolingly. "Luisa is too independent to be anyone's guest."

After this piece of understatement Beverley Mayne took himself off, for he too was staying at an hotel. Isotta pressed him warmly to visit them again on the morrow. "You have been so good to me," she said. Mayne protested that he was charmed; bowed over Isotta's hand, Maria's, Carla's and lastly Cristina's, who had not put herself forward as hostess. It was in any case difficult to do so when her mother-in-law was present.

On the day Jake was expected to arrive the three young people, Jacky, Carla and Will Cosgood, were sent off with Mrs Sim to explore the Zoological Gardens. They had taken a picnic lunch, as the weather was fine, and would not be back till evening. Will in particular was avid to see the animals, for Maria's silent boy had his passions. Mrs Sim, of whom he had made a friend, had already told him about the giraffe from Windsor which had been a present from the Turks. "Old King George loved that giraffe and used to feed it himself daily, but in the end it died, of the cold most likely. He used to say it had eyes more beautiful than any woman, and the King was a great one for the ladies." Mrs Sim did not amplify this statement. The day went well, and it was evening before they returned, almost in time to witness the *dénouement* at the house off Piccadilly.

"We was married all right and proper, but I promised I wouldn't say nothing till Jake came back, and I haven't," stated Cynthia vigorously. Safe on her tall, fair, handsome husband's arm—in fact Jake shuffled his feet and looked at the carpet, and Cynthia was the one who took on all comers—she had somewhat shed the mousy appearance of the plain young woman bent over the books day after day at the shop. Her head was up, her gaze returned everyone's squarely, and nobody tried, perhaps from astonishment, to interrupt what she had to say. A silence greeted the end of the speech; the first to break it was Isotta.

"Then this child that you are to have, it was conceived in wedlock?" Cynthia came as near to tossing her head as any human can to so equine a gesture. "That's our affair, begging your pardon. But it'll be *born* in wedlock, and that's what counts with the law. I'd have said as much to any of you, and to father looking down his nose, but Jake said I wasn't to."

Isotta swallowed. "Then—then—"

Marcus stepped in; he had an admiration for Cynthia and the

silent battle she had fought, and wondered how she had contrived to get his dilatory brother to the altar. "I think, Mamma, that it is our duty—and our pleasure—to welcome Cynthia into the family," he said gently, and Isotta roused herself to permit the young woman to give her a peck on the cheek. Cristina followed, but her kiss was warm. Maria did not budge; she had been among the harshest critics of Cynthia, and would not change her mind. It did not matter greatly; she would soon go back home, having waited only to make young Will known to Carla and Isotta.

That lady accepted the inevitable; she was never again heard to complain of Jake's marriage, bitterly as she might resent it within herself. At least, she thought, the child could be taught to speak properly and could be introduced to company without revealing his distaff ancestry. It was too late to do anything in this way about Cynthia; one could only hope that she would stay in the background as much as possible now that she had had her way.

Marcus had been giving much thought to the problem of employing Jake in the store. At present he could take Cynthia's place at the accounts table, but soon it would no doubt be necessary to provide him with a senior place, and the only one available belonged to Laxton, who was a good salesman and had wheedling manners which opened the purses of women clients rapidly. It was impossible to see Jake in this role; he would merely stand there. Yet finances could not, at this moment, stretch to another full salary. Marcus shelved it, keeping the possibility of Jake's having to replace Laxton in his mind. He would regret it, but it must, sooner or later, be done, if nothing happened to make the change unnecessary. Perhaps, as so often happened, fortune would take a turn. Meantime the newlyweds had found a modest house to rent within walking distance of the store, and Jake appeared with a sailor's punctuality daily at half past eight.

Carla reflected, towards the end of their English visit, that she would be sorry to return to Italy with Mamma. Indeed it seemed odd that they must do so, for Marcus spoke of hiring a tutor for Jacky whom she herself could quite well have shared. But Mamma had been cross when she suggested it and had said firmly that there was no question of staying here. Was not Carla to be a bridesmaid at Luigi's wedding?

"That is not till next summer, Mamma." She felt pensive about the wedding; Luigi was one of the people she had always loved best, so handsome and gay; it was hard to think of his having to marry little Teresa, who was neither amusing nor pretty. Carla let her long eyelashes droop over her cheeks; she knew very well that Mamma would have liked her to be the bride, not the brides-maid, but there was all Teresa's money which would be of use for the firm. Instead, Mamma would try to push Carla into the company of young Filippo, which was nothing like the same thing. If Jacky were left behind in England, she would no doubt have to rely much more on Filippo, who was almost her only friend; cousin Margherita's horrid children did not count, and Mamma did not encourage company outside the family, except of course for Sir Beverley Mayne. "He is her *cavaliere servente*," thought Carla with a little smile; Jacky had told her that and it was, somehow, wicked and on no account to be repeated in front of Mamma.

Before parting, the two exchanged locks of hair, and Carla laid them side by side on her palm. They were almost identical, rich, dark, shining and curling; she would put hers in a little silver locket she wore "but you cannot wear such things," she said to Jacky. He laughed. "I will make a bracelet of it and wear it round my arm," he said. He rolled up his sleeve, bared the white-fleshed arm, and let the lock of hair curl about it; he was very strong, and the muscles he had showed were hard with running and leaping. He was not totally immersed in the parting with Carla, though he was sorry that she was sad; Papa had promised such wonderful things, besides the new tutor who would be a bore; he, Jacky, was to learn to hunt, which he had always longed to do, and there were sights to be seen and places to go in London; he would not be dull. Also, Cristina seemed kind; he could not think of her as a stepmother. Altogether it would be an improvement on Florence and the company of Grandmamma, who had nevertheless been good to him. He suddenly remembered Carla, and that she would be gone tomorrow; he would miss her, she was sporting for a girl; he was not himself quite clear what he meant by that, but he saw that there were tears in her dark eyes, and quite spontaneously he leaned across and kissed her. "I'll come to see you," he promised.

"You won't forget?"

"Never." Neither could foresee the circumstances under which they would meet again; they would be very different.

I want you, wrote Luigi in one of his letters about then, *to look out for any work by a certain Frenchman, Claude Monet. He does not paint leaves but the light on the leaves. He will not become the fashion yet. If you find anything of his, inform me.*

Marcus folded away the letter, aware as he always was of Luigi's gift of foresight; he had seldom been wrong about coming painters. Also, Marcus was grateful to him about the business of Jake; Luigi had agreed to pay the latter a salary meantime till it was seen how he shaped. The store was popular; several paintings had changed hands in the past six months, and the House of Cray was becoming a focus for good taste in a way that would have gladdened the heart of the elder Marcus. All in all, but for Dorothea, life would be placid and profitable.

She had given birth to a son, who resembled his father. Far from concealing the fact, she had taken to driving about with the baby in her carriage, a great mastiff guarding them both. It was impossible that polite London did not know of the liaison; perhaps for Cristina's sake, nothing was said or implied by anyone. Marcus was pleased that his gentle Italian wife should have been accepted in society; she made no mark, but neither did she offend. She would know, of course, about the birth; it was one of the things they did not discuss, especially since Cristina's miscarriage in the autumn. That had grieved her; he had, as he had promised, stayed by her bedside, feeding her chicken and wine; and had comforted her. Young Jacky was with them, very much alive, and his son. Why should he fret for more? And Jacky, he knew, would be dearer to him than ever Dorothea's boy could be. Yet Cristina still pined, and wanted children.

He arrived home to find her also reading a letter; it was from Maria, back again in the north. "Mamma has written to ask her to find a governess-companion to practise English with Carla," she said, raising her head from the letter for his kiss. "She asks if we can have the young lady to stay overnight, then see her on to the ship. May we do so?"

"Of course." He was glad to learn that Carla was to have a companion, and hoped that Maria's choice would not be too grim. He had taken a great liking to his little sister, so seldom seen by him; he wished it was possible to go to her more often, but the business forbade. Perhaps when Jake had found his feet he himself, and Cristina, could take a holiday together in Italy. He watched, as if absently, Cristina pouring his tea from a silver pot, took it from her, and drank it gratefully. A fire burned cleanly in the grate; it was peaceful, his home, to return to. If only he need not be constantly troubled over Dorothea! But that lady would not allow herself to be forgotten.

The governess arrived, and was duly met at the station; she carried her few possessions in a basketwork trunk. She was a shy, palely pretty, fair-haired young woman named Hester Fenton, and this was her first appointment. Later they were to learn that her mother had been a lady, but that the first marriage, of which Hester was the result, had been impecunious and the second, after the death of her young husband, frowned on; in fact, Hester's stepfather was a baker. There seemed no evidence of coarseness, however, in the young lady herself; she sat quietly by Cristina in the carriage sent to fetch her, and behaved with decorum during her brief stay in the house. Marcus contrived to have a few words with her before she left, sending his best love to his little sister, also a sapphire and pearl pendant he thought might please Carla; it was made like a basket of flowers, and he had picked it up for very little. "How kind," said the young governess, and her eyes filled with tears; afterwards he wondered if, in her life, kindness was rare. Later they heard that she had made the voyage safely, and that both Isotta and Carla were pleased with her.

Luigi was duly married that summer. The bride was dressed in oyster-coloured satin, her gown and bonnet trimmed with blonde lace, so that her plain little face peered out short-sightedly. Carla wore white, as the chief bridesmaid; her dark prettiness was enhanced by a wreath of real flowers, cunningly interwoven by Hester, who had not been asked to the wedding. Filippo Pelosi's daughter from his second marriage was the bridal attendant, aged six. Her name was Margherita and her hair like primrose silk, combed straight over her shoulders. Everyone exclaimed with delight at sight of her; she attracted more attention than the bride.

Carla had followed Teresa to the altar nervously, in case she herself spoilt the ceremony somehow: Isotta had drilled her in the part she must play, but she was filled with misgiving. Suddenly at sight of Luigi's slim upright figure waiting at the altar she knew why. How long had she been in love with Luigi? It was hardly a suitable time to make the discovery, no doubt. There was nothing to be done, and Teresa and he were made man and wife while she watched; later they drove off on the wedding-trip and the guests remained to consume wine and small sweet cakes. Carla stroked her bridesmaid's bouquet, neatly made up and tied with white ribbon. Someone was watching her; she sensed it before seeing it. It was not surprising, for she knew she had grown prettier of late; and she was dressed finely today. But it was unexpected to have aroused fire in the bosom of young Filippo, with whom she generally quarrelled.

Filippo's elder namesake, watery-eyed and flabby, had given the bride away while his harsh second wife sat in the congregation; their only surviving son, a little boy named Angelo, was said to be not quite right in the head. Carla watched them and let the younger Filippo watch her, and at his insistence gave him a carnation from her bouquet. Then she forgot him while they all posed for more photographs taken by the Milan studio manager who was now a part of Bondone Figli; old Filippo had retired from active business.

The descent on London of Luisa and Margherita did not take place for some months; in fact, they came at the worst season of the year, bringing with them Margherita's daughter Anna-Maria, a thin whining child of eleven. Huddled over the hotel fire and wrapped in warm clothes, they wrote to invite Marcus, Cristina and Jake to luncheon. As Cynthia was left out of the invitation, perhaps by accident, Jake refused to go; in any case his wife was heavily pregnant by now and disinclined to walk on the slippery roads. Jake was left, accordingly, with Laxton in charge of the shop; the two did not get on, and Marcus abandoned them thankfully. It was not, as he confessed to Cristina, all roses having his brother in the firm and he often heartily wished Jake back at sea, where his peremptory ways would be an asset. More than one customer had been offended by him, and knowing clients now asked personally for Mr Marcus Cray.

The luncheon went off uneventfully and was good and well served; Luisa said she understood now why the English ate roast beef. They chatted of family news; Teresa was to have a child, and

Carlo, Margherita's second son, had decided to enter the Church, which pleased his mother. Margherita did not have many pleasures in life; she seemed unable even to enjoy the change of scene, for Anna-Maria was spoilt and gave her no peace. Cristina wondered if a governess would solve the problem, and timidly asked how Miss Fenton was faring with Carla and Isotta. Very well, they said; she did not put herself forward in any way.

Marcus and Cristina left at four o'clock, with an invitation to the ladies to come and be shown over the House of Cray next morning. Accordingly, they arrived, in a cab; Luisa was resplendent in sable furs, draped over a green wool and velvet ensemble with a matching hat; she was a fine figure of a woman, still bright-haired, six feet tall, chattering as always, and with the Bondone hook-nose added to her air of total command. What happened next was all the more extraordinary; but, as Marcus afterwards said, life being what it is they ought to have been prepared for it, or something like it. It was still, and would be for a long time, incredible.

When they arrived Marcus had an important client, and accordingly turned them over to Laxton to be shown round. He saw from the corner of his eye that they toured the picture-gallery and then disappeared in the direction of the coffee-shop, Anna-Maria tagging behind. He did not see them again that day; Laxton returned, looking as usual, and the hours passed as they generally did. Marcus enquired if the ladies had seemed satisfied, and was told that they had, and had departed to look at other shops, as the snow had stopped. Not a word was said by Laxton about his own invitation to luncheon next day, which was a Sunday.

Thereafter he was quiet, not even a gleam appearing in his eye or a cocky angle to his little red pointed nose; he wrote up his sales, did his duty, and forbore even to quarrel with Jake over trifles. Time passed, and it seemed to Marcus, thinking of it absently, that he had seen very little of his cousins on their visit and that this was some relief, as Dorothea was being *exigeante* and he could not call his time his own. Accordingly, when Laxton came and asked him for a day off, he was unprepared, and queried it rather sharply.

"You had your holiday in the autumn. What is it; a funeral?"

"No, sir, a wedding; my own."

He smirked a little. Marcus raised an eyebrow; Laxton's bachelor habits were so pronounced that his news was unexpected as if an anchorite had announced his engagement. Marcus tried not to smile too broadly; there was certainly, by now, a gleam in the little man's eye, and he drew up to his small height with some dignity. "Do I know the lady?" Marcus said absently; he was not interested, and afterwards things could go on as before.

"Assuredly, sir. She is your cousin."

"My—" He gaped, like a boy, with incredulity; subsequently he was able to make some intelligent comment, and listen to what Laxton chose to impart, which was not much. Luisa and he had seen one another daily "and, of course, sir, she knows how I fought with Garibaldi some years ago, and it was nice for her to be able to talk in her own language; not many know it here. She told me straight out that she'd fancied me from the beginning." He smirked again, and Marcus was left with an impossible mind's eye vision of the marriage-bed; it would be like mating a tapir to an elephant. He muttered the correct things; asked where the church was, and said that he and Cristina would certainly be present; he did not offer to give away the bride, for already, at this stage, warnings sounded in his mind of Luigi's probable fury. Luisa was the heiress of old Gastone, and her portion was large. That, of course, was why this knowing little adventurer—half-an-hour before he would not have applied such a term to Laxton—was, to put it colloquially, taking her on. His old age would be comfortable. After all, why not? Luisa was of age. And yet—

When he had got rid of the prospective bridegroom, Marcus went to send a cable to Luigi. The reply came the following afternoon. DISMISS SALESMAN IMMEDIATELY PROPOSAL IMPOSSIBLE PREVENT WEDDING LUIGI.

By that time, it was too late.

Jake was by now enabled to undertake his full share of work at the shop, for Laxton handed in his notice, which he did not stay to work out. The newlyweds were not seen again by Marcus and Cristina, but Margherita was; with the child clutching at her skirts, she called tearfully at the house one early evening, when they had just finished tea; Cristina at once sent for a fresh pot to be made, but Marcus wondered if a small glass of brandy would be more agreeable; Margherita was not only frozen, but distressed.

"He is so *impertinent*. He orders Luisa about like a drudge, and she—she likes it, or anyway puts up with it. Nothing is comfortable now; everything he wants is done or bought, and she's ordered him suits of clothes and I don't know what else. It would be just as well if we were not there; I'm only in the way." She sniffed dolefully, drinking the tea. "All these years I've hardly been alone with Luisa, with my marriage as you know it was, and now this. I do think that at her age—" Some of the misery was, no doubt, due to the probable loss of any sums Luisa might have left her sister in her will; but by custom as it stood most would have gone to Luigi, and now—Well, there was nothing to be done, except wait.

12

Carla had not been well, and Isotta had managed to afford to hire a little house by the sea near Rapallo for four weeks. It was pleasant weather and they wore old clothes; Hester Fenton and Carla walked along the beach looking for shells, their skirts whipping about their ankles with the light breeze. Hester was happy nowadays; she had been received into the Catholic Church, and her timidity had a staff on which to lean. "Will not your family be angry and refuse their permission?" Isotta had asked her, and the lovely colour had come up in Hester's cheek.

"There is nobody now but my stepfather, and he may be cross, a little, as he is a sidesman. But he will not care greatly; I do not expect to visit him again."

So she went without cares today, limping a trifle as she always did after a riding accident in childhood. Carla had found a shell she wanted, and stopped to examine it lying in her pink palm. They found a place to sit, and watch the sea with its changing colours of turquoise and blue. Carla sniffed the air; she had felt better since coming here. If only they need not go back to the heat of Florence!

They sat in silence, for they were good enough friends not to have to make conversation. Carla was thinking, as always, of Luigi, and from there she remembered Luisa's odd marriage and how she had brought her nasty little bridegroom home. Luigi, who Mamma said had not been pleased at first, had offered him a place in the firm which Laxton had refused, saying he did not now need to work to live. Perhaps that would be all that happened; but knowing Luigi one somehow expected more. As for Luisa, she ministered to her little man in every way; they no longer lived with the family, but had hired a flat in the city, where Laxton was said to be running up huge bills. But that is all family gossip, Carla thought. What would one know, where would one be, without the family? Perhaps like Hester, cast on the world. Impulsively, she said aloud, "I am glad you have come; it affords me company." She sat still looking at the shell, with the wind stirring her hair, curling and loose about her shoulders. The shell was curved, in shades of rose; she would take it back with her to Florence and put it on her dressing-table where she could see it daily. The holiday was almost at an end.

They walked back slowly, and noticed a carriage waiting near the house. "It is Aunt Anna's," said Carla flatly. She wondered what had induced Anna to stir abroad, indolent as she had grown of late years. One thought of her always as a stout perfumed black-clad shape in dim light, with the blinds drawn to prevent headaches.

But the shape sat in the room now with Mamma, and there was a third visitor; Luigi's wife Teresa, stolid, rouged, and thickening with Luigi's child. Carla suffered herself to be kissed on the cheek by both women. Everyone was smiling, as if in conspiracy.

"We will not stay overnight, Isotta," said Anna, who sat holding her daughter-in-law's hand in a way Carla found disagreeable; but no doubt Teresa was doubly dear to Anna, being also her niece. Luigi's wife said nothing during the visit, chiefly because she seldom had anything to say. She showed no interest in the room or the sea outside, but stared at nothing, or else at her skirts. They had driven down today because Aunt Anna said the drive would be good for her; certainly it had done her no harm. She heard the small-talk of the older women, ranging through everything from food to a cure for insomnia, from which Aunt Isotta suffered so badly. Teresa could not understand why one should not sleep when one was tired enough. She herself had few ills, and no interest except Luigi, who both terrified and fascinated her. Since he knew the child was coming he had kept away.

"Aunt Anna has something to say to you, my child," Isotta told Carla, smiling. Carla was bewildered; what could it be? Was there a message from Marcus? That was all she wanted to hear about; or word from Luigi, but the latter never thought of her. Anna still smiled also, her full pale lips drawn up, her eyes intent beneath the bonnet.

"It is on behalf of my son Filippo that I am here, my child," she began. Then, with the smile broadening, "He is devoured with love for you. He begs me to ask you if you will consider becoming his wife. It would make him very happy."

They smiled on; the whole world was smiling. Hester had not

come into the room; Carla knew a sudden need for her. What should she say? It was evident that Mamma was favourable to the proposal. But Filippo . . . she had never thought of him as a possible husband. He was not interested in young women and had never kept a mistress, as Luigi had and still did, as well as remaining very much interested in Massini's plump, married and opulent niece, Signora Grassi. Filippo to order her life, share her bed . . . it was not too welcome . . .

"Dear child, we will not hurry you," said Anna smoothly; then to Isotta, "She will require a little time to think of it; this has been a shock to her."

"It is a great compliment, Carla," put in Isotta, frowning a little; no doubt she thought Carla's silence was discourteous. The girl stammered something; yes, she would be grateful for a little time, and to talk it over with Mamma and, she almost added, Hester. But Hester was out of these women's reckoning.

Anna rose, and touched Carla's cheek. "Send us an answer soon," she said gently. "Filippo is anxious to know what has been decided. Now, Isotta my dear, we are going on to stay with friends at La Spezia; I will not take this child back all the way to Fiesole today. Is she not well? Luigi hopes greatly for a son."

After they had gone Isotta sent for Carla, who came unwillingly; perhaps Mamma was going to be angry with her. But the voice was calm. "It is a handsome proposal," Isotta pointed out. "You must remember that there is nothing for you in the way of a dowry, except what Marcus may choose to give you; and he, God knows, has many expenses of his own." She knew all about the establishment in Clarges Street. "If you marry Filippo, you will see a great deal of Luigi himself, and will be in a position greatly to help both Marcus and Jake."

"Yes, Mamma." She hadn't thought of it; of course, to help Marcus was what she greatly desired; dear tall, humorous Marcus, easy-going, generous, lazy Marcus, whom she loved more than she could tell. And there was Jacky, whom she would help also.

"You have not answered, Carla." The voice had grown a little sharper; if the girl proved difficult, this very advantageous offer would go to the winds. She had always prayed that there might be a marriage, either with Luigi—but that had been unlikely—or with his brother. The foolish child must not be permitted to waver indefinitely; Filippo might be in love. Had it happened at the wedding, when the child had worn flowers in her hair? But Anna was proud, Luigi also; they would want an answer soon.

She stood up. "Am I to write to your aunt, saying that you accept Filippo's proposal with pleasure? Or am I to refuse? That will place us all in a very awkward position. The family have been good to us, and you—"

Carla flung her head up. "Do not trouble, Mamma. I accept the proposal. As you say, I will be able to help my brothers." She was pale and still.

Isotta came and kissed her on the cheek, as the relatives had done. "I am glad of it," she said. "When you are married you will have much more freedom. We must begin to think about clothes."

Carla was married to Filippo Bondone in the autumn, when the colours of the trees and flowers had changed to flame and brown. She looked pale and, for the first time, Isotta had thought of putting a little rouge on her cheeks; but had decided against it, as the bride must not look tawdry. Her dress was simple and suitable, and there were no attendants. Luigi gave her away, and it struck Isotta that they made a handsome couple; but Filippo was not ugly either, and when the pair returned after the ceremony everyone, all the relations, Anna, even Teresa, and the elder Filippo's wife (the old man was ill, and had not been able to come to the wedding) said how pretty a pair they made; that was a word much in use; they looked pretty.

They were driven off in the beribboned carriage: and almost as soon as they had gone, perhaps sooner, a buzz of talk broke out concerning the scandal about Luisa's husband. Neither Luisa nor, naturally, the husband had come today. The details were not fully known: all that was certain being that Luisa's husband had suddenly left Florence.

13

It had happened without fuss. Anna and Teresa had, of course, paid a courtesy-call on the newlyweds, and had found Luisa adoring her spouse in the parlour, wherein was being poured excellent coffee; they had stayed to partake of it, but afterwards compared notes unfavourably; Luisa's choice was agreed to be anything but handsome; so small and skimpy, and that red nose! What could have induced Luisa so to cast aside all prudence? "And," added Teresa in one of her few recorded statements, "he is not even polite."

"We poor women like to be bullied," said Anna.

Some days passed, in course of which Luigi had dragged full details of the meeting from his wife; subsequently, a note was brought round to the hired flat to the effect that Signor Bondone would appreciate a few words with Mr Laxton, alone.

"Am I not to accompany you?" begged Luisa, who could hardly bear to let her little man out of her sight. His ugliness was nothing to her, his manners engagingly brusque, as befitted a hero; after all, he had fought with Garibaldi. She was happier than she had ever been in her life, fulfilled, conquered, and temporarily quenched. "No," replied Laxton, "it's a man's talk," which he assumed would be held on the lines of some offer, perhaps, of a directorship; he had shown sense in declining the earlier offer of a job in the store. He'd bettered himself, that was it; and these Bondones had best know it, just as the Crays had had to do. He set off, almost strutting, for the office was within walking distance of where they lived. Luisa watched him from behind the lace curtains, then turned away with a happy sigh, and went and sat down on the cushions; truth to tell she was a little tired, the speed at which they lived bearing small resemblance to her former maidenly seclusion. He would return for luncheon; and she had made sure to order a good one.

Luigi was waiting for Laxton in the office, and indicated a gilt chair, which the caller took. Luigi then sat down behind his accounts-table. He had not taken his eyes off the arrival since Laxton's entry, and continued to pierce him with that oblique, golden gaze, hard as a stone, which employees had cause to dread. But Laxton was not an employee, so he told himself; and began to chafe under the continued silence and the unswerving gaze. He decided to assert himself.

"You said you wanted to see me," he observed, "and I've come. I haven't got too much time, so if you'd oblige—" He let the sentence taper off into mid-air. Luigi took some papers from a drawer and put them on the table.

"I too have very little time to spare," he observed evenly. "I was in touch, as recently as three days ago, with an old friend of yours; his name is Bronzetti."

He paused, with his hands still on the papers as if to keep them to himself. Laxton had raised one of his thin eyebrows, but made no other sign. "I don't think I remember anyone of that name," he ventured. "We hadn't much truck with names in the war; it was every man for himself." He preened himself a little; Luisa had made him, over and over again, relate the part he had played in the fighting, especially at San Antonio. It had made him believe he was even more important than he had always thought; very possibly, they would not have won the victory at all without his help. These Italians were all very well, but full of talk; they talked more than they primed their carbines, whereas he—

"Bronzetti," Luigi said, "remembers you. I have the proof here, in photographs. There were a great many taken during the war of liberation, mostly of ruined buildings, a few of officers."

He held up a photograph, in which a group of men was seen; they wore the dusty tunics which now, without colour, looked drab; all the men were bearded, but Laxton was recognisable by his small size, among the officers. Beside him was a tall man.

"I don't remember," began Laxton. He started to bluster; he couldn't say, there might have been somebody. He thought he could remember now, but as for knowing the man again—

"That will not be necessary. I myself can identify Signor Bronzetti. He and several others would be most interested to learn that you are back again in Italy, Mr Laxton. They may even hope that you intend to repay the sums you stole; embezzlement, *signore*, of money which was badly needed for stores and carbines. You were clever enough; nothing was discovered until you were out of the country, and then there was not much hope, the times being what they were, of ever cornering you for long enough to regain it. But that itself would not suffice these gentlemen, you know; they are Italians, and every Italian has a long memory, and a moderate thirst for revenge. I would not wager a long or comfortable stay for you in Florence, *signore*, if I tell certain ex-officers where you are to be found; at the moment, they have no notion, for I was discreet in my enquiries.''

He smiled with closed lips, while the eyes gleamed; Laxton had paled, his usually crimson nose standing out almost greenish in appearance against his cheeks. His hands clasped the arms of his chair; the knuckles had whitened. He said nothing.

"You are a hardened little rascal, are you not?" said Luigi softly. "It will not be prison for you, *signore*; sentences for war wrongdoing are not easy now, and the process of justice is long, especially as you are not a national. You know what will happen instead to you, do you not? They will find you secretly, if I say the word, and kill you; perhaps not pleasantly.''

"I—" Laxton paused, wet his lips with his tongue, and gave in. "What else did you want with me?" he said, his voice hoarse in his throat. "Why did you send, and—and tell me all of it? If they're going to shoot me, they will. What's it to you?" He slumped back in the chair, breathing hard. It was increasingly evident that he was no longer a young man.

"What I want is for you to go, at once, away from Florence, out of the country, and never see or correspond with my cousin Luisa again.''

There was a silence. Then "What'll I do?" said Laxton. "Where'll I go? It's not to say, once they're on the hunt, they won't find me anywhere. And I can't go back to Cray.''

"I would not permit it. But they will not find you, for I shall tell them not to do so. Also I have a place ready for you if you will take it. It is perhaps less luxurious than you have grown used to in recent weeks, but it is employment, of a kind. You may go to Brest, where my cousin Enrico Bondone has a shipping-office, and arranges for consignments to be sent to England and elsewhere. You may work in his office, if you choose, under an assumed name; no one will question you, although you will be supervised. It goes without saying that, if you leave to go elsewhere, the protection is withdrawn and you are thereafter at your own risk; but perhaps that will not be strange to you. You are a man of resource, Mr Laxton; but I do not want such a one in the family."

"—your family," said Laxton coarsely. "Who the hell are you? You used to be grocers. I wasn't doing no harm where I was, and everything comfortable, and now—"

"All good things come to an end," said Luigi.

Nobody had thought particularly of Luisa, but when her husband failed to return she was at first half-crazed, then inconsolable, and shut herself up for several days. Later, she sent for her sister Margherita, who tried to comfort her, and later still for Carla and Filippo, who had returned from their wedding-trip to Rome. Carla was fashionably dressed, with her hair *à la mode*; she seemed happy, and Filippo still devoured her with his eyes. By then, no reference was made to the missing Laxton, who at first had been supposed to have met with an accident, but Luigi had caused word to reach his bereaved cousin, discreetly, that the little man was safe but elsewhere. There was nothing more to do, it was evident, except make polite talk; and poor Luisa blinked through her tear-reddened eyes to take in Carla's fashionable gown. Everyone, it seemed, was allowed to be happy except herself; and a shrewd thought had already come to her that Luigi might not have been as harsh had she been past child-bearing. He would not want another heir to Gastone's inheritance. It was hard and cruel, and she was the only one to suffer; instinct assured her that her little man would end in equilibrium wherever he was, perhaps even enjoying himself. The thought made her frantic; but she could do nothing except hope and pray. At the least, she was no longer an old maid; but if only they would let Laxton come home! She would remember him for ever, and never cease to worry Luigi about his return; that was her duty, as a wife.

Carla and Filippo held their first dinner-party shortly, and the guests were not all from the family, though Luigi and Teresa, by now going out very little, came; and an acquaintance of Luigi's who was briefly in Florence on leave from the British Army and had come to Bondone to buy a crayon drawing: Hester, to Filippo's slight annoyance, for he considered her a servant; and the new sub-manager at Bondone and his wife, both French. It promised to be a lively evening as Stéphanie d'Eute, the manager's wife, was said to be witty, and was certainly beautiful;

she arrived in a toilette which made Carla feel like a schoolgirl. But Filippo had approved Carla's dress and had himself pinned a white hothouse flower in her hair, then stood back to assess the result, rather like a portrait-painter. He had also arranged the flowers, silver and crystal, much of it wedding presents. The table gleamed and reflected the candlelight on which Filippo had insisted, as he said their new gaslight was hard and did not flatter. He was adept at this kind of thing, and when he had finished the dining-room looked like a work of art; it was ungenerous to think, as Carla tried not to do, that such talents belonged to a woman.

D'Eute himself was saturnine, half Spanish, and kept his eyes on his wife. The Army acquaintance was called Arnold Guisborough, and came of an old Wiltshire family. "He will be able to talk English with you," Filippo said to Carla. The young man was very tall, with fair hair and sunburnt good looks; he did not in fact talk much, and Carla hastily rearranged the seating in her mind, for it would not do to put Guisborough between dull Teresa and shy Hester. In the end they were all assembled, and Stéphanie began to chatter at once, in a high wheedling voice that came as a surprise; her beauty was so perfect that one would have expected tones of velvet. But she was amusing, and set everyone laughing; it started the evening off very well. The cook had excelled herself, and by the time they reached the ice-pudding everyone got on with everyone else. "Icy inside, icy out," Stéphanie observed, for it was freezing weather. "But the room is warm," put in Hester quickly; she was afraid Carla would think her guests were uncomfortable. This kind of thoughtfulness was typical of her; Stéphanie sometimes hurt others with her sharp wit. Carla only smiled; the wine had flowed, and she was pleased that her party was a success. It was easier without Isotta, who had gone with Aunt Anna to Milan to visit Uncle Filippo, who was dying.

They went into the drawing-room, and after coffee it was suggested that there should be some music. Filippo was an adequate pianist, and he had made Carla practise a song to his accompaniment; she was shy about performing before anyone, as she knew her voice to be true and sweet but not strong, or at least not strong enough for Rosina in *Una voce poco fà*, which was the chosen item. A guest should sing first, she tried to insist; but the others clapped, and called to her to begin. Filippo rippled off some chords, and she made the best of it; but during the singing

175

her eyes happened to catch those of young Guisborough. His gaze was fixed on her, burning, undoubtedly ardent; she blushed, and looked away. Where could one fix one's eyes with safety? Not on the cool gaze of Luigi, who watched her intently also; not on poor Teresa, who Filippo had unkindly said might give birth at any minute on the sofa; fortunately the aria was at last finished, and she was able to sit down and listen with the rest. Filippo played on, but presently Luigi said, "Stop; our friend here plays better than you do."

Guisborough shook his fair head, colouring like a girl beneath his tan; but he was persuaded to play, and at once Filippo threw up his hands in despair; here was a professional. The English officer played a Chopin mazurka, then a couple of studies by Schumann which the Italian listeners had not heard before; then a melody by Queen Victoria's husband; lastly he turned to where Carla sat, withdrawn a little from the company, her hands clasped in her lap.

"I have a song for you to sing," he said in his deep voice. It was one she knew; sugary, a little, too well known, but it suited her register; *On Wings of Song*. She found her courage return to her with the easy air; she sang well, and again Luigi watched intently. She made herself turn away from him—it was distressing to her—and fixed her gaze on the fine broad shoulders of Guisborough at the piano; and his long, sensitive hands on the keys. There was no doubt that he was a handsome young man; the fair hair curled at the nape of his neck like a child's, and the flesh was smooth and young above the stock he wore. He was not allowed to stop playing, but Carla refused to sing again.

The evening passed too quickly. As they left Luigi said to Carla in a low voice, "I shall call for you tomorrow morning, about half past ten, for a drive," and then went out, taking Teresa, a stout muffled form in her cloak. Last to leave was Guisborough, who murmured jerkily as he kissed her hand; the difficult words were masked by the noisy departure of the d'Eute pair, who were bantering with Filippo, by now a trifle drunk: there was laughter.

"I love you passionately," said Guisborough in a low voice. "I have to say it; do not answer, yet, I must see you again; pity me and let me visit you. I must so soon go back."

She had heard that the English were cold; this was different, assuredly. But she withdrew her hand. "Do not mock me," she told him. "I will be glad to see you at any time, but do not speak of

176

love."

They all left then, and the night fell silent. She became aware, as she followed Filippo back into the warm house, that she was tired; it had been a strenuous evening, although she was glad it had gone well. Filippo was looking at her a little spitefully, his eyes sparkling like lit coals.

"All the men are in love with my wife," he said, "except d'Eute. He has his own troubles; that woman will lead him a dance some day."

She was glad that the mention of Stéphanie had led his mind away from herself. The burning gaze of Guisborough had disturbed her less than Luigi's long, cool one; she knew he was intensely aware of her, as he had never seemed to be before.

Luigi arrived next day in a double-caped greatcoat, and said that Teresa had started her labour.

"And you left her?" She had been waiting ready for him; she wore an outfit which Filippo had chosen for her in Rome. It was trimmed with white fur, and had a matching bonnet.

"Certainly. The husband is useless in such circumstances." His voice was cold, as if the matter did not concern him. Carla felt guilt assail her as he tucked her into her place beside the driving-seat. It was a low-slung curricle, hardly heavy enough to balance the fine paired greys he drove; but she knew that she would be safe with him. She questioned herself immediately: how did she know? Filippo was at the shop, where Luigi ought to have been. He ought to be anywhere except here, with her. He gathered the reins in his gloved hands and they started and soon got up speed on the clear snowy road. He headed out of the city. She abandoned herself to pleasure at feeling the smooth snow glide past under the carriage-wheels. Luigi drove as if he were not afraid. "And you are not," she said softly. He turned his head, while the greys galloped on, and looked at her; she flinched beneath the hard desire in his gaze.

"I am not . . . what? What did you say?" He caused the greys to slow, and they glided up and on into the hill roads where the snow lay deep and undisturbed; the trees were festooned with whiteness, which had not yet begun to melt. It was a mad journey; she felt at once that both he and she herself were mad, for the time. One did not do such things. "I said you were not afraid," she told him. He let the reins hang loose, and turned to her.

"Of what should I be afraid? Of Filippo? Answer me, is he a husband to you?" His voice was fierce; she flinched a little. "Yes," she said. "I—I think that I am to bear his child. Say nothing of it yet; I may be mistaken."

"It half kills me to think of you in his embrace. I have to tell you this; you knew, did you not, that I would tell you of it, Carla?" His voice dropped over her name as if he caressed it, and her. She drew a hand from her white muff and raised it to her cheek; the colour glowed there already with the cold. "I knew," she said, "last night, at the dinner-party."

"Not sooner? I have loved you since I saw you coming to the altar behind Teresa, with white flowers in your hair."

She knew a singing of pleasure in her heart; he had not, then, been indifferent. "Yet," she said, "you did not forsake the marriage, and come to me."

He gave an impatient movement. "A marriage is made for financial reasons; it would have caused great offence, and a rift in the family, had I cancelled everything. I could not behave in such a way. Yet now you, and I, are here, and we—Do you love me, Carla?"

"I have loved you ever since I was a little child; you were so assured, so godlike, and there was no one like you, except perhaps—"

"Yes? Who is this other?"

"Marcus. I love him better, I think, even than I love you. Yet I love you very much, Luigi. Without you my life would be meaningless. I live for the times when I may see you again."

"Marcus is your brother," he said, letting the greys walk; their hoof-treads sounded in the crunching snow. She fixed her eyes on the horses' backs, and on Luigi's hands, strong and controlled, easing the reins. "And Filippo is yours," she said softly. He jerked suddenly, so that the horses stopped in the snow and then started again. "And so?" he said. "I take what I want, Carla; you should know it by now."

"I do know it. Yet to Filippo you are also a god. He copies everything you do; I even think he married because you had done so. Do not fail him, Luigi."

There was a long pause, and then he said, "I will not. But I must see you, almost daily. How can I do it if you will not love me, give yourself to me? It would be foolish to call, and call, and make polite talk; there is enough of that already. My mother talks to my wife, and to the neighbours; everything I do is public property. They have nothing else to do but talk of me. How then can I see you, if . . ."

"If I were your mistress, their tongues would wag till I was driven from Florence."

"I would not permit it," he said, as he had said it to Laxton. She laughed a little, sadly. "No," she said, "we must think of something else. I too want to see you . . . daily."

"That is something. We could say," he said savagely, "that I call to advise you on picture-hanging. But that will only suffice for a little while. What next? What can your inventiveness suggest? I did not know you were a minx, Carla." He turned and took her chin between his finger and thumb: his strength pinched her flesh, so that it reddened. His golden eyes were close to her; she forced herself to meet their gaze squarely. "I do not think," he told her, "that Filippo has awakened you. It should be my pleasure, but you forbid me. How can we live, without each other?"

She shut her eyes. "We can live as we have always lived, and as we must live on, Luigi. The Church says we are brother and sister. For us to love physically would be sin. It is not as it was in the days of . . . Signora Grassi and her sister."

He turned away impatiently. "You speak as a child. The Church has her old saws, to which she must conform. I own no master, and you—"

"And I would be most unhappy, if we sinned and if we hurt Filippo."

"Filippo," he said thoughtfully, then "There is a young woman in your house; what is her name? Feston, Fenton."

"Hester? You noticed her last night at dinner."

"No, I noticed nothing but you. She will suffice for our need. What is she, a sewing-woman?"

"A companion. Filippo was angry when I made her come, but he endures her. She troubles nobody; she is very shy, and has no family."

"She will suffice," he said again. "I will pretend that I come to see her. She is pretty enough; I remember now, she has fair hair, and limps slightly. Why does she limp?"

"From a riding-accident in childhood. Do not be unkind to her," said Carla. "If anything hurt her, I should never forgive

179

myself."

"I am never unkind, and have never hurt anyone," said Luigi.

When they returned from the drive it was to receive news that Teresa had been delivered, at about eleven o'clock, of a fine son. On hearing of it Luigi hurried off to be with his wife. Carla dragged herself up to her bedroom and lay down on the bed, flinging her bonnet aside. Presently Hester Fenton came in quietly, to ask if her employer needed anything. Her movements were silent, her expression timid and loving.

"I need nothing," said Carla, and after the other had gone away began to cry. It had all of it happened at the wrong time; and there was nothing to be done.

14

"I have always said Mariana was a hard woman," pronounced Isotta, sipping coffee before the fire in Carla's morning-room. "Even when it was time to view your poor uncle's corpse she showed no emotion, though little Margherita wept bitterly for her father. Of course, there was a good deal of difference in the ages of husband and wife. And poor little Angelo will never be like other children. Teresa naturally could not attend." She set down the cup, thinking with approval of the cause of Teresa's inability. "Baldassare's death was a tragedy," she reminisced. "His father never recovered from that and from losing Caterina so soon afterwards."

She sat back and began to nibble an almond biscuit; dear Carla's house was well-appointed, and little comforts of this kind could be taken for granted; such a mercy that the dear child had married money! It had been the wisest course to remain in Italy all these years, leaving Marcus to manage his own affairs as a man should; had Carla been over there she would no doubt by now have been married off casually to some Englishman with a brief passion for a pretty face. Fortunate as her own marriage had been, Isotta firmly believed in arrangements, particularly on a sound financial basis, whatever one might feel about second wives like Mariana Pelosi.

Otherwise, the family prospects had never been better, with dear Luigi being obliged to take on a sub-manager owing to the press of business. As for the baby, he was a fat little fellow with fair hair, rather like Jake had been. No doubt he took after his mother. Isotta was matriarchally happy; Carla had mentioned her own hopes, now virtually certain. The dear child looked peaky and pale today; that was as it should be, and meant that the pregnancy would proceed quite uneventfully. The late summer, they thought.

The manservant had come to the door and hovered over the coffee-tray. "Has the carriage come yet?" Carla asked him. Isotta pricked up her ears. "What carriage?" she said. She herself lived on the second floor, and needed no conveyance.

"The carriage to take Hester to the studio."

"What studio?"

Carla was exasperated; she felt queasy and ill, and Mamma could be impossible. "The studio of the miniaturist who is painting Hester's portrait for Bondone Figli," she explained carefully. Bondone meant, of course, Luigi himself, but Mamma must be prevented from knowing that quite yet. It had been a scheme of their own to get Hester away from the house to a place where she might meet Luigi casually. He had talked a great deal about the ideal of English beauty, and Hester had blushed like a rose. No doubt Luigi had watched the progress of the miniature with close attention. Why was she herself so cross about it? It was she who had suggested the whole deception in the first place. But was it still a deception, or was Luigi in truth attracted by Hester Fenton? It began to seem like it, and she herself was left feeling foolish.

"There is the carriage now, *signora*," the servant told her. In the hall, Hester came and slipped on her cloak and muff; they heard the light, uneven footsteps going out, then the sound of the wheels driving away.

"Miniatures! Carriages! And all for a paid companion," scoffed Isotta. "You are far too good to her, and she will never return to her place; such people do not repay favours."

"Hester is not a servant, but my friend," replied Carla loyally.

The studio was not in fact far from that where Ravallo had once painted Gabriella Strada, and the height above the street was the same; but now it could be viewed through clean glass. This was a prosperous artist's abode, half workroom and half reception-room. The costly materials used by miniaturists, the sable brushes and ground colours and ivory boards, lay tidily on a table by the door; the wooden roof-beams were clean and polished, while rugs lay on the floor, the clear north light picking out their rich colours. Across them Hester Fenton stepped, her gait almost fearful.

The artist was absent, as had been arranged. Hester stopped for instants to look at her own portrait. It had been finished for some time, except for the background. Swathes of plain colour had been laid on this, outlining the fair, smooth head and delicate features; the painted likeness smiled contentedly. There was a cynical permissiveness in its being still here, deliberately unfinished; the artist knew there was no hurry; the excuse for which the painting had served was no longer used. Now she came, and left, unseen.

She went across the main room and opened a small door in the wall. Beyond was a bedroom, plainly furnished but clean. The great brass bedstead and counterpane were new, the sheet already turned down. Across the bed lay an expensive night-gown of silk and lace, such a thing as Hester had never owned before; a harlot's dress, a kept woman's. So she told herself as she slipped, quickly and ashamed, out of her clothes, not stopping to watch her revealed nakedness in the mirror. The cool pale silk went over her head, and when it was on her she picked up her discarded clothes and laid them neatly over a chair. She let down her hair and combed it with an ivory comb which lay on the dressing-table; there was provided the whole set, brushes for hair and clothes, a jar for pins, a hand-mirror. They had been presents from Luigi. When she and he were away the cleaning-woman tidied the room, made the bed, dusted and polished the furniture and brushes and jars. It was part of her duties for the studio.

Hester's hair hung about her like a golden veil. She sat for a time on the edge of the bed, unwilling to get in. One of her feet was thinner than the other. She sat staring at its defenceless whiteness, magnifying to herself the fact that she was lame. Why should he love a lame woman? Yet . . .

Her hand went to her breast. There were sudden footsteps in the studio, eager, confident, hurrying towards the door. It opened and he was with her. For an instant she saw his face and body, handsome as a god's, irresistible, the dark curling hair and golden eyes glowing and vital, the proud mouth smiling. Then he had come to her and was kissing her, her mouth, her throat, her breasts. He pulled away the silk from them until they were naked, then held them in his hands. He lifted her then, easily and laughing, and laid her on the bed. She was shivering by now, and he soothed her.

"Why are you still afraid?" he asked her. "Always you shiver like a little rabbit when it is caught. No harm will come to you; trust me." He had begun to undress, with swift accustomed hands; as she had not done, he left his clothes lying, and stood naked for moments, his body taut and powerful, the flat belly showing an apex of dark hair above the ready genitals, the legs muscular, an athlete's. Then he was upon her, a god taking a nymph. She flung her arms about his neck and drew him close to her. She was weeping, as she always did at such times; the bright tears sprang in her large blue eyes and spilled over on to the roseleaf cheeks; he kissed them away. It always entranced him that she could cry thus, without a sound, almost without effort. He smoothed the trembling limbs, settled himself between them, took her swiftly, then more slowly, bridling his passion for her sake. Presently, warmed, she began to emit small whimpering sighing sounds, like a little animal. He laughed, and lay within her while her climax came. It diverted him to watch her thus, abandoned, without her modest ways, her—he smiled—careful gentility. She was unlike other women he had taken, always greedy and eager for him and what he could give them. Hester on the other hand asked for nothing but to love him, and not to be discovered in it.

He had finished. He began to play with her hair, loving its golden shining cleanliness, its silken softness against his cheek. She was silent; she never troubled him with talk.

Afterwards, they dressed together; he aided her with her laces. They would leave the building separately, he to his carriage, she to hers. The room was again empty except for the rumpled bed, while the sunlight travelled slowly across the disturbed counterpane.

Isotta had always kept up the English habit of tea in the afternoon. It was not often, however, that Anna Bondone invited herself, for she seldom went out now except to church. Accordingly, Isotta knew that there must be some special reason which brought her sister-in-law here; and poured the tea when it came, passed little cakes over and waited. They made conventional talk about the state of affairs—in this they were fortunate, for there were no husbands to forbid them to read the newspapers—the progress of the baby Luigini, Teresa's recovery, which had been good, and the health of Carla, which was equally interesting, though Filippo—Isotta was tactful enough not to mention this to the guest—was no longer attentive. They then strayed to the matter of the English companion, about whose conduct Isotta expressed herself dissatisfied.

"She takes the carriage whenever she chooses, and Carla permits it; where the creature goes I do not know, but if it is to the shops then she is spending a great deal too much money for a person in her situation. I have spoken to Carla, but it is useless; she can be obstinate, especially now when she is not very well. But to call the other girl a companion is begging the question when she is hardly ever available." Isotta exaggerated, knew that she did so and that the other would understand why. Anna took another mouthful of cake, chewed it carefully—her false teeth did not fit well, and she must again visit her dentist—swallowed, and gave her verdict, which purely by coincidence concerned her son.

"Young people now are very erratic," she said. "Luigi is never at home, although of course he may be working at the office; he goes out very early each day, in time for eight o'clock, and stays till late. I know that he works hard, for Madame d'Eute, the new sub-manager's wife, who as you know has the apartment opposite, sees his light burning. She is very amusing and makes me laugh, which is pleasant at my age. By the way, she needs an English governess for her little Antoine. Would this idle creature of Carla's be better in that situation? Perhaps she has not enough to do. I met her the other day coming out of the confessional at Santa Maria Novella, bathed in tears; perhaps a man is involved."

Isotta pursed her lips and poured more tea. She did not feel inclined to help Miss Fenton to find another situation; it would be better if she took the boat home to England. A certainty that all was not well had already come to her; she gazed, as if for advice, at the daguerreotype of her husband, which hung above the fireplace. But all this intrigue would be below Marcus' integrity, his dislike of the commonplace. Had she herself failed him in becoming what she was, just another gossiping old woman? Her eyes threatened tears, and she blinked them away.

"Another cup, dear Anna? It is agreeable to have you with me; the young ones have their own affairs, and I often feel lonely. Perhaps I should go to England to visit Jake, but that wife of his displeases me. They should never have married, although the new baby thrives. Marcus writes that she is very pretty, with dark eyes and hair and the loveliest little hands, and is to be called Maria after her aunt, which is unexpected, for my dear elder daughter never approved of Cynthia while she lived. Her death was a great shock to me, and no doubt to the poor little boy—of course he is almost a young man now—left alone with very odd guardians in the north."

Anna nodded comprehendingly, at the same time thinking as she always did how extraordinary it was that dear Isotta always showed more interest in her second son than in her first. "No sign of children yet for Cristina?" she enquired, but was met by a shake of the head.

"I have no doubt Jacky makes up to her for everything," said Jacky's grandmother. "Dear me! He too must be quite a young man; the years fly so fast. He never writes, for he is not fond of that; Marcus says he is always out and about, riding, or walking in the country with a dog—I cannot imagine whose, for they have none—or skating on the ponds in the winter. He hopes to enter the army; he has no ambitions in the firm."

"He must be a very handsome young man, for he was a beautiful boy," said Anna. Presently she took her leave, adjusting before the gilt-framed mirror her bonnet's ties, which had slipped a little and revealed too much of her sagging jawline. Isotta watched her with compassion. Poor Anna, who had once been so beautiful and was now so stout! But her religion consoled her. Isotta rose to bid her guest farewell and for instants they were both reflected; the stout tall woman, the wizened small one, both in black. The years had flown indeed, sparing nobody.

Carla listened to the sound of sobbing; she was beginning to be impatient. If one were loved by Luigi that was, or should be, an occasion for joy. At least, she would once have thought so; but for a long time now she had as it were stood back from herself, watching her own responses; things mattered less than they had done when she was a child. But this dreary creature would neither forgo her own occasion for sin nor, after it was taken advantage of, rejoice. Luigi would soon tire of tears. Hester had been, as one might have predicted, again to the confessional: there was a priest at Santa Maria Novella who spoke English. "He said," sobbed Hester, "he said—he was harsh—that I must go away; that I was doing harm to myself and to the marriage."

"Then leave and be done with it, if that is the way you feel." Her own voice sounded flat and unsympathetic; she had not meant that, but this scene, again, was not the first, would never be the last, and she herself was troubled and ill.

"I love him so! I love him so!" That was about Luigi, not the priest; one's detachment could sometimes be almost, if not quite, amusing; as though one were like Madame d'Eute, mocking at everything from a safely removed distance. "Then if you love him, give up everything for him, and stay," said Carla. "It is either one thing or the other; you cannot continue in this way, tearing yourself apart." Who would have thought, when in another lifetime she herself had so lightly hatched the plan with Luigi, that all this tormented depth would have come to the surface? Perhaps she herself needed a confessor. She bit her lip, and was silent. The dishevelled girl lay face down on the bed, shaken with crying.

"I mean to go," she said. "I have written him a letter of farewell."

"Where will you go?" She herself would lend the fare, she thought. "Have you other employment in prospect? How will you live?" It was necessary to ask the fool such things; she would never think of them.

"I—I do not know. I have not thought. I will go to England for a little while, to my stepfather."

And that, from what you have told me, will be a sorry welcome, Carla thought. Who else was there? Kind Cristina would undoubtedly help the girl, but Marcus might be angry with Cristina. Aloud Carla said, "And from there? You will be quite alone, remember, while here you have friends. Have you no one else in Italy to whom you may go?" Idly, through her mind flitted something Mamma had said about the d'Eute couple needing a governess. But that would be too near Luigi.

"I want to go home," said Hester, like a child. "I will go to England. I do not want to think yet what to do. Perhaps I could enter a convent."

"You could do that more easily here, if they will have you. There is the one where Mamma was at school, in the country near Arezzo. It is not too strict. I could ask Mamma to write, and send the letter with you, and they would perhaps let you stay while you thought what to do next. I cannot think that it is wise to return to England when you have no prospects there." Now I sound like an old woman, she thought; and soon I will be one, and so will she. If only she had a particle of common sense! But in that case the affair would never have reached this stage. All women were fools over men, no doubt; she need not blame poor Hester.

Hester left for Arezzo the next day. Isotta had asked no questions in providing the note to the Mother Superior.

Next day again came Nemesis. Carla knew she might have expected it. Luigi stormed into the house, looking ready to horse-whip anyone; in all her life she had never seen him in such a rage, but of course his wishes were seldom thwarted. He had thrust in past the servant. Carla had been crying—tears were everywhere in this business—but he did not notice or, if he did, cared nothing. His eyes blazed.

"Where is she?"

"She has left here. She is no longer in Florence." Useless to feint or prevaricate; she began to be a little afraid. He stood over her, having declined a chair. Almost, there might have been foam between his lips.

"I asked you where she had gone, not where she is not. If necessary I will have the whole country searched. Has she gone abroad? If so I will follow her."

"There is no need to go to such lengths," she said drily. "As you insist, she is in the convent near Arezzo where Mamma went long ago to school." It would have been useless to try to prevent his finding out; as well save time and effort. He scowled down at her.

"So," he said, "you and my aunt arranged this. You—to spite me, after—" He almost spluttered the words; suddenly, she saw them, the pair of them, himself and her, as they must appear to an outsider; and laughed a little. He rounded on her at once. "To make a jest of it!" he said. "You have no heart. To mock *her*, when you know she is as defenceless, as gentle, as—as a fledgling bird." He stopped abruptly, afraid of talking like a fool.

"The bird took wing on her own account," said Carla, her voice wry. "If you get there quickly, you may contrive something before the story is known all through town. What you say to one another is your own concern; I will know nothing."

He thrust out a hand suddenly. "Carla, I—I am grateful. You know it." He was not only speaking of the news about the convent. "I must follow her," he said in a low voice, "and bring her back with me. The poor child will be in great distress."

"And quite alone," said Carla; her words followed him to the door. "And Mamma, who wrote her letter of admission? Do you suppose she will not gossip with Aunt Anna about the matter, and Hester's going and then returning here? She cannot stay here now, Luigi. If you bring her back, you must find somewhere for her to go, if she will." If he set Hester up as his kept woman, she was thinking, the girl would be wretched; every slight she received would brand her soul. But what else was there to suggest?

He grunted. "Have no fear," he said. "You will not be asked to house her," and went out.

He was not heard of for three days, during which time he had reached the convent, persuaded the porteress to grant him an interview with Hester in the parlour, talked to her, dried her tears, kissed her, and brought her away with him. They had spent the intervening time at an inn, making love. Now he had left Hester in an hotel room in Florence, and came striding into the Bondone office, mouth set, in no mood to answer questions. But he did not have to. Providence already sat there in the person (in russet grogram with a wide bertha of écru lace, which showed off her ear-rings) of Stéphanie d'Eute, who was consulting her husband about some minor matter. On Luigi's entry she smiled, banished d'Eute, and addressed herself to the angry young chairman of Bondone Figli as if nothing at all were wrong. Not many women could have spoken to him directly on a subject which at that moment occupied him to the exclusion of all else, except business.

"So you see, Signor Bondone, I am looking for a *gouvernante*, but the person who undertook the task would have very little trouble, and almost no duties. Antoine already has a tutor who gives him his lessons, and he is a quiet child; when he is not at his books he occupies himself with toy soldiers. It would simply be a question of being there in the house when I am out. And there would be a separate room for her; the flat, as you know, is large."

His first prick of anger—how the devil did the woman know what he wanted?—changed, after a moment, to a rush of gratitude such as Luigi Bondone seldom felt, for he seldom had cause. He had always been sufficient to himself, expecting help from nobody. Now, this gracious and amused personage—and it suddenly came to Luigi how long it was since he had heard anyone laugh—this beautiful and worldly woman seemed prepared to help him out of what was, he had already realised, a very difficult situation indeed. Hester could not be left alone in some apartment as his mistress, exposed to the snubs and jests inseparable from that position in Florentine society; she would die of humiliation after a week. But to have this lady's protection, which was virtually what it meant, and to know that Hester was being cared for, fed, and spoken to normally whenever he was elsewhere—

The golden eyes surveyed Stéphanie, who appeared undisturbed by them. "*Madama*," said Luigi, "I am everlastingly grateful."

Afterwards Stéphanie d'Eute smiled to herself. It suited her purpose very well to have, in the first place, this rich and powerful young man's gratitude; other things would follow. He was a man who liked predictable situations, and also to be made to laugh. She had studied him for long, and by now had almost despaired of obtaining his notice; but after today he would remember her, and the right cards could be played at the right time. Meantime, she must smooth matters over for this Hester, who would soon bore him. What a goose the young woman must be!

Jacky was grooming the mastiff puppy he had called Zefiro, and who was to be a present for Carla. Zefiro was out of a bitch owned by the most beautiful woman in the world, who lived in Clarges Street. Jack had met Dorothea and had been entranced, and she herself, not getting any younger—they said her husband had become a monk somewhere on the Continent—had luxuriated in the handsome young officer's admiration. Reclining in satin and lace on the chaise-longue, her abundant hair aided with a little gold dust, her face with a little paint, she surveyed the young man, slim and upright in scarlet regimentals, an Apollo in chains. He cast an experienced eye over the great mastiff bitch and asked when she was due to whelp. "In six weeks," replied Dorothea, "and if you have been to visit me often enough, and have made me laugh enough, you shall have the pick of the litter." And so it had turned out; and Jacky, who worshipped dogs, had got down among the fawn-coloured mass of heaving wriggling intent pups, and had selected one, a dog; he would have good bone, a square muzzle and direct hazel eyes. "This one," he said.

"What will you call him? They answer early to their names; I can get him ready for you."

"Zefiro. It means a light wind."

She laughed, throwing her head back to reveal the strong

teeth. Jack's visits always cheered her; his father cast an eye in other directions now, and it was pleasant, while her lover entertained little shopgirls, to laugh with his magnificent son by another woman; to a degree handsomer than her own, who was in his last year at school. How well this wretch had turned out! On the stage, she thought, Jack Cray would make a fortune; but she knew Marcus was proud that his son had been admitted to Woolwich, and had later passed out with commendation. It was also fortunate that Jack had a taste for the army; he had been hurt, a little, when his father refused to give him a place in the firm.

"He speaks as if it is Uncle Jake's inheritance, and by rights it is mine," he had said, full underlip thrusting. "Uncle Jake hasn't the feeling for . . . things . . . that Father and I have. He bores the customers so quickly that they buy something in a hurry in order to get away. That isn't good for the business. People talk to each other."

"Your uncle will be your enemy if he learns that you say such things."

"He dislikes me in any case. He behaves as though he has the right to Papa's affection and I have none. In fact we seldom meet." Jack flushed darkly. There had been an incident, a minor sexual triumph, he had won a girl Uncle Jake fancied, and had made a fool of the older man; it would not be forgiven him.

Dorothea changed the direction of the talk. "You look much better in uniform," she said. "The shop would have bored you."

"Never."

After he had gone she frowned a little. Why in fact did Marcus refuse to have his son in the store? It would have meant far less outlay than sending him to a military college, and Marcus was forever pleading shortage of money whenever she wanted her own little luxuries, such as a set of amethysts she had fancied, and got in the end; they set off the glints in her gold-dusted hair.

That had been three months earlier. Now Jack sat with the young dog, made ecstatic by his attentions, at the home of his commanding officer and great friend, Arnold Guisborough. The gentle Wiltshire landscape was filled with soft green; he would miss that when he went to Italy for the rest of his leave. But he would be glad to see Carla again. He frowned. From her letters she didn't sound too happy, despite the birth of a baby girl last year. "If that little rat of a husband ill-treats her, I'll thrash him stupid," Jack promised himself. In fact Carla's letters seldom mentioned Filippo, or any of the family except, occasionally, to say that Grandmamma seemed quite well, but hardly slept at all nowadays without laudanum. The baby was pretty and had been christened Susanna. "You guard them, good boy," Jack murmured to the dog, who had grown responsive and lovable, with a dark mask and ears of sable silk. The young man laid down the grooming-brush and ruffled Zefiro's neck, kneading with his fingers down to where the shoulder-blades protruded; the great face grinned up at him, pink tongue lolling. Jacky hoped the dog would be happy with Carla; it had quickly learnt devotion to himself.

But Carla could charm anything, man or animal. Not long ago a curious thing had happened; he had been talking to Arnold, and they had already established the fact that he and Carla had met in Florence. For some reason Arnold had had to take out his wallet, and inside, among other things, was a photograph already turning brown. It was of Carla in the garden, leaning against a sundial. Jack had not disguised his having noticed; he kept nothing from his friend. The latter had, instead of attempting to conceal the photograph, taken it out and looked at it reverently, the sun shining on his fair hair. "You're fond of her," said Jack gruffly.

"She is the only woman I have ever loved, or ever will."

A pity Arnold couldn't come with him on this Italian leave; but he had to return to the regiment.

He sat with Carla in her drawing-room, the puppy by him; admiring the way the room had been redecorated lately with light, pastel colours; Carla, in a grey silk dress with touches of acid yellow, her face powdered, enhanced the scheme. She looked pretty, but not, he thought, very well or very happy. But when he tried to introduce the subject she only laughed, and brushed off any sadness as though it had been a gnat, in the evening air. She was restless, and wandered about among the great vases of arranged flowers Filippo favoured and often, even these days, did himself. Filippo was still at the office; Jack did not look forward to their meeting.

"He likes his work, and it suits him," said Carla, caressing the puppy. "He is very knowledgeable about such things as cameos—when we were married he got me a fine set, signed by

Giramotti—and small things; a great deal of the exchange at Bondone is small, and very precious. Lately they sold the Contessa di Mirafiore's moonstones for her; the price they fetched was enormous." She passed the time at first with practised, artificial conversation in this way, as though he had been a stranger. Suddenly she looked at him and tears rose in her eyes: she set the dog aside, and turned away.

"I talk, and talk," she said. "It is a habit; it helps time to pass. The truth is that Filippo has a dynastic mind; he hopes Luigi's little son will die, so that his may inherit. Teresa has had no more children. I have had two miscarriages, but this time—" she touched the pale wooden rim of the table—"it may be all right, and it may be a boy. Susanna is nearly two now; tomorrow you shall see her, when the nurse takes out her. She is like Filippo, but prettier." She laughed a little. "You must make the most of your time here, not waste it on me; tomorrow you are to go to Bondone's offices and be shown round, and the manager's wife Madame d'Eute—we all call her Stéphanie—wants you to come across for coffee at half past ten. She is very amusing." The voice sounded tired, as if it recited things for the hundredth time. Jack tried to summon enthusiasm for the visit to Stéphanie d'Eute. Zefiro thumped his tail on the carpet, afraid of being forgotten.

Next day, Jack saw Madame d'Eute; and was dazzled, a little, by her beauty, as he had been by Dorothea's. She dispensed the coffee from a machine which she said had been lately invented in Scotland; Jack watched its mysteries, sipping, at last, the syrupy dark fluid with enjoyment. He had managed to be civil to the wretched little Filippo; had spoken at some length to Luigi, who asked about his military prowess; and had been intrigued by d'Eute himself, whom he decided resembled the devil. The latter was not present at his wife's coffee-dispensing, and Jack had her to himself, listening to the high unexpected voice retailing amusing gossip such as he could understand and laugh at; there was nothing recondite about Stéphanie.

After some time a disturbing thing occurred. There was a door at the further end of the drawing-room; it opened, and a young woman came out for an instant; she was heavily pregnant, and when she saw the company blushed in confusion, and went back into her room, closing the door quietly. Stéphanie d'Eute gave a little shrug, almost to herself, but it was noted by him: he did not like her quite so much as he had been prepared to do. Presently Luigi came in, as if by custom; the hostess handed him a coffee-cup, and he sat down on one of the striped Empire chairs and listened to her talk, at times laughing heartily. This went on for about twenty minutes; then Stéphanie put out her white ringed hand, slapped Luigi lightly on the knee, and said, smiling, "You naughty man, go and visit my poor Hester." He made a *moue*, got up, drained his coffee-cup, and went towards the closed door, going in without knocking. Jack was aware of shock; was this state of affairs customary?

Luigi did not reappear, nor did he himself comment. Later he told Carla, who raised a hand to her eyes. "So that is the way of things," she said presently. "I should have known, and prevented it while I might still do so."

"You could not prevent anything of the kind; how could you?" he asked, bewildered. She looked across, smiling a little, her dark eyes shadowed beneath the lids; it occurred to him that she was often ill.

"Once I could have done so," she said, "or perhaps not. It is, after all, human nature, and one cannot alter that. But it is cruel if it is as you say: wicked and cruel."

He did not go again to visit Stéphanie d'Eute, although she had pressed him to do so before he returned to England. Another event blotted out social exchanges: while he was still in Italy, Isotta died.

She had not been ill. The first Carla knew of it was the terrified sobbing of the Italian maid, who ran downstairs crying out that her mistress was dead in bed. Later it became clear that the maid had acted foolishly. Isotta had always taken sleeping drops, and they were put out each night. On this particular night they had been forgotten, and the maid poured a strong dose and woke Isotta up to make her drink it. "Why wake a sleeping person up to give them laudanum?" asked Filippo reasonably, when he heard. Isotta had gone back to sleep and had never wakened again. The maid was beside herself; she had killed *madama*. There were hastening footsteps everywhere, the doctor came, and then left as there was nothing he could do; then the undertakers came. Carla, sitting by her dead mother in a state of shock, knew one thing clearly, looking at the peaceful face; Mamma would want her body to be buried in England, beside Papa's. It must be arranged; they would have the funeral service here, and the parish priest should hold it in the church; then Jacky—how fortunate that he was still here!—should escort the small coffin overseas. Already a blank feeling of loss was numbing Carla; Mamma had been always there, as long as she could remember; difficult at times, possessive, scheming a little, but always loving. Now she herself was alone; she examined the thought, which was strange; after all she had her little girl and her husband. But there was no one now to whom she could talk except Jacky, who would soon be gone; and Luigi. She turned away from the thought of the latter; they had not met since Jacky had told her of the situation with Stéphanie d'Eute. No doubt she would encounter Luigi, and Stéphanie, at the funeral.

It was well attended; no one had realised how many acquaintances the tiny unassuming old lady had had, both aristocrats and tradesmen. Beverley Mayne, ignoring the whispers that he had been Isotta's lover, was present in full black; all the Bondone staff and directors came, and there were crape bows hung over the shop doors, though it would re-open in the afternoon. Poor Luisa was there, looking old, miserable and lonely: Margherita had not come. Jacky, wearing a black cloak Luigi had lent him, helped to carry the coffin into the church to lie there overnight; everyone had been edified by the excellent sermon the priest preached next day, for he was an old man who had known Isotta well. Anna sobbed in her place; like Carla, she was alone now and frightened, for her body was suddenly full of pain and she was losing weight, so that the skin hung in folds, and it would have been pleasant to discuss such symptoms with dear Isotta, who had always listened with interest. Teresa, silent and unmoved as usual, sat by her; aunt and niece were close, but there was not much satisfaction in a relationship where only one partner talked, and Teresa only opened her mouth to complain about Luigi, who might have been expected to be unfaithful. But one must wean one's mind from all that, and think of the dead woman. Filippo in fact had the last word.

"Thank God the old bitch is dead," he said in a low tone to Luigi. "Now I can feel free in my own home; I tell you, she spied on everything I did." He looked with sudden, bright-eyed ferocity at Luigi, standing by him, outbidding him in height, attraction, everything. "You had a fancy for Carla for a while,

195

didn't you?" he asked spitefully. "Never think I noticed nothing. You don't come to the house so often now." As soon as it was said he regretted it; he loved his brother, perhaps no other love had ever entered or would enter his life; if Luigi were off-hand with him, he would sulk, and weep when he was alone. He cried easily, like a girl.

Luigi's profile was unmoving as that on a coin, the proud bones clear. Presently he said, "Your wife is an attractive woman, and I am a man," and fell silent. Filippo's voice almost squeaked in rejoinder. "And I am not? Is that what you are trying to say? I tell you, I give Carla a child every year; it is not my fault if they do not live to be born. The Crays are a sickly family; look at the way all the children died in England. It is only because Carla lived here that she grew up."

"Keep your voice down," said Luigi evenly. It was time to lift the coffin by its cords, and they went with the rest and did so; its weight was light.

Jack departed after that, taking the little coffin to the ship. Arrangements had been made by telegram for Marcus to receive it at the other end, and thence to a short, second burial service by the grave of the first Marcus Cray.

The journey was unremarkable, and Jack spent the time on deck, watching the sea. By the time he reached England it was drizzling, and the mourners held up black umbrellas like a uniform. Cristina had a cold, and kept her face in her black-edged handkerchief, so that everybody thought she was weeping for her mother-in-law. Marcus stood and cast the first earth to fall on the coffin, laid in its grave. His thoughts were compassionate and pitiful. Poor little Mamma had gone to her account, and there was nothing more to be done for her, except pray. He examined the subject of prayer, about which he thought at times. Opposite, Jake stood gravely silent. He had left his wife with the other women; Cynthia was pregnant again. The two little girls, Maria and Annie, had been told to stay at home with their nurse, being too young to come today. Jake was a faithful father but a bad husband. He took comfort in the thought of his children; he was fond of them.

At almost the same hour, in Florence, Hester Fenton was delivered of a daughter. Instantly—she hardly took time to let

196

them sponge her after the birth—she had the child handed to a maid who took it, by previous arrangement, to a wet-nurse in the country. Hester herself sat up and made them dress her and lace her stays. Then she walked unsteadily through to the drawing-room, and sat down by the fire, her cheeks already showing two patches of bright, feverish colour. She had intended to go out and walk, but found she was too dizzy; perhaps someone would come in, a visitor, anyone, and see that there were no grounds for rumour. In fact two friends of Stéphanie came in, talked for a little, then left; they spread word round that the English governess seemed very odd, almost as though she were ill; one hardly ever saw her.

Luigi came in as the visitors were being shown out. He frowned impatiently; if Stéphanie were at home he would have to spend time talking with her, and he had wanted to devote himself to Hester and to the baby. His affection for his mistress had strong roots; he would never consciously see her mocked or deprived, and he looked forward greatly to the first sight of his child. Teresa's son Luigini was afraid of him, and this had left him more at a loss than he knew; like most, he craved affection.

He was shown into the drawing-room, and prepared to hurry across it to the further door. But Hester was sitting there openly by the fire, bolt upright and fully clad, the colour burning in her cheeks. He drew an involuntary breath of incredulity, disgust—it came from deep within him—then went to her. "You should be in bed," he said. "Where is the child?"

"No, no—she is well, I am well—they must not see—or know—" Her hands fluttered up whitely, protestingly. He bent down and lifted her, carrying her to the bedroom and, once there, laid her on the bed. He began to unfasten her gown and undo her laces. When she was in her chemise he put her between the covers without speaking further, went over and raked the stove which stood there, then when it burned brightly turned to her again.

"Where is the child?" he asked. "I came to see it—and I find— good God, you may have killed yourself by acting in such a way! Does the world's opinion matter so much?"

"Do not be angry, Luigi." She had begun to weep; she felt tired and ill. He came, as if to a pet animal, and comforted her; she gave him the name of the place where the baby had been taken. "She

197

cannot stay here," she kept saying. "She cannot stay here, where people will see her, and talk."

He left her with a promise from her that she would try to sleep. Before leaving he instructed Stéphanie's servant to go in and keep an eye on her, and on no account to let her leave her bed. Then he went away, much troubled.

It was almost two weeks before he had leisure to go and visit the baby. In that time she had changed from a mewling red-faced thing to an exquisite, precious possession; her hair was fair, and curled lightly, and she had great blue eyes. The woman had kept her clean, and looked on with pride; few fathers took the trouble to come to see her charges. This young man loved his daughter, she could tell; he held the small warm bundle to him, while his eyes never left the babys face; presently he teased her with a finger, and made her smile. At the end he kissed her, and took his purse and found a gold coin; he gave it to the wet-nurse.

"There will be another if she is well next time I come," he said. "Look after her carefully."

She watched him mount his horse and ride off, staying at the door till the hoofbeats were out of sight and sound. He had looked fine in the saddle, that young man. She wondered what the story of the birth was; but knew nothng other than what she had been told.

15

Informed parties took it for granted that Jack Cray would propose to Lavinia Hope-Churt at the regimental ball. They included Marcus, who had engineered the whole thing with an eye fixed on Lavinia's expectations and estate; and the young woman's mother, Lady Luttnor, a plump easy-going matron who had married twice, and who hitherto had worried somewhat lest Lavinia never marry at all, or else unsuitably; the heiress was arrogant and difficult, and most reputable young men shied off, despite the money. But Lavinia herself seemed to fancy hand-some Jack, and indeed, my lady said with nostalgia for lost youth, it must be almost impossible to resist him. So she watched with indulgence as the couple waltzed among other couples, the women's pale bell-like skirts swinging in time to the rhythm of the scarlet-coated band. The Colonel's wife was dancing with young Guisborough and evidently enjoying it. Afterwards she brought him over to be introduced to my lady and to the few non-uniformed guests, one of whom, a tall Italian named Count Belloni-Negri, seemed bored with the whole proceeding and had not danced. "Like Lord Byron," her ladyship murmured vaguely; but poor Byron had at least been handsome, whereas this Count, besides having too good an opinion of himself, was goggle-eyed, a great misfortune; and though his English was good the things he said were often lacking in fact. In short, nobody liked him.

Arnold Guisborough, magnificent in gold-braided scarlet, bowed, and said he knew Italy. Having handed the Colonel's lady to another partner—it had been an exhausting dance, and her corset-bones had jabbed him painfully—he began to make polite talk with the Count, as was civil. They discovered one or two acquaintances in common and when he could, Arnold men-tioned the Bondone clan, particularly Luigi. "He is very know-ledgeable," he said superfluously. A sudden wish took him to be under those clear skies, near Carla; even to see her passing in her carriage would be a delight. The Italian smiled unpleasantly, turning the whites of his eyes up.

"Bondone," he said, "loved his sister-in-law perhaps too well. It is an open secret that they were lovers, and that the children are perhaps his, not his brother's."

Arnold sprang up; he was white about the mouth. "You lie," he said. When the Count was on his feet Arnold took the back of his hand and struck the Italian across the face. The blow was seen by everyone, as he had intended. The music had stopped; it seemed that everybody in the hall was turning and staring in their direction. The Colonel came up, fussily.

"As my guest—" he began, but Belloni-Negri cut in. He was as pale as Arnold, with a red weal across his mouth where the gloved hand had struck it. Arnold stood stiffly to attention.

"You have called me a liar," said the other. He had recovered his poise and almost sneered; his mouth and nostrils twitched. "For that, honour demands—" He looked about him; he knew nobody well. "My second will call on you," said Arnold clearly. A nearby officer, whose name was Lingard, put in "Don't be a fool, man! You will be cashiered if it comes to that."

"I forbid it, and that is an order," said the Colonel, and turned on his heel.

"A lady of my honourable acquaintance has been insulted, sir. It is my privilege to defend her."

Jack had come up, with Lavinia on his arm. She was a pallid creature, dressed fashionably, slim and with pretty fair hair. He took her to her mother, then rejoined Arnold Guisborough. "What's up?" he murmured, and was told without delay. He frowned. "I'll act for you, of course, but it must all be kept quiet, or we are both in hot water."

The Italian had turned away, followed by Arnold's eyes. "Find him a second," he said.

"They say he's a crack shot, old boy. Perhaps we can get him to apologise. It was said without thinking."

"I will not accept an apology."

"Damn it, Carla's my concern if anyone's—"

"She is nobody's concern except mine. I will take no withdrawal. Find him a second, and arrange when we may meet."

The music had started again, a quadrille. Lavinia turned her pale, close-set eyes to where Jack stood, the handsomest man in the room, slim and elegant in his regimentals, the heavy-lidded eyes brooding. He had just asked her to marry him, and she had

200

accepted; but it didn't seem quite the moment to tell Mamma. Most of the company proceeded with the dance, anxious to cover up any unpleasantness; the Colonel had done his duty, and now knew nothing. Jack and Guisborough drew away, and presently, with a word of apology to the ladies, went out. Nothing was to be officially known, that was evident; the dancing continued, decorous and exhausting, with the lavender night pressing against the windows.

Arnold Guisborough and Count Belloni-Negri met two days later in the early morning, when the mist still swirled whitely among the thorn-bushes on the heath. The seconds—Lingard had been persuaded by Jack to act for the Italian—inspected the pistols, measured paces, then stood back. The two antagonists waited in the silence, then, when the word came, fired.

The Count was hit; he clapped a hand to his shoulder and swore. Arnold did nothing. He had dropped his right hand, from which blood was already spurting. Later they found that the two middle fingers had been shot off. It was the hand that had struck the blow at Belloni-Negri.

At least the Count would find it difficult to be as accurate for some time to come, Jack muttered; his shoulder-joint was shattered. They tied up the wounds as best they could—it had been inadvisable to bring a surgeon who might report the matter—and when that was done, Jack turned to Arnold to try to relieve the situation.

"It's a queer time to announce my engagement," he said. Arnold grinned at him, clenching his teeth against the pain that had come when surgical shock was past. He would never play the piano again; that was his only regret.

"Allow me to congratulate you," he told Jack. Neither young man was anything but clear-sighted. Jack knew that Arnold's army career was in all probability finished; Arnold knew that Jack was not in love. The money would be useful to pay his debts, which with the life of an officer and a gentleman had become pressing.

Arnold was cashiered. The plans for Jack's wedding went on apace, for the bride was possessive and the bridegroom's eye already roved. If Jack had been able to see into the future, matters might have gone differently; not long ago he had encountered a little girl of fourteen with red-gold hair, visiting the Cray store with her mother, who was trying to sell a painting which might or might not be a Guardi. In course of the negotiations they had encountered Jack, lounging in the inner office; he had talked to the child and had shown her round the gallery, unaware that his image would persist in her mind long after other things had faded. But for the time he forgot Harriet Grove, and married his pale heiress.

PART THREE

16

Marcus always disliked shareholders' meetings; they made him answer direct questions, and he was too indolent to relish the exercise of his mind these days. On this occasion it was a fine day, with the sunshine accentuating the slight, dusty film on the outer windows; everything was made tawdry by that and by the inevitable film of tobacco-smoke. He began the proceedings in the usual way; the clerk's voice droned on with the minutes of the last annual general meeting. Jake was not here today; Cynthia was very ill. He reflected that illness occurred in bouts; from Florence had come recent word that Anna Bondone was dying.

One of the public members, Mr Oates, got up to speak. He was an unpleasant-looking fellow with a long clean-shaven chin and black hair, his clothes none too immaculate. Nevertheless he numbered himself among the *cognoscenti* and was often to be seen in the shop, though he bought little. The bumbling voice raved on before Marcus realised that he himself was being called in question, not pleasantly. He raised his head and regarded the speaker, who must be as tall as he was himself; few men were.

"—and this lady also told me that Mrs Marcus Cray bought a garnet necklace at a larger discount than ought to be allowed to members of staff and their dependants."

Poor Cristina was in Sussex, where she had hired a little cottage. He felt guilty towards her; she knew about his women, Dorothea—of whom he saw less now—little Helen White in the beauty-lotions, winking and dimpling behind her bottles of orange-flower water and pots of creams. Nell was fun, and his times with her after hours did no one any harm. Maybe he had let her buy one or two things . . . and the others. But this long-chinned shark would not be given satisfaction.

". . . and I say that the books ought to be examined by an independent auditor."

There was a murmur from the crowd, whether of agreement or discord it was hard to tell; their faces, so many expectant blanks, were turned to the table. Marcus stood up and replied that if Mr

Oates was prepared to meet the required fee of an auditor, he was welcome to employ one approved by both sides. A snigger came from the crowd; they did not like the fishlike man, but some agreed with him in principle.

"And the same has happened with Mrs Jacob Cray, at different times; I can produce instances. Where is Mr Jacob Cray? He ought to be present."

"Mr Jacob Cray's wife is ill. I think even you, Mr Oates, would agree that he has sufficient cause for absence; she may not live more than a few hours."

Sympathy was on his side now, and some cried out "Shame!" Oates did not get up again, but they had not heard the last of him. Another man rose and criticised the policy. These dabs of paint, as he called the French Impressionist paintings in which Marcus, at Luigi's instance, had been investing were a waste of money. "They've been in stock now for a long time, and there's no great demand. But when I ask for an English artist's work it's diffficult to find. We needn't be browbeaten by foreigners. There's a new school, as everyone knows, turning out good stuff in London, but when you ask, it ain't here."

Marcus rose again and pointed out that Morris wallpapers and textiles were available in the shop. He himself disliked the anaemic young women of Burne-Jones and Rossetti and Millais, and as Luigi had no interest in them either they had not been included. Now, perhaps, he would have to buy; and certainly they would sell. He indicated to the speaker that his point had been taken about the English paintings. "But anyone who buys an Impressionist work now makes a good investment; in twenty years they will be worth a fortune."

"So you've got yourself some at a discount, eh?" yelled Oates. Marcus ignored him and continued with the business of the meeting. It would be unpleasant if such a fellow were allowed to gain credence here; especially so—and he found that he cared about this—for Cristina. He missed her about the house; he would be glad when she came home.

Cristina in fact travelled up to visit Cynthia, who had not died that day, though it would not be long. She lay in bed, the monstrous outlines of her body outlined by the bedclothes; her face was thin and pale; she had a tumour on the liver, which could not be removed. The two little girls were brought in to say goodbye to her and then were taken away. The sick woman turned her eyes after them, knowing that she would not see them again. Maria would be a beauty, with great dark eyes. Little Annie was fat and plain. Cynthia turned back to her husband, who had stayed by the bedside. She opened her sick yellowed eyes and stared at him, as if seeing him for the first time. He would marry again, without doubt; somebody of his own class. She could not pretend that they had been very happy. If it were all to do again, would she? At any rate the thing was done; perhaps by tomorrow she would be dead. "Don't fret yourself, Jake," she whispered. "I know you're busy; go away and leave me."

"No." He would stay with her. He found his feelings rising in his throat, but with his usual difficulty of expression could not voice them. He would have liked to tell Cynthia that he was still fond of her, that the other women hadn't meant anything. And it was sad that she had had so many miscarriages and dead children. There had been a son, who had lived for a little while. If only he could have been spared! Perhaps in the future—he found his thoughts running ahead shockingly, and fixed his eyes on the face of his wife. It was her brain that had attracted him long ago, he knew; she was clever. Old Cussen had died last year.

The door opened and Marcus came in, bringing Cristina. She knelt by the bed and leant over and kissed the dying woman. "It was good of you to come, dearie," Cynthia whispered. "Shouldn't have cut short your holiday." Her mind was still clear.

She indicated soon that she wanted to be sick, and that they should go. While she was vomiting she died, lying afterwards with a trail of yellow matter issuing from her mouth. They cleaned her and tidied her up for burial and then sent for the family to see her for the last time in her coffin. Afterwards the tumour burst. It was not a dignified death; poor Cynthia had never been permitted much dignity. After the funeral Jake went off by himself; he might or might not be going to a woman. Men found strange comfort, Cristina thought; she herself would go to the two little girls, and talk to them about their mother. They were old enough to remember Cynthia clearly. Then she would go back to the Piccadilly house. It made her happy that Marcus had asked her to stay by him.

In Florence, the room had drawn curtains; another sick woman's bed lay in shadow, so that one could only dimly see her face. In the room scented pastilles burned in a silver pan, to dispel the odour of sickness. Luigi and Teresa knelt by the bed; the rest had come and gone. Presently the priest would arrive with the viaticum.

Anna stretched out a thin arm; she had lost so much flesh in the past weeks that it was skeletal. Her hand touched Teresa's forehead gently. The young woman seized it and kissed it; there had been great devotion, beyond the blood-tie, between her and her mother-in-law. "I want you to go now," said Anna with difficulty, as if saying the words hurt. "I want to speak to Luigi alone. Do not let anyone else come in until we send."

Teresa went out, weeping. She was losing her only friend. In the room, the dying woman turned to her son. He leant closer, as if to catch the words which she would utter so that not one might be lost. "What is it, *mamma mia*?" He had not used that name to her since he was a little child. She straightened the arm that had dismissed Teresa and began to fondle Luigi's hair with the thin hand; it felt crisp and vital against her dying flesh.

"I have a thing to tell you which no one else must know until you yourself are on your deathbed, if you choose to reveal it then. It is . . . this . . ."—she struggled with weakness that threatened to silence her—"you are, it is probable, not the son of Luigi Bondone. I believe your father to have been Riccione the lawyer, your guardian in your youth. I . . . am not sure. I have kept the secret all these years. Your—my husband—may have suspected, but could not be sure. I do not think you are like him; you have too much love of life. This had to be told to you before I may die in peace."

He had stiffened; now he made himself speak to her again, the shock of what she had said having alienated him for instants. Later he was to calculate, within himself, what it meant to him to be no longer of the blood of Enrico Bondone. She had said she was not sure, but if not, why had she told him at all? "How did it happen?" he asked, but Anna only smiled.

"I will not tell you that," she said.

"You were in love with Riccione?" Remembering the dry, grey lawyer it seemed incredible; Riccione could have been no longer young when . . . Still he refused to accept it.

Anna said dreamily, "I was never in love except once in my life,

208

and that was with George Massingbird, the Englishman. He is dead long ago. Perhaps now, again, we will meet."

She grew drowsy, and out of pity he left her, and went and told Teresa to send in greater haste for the priest in case he came too late. Then he went out. Anna after her last confession would not want him in the room again; he would leave her to die in peace. His thoughts whirled in chaos; to calm them, he took his hat and stick and walked about, seeing nothing and staring through acquaintances whom he passed by. He felt as though the tiger's strength in his body would only be appeased by walking, walking; later he found himself in the office, which was empty today because of Anna's illness. He made himself touch and finger the paintings, the *objets d'art*, everything for which he had worked so lovingly over the years. Bondone Figli; and he no son of Bondone.

Who was the heir? Filippo; under whom the business would wind down in a year. Also, the truth nagged at him; by rights, much should be the property of Marcus Cray, in England. That will of Enrico's he had burned long ago had contained justice, if he had known . . . but he would have acted no differently. He would act no differently now; when he returned to the house, they would tell him Anna was dead. The secret remained between himself and her: the priest would reveal nothing of any confession.

All these years, and he an impostor. The wild resentment, the blow to his pride, unmanned him; he was about to seat himself at his desk and lay his head on his arms, an instant only, till he regained sanity. He had begun to go towards it, and saw the door open. Stéphanie d'Eute stood there, in a walking-dress of plaid taffeta. He knew she had come of deliberate purpose; she made no excuses, and in her eyes was open invitation. He went to her and seized her in his arms. He would take whatever solace she could offer. Afterwards, life would resolve itself; but for now, there was this. He used her, as he would have used a whore.

Later, undressing to go to bed that night, he was to stare in astonishment at the bite Stéphanie had left on his shoulder. He had not felt the pain at the time, tiger and tigress as they had become together, on the office sofa.

17

Cristina had not been well, and after her convalescence Marcus decided to take her to the theatre. They chose a variety show at the Palladium. Marcus had seen it before, but decorously sat by his wife and applauded with the dressed-up chattering audience. They clapped with especial vigour for a young Welsh singer who had also danced during her act, kicking up strong legs in black net stockings. She was plump and pretty, with the somewhat harsh timbre of the Welsh hills in her singing; otherwise she was not notable, and Marcus was surprised to see, seated in the audience and regarding her with fixed attention, his cousin Robert Platen, his harsh face set. The crowd shouted "Peggy Williams! Welsh Peg!" and the pretty creature came back to take another bow. The place was crowded and when Marcus asked Cristina to excuse him while he went to the bar for a drink, he had to struggle through to the open space at the side of the auditorium. There he found both Robert and Jack, not together; the latter was with the handsome young woman who had, Marcus knew as a matter of course, formerly been one of Jake's mistresses. He chaffed them all, drank his brandy and returned to Cristina in time for the rising of the second curtain. Afterwards they went out together into the cool night air; Cristina said she would like to walk home, and they strolled arm-in-arm down the street among the pouring crowds and jostling flower-sellers, their baskets bright with posies under the gas-flares. Robert was before them, buying violets; he would no doubt wait with these at the stage door, or did he already have the *entrée* to the dressing-room? They both laughed; at Robert's age, spring in the blood was not to be expected. But one never knew.

"He was always alone," said Cristina. "It will be good for him." They had once or twice seen him with the little fair-haired boy, Dudley, who was now at school; as for the Irish housekeeper who was Dudley's mother, there had been no news of her for long. Robert seemed to need solitude with which to refresh himself; however, here he was in love, and when their laughter was over they both had the same thought; so young a woman might well make a fool of him, and hurt him badly.

Next day, Marcus forbore to chaff his cousin in the shop; Robert could erupt into violent rages or else continue for weeks in an icy silence if he were displeased. Marcus had better tactics; he went to his own mistress, Nell White, who no longer served in the shop and knew everybody in London. She gave her kindly laugh. "The old one's a goner, all right," she said. "He hasn't missed a single performance since he first went. They say that show will stay for a long time. Must be running out of money, the old gentleman, what with flowers and all."

"Perhaps she will be kind to him," said Marcus, but what hope was there of that? There would be younger and richer men after Welsh Peg; she would never consider an ageing, irascible soldier with a scar on his face and an illegitimate son.

But a few days later—it was a Sunday, and the crowds after church had thronged to greet the sunshine in the Park—Marcus and Cristina met a couple strolling beneath the trees; Robert, who raised his tall hat to Cristina, and Peg on his arm, fetching in garnet-coloured velvet and a hat with a feather, which set off her dark curls. They passed on, as an introduction would not have been correct.

Later they learned that Robert had set Peg up in lodgings, and was often to be found there with her. Still later, there was a baby, a little girl whom they named Roberta, after her father. She was very pretty, and as she grew older turned out to have inherited her mother's comic talent; she could imitate anybody she had met, and Robert learned to laugh heartily, sitting in his chair, idolising his daughter whatever she did. In fact he favoured and loved her far more than his son, which did not mean that he neglected Dudley; when the boy had school holidays they would all live in the house together, with Peg unlaced in a wrapper, her hair tumbling down her back. She was fond of Robert and the children; but as time passed she began to be bored a little, and longed to go back to the theatre. She could still dance and sing and mimic with verve. One day she broached the subject with her quick-tempered old lover and found him surprisingly amiable.

"It's just that I feel I might as well, while I can," she said. "You've got the children. And I'll be home now and again."

"As you will," he said, but he no longer followed her to the nightly performances. As Peg herself said, he had his own

211

theatre at home. Certainly it was impossible to be dull in the society of Roberta. About this time Robert retired from service in the shop, and could spend all day in the child's company.

Carla came downstairs slowly from the nursery. It made her sad to visit it these days; little Simone had formerly been waiting to rush to greet her and fling his arms about her neck, showering her with kisses. It was only a fortnight since his funeral and she could not yet feel anything but numb grief at the vacant place; she tried to be gentle and patient with Susanna, who had grown noisy and difficult, while the baby, Annina, had nothing to say yet, her fair hair shining against the nurse's starched apron. The nurse herself was competent and would see to it that Carla, like other women of her class, knew little of her children if that was what she desired. At present she had no desires, only weariness. Since the sad news of Arnold Guisborough's maiming she had had no joy in life.

She could hear the voices of Filippo and Vecelli, the secretary, murmuring as she crossed the hall. She shut her eyes for a moment and then went in. They were together as always, Vecelli's white face and thin cruel lips making him look like Mephistopheles; Filippo snuggled—it was the only word—near him. In Filippo's hand was an opened envelope which he tossed casually on the table at sight of her. "It is yours," he said briefly. She recognised Luigi's clear handwriting and knew a stab of anger.

"If it is mine, why was it opened?" Useless to ask, as she might have known by now. Filippo sniggered. "A husband has a right to open his wife's letters," he said unctuously, and over Vecelli's face crept a sour smile; he had no natural pleasure, only contempt for everything and everyone. Carla felt the flush that had risen to her cheeks die away; she turned her back on them both and took the letter to the window. It was formal and correct, and could have given the reader no especial satisfaction. Luigi desired her to come to see him privately as soon as it might be convenient for her. "And if I refuse my permission?" enquired Filippo, and he and his beloved—she had known for long how it was between them—burst into gales of laughter, turning to each other like two schoolboys, or as her mind told her, a girl and a man. She was not certain how long she had lived with the knowledge about Filippo.

212

She called for the carriage and went to see Luigi at once. She was not eager to visit him; he was being very cruel to Hester. He had finally taken a house in town and installed Hester openly in it as his mistress, with the little girl and a small staff of servants; and Stéphanie d'Eute paid frequent visits to her friend. It would not have done for the polite world to know that Luigi Bondone was having an affair with a married woman; this was their way of getting round public opinion. Hester herself must be in torment. Carla had not visited the house and had no wish to, but she had twice taken Hester for carriage-drives with the little girl, Rosa Maria. The latter should have kept them lively and amused with her chatter, and the sight of her exquisite face beneath the frilled hood she wore; Luigi adored her. But Hester herself sat woodenly, expressing no pleasure at the sights they passed of water and trees and gardens. She was like someone who has passed beyond suffering, and even the child did not move her to smile or answer.

Luigi sat at his desk in the office beyond the gleaming show-rooms. He rose when Carla entered, gave a little bow, and drew out a chair for her. He then signalled for coffee to be brought in. Carla had no great wish for it, but all of Luigi's gestures now were grand and important; it would have disrupted some schedule or other to have refused.

He sat down again and the golden eyes fixed themselves on her. I am no longer a woman he loves, she thought, not even one he has once loved. I am simply here to do his bidding, whatever it is. She knew that if she waited in silence she would soon hear; but what he said astonished her, joyfully.

"It is my intention to send you to visit your brother in London. You should start as soon as possible; before you go, come to me and I will give you a certain package, which you must keep always with you until it is in his hands. It is of great value and I would not send it by the ordinary post, or by any other messenger. You I can trust."

She had taken off her gloves; now her hands strayed to her furs, feeling the soft deep texture with a new curiosity. Why had he chosen her? She would not ask him; and it would be a delight to see Marcus again. The hand fell back to her lap and she said, "What about Filippo? He will not take it kindly if I leave alone." Filippo would be afraid she might meet Guisborough in England:

he was insanely jealous, despite the situation.

"You may take your maid. I will deal with Filippo." Luigi's tone was dry and she knew that, however he had found it out, he was aware that her marriage was wretched. She fought down resentment at this all-knowing faculty; she herself had tried valiantly to pretend to the world that everything was as usual.

They discussed dates and sailing times, and she knew her orders were complete; she would have preferred to know what it was she carried, but no doubt Marcus would tell her. Warmth flooded her at the thought of seeing him again. They had corresponded over the years, but he still thought of her as a young girl whereas—she shrugged it off—she was twenty-six. Cristina too would be glad to see her, and to have news of home.

She drove away thoughtfully, focussing her mind on clothes. There would just be time for the dressmaker to fashion her a new travelling-gown. And the little Mantuan maid, Lisa, would enjoy the journey; she had great sparkling blue eyes, one a trifle cast so that Filippo said she squinted. She was quiet and deft, and would be an asset on the voyage; Carla prayed for a smooth one and that they might not be seasick.

She was troubled about leaving the dog Zefiro, who went everywhere with her; he would allow no one to approach her unobserved. She could not make up her mind to leave him; and yet it seemed unnecessary to take him on so short a visit. The decision was made for her; on the day before she must leave, the old groom who was also a gardener came to her with anxious eyes.

"It is the dog, *madama*. He is not well."

He was lying in his kennel, head lolling, and although he wagged his great tail feebly he could not rise to greet her as he would always do. Carla knelt down and took his head in her lap; his eyes were already glazing, and as she held him he died, the great body growing limp and powerless in seconds. She was so shocked that she could not believe it had happened, and kept caressing him and calling his name. The groom tried to comfort her.

"He knows nothing now, *madama*. He waited for you to come before he died. I have seen it happen often with such dogs; they have a great devotion."

She was crying now, soundlessly. She knew Zefiro had been

poisoned; and she knew who had done it, and why. She gave instructions for the body to be taken away and buried or burnt; Zefiro no longer inhabited it. When she went back to the house she said nothing of the matter to Filippo, and kept her face stiffly unconcerned before his minion. They had done this to hurt her as much as they might, to ruin her English holiday. Well, they should not; but there would be no friendly dog to return to, tail wagging and tongue lolling with joy that she had come home. In fact, this no longer was her home. She belonged nowhere; it did not matter. Nothing mattered except that soon she would see Marcus again.

Her prayer about the weather was answered at any rate; the sea was like glass. She stood on deck looking out to sea, the stacks and piers and anchored ships of the seaport fading behind her. It was as though she could already visualise England. Was she not, after all, an Englishwoman, coming home? Home was not the place she had left; Filippo had been spiteful and had devised all possible ways to torment her, besides the poisoning of her dog; he took no pleasure in her company but was jealous that she had been chosen to go. He had even—she shrugged again in contempt—tried to make her pregnant, saying that if so she could not travel. It had not happened, that was all. The children had not understood where she was going; Susanna had been told she was to send a kiss for Uncle Marcus, and had refused; baby Annina had stared wordlessly. Children were not enough; one needed adult company, and she herself had had none for years, unless Luigi could be counted. Now she would relish Marcus' wit, his careless generosity.

The maid Lisa watched from the stairway hatch, pulling her hood close over her curls; she did not want her fair skin blown on by the salt breezes. In her hand, cast over her wrist by a thong, was the *signora*'s jewel-case; Carla herself kept the key. Inside was the package. It was amusing to be going to England. Lisa, who had begun to improve herself on obtaining this pleasant Florentine post, would take full advantage of whatever was of value there. She had been practising English phrases from a little book. She could read and write, which many other servants could not; and had a strong notion of how to please men, though she had kept herself carefully chaste. One day she would have a rich husband and she must come to him without reproach. How

215

pale *madama* was! Perhaps after all the unpleasant little *uomo*—Lisa had no illusions about Filippo—had done some harm. If that were so, Lisa knew of a *tisane*. But she would not offer it yet; there was a time for everything. She would be glad when they were off the ship, which smelt of oil and stale herrings, and had their feet on firm ground, English ground. London was a great city, larger than Rome.

Carla was still at the rail, staring seaward. "Best come in, *madama*," called the little Mantuan softly. "You will take cold, and be ill, and that will not do."

Carla smiled, and came. She permitted this maid a good deal of freedom; Lisa's ways were ladylike and she was careful with her speech, and did not make a fool of herself over men. It was growing dark, and they went below. Next morning there was a pink flush of sunrise, and the coast of France could be seen, flat and green against the Channel water. This was the dreaded crossing, but today it was calm. It was as if the weather itself favoured her meeting Marcus again.

18

Marcus was waiting to meet the boat, and at sight of the tall swarthy figure she felt a spring of gladness rise she had thought was dead. She hastened down the gangway, bidding Lisa keep close; the precious jewel-case must not be mislaid or stolen. It was at the back of her mind even while she felt Marcus' strong arms about her, almost lifting her for his kiss. His face had grown older; disillusion had carved deep lines from nose to mouth. But his eyes shone at sight of her; he held her away from him.

"You are pale, my dear. Was the voyage bad?" Already he had seen the little maid, standing demurely behind Carla; his heavy-lidded dark glance flickered over her. "No, smooth as glass," Carla answered, and he took her arm in his and led her out of the crowds on the quay, Lisa following. Carla turned once. "Do not let us lose that child," she said, "she is carrying a present for you."

"We will not lose her. I have reserved a carriage, so we may talk in peace. Does the child speak English?" He turned his head to where the maid followed them; Carla saw his cheek grow convex as he smiled back. She was amused; Marcus had always had an eye for a pretty girl. "Not enough to trouble us," she said. "She knows a few phrases; she has been learning them for the voyage. If we speak rapidly, it will not be understood."

"I am glad. I would not have liked such a child"—his smile widened at the name he would always give Lisa—"to be thrust into rough company in other carriages."

"No, for her mother has bidden me watch her strictly."

"Is she flighty, then?"

"No, she is level-headed; but London is considered to be very dangerous." She flashed a glance of her own up at him; so many years, and they were talking about her maid! "Is Cristina well?" she asked him.

"A little tired; she is very tactful, and let me come alone today, knowing we would want to talk together. She is waiting to welcome you, and sends her love."

They entered the carriage and Marcus made his sister comfortable with wraps. He said to Lisa in Italian, "Will you be warm enough?" The blue, lightly cast eyes looked up at him. "*Molta, signore*," she said.

"We shall be speaking in English. Will you understand?"

The child dimpled. "No, *signore*." She had given the jewel-case to Carla; now she smoothed her own wrist, where the white skin had been reddened by the carrying-strap. Marcus placed his fingers over it for an instant. His back was turned for a moment and Carla did not see the swift gesture. To touch the wrist like this, gently, was a professional caress. Lisa said nothing, but smiled on, and tucked her freed hands safely in the folds of her cloak. She did not speak again on the journey, effacing herself as a good maid should. But she was not unattracted to the tall dark Englishman, although she could tell he was much older than she. It would not displease her if they made love, she thought; but there would have to be certain financial arrangements. She remained in a pleasant glow of anticipation during the journey; she had already been on trains in Italy, from home to Firenze and from there, lately, with *madama*, to the boat.

Carla was certain that Marcus had some notion of why she had come. "I am in the dark regarding it," she said, "but Luigi would have me bring this package myself, to give to you personally." She took the small key and unlocked the jewel-case; inside, above the velvet-lined partitions and small drawers filled with gleaming carefully disposed stones, there lay the package. She drew it out and handed it to Marcus, her gloved fingers delicately clear against the buff paper. Marcus murmured an excuse and tore it open.

There was silence. Carla looked out of the window at the grey sky; dear England, where to see the sun at all was an event one noted! There were placid cows grazing in meadows, the flat rich green of the south; there were telegraph-poles, soot flying, all the things that made up railways; the clatter of the train as it journeyed soothed her. How pleasant it would be never to have to return! If it were not for the children, she need not; but such a thing must not be thought of. She would enjoy this visit, cherish it in her memory afterwards for many years, till she was old.

A stifled sound from Marcus brought her attention back to him; he had paled, and his fingers shook. "What is it?" she said. "May

I know of it? Do not say anything if it is secret."

"It is secret, but you may know. Luigi has sent me a draft for a million pounds. He says that I am to buy the business outright, that it has taken him many years to amass the sum, but that it is mine. What can have induced him to do this? Is he mad? I have done nothing to deserve—"

"If he said it, he has a reason. I am happy for you. It is what you would like, is it not?"

Marcus was thinking rapidly. If he could appropriate some of the money to pay his personal debts, pension off Dorothea, redeem some of the jewellery he had been forced to pawn over the years, and then buy the House of Cray—

"It is indeed what I should like," he said smoothly. Luigi had been trusting; it was unlike him. There must be a reason, as Carla said. He stared at her pale little face and wondered how much she knew, if it were in fact true that she knew nothing, and if she would report his present behaviour to Luigi; he must show more enthusiasm. He smiled suddenly, knowing his smile had unfailing charm.

"Luigi is generous," he told her. "He will not regret it."

"He may have sent me with the paper in case you were too proud to accept by letter. I cannot think why else."

"Let us stop thinking of whys and wherefores, and enjoy our . . . heritage." He had almost called it a windfall, but that would have been to underrate Luigi. He was still certain that there must be a reason, not yet disclosed. But he was in delightful company—he turned again to smile at the little maid—and the future was clear of debt, challenging, alluring.

Carla stayed three weeks. At first she was glad to sit with Cristina in the house, close to the fire, and rest; the journey she had made was far longer than anyone knew; the years had tired her, and she almost felt now that she had regained her youth. Marcus took a party to the Haymarket, and for that occasion Carla dressed splendidly, having her hair curled by Lisa's adept fingers into a modish coiffure, with diamonds hung about her throat and in her ears, sparkling against her pale blue satin gown. She could not afterwards recall the play; it was nothing notable, and she and Cristina had taken pleasure in looking at the other dressed curled bejewelled women in the boxes and stalls. Did they have their troubles, griefs and secrets? Did they love as she had once loved?

One could not tell; nor would anyone surveying themselves in turn have a better answer.

In the second week there was a dinner-party for the family. Jacky—she still thought of him by his childhood name—and his wife came, Lavinia in diamonds that rivalled Carla's own, but with her face hard, pale and narrow above them; the regiment was ordered to India and Carla thought wryly that Lavinia would make the perfect memsahib. Jack himself talked to her over coffee, and seemed resigned enough; but Carla regretted his marriage with a woman he could not love. He should have married a fairy princess, an angel. The world was cruel.

Jake was present without a partner and it was easily seen that he and his nephew did not deal together; he and Jack never exchanged words, and avoided one another studiously. Jake had called earlier at the house to kiss his sister and talk with her, and Carla had thought then that he seemed even stiffer than in former days, and certainly unhappy. "He needs a wife," she said afterwards to Marcus, who grimaced.

"It is no doubt my fault that he has not married again, for all those he chose for himself were unsuitable. I told him that in the position he may expect to hold he must take a wife whose breeding and income will enhance the business; and I do believe that notion has entered his thick head and has made him wary of other comforts—which before he was not."

She was regarding him steadily. "You speak as if Jake were your heir."

"So he is." His tones were curt, and she braved his anger and said "What of Jacky?"

"Jack has his army career. He is provided for."

"But, Marcus, he is your son."

"He is possibly illegitimate. That handfasting meant nothing. He understands that clearly—or should, since I have myself told him of it."

"You and Grizel—" She pronounced the unfamiliar name carefully; it was not possible to put a face and form to the name of Jack's mother, back in the shadows.

"Had no marriage lines, and no clergyman. Do not speak of it any more, Carla; my mind is made up."

Nothing would move him when he was in this mood, and she left the matter; in any case, another came to disturb her more. Arnold Guisborough called, and she had to force herself not to condole with him over his ruined hand; tears rose in her eyes, for she knew from Marcus' letters that it had happened for her sake. She could not do as she would have liked to, and raise the hand to her cheek. She could only murmur, mindful of the others in the room, "I believe I owe you thanks."

The blue eyes burned down at her. They had so seldom met, and yet he would never love any other woman; as for herself, had she been free to love, would she have loved Arnold Guisborough as his wife?

It did not bear thinking of, and she saw him go, knowing that there would always be a silver thread spun between him and her, however far their ways lay apart. Love did not end with death, but she had the certainty, from whatever source, that she would not see Arnold again.

Her mind sought to occupy itself with some other matter, and she began to consider Jake's widowed state and what might best be done. There was a shy young girl she knew in Italy, Beatrice di Lupo del Pela, of the old family, who desired to enter a convent but her parents were unwilling that she should, because her dowry was considerable and they grudged its loss to the Church. Would Jake be a suitable bridegroom? He was, it was true, many years older, but kind, steadfast and handsome; he should be a welcome suitor for a child who no doubt was afraid of younger men. She spoke of the matter to Marcus and had the satisfaction of knowing that he approved of the idea; he would write concerning it to Luigi, who would arrange everything. "Jake could perhaps travel back with you," he said, and Carla welcomed the thought; it would be pleasant to have Jake's solid presence by her when she again confronted Filippo and his catamite. Whether or not Jake understood the true state of affairs there, he would mean protection, for the time.

She sailed at last on a day of blowing rain, Jake by her. With them was the little Mantuan maid. Before going Marcus had come to her pleadingly, to ask if she would leave Lisa behind. Cristina would be glad of her services.

Her eyes had raised themselves to meet his; neither pair held any expression. "No," Carla said, "I promised that I would take care of her and would bring her safe home." A swift memory had assailed her of driving lately with Cristina in the Park, and encountering in a carriage a painted, ageing woman with dyed hair; it was Dorothea Wainfleet, with her young son by her who looked so like Marcus that his parentage flaunted itself. Cristina had not even stiffened, but Carla knew that she knew; it would have seemed impossible to speak to her of it, but later she had raised the matter for herself.

"Marcus is kind to me," she said. "I am his barren wife who brought him no dowry. What pleases him must be acceptable to me. When I was younger it was different." She had flung out her narrow hands in an expressive gesture, smiled, then fallen silent. Carla knew admiration for her, and had in any case a curious certainty about Marcus' own feeling for his wife. It would outlast that for other women, and was a kind of love. But she would not insult Cristina by leaving the little maid behind. Marcus must conduct that part of his life for himself.

"He will need to marry money, for he will never make any."

Luigi, standing before the newly acquired Sansovino Bacchus, frowned thoughtfully at its exuberance, traced with stone ivy. Carla, who had come to Florence at his request, and was to be driven later to visit Teresa, listened in silence; after all, there was nothing to say. Marcus himself was in some despair at Jake's inability to appreciate, or express his appreciation to possible clients, or even friends; he remained as he had always been, self-sufficient, decent, brave, and without humour. Recalling Jack's warm sympathy and charm, she regretted again that he would not inherit. But it had been useless to try to reason with Marcus; his mind had continued obstinately made up. She did not explain this to Luigi; the thing to do with Luigi was to listen.

"I think," he said, "that I can arrange a meeting with the girl Beatrice. Teresa must write, inviting her and her mother—the mother is formidable, a niece of Massini—to visit us. What form should the visit take? A stay, or a luncheon party? They were related to old Nardini, and we have a slight acquaintance though him."

Carla looked at the Bacchus also and his laughing face gave her a notion. "It is too hot in Florence now," she said. "Any courtship would wilt. Why not an *al fresco* party at the Nardini place? We could meet there, and Jake could row them out on the lake." Memories of that earlier picnic for Marcus' betrothal were with her; the remembered scent of the pines came to mind. Marcus

222

had been strange then, withdrawn into himself as they drove home. Dear Mamma had been there. At thought of Isotta her eyes filled with tears, and she looked away to brush them off unseen with the back of her glove. Luigi had enough weeping to contend with; she would not add to it; one got one's own way more easily if one appeared cheerful. She heard his approval of the *al fresco* intention, then launched into the subject of Vecelli the catamite.

"Luigi, that creature must go; if he does not, I will leave with the children and take them to England." Conditions at home had been more than ever intolerable on her return; by now she might be a stranger in her own house. Filippo hardly addressed her, and the servants had been changed and those who replaced them were Vecelli's choice and obeyed him rather than herself. She tried to put the matter calmly to Luigi, whose mouth tightened a little; he had lately lost a tooth, and it came to her that he was no longer a young proud Caesar but a middle-aged art dealer, all eagerness gone. Yet what he said would be done, would be.

"Vecelli shall leave," he promised her. "You realise that Filippo will not be easy to live with afterwards."

She shrugged. "At least the house will be clean. I tell you, coming back was like breathing sick air. I was glad to drive out today."

"Come to Teresa," he said. They went out and into the waiting carriage; absently she noted the bustle there always was at Bondone nowadays, with interested customers moving from one to the other object of beauty, or else spell-bound before the one they wished to buy. D'Eute was not present, but there were enough members of staff to watch discreetly without troubling the buyers; thefts seldom occurred here. It was a magnificent place, a meeting-house for the knowledgeable of Florence. As a member of the family she was proud of it. She sat in the carriage erect and smiling, the curled feather on her bonnet crisp and blue, her pelisse a matching colour. She had the comfortable assurance that Luigi was flattered to be seen with her as they drove. Now and again she nodded to acquaintances; she had many, and her reputation was unassailable, the old story about Luigi long forgotten. In time, perhaps, she would become a matriarch, as Anna and, in a way, Isotta had been; the thought amused her. Would Luigi then be an old, toothless man, his hair grey?

In the house there was discretion, but no welcome; certain

sounds from the schoolroom told one poor Luigini was being whipped again. Teresa's face as she dispensed coffee was ugly with weeping. Carla could not ask what was the matter, because Luigi stayed, accepted his coffee from his wife's plump pink hand, made polite talk, and later escorted Carla back to the carriage and drove her home. As soon as they were out of hearing she said to him, "Why is Teresa unhappy?" She would like also, she thought, to speak to him about the boy; his harsh tutors were reducing him to a state of cowed stupidity. Luigi always said he believed in discipline, but there could be too much.

He frowned, keeping his profile unmoved. "Teresa cannot understand that a man must have his pleasure, and she provides me with none," he said. Suddenly he slackened rein and let the horses walk. "I want to ask for your help," he said, "it has come to that. Stéphanie d'Eute is to have a child, which is mine. Estéban has already left her. It is not known yet, but once the gossip starts it will be bad for business. What are we to do? I have let it be given out meantime that d'Eute has been sent to Brest and will return, but that excuse will wear thin."

It was like him, she thought, to consider the whole matter in the light of its effect on the firm. "When is the child to be born?" she asked him. It was pointless to scold; he had listened to no advice since Anna's death.

"In three or four months. I cannot ask Hester to rear it; she has endured enough." His tone was weary, as though Hester's tears were a reproach even to him. "No, you certainly cannot," Carla said warmly. "Have you no discreet person to whom you could give the child, if Stéphanie will not acknowledge it?" That lady must have indulged in tight-lacing, she was thinking; she herself had noticed nothing.

"There is one; the terrible Signora Pazzi. You may have noticed her today at the desk. She is the widow of a failed poet, who was an invalid. Her life has not been easy. She is intelligent, however, and would perhaps consider taking a house for our purpose if I pay for it. The child could be nursed there, and afterwards be understood to be under the *signora*'s guardianship, after which there would be no more questions."

"Is she fond of children?" Carla remembered, now it was mentioned, a plump dark woman in the office, the spiritual successor to Isabella. She had worn a silver crucifix over her blouse, and had had a reliable air. The situation was fairly desperate, as while Luigi's affair with the unmarried Hester Fenton might be overlooked, Catholic Florence would disapprove of adultery. It was astonishing that the liaison with Stéphanie had not already been remarked. The husband's going would soon start gossip; he must be placated, if one could placate a tiger whose lair had been invaded; so Carla thought of d'Eute. He would not be given to taking such matters tamely.

"Fond of children? I do not know," said Luigi. "I do not like her, but she is a useful employee. It might serve. I will come in with you now and deal with the matter of Vecelli."

This he did, in the space of a quarter of an hour; presently she heard the carriage drive off, and Filippo came to her in screaming madness, crying like a baby.

"It is your fault," he said, "all your fault. I wish you were dead, then he could come back."

She leaned against the sofa, weary in every limb; the good of the London holiday had already left her.

The planned picnic to Nardini took place on a warm calm day in early autumn. As before, they took iced wine and cold food with them. Jake drove one carriage, and it was some indication of the importance of the occasion that Luigi drove the second; he was seldom to be bribed from the office nowadays in daylight. Teresa had come, her face veiled from the rays of the sun; she sat beside Carla, who had brought Susanna, and the child sat obediently enough in the seat facing the horses: like many children she was prone to travel sickness. Carla herself had a headache, and would as soon have stayed at home. But it was of importance to give a warm welcome to Beatrice di Lupo del Pela as Jake's probable betrothed, and to make the shy girl feel at ease.

Beatrice and her parents waited beneath the pines, for they lived at the *castello* about five miles off. The Contessa was a stout woman with fair hair curled elaborately; her husband was slight and small. Beatrice herself was beautiful, with long eyes black as jet beneath sleepy lids, and black hair confined by a ribbon. Her figure was tall and slight, like a young tree, and she was dressed modestly. Carla saw Jake look earnestly at his intended bride, then subject himself to being addressed by her mother. That lady was voluble, having no doubt few listeners as a rule. The trio walked slowly round the rim of the lake, whose waters today lay turquoise in the sun.

225

"Uncle says we are to row out in the boat," called Susanna, her dark curls bobbing cheerfully. She loved all action, and was happiest out of doors. "Mamma, may I take off my shoes and stockings and wade in the lake? Uncle Jake says it is safe." She found Jake pleasing and reliable after her Papa, who had not come today.

"Uncle will row you out in the boat presently, and you want to wear shoes and stockings to look like a young lady." Carla tried to speak lightly, but her headache had worsened and almost seemed to blind her; it was difficult not to be short with the child. Susanna pouted and ran back to join the others; Carla raised a hand to her forehead and wondered where she might go out of the sun. No doubt the house would be shady.

She found the way and mounted the steps slowly, remembering that other time among the roses. How quickly youth went! The young Cristina and Marcus had gone off together among the pines, long ago, as the three were going now. Now—well, now all of their lives were different.

The house was cool, the great door standing open; since the old Count's death only servants lived here. Carla walked slowly into the arcaded hall which had been built for six centuries; and came face to face with a young man's portrait. She stopped before it; it might have been Marcus in the flesh, at twenty. A certain thought came to her; had it indeed been so? And Mamma, as a young girl, and this youth her lover? If it were so indeed, and Marcus knew of it, he had determined—she saw it all now—that Jake must be the Cray heir. The thing still seemed incredible; Mamma, the devoted widow of later years, which was all one could remember . . .

A light footstep disturbed her; she turned to find young Beatrice staring at her. "I did not want to go with the others in the boat," she said in her soft voice. Carla made herself smile and talk; this beautiful child must be made to feel at home among them. Yet she remained conscious of her own headache, which did not lessen; and of the strange truth, if it were truth, contained in the portrait of Felice Nardini, dead these many years, and his unacknowledged son.

Misfortune had overtaken the party in the boat, rowed out as in an idyll on the bright water. It had sprung a leak, and there was much haste to get everyone back to shore; before they contrived it the water was pouring in, and Jake knew that he could not continue to row in safety. He and Luigi hauled at the anchor, and once it was bestowed Jake jumped out of the boat, among the screams of the ladies, and carried them one and all to shore, wading back and forth until everyone was safe. Then he, Luigi, and the Count, who had all acquitted themselves bravely, took themselves and their sopping clothes back to the carriage, where unseen by fair eyes they shed, wrung and shook them and let them dry in the sun. It was the kind of practical adventure at which wordless Jake excelled; he could not have made a better impression on his future mother-in-law. Laura di Lupo del Pela had never in her life been carried to safety by a tall handsome man with greying fair hair and strong arms which took her weight easily, letting her second best silk dress cascade over his arms without even getting it wet. From that hour she would never cease to sing Jake's praises, and the betrothal was as good as made.

Teresa had been included in the adventure, and she and the rest of the ladies sat afterwards about the lake shore, letting the hot sun dry them if their clothes had dipped briefly in the water. The repose, at any rate, was pleasant. Little Susanna, who had managed for herself, ran about crying, "Where is Mamma?" her slender limbs active, her muslin skirt bedraggled with the wet. Later they would remember the food, and would eat and drink, thankful for the coolness of the wine on its ice from the deep cellar. Carla and Beatrice had rejoined the party by now, glad to have escaped the watery adventure; but everyone felt at ease, and pleased with the gentlemen, who were still prevented from appearing and who consumed their share of food privately near the carriage. It was hardly, as someone said afterwards, a very romantic wooing; but the shy betrothed was perhaps won more quickly by Jake's absence than if he had been assiduously present, with his notable lack of address.

Carla had gone home and lain down on her bed till dinner-time; she did not feel well enough to eat but would dress for the meal. It was no doubt, she thought, a touch of the sun. Her temples throbbed and the little maid Lisa rubbed them with eau-de-cologne; her touch was light and soothing. "I will draw the blinds for *madama*," she said, and did so: the shadowed room grew quiet as she slipped gently out. Carla closed her eyes; behind them, her

227

thoughts whirled and she tried to bring peace to her mind, but could not. The memory of the bright water, the dark pinewood and its eternally chirping cicadas turned in a kaleidoscope of colour and sound, and always before her eyes was the portrait of Felice, as though his dead face mocked her. How little one knew of anyone! Mamma had been a faithful wife and, except perhaps for Sir Berkeley, a faithful widow. Now, it was as though the stability of the entire family were threatened. Of course it would not be; she would keep her own secret. Did Marcus indeed know? Would young Beatrice, on meeting Marcus after her marriage, see in his face that of his true father? It was useless to ask oneself; there was nothing to be done, and she felt tired, so tired, as though her very blood were water.

She made herself rise, and be dressed, and go downstairs to face a sullen Filippo lacking his Vecelli. He had scarcely addressed a word to her since the creature had gone, and she was relieved at this; it would not be necessary to make polite talk. She picked up a fork and toyed with her food, eating little, forcing down some. She was certain now that she was going to be ill; she felt sick, and laid down the fork. Suddenly an agonising pain shot through her body. She bit her lip, and laid a hand on her abdomen; it felt taut, and the pain was central and had not gone away. She felt beads of sweat break out on her forehead; she would have risen to walk to the door, but could not. The pain was insistent, and in the end she gave a little cry of agony. The servant who was handing the courses laid down his dish. *"Madama,* you are ill? I will summon help."* He left, and returned with two menservants and Lisa; between them they aided Carla out of her chair, and the coachman, who was strong, lifted her up in his arms carefully. Her head was turning from side to side with the pain. Filippo had risen from his place and stood staring at her; she knew that the last thing she would remember would be his dark, bright eyes, their whites showing like those of a nervous horse. She closed her own, willing herself to endure the pain as she was carried back upstairs. They unlaced and undressed her, and put her to bed; the doctor had been summoned. When he left, his face was grave.

"There is nothing to be done," he said in a low voice to the waiting group, Filippo among them. "The relatives should be informed. Meantime give her warm milk, if she will take it." He had given the sick woman laudanum and opium to deaden the pain, and her grey lips had thanked him; she was still fully conscious.

Carla continued in agony for two days before she died. With her at the last were Luigi and Teresa, the former holding her hands; the priest had already been and she had made her last confession. Filippo stood about, aware that he did not fill the place of a mournful husband; he left what had to be done to others, and from time to time raised his eyes to stare at Carla's now changed face. No one spoke to him and he appeared not to notice it. Once he went to the school-room and said to Susanna, "Your mother is ill; you must be quiet and not romp."

Susanna stared at him; she had no respect for him and very little love. "I am sorry," she said politely. "Will she get better?"

"They say that she will not. You must prepare yourself. The priest has been with the viaticum. Say a prayer for her; that is the best thing." He found himself suddenly wise, old and comforting. Susanna's eyes filled with tears and she turned away. If Mamma were going to die, she would miss her; she had not previously ever thought how much. She had not always been kind to Mamma, and now it was too late. Would they let her go into the room? She would like to kiss Mamma before she died.

They led her in. The other child was too young to know anything. Susanna pressed her full young lips to Carla's inert hand; she was suddenly afraid to look at what had been Mamma, so still and grey. After she returned to her own room she started to tremble, and continued so for long enough to hear the sounds of the undertakers as they came in. Then she went to the window and looked out, watching the carriages in the street. They had laid down straw because Mamma was sick, and the passing wheels made no noise; there was no noise anywhere, except for the footsteps moving about Mamma's room.

When Marcus heard the news in London he shut himself in his own room and refused to see anyone. Cristina waited through the long day and then the night; but he did not come to her. She knew that to go to him, offer him comfort and love, was valueless, as all things were except to leave him alone and silent. She made herself see to small everyday tasks about the house, give the servants their orders; she tried to read a book from the subscription library, but the words on the printed pages passed before her eyes without meaning, and she put the book aside.

She rose once and came face to face with her own reflection in a mirror; she saw a woman no longer young, having put on flesh lately, so that her eyes were her only telling feature, almond-shaped and bright, but not with tears; it had been useless to weep for Carla, whom she had loved because Marcus loved her, and who had been still young.

She thought of a thing to do; she went to her writing-desk and sat down and wrote to Arnold Guisborough, far away in India. It was better that he should not receive the first news from the papers, late as they would be in reaching him and Jack.

Marcus also was writing a letter. He had undergone his own agony and by now, the silence was itself unbearable, stifling him like a cloak. He wanted to go out and walk, and walk; but first this letter must be written. It was addressed to Luigi, and contained no condolences; it concerned the little maid Lisa, returned to her parents in Mantua after the death. If Luigi would write with the offer of paid employment in London and arrange the passage, he would be grateful. After the letter was written he stared at the page for a long time before sealing it. He knew that the girl was the comfort he desired; if she refused to come he would be desolate, but he did not think that she would refuse, for there had been an understanding between them; perhaps, also, she would be a link with Carla. He laid his head on his arms; sluggishly, at the back of his mind there stirred gratitude to Cristina for not disturbing him with trite solaces for grief, tears, attempts at comfort. She was a woman in a thousand; he should use her better. But the Mantuan girl was what he needed now Carla was gone. He would ask Cristina to write a formal letter of condolence to Filippo; he himself wanted nothing to do with the pervert who had been Carla's husband.

Lisa from Mantua was in London within the month, and Marcus installed her in the house once occupied by Dorothea Wainfleet, who had left it some time ago. He found distraction there from his grief; once or twice, at the beginning, he was surprised to hear the sound of his own laughter. He delighted in dressing the child in grand clothes; she took to paint and powder like a professional, turning her talents now to embellish herself, instead of a mistress; in fact, she had a maid of her own to curl her hair modishly, brush her clothes and iron her linen. Marcus bought her a little dog, an Italian greyhound which Lisa liked at first to have sitting in her lap, her white fingers caressing his smooth coat. But she was idle, and would not exercise the dog; shortly she tired of him, and Marcus took him home. He could never resist any animal, dog, horse, waterfowl; they were necessary to him, like his women. Lisa herself made the perfect mistress; she was fresh, spontaneous, gay; at times, despite the years between them, he could have sworn she loved him. He would have her painted naked, to remind him of her body, with its pert charming breasts and plump thighs. She gave him more delight than any other woman had ever done; he would never tire of her, and she spent his money like water. He acknowledged the fact humorously, and did not reproach Lisa; it would have been like slapping a child who had been given a toy, and he had in any case no heart for it.

Cristina guessed that there was a new woman. Using the discipline to which she had long since schooled her mind, she tried to be glad, and in a way was so, that Marcus was happier. The seared lines of grief had almost left his face. They spoke together of ordinary things, and she stroked and fed the little greyhound Lisa had abandoned; it attached itself to her, and even brought her comfort.

Jake married Beatrice di Lupo del Pela in October; the wedding was quiet because of mourning, and moreover the bridegroom was in haste to return to England. He had meantime made the acquaintance of Rico Bondone, who called in at Luigi's office one day over the matter of shipping certain paintings to the London shop. The two men liked and respected one another; taciturn Jake could be coaxed to talk of ships and the water easily enough. Also, it was of interest to watch old Bondone's bastard son and see, as they said, a speaking likeness of the founder of the firm, with his great hook nose and upturned mustachios; but Rico was more reserved than his father had been, and displayed no interest in women.

One subject discussed was Laxton. The little man had made himself useful enough in the Brest office, and Rico would be almost sorry if he left it; but the pathetic sight of Luisa, the ageing grass-widow, still pleading for the return of her beloved, touched him. He opened the matter—possibly the only person who

231

would dare do so—with Luigi, and said a cunning thing, his eyes wrinkled with laughter at the corners; he knew the state of affairs well enough.

"Could not Luisa be induced to make a little legacy to some project you cherish, in return for the person of her husband? She will pine away if she is made to wait any longer; poor soul, she will never have children now."

Luigi's eyes narrowed. His swift mind had fastened on a project at once; no less than the crippled son Stéphanie d'Eute had borne him, who was looked after by Signora Pazzi. The *signora* loved Bobo like a mother; the fact had lessened Luigi's dislike for her, and they were now almost allies; he visited his lame child frequently, reproaching himself and Stéphanie, whose tight-lacing during pregancy had perhaps resulted in the deformed limb; one could not be certain. But he himself, after family commitments were met, had little enough left to leave to Bobo; and certainly d'Eute would will the boy nothing, still living as he was in dudgeon by himself with young Antoine. What if he should suggest to Luisa that Laxton might return if she made a will leaving her money to Bobo? As before, any withdrawal from the conditions could meet with swift reprisal.

He saw Luisa, and remained untouched by her blubbered face; no woman should cry who could not do it attractively, and Luisa's nose grew red and her cheeks smeared, while her voice was as harsh as ever and between sobs was unendurable. He sent off word to Laxton that he might return, and did not stay to watch the reunion; he rode off for some days into the country, taking neither Stéphanie, Hester nor any other woman. He spent the time quietly, resting and observing the hills; in fact, he knew what troubled him. Hester was talking of entering a convent, and it had not previously occurred to Luigi how unwilling he would be to let her go.

She had practised the rule secretly now for almost two years, wearing a harsh spiked girdle next her flesh, reading the offices and going to Mass daily. She had never taken pleasure in her little girl's company, seeing her only as the child of sin; as a result, Rosa-Maria grew up insecure and full of tantrums, unmanageable to governesses. However she was so pretty, and could wheedle so well, that much was forgiven her. She would be old enough now to be sent away to school once Hester was no longer present to look after her; but the convent would not accept a mother in charge of a child, however shameful. Hester prayed with tears falling, and on one of Luigi's rare visits—he was no longer her lover nowadays—asked him if Signora Pazzi might not look after Rosa-Maria, as she did Bobo; the half-brother and sister were good enough friends. Luigi distressed her by his cold reception of the idea; in his strange mind, such an association ranked as improper. So matters continued as they were, except that the Laxton couple were reunited at last; but not happily.

He had had other women in Brest. Luisa was sure of it, and would have been so in her jealous mind even had it not happened. He looked the same, though his hair was scanter, greyer and he had lost his pegs of teeth; but she loved him, would always love him, and he found it unrewarding, particularly since being informed of the contents of the new will. He had been happy enough in Brest and it was no reward to be brought back to the bed of this ageing, ugly woman, with her possessive passion; in especial as there would be no financial reward after it was all over. He began to be insufferably rude to Luisa, taunting her and making sharp cruel answers to her pleading for his love. The passing of time grew bleak and unhappy; she was often left alone, crying hideously in her room.

Luigi rode home, and matters went on as before; except that he broached the matter of Rosa-Maria with the *signora*. "But of course," she replied calmly. "I love children, and it will be good for Bobo to have a companion; an only child is at a disadvantage and often finds it difficult afterwards to go out into the world."

He gazed at her, realising that in all their association he had hardly looked at her as a woman; he had always thought of her as ugly, but she had magnificent, gentle dark eyes and a natural dignity. He remembered hearing that her own background had been poor and her childhood troubled; no doubt that gave her sympathy with children. "We will see," he murmured, using a phrase that he commandeered fairly often; it involved one in nothing while allowing for graceful withdrawal. But he would think about the two children; how fortunate he was to have so excellent a guardian for them! Stéphanie's rages had made her an exhausting companion of late years, although her body still fascinated him and her wit was as sharp as ever.

233

Cristina and Marcus had formally visited Jake and his new wife, and the two daughters by his first marriage who now lived with them. It could not be an easy situation for the young bride, who as yet spoke little English. Cristina was planning a drive for her, as a treat, but had not yet written the letter when the servant announced that Mrs Jacob Cray had called at Piccadilly.

The girl was shown in, and did not look happy. She was carefully dressed in an outfit made of brown velvet, with black braid trimming, and a hat with a curled black feather, framing her face. This was a pale oval, and the magnificent eyes looked out at Cristina in a kind of wordless appeal. Marcus' kind wife rose and went to Beatrice and kissed her on the cheek, drawing her towards the fire. The jewelled eyes of the little greyhound followed them.

"Warm yourself, my dear, for you will find England cold, as I did when I first came." She made the girl comfortable with cushions and a chair; but Beatrice sat on the edge like a schoolgirl, and suddenly burst into tears.

"It is nothing," she gasped, as Cristina bent again over her. "I am—foolish, that is all. But where we are I cannot cry; there is always someone watching, the girls, their governess—" She sat back, wiped her eyes and tried to smile. "Forgive me for troubling you, *signora*."

"You must call me Cristina, and I will call you Beatrice. Now tell me all of it; never fear, it will go no further. I am not a chatterer."

Beatrice twisted her slim fingers among the handkerchief's lace-trimmed folds. "You will think I am a fool," she said again. "But as you may know, I wanted to take vows. Mamma was angry, and I always obeyed her, so—" She shrugged a little. "It is no one's fault but my own, but—ah, this state of marriage! I cannot accustom myself to it." She flushed, and fell silent.

Cristina was regarding her wisely. "But your husband is kind, is he not?" Jake was very kind to his own daughters. When he had brought this child home as his wife he had taken her to them and had said, "Here is a playfellow." Marcus had told her of that. Jake had no doubt meant well, but the girls probably resented so young a stepmother; they were not straightforward children and Cristina herself over the years had made very little headway with either Maria or Annie. The one was after all beautiful, the other not; both were perhaps a little stupid, like their father.

Beatrice agreed that Jake had been kind. "When he came to me the first night he said, 'Do not be afraid' and I tried not to, but—but I cannot like—"

"When you learn to love your husband, you will want to please him. At the beginning it was strange, no doubt. And perhaps you will have children." Cristina's voice held no tremor as she voiced what had been hopeful for her once, then bitter. The blush had receded on Beatrice's face and left it white and wan.

"I think," she said, "that I am going to—I do not know—tell me . . ."

They discussed dates and seasons. All the time Cristina sensed the girl's wonder and gratitude at having the facts of the body spoken of without prudishness. Her mother must have been a harsh woman, lacking in understanding or humour. Finally Cristina persuaded Beatrice to laugh at herself; the child might be born in the summer. "If it is a girl," Beatrice breathed, "we will name it after you."

"You must let Jake think he has suggested that. It pleases men greatly to think that an idea, a suggestion, has come from them when it is really your own."

Beatrice's white teeth showed in a sudden smile. There was hope for the marriage. After she had left Cristina wondered at the wisdom she had herself dispensed; she had not known that she knew it. The years of waiting had paid dividends, after all.

When Marcus came in she told him of Beatrice's visit, without betraying her confidences. "Poor child, she is lonely, no doubt," he said. "I will take her about a little, I believe; she is very pretty, a pleasure to look at. Jake likes plain women, and will not appreciate his good fortune. I do believe he loves no one in the world but young Maria; when he talks at all, he talks of her, her pianoforte playing, her painting, and so on. No doubt she will be a reigning beauty in a year or two." He moved to the fireplace.

"Then you must take her about also."

Marcus looked sharply round; it was not often that gentle Cristina made him a repartee. He grinned, showing unspoilt teeth. "Well spoken, my love," he said. "I do believe that you are the perfect wife for me."

She was happy afterwards, thinking of that, when he had gone out again, to visit Lisa, or perhaps Nell. The latter had borne him a son lately and no longer remembered working in the shop, but she was not kept in luxury like Lisa; Nell remained what she was, an honest Cockney, and knew more than anyone else how to make Marcus laugh. As the years passed he had become avid for laughter; he was growing old, and his son Jack was far away; by his own decree Marcus would not bring him home. The rare letters—Jack was bad at writing—told them little except news of the hill stations and of polo. Lavinia was seldom mentioned, and doubtless led her own life with tea-parties and polite visiting.

Marcus was as good as his word, and took Jake's young wife out driving, in the Park or once, wrapped in furs, when business was slack, into the country, where even at this time of year Beatrice exclaimed at the differences between the lush flat fields and those of hilly North Italy, with their brown sparse harvests. Marcus found her shy at first, but an agreeable companion, and he could talk to her in Italian, which pleased Beatrice as she seldom heard it nowadays. He took pleasure in teaching her the English meanings for the things they discussed; she was quick and apt, and even Jake noted that her speech was improving and that she appeared, despite her pregnancy, to be blooming with health even though it was winter, with damp fogs and cold. Others watched less pleasurably. Strollers in the Park noted one more pretty woman by Marcus' side, and drew the usual conclusions; they would patronise his shop, as it was known to be unique and everyone was to be found there; but his womanising gave them rich gossip, and sympathy was felt for his wife. For Cristina's sake, she and he did not suffer socially; and in any case a reprobate is always more beloved than a bore. Few liked Jake Cray, whose affairs were rightly supposed to be dreary—he had kept a long-nosed mistress out near Barnet for some years despite his second marriage—and he would not be forgiven as often or as readily as Marcus would be. Both brothers continued on their chosen way, irrespective of talk; though Jake tried at first to be outwardly faithful to the child he had married. But it was, as to his credit he never told anyone, like going to bed with a nun; and he soon returned to his old haunts, though not as flagrantly as his brother.

Meantime Marcus would drive Beatrice home, and hand her down gallantly from the carriage. From an upstairs window, two set young faces watched. Maria, as the elder, was the first to speak.

"I don't think they ought to drive out together alone like that. It isn't proper." Her rather heavy face, with sleepy dark eyes that betrayed her Bondone blood, had coloured. "Papa is too good-natured; he ought to put a stop to it." She was in fact jealous at not having been invited.

"I think they flirt," said Annie righteously. She was a stolid child who resembled nobody, except that she had Jake's grey eyes set in much flesh. She was careful with her affections, not even loving her sister very greatly; their talents were too un-equally bestowed. Annie loved instead with passion her friend Sally Mountford, a red-gold blonde creature who came for whirl-wind visits, ordered Annie about and criticised everything. Sally would have plenty to say about their step-mother's carriage-drives with Uncle Marcus; she knew the world at twelve years old.

Marcus returned home to find a letter waiting, and saw with pleasure that it was from Jack. He excused himself to Cristina, tore it open, and then his face changed to an expression first of astonishment, then black anger. He flung the letter down. "The fool," he said, "the damned fool!"

"What has happened?" asked Cristina gently. Marcus was not often angry, and when he was so it meant that he had been hurt. She rose and came to him, but he turned away.

"Read it," he said, and jerked his head to where the letter lay on the table. Cristina picked it up, smoothed it, and read. Presently she laid it down.

There was nothing to be said, she thought. Jack had sent in his papers, had eloped with a young heiress named Harriet Grove, and was on his way home.

19

Luisa Laxton was having servant trouble again; the house had become a byword and it was difficult to persuade maids or footmen to come to it, as Laxton treated the servants so offensively that they soon left, and word had gone round. She resignedly interviewed a young peasant from the provinces, decided to accept her despite her shortcomings, then having made arrangements about paying the girl went wearily to her sitting-room. She had little leisure time nowadays and would have been glad, she realised, of a return to the old times, when she could have driven over to gossip with her sister Margherita when the morning's tasks were done. They had not seen one another for some weeks; she was too weary to drive out so far, and Margherita, free now of her impossible husband, luxuriated in being alone; no doubt it was a luxury.

Luisa rang the bell and when no one answered, went herself into the dining-room to pour herself a small glass of aqua vitae. She had become addicted to a little nip in the afternoons, though of course it was never spoken of and one would not wish the family to know of it, even Laxton. Fortified by the burning in her throat, she returned to her sofa, and sat gazing at the lit stove, noticing that its tiles were smeared; the housemaid had not carried out her duties properly, and must be taken to task; the prospect almost daunted Luisa, who felt as full of troubles as Pandora's box. How fortunate, if she had only known it, she had been in the days of dear Papa, when all problems were resolved for one! Young girls did not realise their good luck. And even a little later, when she had been free to make the trip with Margherita to England, consulting nobody!

The door slammed and Laxton came in; he had been shooting with acquaintances, and was splashed with mud, his boots and trousers indescribable. Luisa bit back the request that had come to her mind about preserving the carpet and furniture; Laxton did not care for such things when they interfered with his own comfort. She had long ago had to admit to herself that he was

238

dirty, greedy, devious and overbearing; indeed she herself had endured more from him than she had ever thought to suffer from anyone.

She looked at him, for the first time, with a dispassionate eye; his sharp nose was red with being outdoors, and he brushed away a drop of moisture with the back of his hand quite openly. He then rubbed his hands together at the sight of the fire in the stove, and came over, standing for a while, his clothes steaming. Presently he sat down and began to unlace his boots. They were thick with mud, and he threw them aside and sat there in his stockings, steaming with sweat and damp.

"Where is the fellow?" he said. "I rang, but no one came."

"He has left."

"Damn it, then someone must clean my boots; you had better do it." He kicked the unlovely objects towards her, and reached towards a box of cigars which stood on the small inlaid table by his side; presently he would light up and puff the smoke all over the sitting-room, not excusing himself or asking her permission. Other women made their husbands smoke in a room set aside for the purpose; Luisa contemplated it, and realised that she did not care where Laxton smoked, or if he smoked at all.

She stood up; there was a certain majesty in her bearing. "You can clean your own boots," she said clearly. She went out and closed the door. Left behind, Laxton was prey to astonishment, some regret, and belated awareness of his own folly. Luisa would have died for him, and he had misused her. He should have been more careful; women were touchy. It was comfortable living here, and he had put it in danger; he must make things right with her.

But this proved impossible; Luisa was a Bondone, and once she had decided on any matter, that was that; she never admitted Laxton to her bed again. They went out together, as the world would have judged them adversely if they did not; but there were no more payments of Laxton's casual debts, no more pampering of his person; he became a suppliant in his wife's house, thankful for small mercies such as food. Luisa began to treat him disdainfully, as he had once treated her; she no longer considered his needs, or in fact considered him at all. He suffered, and it served him right; but he let nobody know his feelings. Presently he put out feelers to ask if he might go back to the office in Brest; the request was granted, and after that Luisa continued as she had once begun, an independent middle-aged lady of means; she went where she would and did as she pleased, and was much happier.

In the following year she found a lump in her breast. She went to a doctor, who told her the truth; she had not long to live, and for what time remained to her went to stay with Margherita, where in the end a nurse was hired to look after the sick woman. By then it was too late to brood over the wording of Luisa's will, or to divert the money left to Bobo. In any case limping Bobo had now two baby sisters, twins, one dark and one fair, whom Stéphanie d'Eute had lately borne to Luigi. They were housed, like Bobo himself, in the establishment of Signora Pazzi, and their father visited them frequently.

Susanna Bondone, Carla's daughter, was playing chess with her cousin Luigini. He was a tall fair boy, already too plump, with his father's nose and his mother's heavy jaw; by contrast, his fairy-like golden curls clustered lightly about his head and his large blue eyes were staring and timid. He was a docile creature, less stupid than his tutors believed, but they had beaten the enquiry out of him; he was a disappointment to his father, his mother did not trouble to exercise her affection for him, and he was often lonely. Susanna, on the other hand, adored him; she told herself that when they were grown up, she would marry Luigini. Did not she know everything he liked, and were they not rivals on horse-back, one of the few pursuits at which the boy shone despite his raw backside? Susanna loved riding, and the feeling of the wind in her hair; one day, Luigini and she would ride freely up into the hills, dismounting whenever they chose to drink clear water from the mountain streams. So she told herself; it had not occurred to her to relate her dreams to anyone; Mamma was dead and Annina too young to understand, and as for Papa, he was futile and broke his promises, and cared for nobody except Vecelli, who had come back again, and lorded it over the household, which was why Susanna had been sent for a while to stay with her aunt and uncle. But Papa was coming tonight to dinner, to meet these new cousins from Scandinavia.

Susanna pondered over the family tree; it was so complicated that had she not been familiar with it as soon as she could understand anything, she would never have unravelled it. Aunt Selina was the sister of Uncle Robert who was the first cousin of

Uncles Marcus and Jake in London, and Cousin Elisabetta—her name was pronounced differently in German, but it did not signify—was Aunt Selina's niece and in some way related to her Scandinavian husband Røs, who had died some years ago. Røs and Aunt Selina had a son named George, who had been sent away to military school when he was old enough, and he had not come on this tour of Italy with his mother and Elisabetta, who had already visited Rome and Naples and were returning by way of Florence. They spoke of visiting Uncle Marcus and Uncle Robert in London on their return, but the tour had been intended to improve Elisabetta's knowledge and they would linger for choice in Italy.

"I take your bishop," Susanna said, and her fingers closed about the figure in carved white ivory. Luigini looked disconsolate: he generally lost.

Filippo was strolling meantime in the garden with Vecelli, their arms linked; it felt as natural as wife and husband. He glanced up adoringly at his *mignon's* tall form. Things had gone very pleasantly of late; no one, not even Luigi had tried to dictate to him or prevent him from again housing his beloved. "We will never be parted any more," he breathed, and Vecelli's lips curled in their thin familiar smile; but already there was a cloud on Filippo's horizon; it had come to him some time ago that he was worth less than his brother, as he had no male heir. If Luigini should die— and the boy looked pasty and sickly, and it might happen suddenly with a fever, or other things—there would be no one, except himself, to direct the future fortunes of Bondone Figli, which his grandfather had founded and which was, above all other things, a family concern. "It is unlikely that Teresa will bear more children now," he murmured, and Vecelli turned his head, the smile deepening; he always knew what Filippo was thinking.

"You yourself could have a son, my dear. Take a new wife, with better fortune," he murmured. The thought of another woman in the house did not trouble him; Filippo would always return to him after the unpleasant necessity of fathering heirs. His place was secure and he could put any future bride in hers. "Marry one with enough money," he said, and Filippo tittered. "There is an heiress coming to dine tonight with Teresa and Luigi," he replied. "She is bringing her aunt, my aunt, everyone's aunt; all these relations! She will inherit the Hanfeldt beer money; I will take a look at her. It might do very well."

"I cannot drink beer," remarked Vecelli. They walked on laughing together, the bright swiftly-fading flowers in the parterres not noted by them; they were intent on one another as always.

Elisabeth Hanfeldt was Selina's favourite niece. From the time when she had been a sharp-eyed pudgy child her aunt had taken to her, and now that she was no longer pudgy she still had wit. She adored Selina, who meant much more to her than her continually squabbling parents had ever done; the tour of Italy had enlarged her already receptive mind; she knew Goethe and Heine and, except for his calculus, Leibnitz; and could discourse on almost any subject. Perhaps accordingly, there were no suitors although she was already twenty-six. She had no beauty and looked like a young man; her skin was clear and her hair a fading flaxen. She had submitted docilely enough to be dressed for tonight in a dove-coloured gown with black bands, which Selina said became her, but her view of herself in the hotel mirror was the same as usual, dreary and gauche. One had to make amends for the defects of the body by polishing the mind. It would be enlightening to meet the fabled Luigi Bondone and to hear his views about art.

They drove up to the house precisely at the time arranged, for Selina was fanatically punctual and considered one minute's lateness to indicate bad breeding. The servant took their wraps, and they were ushered to where Teresa and Luigi waited to receive them. Nothing memorable was exchanged and Elisabeth told herself that Luigi Bondone's wife was very dull and too fat, no doubt with living on pasta. But Luigi himself fascinated her from the moment she saw him. A distinguished man, such as she had hardly ever had the chance to meet! Such a man would have made her an ideal husband; a pity he was already married to that lump. If only Aunt Selina would agree to stay a little longer in Florence! She listened to Luigi's suave talk, and tucked away every word to savour later; his face, with its light lines of experience etched on the flesh, was forever in her mind's eye, even when looking at the other guests who had arrived meantime; one was Luigi's brother, a little man who seemed very ordinary and who was attached to Elisabeth as her partner to take her into dinner, she towering head and shoulders over him. They did not trouble to converse.

The dinner was excellent. Elisabeth enjoyed her food, and ate with gusto, ears pricked to hear what everyone round about was saying. Sometimes when she and Aunt Selina were apart she would write long letters filled with every conceivable thing; Selina kept them in a packet and often read parts of them aloud to acquaintances, telling everyone about her clever niece. If she herself were to stay behind in Italy, what gossip she could write about the Bondone family! She thought she had a drop or two of their blood in her veins, just a little; cousin had married cousin, and when she was alone she would work it all out. "No doubt that is why I have an understanding of artistic values," she told herself with satisfaction.

Her little partner was saying something now, and Elisabeth inclined her head to give him her attention. He seemed pleasant enough, not of the calibre of his brother, but that could hardly be expected. Elisabeth set down her glass and, suddenly smiling all over her bony face, said with intentness, "It must be a great experience for you to be able to see and hear Cousin Luigi daily," and returned her eyes and ears to her host. So that is the way it is, thought Filippo; perhaps, although she is unattractive, this horse-like creature would stay in order to see my brother more often. There would be no danger of reciprocal affection. He himself might do worse, and this mare would certainly breed; but one must move quickly, for Selina's voice already announced the date of their planned departure for England. Filippo watched Selina's confident well-dressed head, embellished with egret plumes, nod and smile to the far side of the gleaming table; her beady black eyes seldom left them, and now and again she would raise her lorgnette supposedly to study the menu, but in fact to regard Filippo Bondone more closely. Carla's widower preened himself; he knew he was handsome still, and that his teeth were good. He began to be attentive to Elisabeth, who answered absently, as if he were a child who pestered her.

The night passed; with the coming of dawn, in the Convent of the Visitation, the novice Maria Dolorosa who had been Hester Fenton was sweeping out the parlour and cells and refectory with a broom. Earlier she had scrubbed the long cool flagged passages. She took pleasure in the hard physical work, which made her hands rough and red and left her no time for tears. It was different in the chapel, where memory and thought would pierce her mind even while she said the prescribed prayers. Luigi's face was constantly before her then, not as she had last seen it, politely regretful, almost estranged, but as it had been when he was her young ardent lover. Already she had begun to pay for her sin; after death it would not be forgotten, and to think of him now was further sin, which she would duly confess, but penance would not cleanse it, any more than uselessly thinking any more about her fair, beautiful hair, which they had already cropped close, so that the silky veil Luigi had loved had slid down to the stone floor, lying there vital, soft, alive, leaving her scalp chilled and bare for the wimple and veil. Yes, he had caressed it often, her hair . . . Now she was safe from further caresses, further occasions of sin. It was after all what she had wanted, had begged for for years, both of the convent authorities and Luigi, that the one would bid her stay, the other let her go. Luigi had been unreasonable for a long time; he did not like parting with objects he had once loved.

She must not grow bitter; that was to disavow her vocation. She must remember him and their child, in the care of that dark dedicated woman, and pray for them to God. She must try to pray also for Stéphanie, who long ago had taken him away. Stéphanie had acted to the end as if they were friends, kissing her farewell when she left Florence for the last time. Now in all the years that lay between today and death she herself must pray and work without ceasing, in order not to remember.

Beatrice Cray, Jake's wife, was unhappy. It was a condition she no longer discussed with Cristina, who had been so kind when the baby, Cristina Laura, had been born and died almost at birth. Jake had also been very kind then, and as a result Beatrice found herself unexpectedly in love with her husband, and bruised by his infidelities, not that he ever made them the talk of the town; but, loving him, she knew very well that he still went to his mistress in Barnet and also, like his brother, had affairs with the shop-girls, whether pretty or ugly did not matter; they were there, that was enough. She must not let herself, as her confessor told her, grow into a jealous and demanding woman; it was right to love her husband, but wrong to harm her immortal soul. Beatrice gave up the attempt to explain the love she felt for Jake, which had small connection, at first at any rate, with heavenly love; she longed for him with all her body, and grudged the times when he was far from her. She had been ill after the birth, and had somewhat lost her looks; now, she tried to remedy them with strawberry-lotion, and even a little discreet paint when at home, under the harsh gaslight. She drove about the shops, saw her dressmaker, and ordered herself new gowns, but to no avail; she could never be sure of Jake. Cristina as she knew had reached a state of calm about her own husband, flagrant as Marcus might be in unfaithfulness; and, accordingly, Beatrice said nothing to her of her own trouble: it would be of no avail to be told to pray, or to have patience and understanding, as Cristina would be certain to do. Beatrice in fact felt that she understood Jake very well already; he was like a brave child, honest, inarticulate, bewildered by the world except when he could be active in it; the fact that he was many years older than she was, and had daughters almost her age, mattered no longer. Sometimes she would go to Maria or Annie in their own sitting-room in the upper part of the house, and try to talk with them if only to practise her English; they were civil enough, having been brought up to be mannerly, but Beatrice never felt that they welcomed her.

So she was lonely, without even the consolation yet of becoming pregnant once again. When she saw from her window a carriage come, and out of it step Cristina in a velvet pelisse and muff, she was relieved; she had not gone to her sister-in-law, but the latter had come to her. They could continue friends.

Cristina was cheerful, seating herself on the red upholstered sofa and looking almost pretty with the colour in her cheeks from the drive. "Marcus has had a letter," she said, "from Cousin William, his sister Maria's son in the north. We have not seen him since he was a little boy, and now he asks if he may visit us in London. Why, he is a young man now; how the years fly!"

Beatrice poured coffee from a silver pot and said nothing. The years might fly for her, too, as they had for Cristina, and nothing to show but a gnawing desire for one's husband, and no heir. She watched Cristina select the pieces of cut sugar to put in her cup; the white hands moved carefully, selecting a first, a second, piece, placing them in the coffee with a little *plop* and returning the silver tongs to the silver basin. The tongs and spoons had each one the head of a different apostle, and Jake had chosen them for Beatrice from a consignment which had come in from

Luigi last month; it was the first time she had used them. She stared at them, trying to take pleasure in the gleaming forms, but could not direct her heart; no doubt the time might come when things would please her more than people; more even than one absent person. But now—

Cristina put out a hand suddenly, her face gentle. "Do not be sad about the baby," she said. "There will be others, and you will be able to watch them grow, and talk. Let me visit you then, to share your children a little."

Beatrice thought of the other's years of patience and lack of reward, and for a time forgot her own dark thoughts. When Cristina left she stood by the window a long time, watching the street, concealing herself behind the folds of the brocade curtain; it was not ladylike to be seen looking out, as Mamma had long ago told her. But rather than feel the room close about her again Beatrice did look, and tried to interest herself in the trees and skyline, the rows of well-maintained houses in the grey square with their mounting-blocks and narrow fanlight doorways, and windows behind which strangers lived their lives. If only she could see Jake riding home down the street, mounted on his bay Sultan, for he loathed closed carriages! But he did not come, and when it began to grow dark she turned away, and sent for a maid to draw the heavy curtains and light the hissing gas-flares.

Meantime Marcus was re-reading his nephew William's letter, which had come that morning.

Longhouses, September 18th.

My dear Uncle, it began,

I hope that all goes well with you and with my cousins. I am writing because I have a proposal to put to you which may not please or interest you, but I hope that it will. I expect you know that I purchased this house when old Colonel Massingbird died; it was in bad repair and much needed doing, so the builders will be here for some time yet. The problems multiply daily.

This is what I had it in mind to write. For some years now I have indulged my own taste for the antique and the curious, and in my travels about the north shires have found several things, especially in old cottages, which often they will part with for as little as a silver coin. Lately I found a unique oak refectory table in a fair state of repair, and again a dresser with lion handles, in a house in Cumberland. There is much old oak to be found in these parts, and although the wood is not at present fashionable or in demand I have no doubt that its excellence will make it so again when the present abominable craze for mahogany has passed. Nevertheless my house is not large, and what I have collected from stables and attics threatens soon to overflow it. I should be much interested in the business side of the matter, if this could be arranged with you. It would of course be preferable to me to be associated with you rather than starting on my own responsibility. You have such experience that you would know at once, were I to bring some few smaller items to London, whether or not they were worth so much pother. May I take myself at my own word, and call upon you? I should like to stay for a few days, but not longer; there is the estate to oversee and I am interviewing tenants for the farms, and must return soon for all this to continue smoothly. Might I call to arrange all this? Might I perhaps call upon you at the store on Thursday week at whatever time suits you, or another near date if this is preferable? I shall be staying at Brown's Hotel and any message will reach me there.

> Your devoted nephew,
> William Cosgood.

Marcus read the letter again with a twitching of his mobile eyebrows; this young fellow was close, and seemed to know what he was talking about. Without further hesitation he sat down at his desk and wrote a reply.

> Piccadilly, 20th September.

My dear William,

I was delighted to have your letter and to have news of my dear lamented sister Maria's son. Busy as we are here we do not forget you in the north, and it will give me great pleasure to welcome you when you come. By no means stay at an hotel, but be my guest here in Piccadilly. Cristina will like to see you, and you must also meet your cousins and Uncle Jake's new wife. We will discuss your proposition at a suitable time after we have met. If you care to send word of your train's arrival, I will have you collected at the station.

> Your affectionate uncle,
> Marcus Cray.

William would bring light luggage, no doubt, and would not stay long; these dour northerners were all the same. If the proposition proved viable, so be it; he himself would welcome the addition of capital to the business, as Luigi's money no longer covered all the expenses, let alone purchases. "Perhaps we may start a fashion in oak," he murmured, to no one in particular, going back to the fire. Later he sealed the letter and sent it off by the servant. He knew a curious feeling of being entertained at the thought of meeting Maria's son again. After Jack's disastrous news, it would be pleasant to meet a young fellow with his head screwed on the right way. As Marcus said this to himself he was nevertheless aware of an almost physical ache of longing to see not William but Jack, whom he had forbidden to visit him or Cristina; he did not know where the boy was to be found at present, in London or abroad, or how he fared.

20

William proved to be a small thin young man with wavy dark hair and the Bondone hook-nose jutting sharply out of his lean face; his eyes were surprisingly full of dark concealed fire under lids that seldom raised themselves totally. He was also a man of few words, and even Marcus ran out of talk and suggested, as a remedy, that he and Jake should take the young man to a music-hall; it might shake the prudery out of him. They took a cab, and on arrival Marcus plied William with brandy; Jake watched silently, sharing in the drinks and turning his head when the act began. The dancer was a pretty girl from Tooting, who sang popular ballads in a raucous voice; the music blared, and even Marcus began to see dancer, lights, and people in an agreeable moving haze, with blurred edges. At the interval between the acts they went back to the bar, and on this occasion William played host and drank and drank, his expression becoming increasingly intent as time wore on. By the time the curtain went up they were still drinking; no one of the three could have told what went on on stage, except that the audience knew the song, and roared the choruses, swaying to the sound of their own singing. By the end, William asked where the green-room was; and regardless of the press of people battled his way towards it, and had to be forcibly restrained by Marcus and Jake, who helped him to the entrance, bundled him into a hansom, and drove him home with Jake by him while Marcus walked.

Next morning William's head was like red-hot plough shares, and when he raised it from the pillow he groaned. Late in the morning Marcus came in, with a magical mixture of his own brewing; he said it was a sovereign cure. William drank obediently, and by the afternoon was recovered enough to rise from his bed; but if at any time a further drinking-session was suggested he prudently refused. Marcus teased him gently about his ferocity in trying to break into the girls' dressing-rooms, but William only smiled primly and made no reply.

It was perhaps not the best introduction to a business talk, but when this was mooted Marcus found his nephew knowledgeable and experienced enough. He had brought with him in his luggage various small objects, carefully wrapped; a pair of seventeenth-century Staffordshire figurines, seated one on either side of a settle, their painted eyes staring; a Sèvres vase, with the history of how it came to be discovered in a cottage in the north; a carved candlestick which Marcus identified as the erstwhile property of the monastery at Jarrow; hallmarked spoons from the time of George III, and a Queen Anne teapot. If Longhouses were full of such treasures, Marcus was interested enough to want to see more of them; he himself might travel north when affairs were less pressing. Meantime, he spoke to Jake about their boon-companion.

"I dare swear it is the first time he has ever been drunk in his life," he said, "and in the ordinary way he is a young man of sense, and knowledge." He regarded his brother's tall fair figure with narrowed eyes. "Would you consider his becoming a part of the family?"

"He is that already."

"Ah, but I meant more closely. He can be immensely valuable to us, and if we let him go he may well set up with some other firm to oust us. Maria will soon be looking for a husband; would you consider such a match?"

"Maria is very young, and has not yet come out in society." Jake was devoted to his daughters, and the thought of losing Maria, who of the two was his favourite, unmanned him; yet he knew he would have to face the matter some day, and although he had not personally taken to the young northerner, it was true Maria might do worse than marry her cousin.

"I will think of it," he promised. Marcus lit a cigar. "Do not think too long, or he may be married off to some raw-boned lass from his mountain fastness. He is, as they say, eligible."

Jake thought for some moments. He was anxious to turn the screw a little; if he agreed to Marcus' proposal, might he use his own concession to extract a promise in turn from his brother? The presence of Jack Cray in England worried him; he already knew where the young man was to be found. If Jack were to come strolling into the store, with his handsome form and face ready to attract all comers, it might be forgotten that he, Jacob Cray, and his children were the inheritors; but, after all, Marcus' notion of Maria's marriage to William Cosgood would strengthen his own claim rather than dilute it. And Beatrice might, this time, bear a son.

"I will think of it," he said again. Marcus' brows drew together.

"Do not take too long. I want to put the idea into the young man's head before he leaves. He must in any case meet Maria. I will tell Cristina that there should be an informal family dinner, to which the girls can come. See that Maria is made to look her best. I have a notion that she may suit our friend very well."

Jake left, having discussed tentative dates for the dinner. He was still unwilling to face the thought of losing Maria to a cold grey house in the north, and a cold young husband.

The dinner was a moderate success. Cristina had excelled herself, or rather the cook had, and William and the two young girls ate heartily. "Who cooks for you at home, William?" asked his host.

The young man did not raise his eyes from his plate, for otherwise they would have fixed themselves, like a traveller who gazes at a star, on the beautiful oval face of young Maria, with her dark hair, put up as it happened for the first time tonight, piled above it and her long sleepy heavy-lidded eyes, dark as treacle, unaware of him, gazing beyond. If only she would look at him, if only he were tall and handsome, with the right words to say! He had already received a hint from his uncle that his courtship of Maria would be welcome. But she was still so young! As one who had to fend for himself from an early age, William felt a protective tenderness, as if he were more her elder brother than her suitor. Was he the latter? Perhaps.

He answered Marcus' question, setting down his knife and fork neatly on his empty plate. There was an excellent pudding to follow; he looked forward to it with a young man's appetite, and the wine had been good.

"I have an old housekeeper, Mrs Tonge, who has been with us since before my mother died. She is not perhaps the best of cooks, but she suffices me."

"When you take a wife, she will remedy that." The celebrated smile had spread over Marcus' face; he felt the shy heaviness of the evening begin to lighten.

"My wife will not be expected to cook," pronounced William solemnly.

Jack propped himself on his elbow and looked down at Harriet,

251

who was still asleep, her bright hair loose on the pillow. He knew that he had never before looked on such beauty; her young face, with the large blue eyes closed so that the dark-tipped lashes lay on cheeks flushed with sleep, had its lips parted a little, showing pearls of teeth as she breathed evenly, soundly as a child. Her skin was like flowers, smooth as milk, not dried and withered like the other women had been in India. India! He and she were well rid of it and of the world, which shunned them now. There had been little to lose; visits and return visits, cards left, white gloves worn, polo played and watched (he had enjoyed his polo), whist, tea, polite dancing annually at the regimental ball. Young girls were brought out there to find husbands, but Harriet had found him; from the moment of seeing one another again they had had time for no one else; the consummation of their love had been incidental. He loved her body, and also her mind and soul; she was his wife before God, as he had truly told her. Lavinia was a pale dry shadow, seldom troubling him except that now he no longer had army pay, any money he could touch was hers. He abhorred this, and had so far permitted Harriet to pay bills out of her own inheritance; but this could not go on, no man of honour would let it happen. Man of honour . . . he, a married man, had seduced a young heiress whom many men would have been proud to marry; she had refused two offers before they met. "I was waiting for you," she had told him, and Jack reproached himself bitterly that he, in his turn, had not waited for her. He should never have married Lavinia; now, he would set her free if she would let him; knowing her vindictive nature and the judgments of society, no doubt she would not.

Harriet stirred, and the glistening eyes opened slowly, to fix themselves on Jack's face. She smiled, and brought up a gentle soft hand to touch his cheek; it felt like the brushing of a leaf. Jack seized the hand and kissed it. She cast her arms about him, still only half awake; they began to make love like two children, lightly, innocently. His hands caressed her face, her throat, her breast, her bare white arms; he kissed her repeatedly, drowning his sad thoughts in sweetness. At the end, though, these returned. "Why are you frowning?" she said to him, and took two fingers and smoothed away the crease between his brows. He hid his face against her shoulder; she laid her cheek against the dark curling hair. He was so beautiful, beautiful as a god, her lover. Nothing else mattered; she was glad to be back with him in

England. It had been hot and thankless in India, with eternal tea-parties and dull gossip about who was to become engaged to whom. How handsome Jack had been in the polo-matches, swinging his mallet from the saddle, his slim waist and broad shoulders turning, swinging, arms hitting at the ball elegantly, surely! She was sorry his polo was at an end; and now he was worrying again about money. He had not had to tell her; she knew; always they knew one another's thoughts. It had been the same when they were apart, with Mamma taking her up to the hill-station for a change of air; she had known when Jack was wretched, and he that she was lonely. Their coming together had been a miracle; they had not waited for the gossip, which would still be buzzing now. Let them buzz; she did not care. "Jack, Jack," she said, against him.

"M'm?" He had turned his face to nuzzle her shoulder; he looked up at her. How handsome he was, with the long eyes opening like buds of a gleaming flower, the brows manly and well-marked, the mouth sweet and full, the chin cleft! What had she done to deserve such a lover? She was far happier here than in some bungalow as its approved memsahib. She would never marry, but live on anywhere at all with Jack; it had come to that; she had seen Lavinia, and had judged her cold and selfish.

"Jack, if you are troubled about the money—which I am not—"

"Troubled? Of course I am. I can't sponge on you, Harriet. I will get me a job. Father will surely speak for me, or my uncle." He grimaced a little; he and Jake were no better friends than they had ever been.

"Go to see your father, at any rate. He loves you, and—"

"Father has forbidden me to see him." That fiat had been undeniable, issued in one of Marcus' rare rages.

Harriet soothed and stroked him with her fingers. "At his own house, maybe, or in the store; but you could see him at his mistress's." She made no prudish play over the name; facts were facts, and she had long ago burst the cocoon in which young ladies were enveloped. "Arrange it with her, and surprise him there. He will be so glad to see you he may forget that he is angry with both of us."

"Not with you, sweet; he is angry because I left the army, and now he has to feel responsible for me."

"So he should; you are his son."

"But he dislikes responsibility."

They lay side by side, he thoughtful, she responsive; he was considering her suggestion, amused that it should come from her; Mantuan Lisa's house would be the best, and she would welcome him because of the old days, in another life.

"He will come here today, as I wrote to you; but he will be cross, and scold me as well as scolding you, Signor Jack."

He cozened her. "He will not be cross with you for ever; he loves you, Mona Lisa." It amused him that she should be so unlike the ideal of the da Vinci portrait, with its remote smile.

She flicked her powder-puff; she was in the act of painting her face, and it was now enamel smooth, the cheeks pink as roses. "He loves you too, but you are a rogue."

"And so are you; we are both of us rogues, and for that matter so is he."

"Tell him that, and see how far you get." She dabbed behind her ears from a little flask; the scent filled the room. At last she turned to face him; her dark brown hair was curled becomingly, she wore a blue silk gown with rose-coloured ribbons, and it was agreeable to be near her. She smiled, the red lips pouting; her eyes were sad.

"And poor Zefiro died long ago. His mother lived to be very old. I cried when she went. I love animals more than men . . . some men." Her glance was that of the professional coquette. She was happy enough, he guessed, with his father. She had never demanded the things other women had, security, a home, children.

"And I love some women," he told her. The smile widened. "You are in love," she said. "It is well seen."

"So much, that my life only began this year. You can understand that, Lisa; if only my father would also."

"Perhaps he does, but he must please his brother and the world."

"Why?"

She held up a finger; a carriage was approaching. It stopped and the street fell silent. "He is here," she said. "Go into the drawing-room and instead of finding myself waiting, he will find you. I shall listen at the door and come in if he is angry."

"May God bless you, Lisa." He rose to his tall height and went out. The drawing-room was full of embroidered furniture with spindly gilt legs, not fashionable in the heavy way everyone liked

254

nowadays. He might have been waiting in the drawing-room of Madame de Pompadour; in the turmoil of his thoughts, the notion pleased him.

The door opened and Marcus came in, unannounced as was his way. At sight of his son he started, frowned, then let a smile break over his face. Jack came forward eagerly.

"So it's you, you damned fool. I might have known; Nell tried to persuade me, and now Lisa has finished me. Ah, God bless you, Jack!"

They were close, his father's long hands gripping hard on his shoulders, his shaven cheek warm against his own. They broke apart, as Englishmen will; but the warmth was still there.

"Come and sit down," Marcus said. "We need not, God knows, be formal at this meeting. How do you fare? Where do you live? You see I know nothing."

"I am at this present time in a hotel with Harriet, and she is paying the bills."

Marcus frowned again. "That will not do. What the devil were you at to get into this coil? I had thought better of you."

"What faults I have came from you. Were I to have the time again, I would act no differently; except that I would not have married where I did."

"Lavinia was harsh to you? I wondered about it. Truth to tell, Jack, it is for money we all marry; it is the way of the world, good or evil. I made a fool of myself over my marriage through no fault of my wife; now you have done the same."

"The past is over. Will you, Father, give me employment in the store? I know some little—" But Marcus was already shaking his head.

"Your uncle would never allow it."

"But I am your son."

Marcus was silent. How could he say to this glorious son of his that he himself had no right to the name of Cray, that all he had was Jake's and must go to him? It was impossible; seated here, staring into Jack's long bright eyes, he knew it was forever impossible. Now Jack was frowning again.

"As long as I can remember, my uncle has taken the place which should have been mine."

"There is a reason. Never ask it."

"But I do ask. Why am I denied my inheritance?"

"I have told you not to ask."

"Father, that is not enough for me; I am no longer a child."

"Yet you have behaved like one in giving up your commission, racketing home with a girl you have seduced, and then expecting me to help you. It is too much; I will not do it." Marcus' face had taken on the gloomy thrust-lip look it had in his few rages; Jack had already flushed scarlet.

"Damn you, I will not be called a child by any man. You deny me my rights. But for that I would not be in this coil, not desperate for money—"

"Send me your bills and I will pay them."

"That is not enough; I have the rest of my life to live, with Harriet."

"Then, damn it, let Harriet support you, for I will not."

The door opened and Lisa came coolly into the room. "You are like two children," she said. "Why do you not give Jack enough to make him independent for his life? That way he will no longer trouble you, and you can please your brother, if that is what you desire." She bent to sniff at a bowl of tiny flowers in a china vase; pinks, heart's-ease and small late narcissus. "Make him a gift, and say no more about it," she counselled. Marcus got up suddenly and gave her a light smack on her neat, plump blue silk behind.

"You are a witch," he said, "and have put me under your spell. What can I do but obey?"

Jack had returned to the hotel when a package was sent to him. He opened it; inside was a square of gleaming ivory. It was the *croce francesca*, no whit the worse for time. With it was a note.

This will sell for a large sum; I suggest you take advice from a dealer, but for God's sake do it abroad. I think it will keep you in comfort. Your grandmother thought a great deal of it; there is a story there, which I do not know and never will. God bless you and your Harriet. Have a care to yourself.

Your father,
Marcus Cray.

Jack took the letter and the wrappings and put them in the grate, where a fire smouldered despite the summer. He watched them burn and Harriet watched him.

"Should you have burned the letter?" she said afterwards. "It proved that he gave it to you."

"It is done, at any rate," said Jack carelessly. He was working out in his mind how much the ancient carving would fetch; the sum baffled him. They would go abroad, as his father had suggested. There would be peace there, and no turned shoulders in the street.

Later he went out and bought a little tree in a pot. It had white blossom which the florist swore would turn to orange fruits. He took it back to Harriet, and watched her pleasure. He would love to shower her with gifts, jewels, dresses, whatever she desired. His love choked his throat.

"We will go away," she said, "and will always be together."

They came into each other's arms, and everything else was forgotten. The carved ivory struck chrome-yellow lights from the sun. It had witnessed many things.

21

"You must consider that should Beatrice bear a living son this time, Maria will no longer be an heiress. It would be better for her and William to marry soon."

The brutal covetousness of his own saying was not lost on Marcus; but he was concerned over having parted with the *croce* and anxious to make up to Jake for its loss, which he hoped would not be discovered for some years, and never traced.

Jake stood looking out on to the feathery spring green of the Park. "I would not want to force her," he said of his favourite daughter. Marcus shrugged. "How many devoted wives have been unwilling brides?" he asked. "The match is the main thing; other matters will sort themselves out." He thought of Beatrice, of Cristina herself; would either of them regret their arranged marriages? Perhaps; but with Maria it was different. Why this should be so was not apparent to him. He went on talking, aware that Jake listened although he made no sign.

"William is an asset to the firm," he said. "He has a knowing eye and sound financial sense. When I am dead he will be of use to you as your son-in-law, more so than anyone else could be; after all, he has Cray blood." The bitterness of his comment was not lost on Jake, who turned slowly round.

"It is good of you to interest yourself in my daughter," he told the other slowly. His speech was often slow, for it was only arrived at after careful thought; he did not waste his words any more than his money. He thought again of the silent, prudent young northerner; no doubt he would make a good husband to Maria, better than some fortune-hunter. And it would—he admitted it—be pleasant to have Longhouses again in the family. "I will speak to her," he said.

"She may beguile you with tears," replied Marcus, knowing women. "Let Cristina speak, or Beatrice."

"Beatrice is too young," replied Jake stiffly.

Maria's tears duly flowed, nor did they cease when William Cosgood journeyed south to make her his bride. She went to church red-eyed, despite Beatrice's having put her arms round her in a sudden shedding of the shyness she had felt since first meeting this beautiful stepdaughter of her own generation. Her warm gesture met with no response; Maria jerked herself away.

"Papa wants to be rid of me," she said, "because you are going to give him a child."

Beatrice flushed; discussion about pregnancy by young girls was not customary. "That will make no difference to his love for you," she said gently. "Do you doubt him? He is as fond a father as I have ever seen."

"Yet he is sending me away from London, and all our friends."

"You will make others," said her stepmother. "And William will sometimes permit you to journey south with him, I am certain." But she did not dwell on the subject of William; whenever he was mentioned Maria burst out into fresh crying.

The wedding took place. It was remembered for the beauty of the bride despite her tears, for Jake's handsome presence as he guided her to the altar, for the bridegroom's dapper looks— William was never slovenly and his cravat, in fact, was a miracle today—and for the sly wit of Marcus' speech afterwards at the wedding breakfast. The guests and the plain young bridesmaids, Annie Cray and a girl named Elizabeth Tallant, watched and listened, perhaps catching the occasional overtone of bitterness. Marcus had just learnt that, in Florence, Carla's widower Filippo was to be married again, to that German cousin of Selina's.

William and Maria were seen off on the train to Longhouses. After the guests had left Marcus turned to Jake. He did not need to say what was in his mind; even slow Jake felt likewise.

"The little rat poisoned Carla, I'm certain of it, the same way he killed her dog. I wish him small joy of his fat German bitch." Marcus had not encountered Elisabeth Hanfeldt, but during a visit of Selina's to England some years back he had been shown a faded photograph of Elisabeth as an infant; in fact, it greatly resembled Elisabeth as she would be in old age, not as she was at present. She would take up her full share of the bed, Marcus thought flippantly, relieving his sad mind; Filippo would be rolled out. Where would the minion, Vecelli, sleep? For Carla had told Marcus everything; he plunged again into a kind of fierce gaiety, pledging the departed couple deeply, talking feverishly. Jake stared at him and the thought came that his brother did not look well; his face had a leaden colour and the lines were etched more deeply than usual between nose and mouth. A sudden burst of affection rose in sombre Jake for his half-brother, remembering his loyalty and generosity over the years. Jake's own sadness at parting with his daughter receded. Maria would be well looked after, and her future was secure. Her sister also must be married soon, no doubt; how quickly time went by, and how difficult it was to think of plump little Annie as more than a child! As chief bridesmaid today she had been in no danger of outshining her sister's beauty.

Beatrice came to him, ready to be driven home. He gave her his arm and they bade Marcus farewell. After they were in the carriage the young wife turned to her husband.

"I think," she said, "that Marcus is going to be ill. Cristina was looking anxious at the wedding. Is there anything we should do?"

"We must wait, that is all," he told her. The thought of the child she was carrying warmed him, and he took her gloved hand. Perhaps sooner than anyone had thought a possibility both sad and glorious would come; he would inherit the House of Cray for himself and his son.

"A husband," pronounced Selina Røs, "is never negligible."

She was seated before the mirror in the best bed-chamber of the Florentine house, where they had been invited to stay after the formal announcement of the betrothal of Filippo and Elisabeth. The latter sat coolly in her chair, ready dressed for dinner, Filippo's ring, an antique setting of sapphires, on her finger for the first time: it had had to be enlarged at the jeweller's. She sat, placid, German, less monumental than she would in time become; only her eyes were alive. Filippo was nowhere in her mind, but Luigi was. She looked forward, once the unpleasantnesses of marriage were overcome, to seeing much of Luigi, hearing his talk and letting him hear hers, which, as she reminded herself, he had not yet done, as an unmarried woman was expected to remain silent. It would be beneficial to both their minds; how shut away she had been at home, seeing no one! Now all the world would be met with here, everyone who mattered in the world of art, and also many rich who needed guidance in their choice. She would gladly assist Luigi in such ways. She had improved her knowledge in museums and galleries since coming to Italy, and could, she was certain, tackle all comers. Perhaps she might even be asked to work in the office as the wife of Enrico Bondone had done. Her own husband did not matter.

If she had known, Luigi himself, not yet home after office hours, sat drinking coffee with Signora Pazzi in the children's house, watching his little lame son by Stéphanie walk towards them, hardly stumbling. "You have done wonders with him, *signora*," he told her eagerly, still with his golden eyes fixed on his boy, while the fathomless ones of the *signora* surveyed him in his turn. She was deeply concerned about Luigi's immortal soul, and had taken counsel from her confessor; she must do everything, the priest said, to bring Bondone to an awareness of his state of sin, and if possible induce him to return to his wife. But that could not yet be done by words; prayer was the answer, and even at this moment Francesca Pazzi prayed for him.

As if he had been aware of some unspoken quality in the silence, he turned to her, spread out his hands, laughed, and began to talk of Filippo's Elisabeth. "My brother is to marry a young German fräulein—I doubt if the word describes her aptly—who thinks herself a combination of Minerva and Brünhilde. It is not possible to evade her tongue; she talks constantly, endeavouring to improve one's mind, while one closes one's ears." In this he was somewhat unjust to Elisabeth, whose talk was neither incessant nor always dull; she had considerable repartee, but in Luigi's eyes this was a gift only for beautiful women.

He looked at the *signora*. She was not beautiful, and yet he did not grudge her her wit. Only lately he had begun to realise the full extent to which he depended on her; it did not only concern the children now, but also himself. She was wise, and any advice he took from her would be honestly given and received, he was certain. Why had he grown so involved with Stéphanie? They would have been refused communion at Easter had they not separately confessed beforehand and lived apart for some time. Yet of what purpose to repent only for the time being, intending, when it was convenient, to return to the state in which one had previously been?

He sighed. "If only you knew my mind!" he said. "It is full of dark thoughts."

"Turn to God. He is the only Light," replied Francesca Pazzi, her dark eyes compassionately resting on this man who once had resembled a god, and who was still alert and handsome; but she steeled herself against the temptations of the flesh. Luigi had, in fact, asked her to become his mistress once, but Francesca had declined gently; she would not be merely one more in a procession of women.

22

At first, Maria loathed Longhouses and her marriage. It had taken her away from all her friends and everything she knew, and she had made up her mind that she disliked her husband. At the first sight of the low, grey flint building with its courtyard and barns, and the fantastic shapes of the Cumberland mountains thrusting suddenly against the sky to the west, she was frightened. What sort of people lived here? But she had been brought up to disguise her feelings in public, and was able to greet the assembled servants graciously, so that William was pleased with her. The servants became devoted within days, except for old Mrs Tonge, who would have been jealous of any wife of William's. Early on, Maria tried to change the courses at breakfast; she had been accustomed, when she came down in the mornings, to the sight of cold ham elegantly carved, grilled kidneys, kedgeree or bacon and eggs in a hot silver dish, and coffee steaming. But "Mr William always likes his porridge," she was told, and porridge it remained; Maria was still too much in awe of her silent little husband to approach him directly on the matter.

For the first few days it rained, which made everything worse. William rode off to see to his farms, and Maria, left alone and unable to go out in the garden for the wet, stood gazing forlornly from the windows. These were small, white-painted in the two-foot-thick walls, the latter built centuries ago; Longhouses had withstood invasion, fire, attack, civil war, change. Nowadays the garden lay well-tended and green, the lawn following the shape of the west wall; there was a ruin nearby with an arch above the gate, where later William would tell her there had once been a bishop's garden. He had tried to follow the traces of it and had succeeded well enough; there were more flowers in the dug beds than in the bishop's day, delphiniums in summer, great red and orange poppies, ox-eyed daisies, lupins, sun-flowers, all protected from the winds by the stone wall. Maria wondered if, when the weather grew dry, she might pick some lavender to bring into the house and put among the linen; but perhaps that would invoke the wrath of Mrs Tonge. Downing her thoughts, she turned away timidly into the rambling old dwelling, finding half-stairs, floors on different levels, all manner of gradual growth and building over the generations and, lately, to William's order, so that a part of the house was new. Yet it had no style in particular except its own, in the everlasting flint, like the long dykes outlining the fields in which hill sheep grazed. Grey, forever grey, this north country; even the sky full of rain. She fought back tears of loneliness and made herself study the portraits that hung on the low walls. Most were stiff and bad, having been done hastily for a fee by travelling brodmen. There was, however, one which intrigued her, of a young girl with an oval face and eyes like a startled deer. She was gazing at this when William came in. She had not heard him come, and was alarmed to hear his voice so close behind her.

"That is our great-aunt Elizabeth, Robert Platen's mother, who married and went to live in Edinburgh. She was a great beauty."

He had taken her hand, and she felt his warm grasp not unpleasantly; he had already dried himself and changed after the ride out in the rain. He led her to another portrait. "That," he said, "is poor Mary Cray."

"Papa told me of her," she said in a low voice. Mary Cray had been accused of killing her husband and eloping with her accomplice; perhaps she had found Longhouses grey too. The truth of the crime would never be known now. Maria gazed up at the long secret eyes and long hands. It was not a happy face. Would her own portrait, showing only unhappiness, hang on the walls here long after she was dead? She shivered.

"What is the matter?" asked William gently. His handling of her had, she admitted, been gentle always; no need to blame him for her own dislikes, her loneliness. He had lived here alone since he was a little boy.

She felt his touch soothe her, as though she had been a scared animal. "It is strange for you here at first, I know," she heard him say. "But I hope you will come to love Longhouses as I do. I can hardly bear to be away from it, even for a few days. I take pride in the fact that I have Cray blood and that that is our great-great-grandmother's likeness on the wall. Perhaps I am too proud and have been too long alone. But I like to think that, in the end, you will have been as happy here as I."

264

"I will try," she said shyly; the colour had risen in her cheeks. It had suddenly been borne in upon her that she need not hate William. The dour silent stranger who had come to London was different here; this was his place, his home.

After having achieved the triumph of Elisabeth's wedding, Selina returned to her not very much enlivened existence in Stockholm. Her husband Røs had left few memories behind him, and their son George had recently taken his examinations in the army. His reports promised that he would make a good officer, but Selina, lacking her other diversion, was suddenly awakened to the fact that as a person George left much to be desired; he was completely unpolished, and however good an officer he might be she despaired of turning him into a gentleman. Perhaps a suitable wife might save him; she remembered that Jake Cray's younger daughter was still unmarried, and accordingly wrote to her brother Robert Platen to beg of him that he invite George soon for a visit to England, to widen his field of experience.

George arrived, and Robert, whose own household was so crowded that he could not conveniently accommodate the young man and had rented him a flat in Kensington, welcomed George after his fashion. He himself was beginning to fail; the old head-wound troubled him and a sore on his leg, also from the days of the Crimea, had opened and made him more cantankerous than ever. He begged Marcus and Jake to make the visitor at home; unfortunately, George knew scarcely any English and on being invited to dinner at Marcus and Cristina's house, immediately laid hands on the parlourmaid. The girl's cries of alarm led her mistress to separate them and tactfully pour the visitor a glass of wine, which engaged his attention for the moment. Gentle Cristina had overcome the monster, but Marcus could not thereafter endure the young man near him, and was discouraged even from attempting, as he had done with William a year earlier, to take George Røs to the theatre and make him drunk; he was bad enough sober.

He and Annie had to meet, and that young lady, occupying a senior place in the household now that her sister Maria had left for Longhouses, surveyed him without attraction, and was even overheard to remark to her bosom friend Sally Mountford that he stank. As for George himself, his small brown eyes roved once over Annie and told him he did not want to go to bed with her;

265

so the pair parted, never to meet again, but for almost a year Sally kept Annie in hysterics with imitations of their bearlike Swedish visitor, and everyone giggled when George was mentioned at all. After he left Robert fell ill, not from grief, and grew worse, so that his son and little daughter were at last called to his bedside and also, after the matinée was over, Peggy Williams, weeping openly for the man who had been everything to her except a husband. Robert died peacefully, and one more Cray household was broken up; the actress went on tour in the provinces, leaving little Roberta in the care of Cristina. Roberta's half-brother Dudley was at school, and would visit Piccadilly in the holidays; it was almost as if Cristina had some family of her own at last, and in old age she would recall their happy times together wistfully.

Others were more fertile than she. That autumn, Beatrice gave birth to a healthy son, with his father's fair hair and her own dark eyes; he was called after Marcus, and, as he grew and toddled and talked, other diminutives were found in order that there should be no confusion; Marco, Marcello, Marcel. In the end the last name prevailed and during his short life his uncle, his aunt and his parents doted on Marcel, who was both beautiful and clever. Jake had a miniaturist, the rage of the day, to paint the child in a pale-blue coat edged with swansdown; the great dark eyes looked out from the ivory apprehensively at last, as if presaging disaster.

It came, and for avoidable reasons. Annie fell ill with measles, and to relieve her misery—she knew she was no beauty, and to be covered with a rash all over one's face as well was too much— Jake, a good father, used to visit her daily, kiss and play chess with her. It could not have been foretold which visit from there to the baby's nursery spelt the doom of Jake's little son. Marcel became ill quickly, wilting like a pale flower; the measles had turned to pneumonia and the child's agonised breathing could be heard all over the house. Beatrice wept by his bed; Annie, now convalescent, prayed for him, for she was devout in her way; Jake reproached himself bitterly, but to no avail. The little boy died shortly after he had learned to walk; his attenuated body—the bones had grown swiftly, seeking to provide enough blood-cells to combat the disease which was suffocating him—measured as much as that of a boy of ten years; when the earth was removed for the coffin the funeral had to wait while they extended the dug

266

pit further. So passed Jake's heir; and for a long time Jake himself was quietly desperate, almost seeking to lose himself in the same oblivion that had overtaken Marcel.

As for Marcus, his own health was shocking; he had spent much of the summer in bed, which irked him, for he liked nowadays to pass as much time out of doors as he could, away from the stuffy office. Once when he seemed very ill Cristina asked him if he would not let her send for Jack, who was still in the country; but he shook his head, and turned his face away.

"I have said goodbye to him," he told her. "We have nothing left to say to one another; he has his life, I mine."

Lavinia was of course in England by then, making the Home Counties buzz with gossip about her absconding husband and his wanton heiress. The girl must be most improper, everyone said; nobody would invite the couple anywhere or acknowledge them did they show their faces; but they did not.

If anyone had known, they were at Longhouses. Jack had ridden there on a winter's night, the snow blinding him and his horse; it was bitterly cold. He urged his horse on, concerned less with the weather than with Harriet, whom he had left very ill at the inn. Her mother was with her; he grimaced a little. Lady Daphne Grove had come to join them a month ago; she did not care what the world said, she told them, but wanted to be near her only child. Harriet and he had made the best of it; Mamma had been instrumental in saving the failing inheritance by shrewd bargaining and management while Harriet was a child, and by now it had been turned from a liability into a respectable portion. For that they owed her gratitude, and now they showed her courtesy; after all, there was less open curiosity and perhaps insult for Harriet than when Jack and she had travelled alone.

But her state now gave him anxiety. The doctor had come, and in a raw northern burr had ended by saying what all the rest had, that he had seen the disease before but could not cure it. It took the form of a bad headache, a blurring of the eyes and tingling in the limbs; Harriet felt weak, and had to stay in bed. Jack had watched tenderly by her for as long as he might, then left her mother with her; it was urgent to see William Cosgood, and he would not be gone long. But the blizzard had come, and now Harriet would be anxious. Jack cursed the weather, and was thankful at last to see the yellow lamps of Longhouses muffled in snow. Dark was already falling although it was not late. He hoped William would give him a bed for the night, if no more; but he also wanted advice. He left his grip on the rein for instants while he assured himself of the presence of the *croce francesca*, well wrapped and protected in soft leather, inside his coat.

He drew up in the yard, and already there was a stirring in the house, as if the softened sounds of the horse's hooves in the snow had been heard by sharp ears used to them. A door opened, emitting a shaft of warmer yellow light, and the small spare figure of William showed beyond, black against it, mottled by the intervening snow. Jack gave the reins to the groom who had come out, and dismounted easily, feeling his soles land hard on the grit which must have been ready laid; William ran his house efficiently. He shouted, thrusting forward against the snow. Within moments, his cousin had gripped his hand.

"Come in, Jack, come in," William had recognised the tall figure at once, although they had not met since childhood: he took Jack's sodden hat, scarf and coat, shook them and gave them to the waiting servant. "The horse will be rubbed down," he said, "my groom is knowledgeable. For yourself, come in to the fire. Have you eaten? No? Well, there is supper here."

Maria had been seated by the fire, and on Jack's coming into the room rose, and shyly kissed him. He felt none of the withdrawal to which he was used nowadays, as a pariah. William's wife had grown in beauty until her skin and dark eyes glowed with it; she was dressed plainly, like a countrywoman; he thought she seemed very happy. William himself was pouring wine from a chafing-dish which sat by the fire. "We mulled it this very evening," he said, and gave Jack his cup. He drank down the warm spiced stuff gratefully; he had not known he was so cold.

"How glad I am to see you!" he exclaimed with truth, and then, setting his cards before them at once, and flushing a little, "I have left Harriet and her mother at the inn. Harriet is ill. She is being cared for, but I—I had a thing to ask of you."

Maria had made a little gesture with her hand, and looked at William; Jack saw the look and interpreted it. William would not permit his wife to visit his, Jack's, mistress; that was unthinkable. She would send comforts to Harriet, no doubt. But William spoke, his dark glance steady.

"You must all of you come and stay here with us, till the weather improves. These snows can last for many weeks. We will send the carriage with hot bricks tomorrow, and bring the ladies over."

"But—" Jack gestured helplessly; what of society and its verdict? Part of his reason for travelling north was to escape, for Harriet's sake, the coldness and ostracism they had met so constantly in the south. It would be no different here yet, and anyone who sheltered them would be included in the ban. He could not compromise William and Maria so. He tried to speak of it; but William, with a moment's imperious raising of one fine hand, stopped him.

"Nobody will call here till the winter's out; we may enjoy one another's company till then. Maria longs to talk with you; it is dull for her here in the short days, with only my company and the snow."

Maria smiled and looked at him, with a sparkle in her eyes Jack noted; he divined correctly that it had not been dull at all.

William had strict notions, and would not in the ordinary way have entertained a man and his mistress in the company of his wife. But in the present instance other considerations arose, and he had known that they would do so from the first instant of beholding Jack's tall dark figure in the snow.

In the first place, he remembered his mother clearly, though she had died when he was a child; and he recalled her saying in his presence—perhaps he had been too young to be noted—that poor Grizel Dalgleish had never achieved her due recognition as Uncle Marcus' first wife. As one living near enough the Border to be acquainted with the Scots custom of handfasting, William understood more of all this than most people aware of the story. Also, he travelled up and down the country on behalf of the firm of Cray, and in so doing, and at the farm-auctions which he also attended, heard a good deal of gossip, some of which he had already garnered in his mind like grains of gold in sand. He knew, for instance, that Lavinia, Jack's wife, had made her husband miserable, and had driven him to other women or at least a woman; the everyday happiness of William's own marriage now made this clear. However, he had a source of guilt of his own; when last in London, he had been unfaithful to Maria, and moreover knew that it might happen again.

She had begged him, while in town, to call on her two great childhood friends, Frances and Betty Tallant, one of whom had been her bridesmaid. They were orphaned, and lived alone now with a servant; left to themselves they would have drifted into old maidhood, for they had not much money. But Betty's sharp mind had found an exact echo in William's; together they had discussed everything under the sun from current news to philosophy. His long lonely childhood had accustomed him to the company of books, and Betty likewise had her beloved authors, Fielding, Browning, Jane Austen, Shakespeare, Thackeray; they would sit talking far into the night, their eyes fixed on one another. Betty happened to be plain, with a squint in one grey eye. It would have seemed incredible to fastidious William that so soon he would fall into, or rather on to, a bed with any other than Maria. Afterwards he did not know why he had done it, lying confused, bewildered and stunned against Betty's flat thin chest. There was nothing womanly about her and, as a man devotedly in love with his young wife, he should not in any case have found himself where he was. He and Betty had parted without embarrassment; she had not tried to hold him or detain him. But he knew he would go back again; that was the worst of it; in the meantime he redoubled his tenderness to his wife.

They should have been ideally happy, except for his lapse and the fact that Maria last year had had a miscarriage and the doctor who had been called had said he feared she might never now bear children. That caused her great sorrow; William did everything he could to cheer and divert her, buying a pianoforte at an auction so that she could play at Longhouses, having water-colours sent from Newcastle so that she might paint. Such things must hereafter take up his life and hers; he knew she was happy enough, with at present no inkling that anything had gone wrong. Accordingly, he was glad to welcome their cousin, handsome Jack Cray, despite his shocking reputation; very soon, however, William was to love Jack for himself.

They spent an idyllic few weeks together, William and Maria, Jack, Harriet and the latter's mother, who tactfully retired to her room often and left the young people to themselves now Harriet had recovered from her dangerous turn at the inn. The snow did not stop, and the long low house became a fortress against the cold world, with log fires blazing and hot food ready, chestnuts hissing in the fire and much wine. They would grow merry with it, seated over the hearth discussing life and death and people and love and art. There was a painting on the wall by a Dutch artist now, showing parrot tulips, hydrangeas and roses in a jar; Maria said William knew how much she loved flowers and had promised that she should have them even in winter, and there they were. Sometimes she would go to her pianoforte and play— she played very well—and one night Jack and Harriet got up and waltzed to her tune, with William, smiling over his wine, watching his wife's flying fingers. The dancers were worth watching besides; Jack had been the finest dancer in his regiment, and Harriet's beauty bloomed against the harsh cold without. They moved together as one, while the easy music played on. It was a moment snatched from time.

Another day Harriet waited indoors advisedly while Jack took Maria, with William's approval, to learn to skate on the small nearby tarn, which had frozen hard. She stumbled at first, then soared into a glide under his expert teaching. They advanced hand in hand, skimming like birds, able to talk together now that the first difficulties were overcome. Maria smiled beneath her fur-trimmed hood, and said, "You never knew it, Jack, but when we were young I was a little in love with you. I never told anyone till now," and looked up at his tall magnificent figure, superb on the ice. Jack did not smile; a child's love must have hurt. "Your father would not have liked that," he said in a low voice. "He has never been my friend."

They fell silent, picturing stubborn, stupid, handsome Jake at whatever pursuit he now followed; accounting meticulously in the store—all debts were paid; going out later to visit his women who were always ugly, Marcus had used to say in jest; coming in again to his wife and children to be courteous and kind. "He is like Uncle Marcus in ways, and yet quite different," said Maria. They both knew why; Jake had not a vestige of his brother's charm and humour.

"How is Uncle Marcus?" she asked, gliding alone on the ice. "We heard that he had been ill."

She staggered, and Jack seized her hand. "Better, I believe; I have not seen him." He spoke absently, and she could not have guessed, from his tone, how greatly he loved and missed his father. To be back in the old days, able to stride into the office when he could! But it would never happen now; too much had come between.

They unstrapped their skates as dark began to fall, and

returned to William and Harriet. William in fact had gone out, making his way through the snow to an appointment with an auctioneer, who said he had plenty of interesting stuff, old tables and chairs and the like, coming up next week for twopence halfpenny, as nobody here cared for them. "William will never miss a sale," said Maria proudly. She smiled. "I believe he would battle his way through the worst weather in the world, or if he were dying, not to be done out of a bargain."

She held her head high, her cheeks still flushed with late exercise. She admired as well as loved her husband, and knew his value to the House of Cray.

William and Jack had discussed the *croce francesca* early in the stay; it had lain exposed, gleaming almost strawberry-colour in the pervading firelight, while the two men brooded over it. William did not know its history; but he recognised it as very old, probably tenth century; his beautiful hand caressed it gently.

"I want to know where best to sell it," Jack said. "Father gave it to me, and I must turn it soon to money; you and Maria are keeping us now, but I had planned to go north later, perhaps to Ross or Sutherland, where we could take a house; no one will know us there."

William was wisely silent, his thin mouth tucked in at the corners; even in Ross and Sutherland there would be gossip, judgment, unkindness. He said aloud, "There is one man to whom you must take this first, Piet Herrema of Amsterdam. He is the great authority on tenth-century carving. I have met him, and will give you a letter. You should go as soon as the weather clears: the earlier the better."

Harriet said she would not leave Jack to go by himself to Amsterdam. "I am well again now, of course I am!" she protested, her hair gleaming gold in the firelight, her round cheeks flushed as peonies. "Let me come with you; we might take a little house somewhere, stay there for a while." Her ideal of happiness now was of some little house, and to be always with him.

Jack kissed her hair. "We will go together," he promised her. William and Maria watched them, both aware of the brittle nature of such happiness; one must live for the moment, that was all.

23

Elisabeth Bondone closed her eyes against the bright morning sunlight that filtered through the window, bent down, groped for the chamber-pot beneath the bed, and vomited thinly into it. Then she lay back on the pillows till the next bout of nausea. She had started Filippo's child at once, and the process was misery.

Also, her thoughts were black and resentful. Her husband did not matter; once her state was announced he no longer slept with her and had, no doubt, not that she cared, moved in again beside Vecelli. No, it was Luigi who was the cause of her bitter wrath; or rather not Luigi but that old woman who ruled him.

"She must be at least fifty," thought Elisabeth with hatred. Luigi consulted Signora Pazzi about everything, even Elisabeth's own stepdaughters who ought, if they were anyone's business, to be their father's and hers. She herself could have given advice about Susanna, God knew; but there had been no opportunity, and she had been duly snubbed when she ventured an opinion. In any case the girl disliked her and she could do nothing. But this proposed marriage for the child was blasphemous; only not, as she had been firmly told, her business to alter or postpone. Perhaps the young man would waken up. And this bride of Luigini's who was to come here by arrangement, bringing a gilded dowry from armaments, might be congenial; nobody could know until she arrived. She was said to be plain, and that at least was laudable; a reigning beauty in the house of Bondone would have been too much to bear, especially when one looked in the mirror nowadays.

Well, there was no point in lying here all day; later, she would relieve her feelings by a letter to Aunt Selina, who was always diverted by news of the old whore, the old tart, the old hypocrite Francesca Pazzi. Pazzi! If one had never heard the name, it might have been possible, after all, to see more of Luigi other than on his brief and occasional calls here, or in Teresa's drawing-room where nobody said anything of interest and the stuffy room was in any case too hot, like this.

Elisabeth flung off the bedclothes and went and opened the window, breathing in such fresh air as was available in this languid country. Why had she not stayed at home, where at least she had her privacy and the frequent prospects of delightful trips with Aunt Selina, or at least a visit to her house in Stockholm where everything was clean and fresh instead of the flies here, and the stink in the streets? Aagh, it had been wrong to think of that; it was going to make her sick again. Afterwards she would send for her maid and have herself dressed and laced, and go for a little while downstairs and talk to Susanna.

Susanna had been huddled in a chair, alone with her own misery, when her stepmother came in; she shaded her eyes with her hand to try to disguise the fact that she had been crying again. It was no use, Uncle Luigi had issued his orders, which everyone had to obey, and Luigini was to marry this rich German girl and she herself, who loved him so, was to be married to . . . Cousin Angelo in Milan. They said he was mentally defective. She had tried to plead with Uncle Luigi, pointing this out, but he had only frowned and said Angelo had been born when his parents were too old to have children, and his father had then died and so he had been under his mother's thumb all his life, never allowed to speak for himself. A wife would do wonders for him, and he had already admired Susanna's photograph. And what about old Mariana, the mother-in-law? Everyone said she was unpleasant and mean. To have to live with her and Angelo! To have to share a bed with Angelo, ugh . . . she knew about it . . . and live in Milan, where one knew nobody! If only she had had a devoted lover, however poor, with whom she could have eloped! If this were a story it would have happened that way, she would not have been left to marry a queer afflicted boy she had never seen, while Luigini stayed on here and took a wife. It was that that hurt most. Luigini had said not a word about her, Susanna, or of how they had been fond of one another all their lives. He could never stand up to his father; nobody could, even Signora Pazzi. She herself had plucked up courage and had written to the *signora* at last to ask her to speak to Uncle Luigi, to let her, Susanna, go into a convent if that would satisfy them instead. It would have been dull to be a nun, dull and cold. The *signora* had sent a letter in reply, kind enough. "You love the world too much to leave it," she had written, and that was true. "Do your duty and you will find happiness." That was all very well, but the *signora* didn't understand love, she was strict and dark in her plain gowns with her crucifix, almost like a nun herself.

"Don't sit there crying," Elisabeth said now, "you make me feel ill." Let her be ill, Susanna thought; nobody cared, not even Papa; he was often rude in public to his wife, and laughed at her behind her back. What a farce marriage was, and Mamma also in her time had been unhappy; perhaps wives were always so.

"Where is Annina?" asked their stepmother. The younger girl gave no trouble, was nervous but obedient; of the two, one preferred her today.

"In the garden, making flower-chains."

"Then go and join her; the air will do you good." Susanna rose and went out languidly, dragging her feet. One could not help feeling a little sorry for her, despite the fact that the Milan marriage was so rich; all the Bondone marriages were so; no doubt the only thing they cared about was money. Elisabeth closed her eyes again and beheld against her eyelids the dark silhouette of Susanna's thin form against the greenish gold of the sunlight, going out. The image faded, and she herself was left alone in the room, with its shadows.

Mariana Pelosi was the widow of old Uncle Filippo, to whom she had been married when she was twenty-four years old. That she was not by then spoken for was perhaps evidence of her haughty and sour temper. This she had inherited from her mother, who when she was twelve had taken her to visit a Capuchin convent to inspect the fine needlework of the nuns. Mariana, brought up strictly to wear coarse linen shifts and thick stockings, fell into ecstasy at the sight of the cobwebby silk and lace, so fine that it would seem in danger of tearing apart at the touch of human fingers, yet so strong that it would pass through a wedding-ring. The girl's lack-lustre eyes shone with pleasure, her heavy red lips parted as though in wordless praise. Would Mamma buy something, just one thing, a shift, a petticoat?

Her mother took her home and beat her black and blue. "That is to impress on your mind the wickedness of worldly things; they are of the devil," she was told. It accorded with her previous teaching not to gaze again at anything beautiful.

She was known to have a fine dowry, for her father, the volatile Paolo Villaverde, had despite the expenses of his numerous women built up a small fortune in exporting tomato ketchup and olive oil, in those days before it was general. Nevertheless suitors lagged, and it looked as though Mariana would become one more Villaverde spinster proud of her name, in a life of make-believe. Then news came that old Filippo Pelosi of Milan, who was related to the Villaverde, was looking for a second wife who would bear him a son.

Mariana was duly married. The house in Milan was full of photographs, most of them taken by the father, of the splendid and brilliant Baldassare, the son of the first marriage, who had died young; and of his mother, curly-haired Caterina, the bride of Filippo Pelosi's youth, whom Filippo would never forget. Mariana settled sullenly to the business of child-bearing. The first child died, and the second and third; then she bore a little daughter, the primrose-haired Margherita who had been a bridesmaid at Teresa's wedding. That gave her hope. Next came a little boy, who lived for almost three years; they called him Prospero, and he used to run about with a little silver bell hung about his neck, so that the nurse would know where he was. He was a delicate child with milky pallid skin, blue veins showing through at temples and wrists; when he was dead the little corpse looked no paler than it had done in life. Mariana was past tears; she had prayed to all the saints she knew of, and they had not saved him. It was unlikely there would be any more children. The upbringing of little Margherita occupied her for some years; the child was brought up to be devout, and looked like an angel. Even her father, whose heavy face nothing could coax to laughter nowadays, would smile at Margherita and stroke her hair. He had the photographer take one or two poses of her, to hang on the wall beside those of Baldassare. Mothers of hopeful children still came to the Pelosi studios among the sundials, draperies, aspidistras and hooded cameras which put together would make a fashionable composition to show in a frame. The photographs made much money.

In the last year of old Filippo's life, Mariana fell pregnant again. She did not dare to pray. She endured nine months of hardly daring to move or go out. Old Pelosi fell ill and she had another woman nurse him; she must not strain herself. Finally a small weak boy was born; looking at him, she expected at any moment to have to part with him to God, and had him christened at once. But it was Pelosi who died; the baby lived, and Mariana called him Angelo.

He was not beautiful. He would never be normal. He was undersized and, beneath the silky cap of apricot-coloured hair, his face was long and pale as an almond. He did not learn to speak till he was five years old. He never could walk, let alone run; his weak shambling legs carried him short distances, with support from his mother's arm. His mother in fact seldom let him out of her sight and hearing; to send him to school was out of the question, and when he was seven years old she engaged a tutor for him, an old priest named Father Rinaldo. It was all Father Rinaldo could do to teach Angelo to sign his name, laboriously with the tongue protruding beyond the overhung jaw; his mouth did not close properly. But he had a sweet nature and did as he was bid. Mariana taught him to pray, and gave him a relic in a gold case to wear about his neck, for there was no need for the tinkling silver bell which had belonged to Prospero. She made her days conform to his in all things, having no friends of her own, never engaging in gossip with the neighbours as other women did; she seldom left the house except to go to church across the street. Angelo always went with her. It was his sole outing, except to the garden where he would not be seen. Mariana answered relatives' questions about his health with cold, guarded courtesy; it was soon guessed that there was something wrong with him, and even Luigi Bondone did not press for information or try to see the boy.

When Angelo was seventeen he did a thing which, for the first time, showed his will as separate from his mother's; he stroked the hair of a young girl who was kneeling in front of them in church. The girl gasped and fled. Tears began to run slowly down Angelo's face, and Mariana did not scold him; but the episode gave her thought. He was developing into a man. Would a pretty wife help matters? If so, the sooner the better; she wrote to Luigi Bondone, who sent back a photograph of a young girl with dark hair. Her liquid eyes gazed out at the beholder; her lips were full, her face oval, her shoulders broad, a sign of athletic activity. Angelo was shown the portrait and demanded to have it in his room. He would spend hours gazing at it.

The matter was arranged. In the meantime Margherita, who had been married at eighteen to a young civil servant in Verona, died in childbirth. Mariana plunged her household into mourning and tried to postpone the wedding. But Luigi insisted that it take place at once; he did not add that Susanna wept day and night for the loss of Luigini and the terror of her own fate.

Mariana Pelosi might have no friends, but she had acquaintances, mostly left over from her husband's prosperous days in Milan. One was Alma Terranuova, a widow who of late years had taken to assiduous churchgoing, where she was to be met. She had never been handsome, but had now, especially since she had lost her teeth, aged into a withered anatomy, whose black-clad form crept in and out of the shadows in the chapel, its face hidden by a veiled bonnet which was like a Maltese *faldetta* in its efficiency of almost total disguise. Mariana went to church one day before the wedding, leaving Angelo at home; he would sit harmlessly playing spillikins with himself, taking pride in building small castles before knocking them down. Mariana signalled to Alma Terranuova at the end of confessions and the two black-covered heads bent together in the porch. By the end, it was arranged; Alma would go to Florence, with her fare and expenses paid, and would bring home Angelo's bride to Milan. "It is not possible for them to come with her, as there is trouble at home," Mariana hissed. The trouble was in fact Elisabeth's pregnancy, which threatened to deliver itself prematurely and kept everyone in a fuss. "And I, I cannot leave my son, and in any case we are in mourning." She indicated with a sketchy gesture her black gown, black gloves, veil. Mourning went on for a year and perhaps more; she was having masses said for Margherita, whose careless Veronese husband would have forgotten her by now, though he had been desolate at the time. Men were all so.

Alma exposed her yellowed china teeth in what might be a smile; it was many years since she had left home.

She arrived, accompanied by her night's baggage in a nailed chest, only to take umbrage; the fiacre was sent to meet her, certainly, but it took her to an hotel. Crisis was still prevalent in the Filippo Bondone household. Alma spent the time grim-lipped, saying her rosary, deliberately not looking at the fabled skyline, the campanile, the Duomo, the bridges. In the afternoon of the next day Filippo himself arrived, with a red-eyed young woman on his arm; her clothes, Alma decided, were shocking. Filippo filled the breach, talking happily; his wife had got over her turn, and there was now no cause for alarm. He would escort the ladies to the train; the carriage waited. He took one on either

278

side, puffed with importance like a mating frog; he was proud of Susanna's appearance; nothing could hide the fact that she was a pretty girl and had a good figure, and he had chosen her clothes himself, with the same inspired care he gave to his flower-arrangements. She was not wearing her very best, as one did not do so when travelling by train; but in the trunks reposed gowns, mantles, bonnets that would make Milan sit up, he promised himself; he had tried to cheer Susanna by talking of them, but she had begged him to be silent. It was more like a funeral than a wedding, with this death's-head as duenna. A pity the young man could not have come himself. Filippo kissed Susanna, who suddenly clung to him from the carriage window; then waved as the train drew off.

"The flowers in your hat will not do."

She had meant to spend the interminable journey in remembering this morning; how they had all said farewell, even her stepmother had kissed her, and Uncle Luigi had given her ten golden coins for her purse, and Papa had been kind, no longer trailing after Vecelli who in any case nowadays had a veneer of age, carefully smoothed and held at bay with face creams and powder. And the sun had shone on sister Annina's fair head as she waved goodbye from the house-steps; she was easily upset, and it had not been thought wise for her to come to the station. And everything else was in a flurry because Elisabeth was not yet well; and—a mere ghost of a thought this—word had come from London that Uncle Marcus was very ill. Susanna was sorry about Uncle Marcus, of course; Mamma had loved him better than anybody, better than Papa or Uncle Luigi or herself, yes, better than her own daughter, Susanna. But this marriage would not have been permitted to take place had Mamma been there to speak for her to Uncle Luigi. Susanna had tried to do so for herself, but it was not considered modest for a young lady to express her own opinions, and Uncle Luigi had quelled her, oh, so courteously, by saying that he could not have done better for his own daughter, and that she must trust him to do the best for her that could be done, and Cousin Angelo was a desirable *parti* who was not marrying her for money. A dig, this, exposing the truth that Papa was only the younger Bondone brother, and everything they had in fact stemmed from Uncle Luigi and the firm. But . . .

279

Annina's little plump arms had waved "Goodbye! Goodbye!" And the child had jumped up and down in her white dress with the puffed sleeves, to be reproved, no doubt, by the governess she still had, Miss Pole, who looked like a pole herself. Susanna on the other hand had grown beyond such things and only this morning, for the first time, Elisabeth's own French maid Victorine had dressed her hair, before the little pillbox hat was placed on it, and the half-veil drawn over her face. "It will hide your eyes, at any rate," Papa had said when he saw her. "You have almost cried your eyelashes off. Try to be a woman of the world; nobody in the world ever shows their feelings."

Well, the little hat was pretty, Papa had chosen it, with its saucy perching bunch of artificial violets, carefully chosen to achieve half-mourning for this dead girl one had never seen, so that all of Susanna's trousseau was made up of greys and violets and lilacs, pretty in their own way; but she liked bright colours best. Now this ugly old crone they had sent to escort her—it would have been useless to expect a maid from Fiesole or Florence to stay long in ugly industrial Milan. Elisabeth had said she must get Aunt Mariana to find one instead—now the old woman was making remarks about her hat, which was certainly impudent. She—

Alma Terranuova rose, leant over and twitched the pill-box hat from Susanna's head, tweaking hard with both hands at the bunch of violets. It came off in the end. The girl she was to take back for Angelo had gasped, but it was of no account. Young women should do as they were bid. Alma seized the denuded hat and crammed it back on Susanna's head, pulling it down so that it sat firmly and straight, without charm. That was better. One could not go to a mourning house wearing a bunch of flowers. It was needless to explain; she said nothing.

"How dare you touch me?" gasped Susanna, outraged that this old horror should lay hands on her. She began angrily to rearrange the hat, but her hair had come unpinned; she had to thrust it back anyhow, at the same time aware of incredulous anger; she had never been treated in such a way in her life. If the train had stopped, she would have gone into the next carriage, where there were other people; but it did not stop, and she sat down again presently, her lips mutinous. Dark fell before they reached their destination; Susanna began to be frightened, seeing the yellow lamplight from distant cottages shine out across the darkened plain. But soon enough there was the great cluster of gas-jets that meant Milan station, and running porters who came to take the baggage, scowling afterwards because Alma tipped them too little. That lady would present it all in her expense account, adding some here, some there. One must look after oneself; having done one good turn to the wealthy Signora Pelosi, perhaps another chance would follow, and another.

A carriage was waiting. Susanna lay back against the straw-smelling cushions and watched the narrow streets writhe past, dimly lit; already she hated Milan. She had expected to be taken first to the Pelosi house and was astonished when Signora Terranuova—what a name, fitting aptly the smelly, ugly old creature like cemeteries and death!—paid off the driver outside a church. "Where are we?" she asked. "My cousin—"

"Is here now; did you suppose I would bring you to the wrong place? You must prepare yourself."

So it was to be now. A lamp blazed over the arched doorway; they went in, to be met by a felt curtain with a glimmer of faint light beyond. There was a smell of age and dust. Susanna looked at the place where she was to be married and shivered a little; it was shadowed by now, and the little lamps burning above the chapels and the Blessed Sacrament were not bright enough, with their still, red flame, to let one see. Presently she perceived a hunched shape kneeling by the altar-rail; and a tall woman rose and came to them.

"I have brought her safely," said Alma Terranuova.

"It is well. We will settle up tomorrow."

I might be a sack of vegetables they have bought, thought Susanna. Terror had taken her at sight of the hunched figure, her bridegroom. What was she to do? She could not go back to Florence, she had not the return ticket . . . and yet . . . Uncle Luigi's present lay gleaming in her purse, and she . . .

Angelo turned round. He could not have told what made him do it; as a rule he was obedient, and his mother had told him to kneel before the altar till his bride came, the girl of the picture. Now he saw her, wide-eyed with fear, her dark eyes staring, her hair piled up as it had not been in the photograph; later he must ask her to loosen it, it had been so pretty, curling on her shoulders. What was she afraid of? He himself was filled with joy. God had spoken to him at the altar, as often happened; and here was his dreamed-of bride. He felt the gladness stifle him, lock up his chest till it hurt; he could not breathe for love.

Susanna saw him then, his pale almond of a face clear in the surrounding darkness. She was trained in kindness and courtesy and did not cry out, as the girl in the pew had done that other time when he stroked her hair. She instinctively moved towards him rather than away; as her gaze cleared she saw his eyes, opaque and mournful, with a kind of query in them: Could she endure his ugliness, could she perhaps let him love her? He had been unhappy, or rather had never known before what happiness was, and if she failed him now might never know again, never, never.

She went and knelt down by him. The priest came and they were married. Afterwards they returned to the Pelosi house and there was pasta, coffee and a bottle of wine, but no guests except for Alma. The two black-clad old women gobbled their food like vultures, but Susanna could hardly eat, even after the journey. She had expected a happier occasion; but the house was still in mourning, she had forgotten for whom.

It could not be a marriage. Whatever she had feared in her ignorance, her innocence, it was not this; that he should lie sobbing beside her, his body jerking with convulsions of desire, bewildered, unsatisfied, searing. Presently she took him in her arms, to comfort him; it was like holding a child. "Do not be unhappy, Angelo," she said softly, and was to say it again and again: "Do not be unhappy." She tried to soothe him with prayers she knew, among them some she had learned from Mamma in English, which he would not understand: but the saying of them over and over seemed to relax him, and she went on whispering them and stroking his hair. It was beautiful hair, silky and soft, already thinning on the crest of the head, as if age had overtaken Angelo before he had left childhood; her fingers told her of it. Presently he slept, his head on her shoulder, and in fear of waking him she lay stiffly, holding him, till daylight came; holding him like the child he would never give her.

In the morning Mariana and the old woman came, tight-lipped, to examine the sheets. They tried to extract information from Susanna but she would not give it. They left then, mumbling and dissatisfied, having laid out a dowdy black dress for Susanna to wear. She did not like it, it was not new and smelled of age and mothballs. She would have put on one of her own dresses, but they had been taken away. One must wear black; the house was in mourning. She heard the refrain beat in her mind, accompanying everything they said she must do. She was rebellious with anger, helpless, lonely, and afraid. There was no way of getting a letter home, or to Uncle Luigi; they had taken her purse away and she had no money, and they would supervise everything she wrote. She had never imagined such an existence, and was outraged now. Later would she accustom herself? She did not think so; her thoughts whirled in her head, uncontrolled; yet already she knew that was dangerous. She must be cold and watchful, except with Angelo. Angelo was her only friend; and perhaps the parish priest who had married them would help; they could not prevent her going to confession. But the priest turned out to be enslaved both to Mariana, who gave money, and to Alma, who put in much attendance; and only told her to endure with submission the station in life to which God had called her. Had He indeed done so? She could not see any way in which her present existence pleased God, except that she could comfort Angelo.

"Do you need anything?" Cristina asked gently, speaking to the shadowed bed; the light hurt Marcus' eyes since the seizure, and he could no longer turn himself away from it. The blinds, therefore, had been drawn in the room, and the white starched veil of the nurse who sat there showed as a crisp shape in ochre, her badge gleaming in the light of the fire. Cristina resented the nurse, but she herself was unable to do the heavy lifting needed to turn the sick man twice daily.

She saw Marcus' eyes stare up at her, and he smiled a little; he could still do that. "No," he breathed, "except . . . I would like to speak to Jake."

Tears pricked at her eyelids; he had already seen his sons by Dorothea and Nell, and all the servants, who loved him; and she herself had remained, seeming tireless, constantly ready to carry out his expressed wishes, his silent pleas. The slim young men bending over the bed might have been the sons that she herself had borne him; she knew all about them, their lives, careers, hopes. Only Jack was not there.

She went out, closing the door quietly, and sent for Jake. He had been sleeping in the house, no one knowing when the last attack might come which the doctors had said would be fatal.

Perhaps it had already happened and they had not known, some blood-vessel in the brain bursting silently. He looks very grey, she thought, as if she were speaking of someone else. Life without Marcus would be unimaginable.

Jake came, and trod carefully across the sickroom carpet, as though his healthy tread would shatter any lingering life. The nurse was asked to leave, and rose bristling. "Only for five minutes, then," she said.

"I will go too," said Cristina. She bent over Marcus and kissed him on the cheek. His hand reached weakly up and stroked her face. "You have been good," he whispered, "always very good to me."

"Forgive me," she said, the tears overflowing and spilling down her cheeks. Forgive her for what? The missing dowry, the absent sons? The hand still caressed her and then dropped feebly. He struggled to speak.

"It is you who should forgive . . . me." All of their strange love was in the saying. She kissed him again and swiftly left, weeping; she did not think, after watching day and night for long now, that she could bear any more. The priest had already been. It would be better if Marcus died beside his own kin, his own heir.

Jack should have been here, but letters had failed to find him. No one knew where he had gone. And in any case, she sensed, Marcus accepted his son's absence; they must already have said farewell.

Jake knelt by the bed, his big frame crouching uncertainly; his hand held his brother's. At this moment of triumph he could still grieve truly. Marcus and he had been comrades ever since childhood; there had been his own absence in the Navy, which had separated them. Then that letter; he still had it. He thrust the memory of it away; Marcus was dying, and must be comforted. Yet it was clear that he too thought of the letter.

"You have given me . . . many years in control. I have to thank you. Now it will all be yours. There is one thing . . ."

Jake leaned closer to the bed, his fair greying hair falling over his forehead. Beatrice he had left crying at home; she had loved Marcus for his kindness to her when she came to England as a bride. The death would sadden her. He gazed down at the changed face, some notion of the loss it would be to all of them stirring in his torpid mind. No longer to hear Marcus' laughter, savour his quips! But those had often been unintelligible to Jake, or, he reminded himself coldly now, in dubious taste. There was going to be a change in many things now he himself controlled the fortunes of the House of Cray.

"Jack . . . I gave Jack, to console him . . . do not blame him, it was a gift from me . . . the *croce francesca* . . . he was almost penniless . . ."

And that is his own fault, thought Jake; he had a career and army pay, a rich wife whom he deserted, an heiress whom he has seduced. He stowed the matter away in his mind till there should be leisure to deal with it, but out of pity stopped to stare down at the grey contorted face, the lips which still moved faintly; these words might be the last.

"I knew that when you came to examine . . . everything . . . you would find that it was not there . . . I had to give it to him . . . leave it, I beg . . . cannot die in peace unless . . . you swear . . ."

"I will see to it." His own voice sounded cold and remote in the room, and as he heard it there were footsteps and the nurse was again with them. She peered at the patient. "I think he is going now," she said. "Mrs Cray should be sent for."

But Cristina could not come, half-fainting as she was with grief and crying as if her heart would break. She did not come until Marcus was dead, the harsh dark features assembled into calm and peace. Then she took his hand and laid it against her cheek. There was nothing more to be done for him; her task was finished.

The House of Cray was closed on the day of the funeral, and after the service was over Jake let himself into the darkened store. He went to the place where the inventory was kept, and traced a finger down it. The *croce francesca* was still in its place on the list. He did not delete it.

PART FOUR

24

That October, Luigi's wife, Teresa Bondone, died suddenly of what had been in the first place a mild infection. It was a month in which several things happened; Luigini's new bride, a young woman with no conversation, fell pregnant almost at once, and was to give birth at two-year intervals to three sons, all healthy. Overshadowed by these events was the fact that Elisabeth, Filippo's wife, had borne a precocious and magnificent boy, without undue trouble despite the difficulties of his gestation. The third Filippo was to atone in large measure for the weakness of his antecedents, and it was his misfortune that he was born into the younger branch of the family.

At a decent interval after Teresa's death Luigi was quietly married to Francesca Pazzi at their parish church in Florence. Thereafter the course of Luigi's life took on a less flamboyant character and he was, in fact, not much heard of personally after the year 1879. Francesca, while appearing to be ruled by him, in fact ruled him always; and if his immortal soul was not saved it was at least scoured. As for Stéphanie, she had grown very fat and was retired on a handsome allowance to a house near Pistoia. All of her beauty had gone and it surprised and vexed her that her husband d'Eute, when approached on the matter, refused to have her back. The lame boy Bobo she had borne Luigi continued to be the favourite of his father and his new stepmother, and the daughters grew up pretty and pampered, though respectful. Altogether it was as if a new, less garish age had dawned for the family of Bondone. The tidings of Marcus' death in London added their contribution to the deepening shadows. England was absorbed in the Zulu war, and it was difficult to obtain news from anywhere about other matters, although from what Luigi could judge, Jake was making a good deal of difference to the House of Cray's returns by his diehard ways; Marcus on the other hand had always ventured to support coming trends, which kept business expectant and in good heart. Now, Jake would not even stock the Pre-Raphaelites' work, and confined himself to established artists; paintings with a moral, paintings which told a story, naturalistic as photographs, were all one could buy from Cray nowadays. Luigi shrugged his shoulders; the deluge would come, no doubt. The Pre-Raphaelites did not interest anyone outside England.

He had forgotten by now about his niece Susanna; his mind was increasingly occupied with his own salvation and with prayer. One day his brother Filippo surprised him by bringing a letter into the office for him to read. He did so, and noted its colourlessness.

Dear Papa, it read.

Thank you for your letter. I am very well and so is Angelo. He sends you his good wishes. It has been a wet summer here. Aunt Mariana sends her greetings. Please give my love to Annina. I was sorry to hear of Aunt Teresa's death.

"It is not like her," Filippo fretted. "She sounds subdued." Luigi himself noted the change from the old active, unruly Susanna, forever occupied with herself and her pastimes, walking, playing battledore with her sister in the garden, riding on the hill roads with Luigini or a discreet companion. "She will not be able to ride in Milan," Filippo said anxiously. He had grown long ago into a fat little man, whom extremes of emotion caused to flush crimson and become short of breath. Luigi looked at him with affection; he knew this brother's faults but had always been fond of him. He pondered over the arranged marriage with Elisabeth Hanfeldt; Had it been wise? Yet there was the beautiful son to show, and Filippo had been paying less attention lately to the detestable Vecelli, whom no one was any longer interested in banishing from the household.

"Why do you not travel to Milan, and see for yourself how Susanna fares?" Luigi asked Susanna's father. Filippo threw out his white, plump, manicured hands. "What can I achieve?" he asked. "Mariana is a terrible woman, a dragon. I could do nothing with her."

"Perhaps Susanna can do little herself," Luigi commented drily. He put the matter away in his mind to think of later; in his heart, he knew well enough that it was his own doing if anything were amiss with Susanna.

Jack and Harriet were in Amsterdam, walking together along the Prinsengracht, with its bell-gabled houses reflected in the flowing canal whereon floated dead leaves the colour of Harriet's new gown. It was sharp enough today, with the autumn wind, for her to wear Jack's present of sables, a pelisse and muff. Her lovely face nestled against the soft fur, her hair gleaming under the small close hat. In her ears were pearls, also of his gift; round her neck, unseen now, was a fine gold chain bearing an amethyst shaped like a heart. Moving together, lost in one another as they were, they might have been in Eden. He had never been so happy; even the sorrow he had felt at Marcus' death was like an old wound, forgotten except for an occasional throbbing. At this moment, he did not remember it.

He thought of the merchant Herrema of whom William had told him, and to whom William had written, causing the wise old eyes to linger long at last over the *croce francesca*, the gnarled fingers caressing it. First with his metal-rimmed spectacles, then with an ebony spyglass, the old merchant had looked carefully; all the time his face showed interest and pleasure. At last he looked up. "It is Carolingian, certainly," he said, "a product of that brief, fated flowering. How did you come by it, *Mynheer*?" He spoke careful English, each word rounded like a pebble.

"My father gave it to me," Jack replied. He did not mention Marcus' name; it might be wondered why the head of the House of Cray was reduced to selling such a thing. "He could leave me no money, so he gave me this."

"And you do not wish to keep it?"

"I would have liked to. It meant a great deal to my grand-mother. But I and my wife must live." He had not brought Harriet with him today; it was natural enough to speak of her as his wife.

"Will you leave it with me for some days? I should like to have a full assessment. I will read Mynheer Cosgood's letter more care-fully. It is some years since I met him. He is well?"

"Very well, and his wife also."

It was William's letter, evidently, that gave him substance; on returning some days later, a trifle worried about the hotel bill, he was overjoyed when the old man made an offer beyond his hopes. He tried not to be too hasty in accepting and to purse his lips; but burst into a laugh halfway through.

"I am a poor bargainer," he said. "It will do very well."

Since then they had enjoyed themselves richly; superb meals at

291

gleaming restaurants, visits to jewellers and furriers, carriage-drives into the flat country, with ham eaten and beer drunk at taverns in sight of the broad endless sea; walking about the city as they were doing now, leisurely, without a care in the world, probably eating later at some brown tavern, treated with courtesy there where few strangers went because of Jack's handsome face and bearing, Harriet's beauty. They would go to one now, and then back to the hotel, to make love. Life was good; as for the future, that could take care of itself.

He did not notice, gazing at the tall colourful houses with their stone signs, that Harriet's eyes had closed briefly; but he felt her feet lag, and turned swiftly. "Are you ill?" he said, anxious; there had been no return of her mysterious symptoms of last year, and he had hoped they had left her. She nodded, then said "I will go and lie down, I think, when we get in. Go and have your meal without me. I hate to weary you."

Her eyes had filled with tears of vexation; the handsomest man in the world for her lover, and she had to be ill! Before the tears had come, again, the strange blurring. She was frightened; what did it all mean? When he said they must get a doctor, she made no attempt to stop him; perhaps a good doctor would cure it, perhaps there were cures here in Holland not known in the north.

The doctor came, bearded and self-important; but when he had examined Harriet he beckoned to Jack to come into the adjoining room of the suite they had taken.

Jack was pale. "It is serious?" he said, fear rising in him; if it had been himself it was no matter, but Harriet—

The doctor inclined his head gravely. "I must be frank with you," he said. "Your wife will be able to walk and to live a normal life for a year, perhaps two. After that she will be an invalid, needing constant care."

"She shall have it," said Jack. His heart was beating fast. "What," he said, "what is the illness?"

"We know only that it attacks the nerves, and that symptoms are progressive; that is all. By the end these patients are bed-ridden, incontinent—I will not hide it from you—and perhaps blind; after that the mind goes, and other things. A good nurse is essential. I tell you this because I must; it would be pointless to go away and leave you in ignorance of what must happen. Let her take pleasure in her life while she may; it is perhaps best not to inform her of all I have told you, or at any rate to do it gradually, so that she knows you understand."

After he had gone Jack stood alone, the horror of it poised above him like an oncoming wave, threatening to swamp judgment, sense, everything except the desire to cry aloud, and that he must not do, for it would alarm Harriet needlessly and too soon. Above all she must be allowed, as the man had said, to savour her life, her youth, until . . . what? What would be the next manifestation of the dread thing? Paralysis of a hand or arm, loss of sight?

He could not bear it, and after a quick reassuring word to her went out, supposedly for his meal, but instead he walked up and down, up and down the places they had lately visited together, as though the view of leaves borne away, of reflections hovering in the still stream, were the last of life.

The future loomed; he began to talk of taking a small house somewhere, for himself and Harriet, and her mother when she returned; Lady Daphne was at present in their house in London, trying to sell it and tidying up affairs. Jack knew he would have to write to her; it would be easier than speech. He found a place, a stone cottage near Scheveningen, where he and Harriet could sit and watch the sea that she loved, and the blowing sand. It had a garden, in which grew thrift, yellow poppies, fuchsia, all the plants that thrived in the salt air; hydrangeas bloomed there in early summer, the colour of the sky; pale yellow cinquefoil, milk-thistle, a spiked purple hedge-flower whose name he did not know. He and she would sit there together, watching the sea. She did not question; she merely thought that he was tired of their city life, and resolved to go wherever he wanted, to be whatever he asked of her.

They settled into the cottage in February, and during the long dark nights he held Harriet close in his arms, hearing the sea roar; once it almost froze, and he and she walked the beaches by day, feeling the freezing spray against their faces and recalling the time he had skated with Maria last year, in the far-off north. "I was ill then," Harriet reminded him. "What a bore I am!" She turned to him, and caressed his face lightly with her gloved hand. They returned to a blazing fire of driftwood; a woman came in to clean and lay the fire, another to cook. They were happy, or would have been so but for his secret knowledge. Often she would say to him, "What is troubling you?" and ease, in the gesture that he knew, the frown from his brow with her fingers. He would seize her hand and kiss it, and make some jest, and speak of their walking again together along the beach, or perhaps making a carriage-journey into town; but she was content here, sometimes sitting in one of the great hooded straw chairs the region boasted, protecting her from the wind and sand. The little pot-plant he had bought in London had come with them; it had made fruit in the winter, as the florist had promised.

Harriet had no more attacks of the illness, but the time came when he knew he must write to her mother; the burden was too great to bear alone. He wrote, putting the state of affairs truly and kindly, saying that Harriet would need a nurse, and that nurse had best be herself. He sealed the letter and laid it on the tray in the hall, where the postman could collect it at the next delivery. He tried to think no more of it; the thing was done that had to be done, that was all.

Harriet had come downstairs, knowing him to be in the small room at the front of the house which served as dining-room and sitting-room; the kitchen was at the back. She looked at the letter lying on the tray, and wondered that it should be to her mother, in Jack's handwriting. A certainty that something was wrong was already with her; he had been tender beyond belief of late weeks, handling her like china when she was in fact flesh. She stared at the letter, at his clear upright writing on the envelope; and on an impulse took and opened it, and read what it contained.

He came out presently, to find her still standing in the hall, the letter in her hand.

"You would not have told me? You would have let me become a mindless vegetable, useless, a burden?"

She had turned away, and he followed her swiftly and caught her to him; she struggled for instants, then yielded. He spoke with his cheek against hers, his arms close about her.

"I love you. Do you suppose that it makes any difference whether you are well or ill, so long as I can be near you? Do not mock me, Harriet."

"To be a burden on you is more than I can bear. Before it came to that, I should kill myself. You are to be free to live your own life, not mine . . . not mine, in such a way . . ."

294

She had begun to cry, the salt tears tasting bitter against his lips. He would not let her go.

"In any way and for as long as we live, Harriet. I swear that I will love you no matter what comes. In the marriage service it says 'For richer, for poorer, in sickness and in health, till death do us part.' I would have married you, as you well know, but for Lavinia."

"But death will not part us," she shuddered. "It will be a long time till death."

"I will die with you; little by little, knowing what you feel, what you are. I have loved your beauty, but that is not all; if you were an old wrinkled woman I should love you still. What difference is it, this thing they say will happen? Love is for life. Trust me, and let the years bring what they will; and it may be years, my darling, it may be a long time."

"In which I am to become more and more crippled, less and less a human being. I cannot bear it, Jack, for your sake. When it gets to a certain stage I shall die, and set you free."

"You can never set me free. I am yours till death and beyond."

She looked full at him, all of her love in her eyes; presently she let him lead her into the room, to the fire, and chafe her hands, and make her warm with his loving. The thing she had lately discovered lay like a black shape in her mind; they would not speak of it again, but she had assured herself repeatedly that before she would become a burden on him, she would die.

Lady Daphne replied to the letter, not as he had half feared with hysteria, perhaps with an unexpected arrival, but with the sound sense that she had brought to all of Harriet's affairs from childhood. She would come, she told Jack, in three weeks. *There may still be affairs to be settled here that cannot be done earlier, and if I cannot finish them, perhaps you, my dear boy, will come to England and see them on their way, once I am with my darling.* He would of course agree to go, once she was with Harriet, who must not be left alone. She must never be left alone again. He would arrange all of it.

Lady Daphne came, bringing gifts from London shops, goose pâté, chestnut purée, redcurrant jelly, caviare, tea. They feasted and made themselves merry, and then he had his gear packed, and made off for the port; there were matters Harriet's mother had not been able to conclude, and he promised to fulfil them, then return. He stood on the deck of the boat trying to make out Scheveningen lying behind them in the sea-mist; the latter had rolled up thick and white, blurring the view, as they sailed. He went below while they crossed the Channel; his thoughts were impatient and he saw England again with no great pleasure; he would be glad when the business was done, and he could return. He heard at last the ropes being flung out to the derricks, and felt the ship bump against the stone pier; he took the small valise which was all he had brought, climbed to the deck and went down the gangway with the rest of the passengers. A woman in an elaborate hat had lost her luggage, and her hysterical voice was the last thing he heard.

The police were waiting for him at the exit; a tall officer stepped forward and barred his path.

"Captain Cray?"

"Certainly." His first notion was that something had already gone wrong with Harriet, and that her mother had sent for him, perhaps by telegram; if so it had reached here very soon.

"I must ask you to accompany me to the station."

He went, dazed, with them as they asked.

25

Jake had worked assiduously in the store-office during the weeks that followed Marcus' death, and certain discoveries he made caused him to purse his lips; one was that Marcus had let the insurances lapse. To rectify this would cost money, and also the place was overstaffed; Marcus had been too kind-hearted to equate profit with employment. As for the stock, Jake undertook a wholesale revision of it, and instituted a sales week in which everything he regarded as lumber or in poor taste could be sold off; unfortunately he made a tactical error and undersold a doubtful Caravaggio brought in for assessment by the Bishop of Portland last year. The Bishop smouldered on receipt of the news and would no doubt bring the matter up at the shareholders' meeting; other complaints brewing in men's minds, would be raised also. Jake worked on in his dogged, determined way, listening to nothing and no one. He was in charge at last.

It accordingly irritated him a little to have to receive a visit from William. The young man said he had taken a flat nearby, and was bringing Maria down. "Are you not content in the north?" asked Jake peevishly; he resented having to listen constantly to William's opinions, which were sound and moreover did not always echo his own.

William lowered his eyes, remembering Maria's unwillingness to leave Longhouses, which she had come to love as he did. "Content enough," he said, "but I feel it my duty to be near the shop. There is a good deal I can oversee here, with your permission."

Jake frowned and shelved the matter, and thereafter was constantly irritated by the sight of his son-in-law peering and poking about the store, although William still went on his forays to sales and old houses where he found what was, admittedly, good stuff. Maria called on Beatrice, who after some years was expecting another child, and often both young women, together with Annie who was now married to a stolid young departmental manager named Williamson Smith, would take tea together, and gossip restrainedly. As before, Beatrice felt both her step-daughters drawing close against her; she refused to talk to them of the coming child, and dwelt on general topics of the day, such as fashion, which inevitably meant the bustle.

Repercussions of the sale died away, leaving the shop-floors cleared; Jake stalked through the entire store, ear-marking places for his own selected new stock. He did not delegate his duties as Marcus had done; every least thing would be attended to by him personally, or else he would give direct orders which could not be misinterpreted. The shophands felt as if a stiff breeze were blowing; but they were paid regularly, which was an improvement on other days.

Altogether, Jake was pleased with himself as he made his way at last to the shareholders' meeting. What transpired there came as complete astonishment to him, and he would never afterwards speak of it.

Events began with the Bishop. His weighty presence uplifted itself from a chair at the back of the room, and he began to declaim, inspired no doubt by the loss of the queried Caravaggio, which had not been recovered. The shareholders, he announced, were dissatisfied; dividends had gone down steadily over the past years; this year, with the insurance claim, and the cost of regaining the Frankish crucifix—according to the newspapers—

"That cost will be met," Jake called; he had the comfortable knowledge that Herrema, the Amsterdam merchant, would appear at the trial, having identified by letter the young man who had sold him the crucifix saying it was a gift from his father. Jake discounted the cost of sending out lists of missing property to known agents here and on the Continent; it had found the *croce* again and the law could now proceed. Whether it would be possible to obtain all, or any, of the money from Jack Cray was one thing; but one's solicitor would enquire. He raised his head, and attempted to deal now with the crisis engendered by the Bishop, which threatened to get out of hand. Several people were shouting at once; the disorder was worse than he had anticipated; he tried in vain to quell the storm.

"What we need is a new managing director," the Bishop roared above everybody. Someone suggested Mr William Cosgood, who at least had practical experience of handling stock. William was not present; he had gone into Derbyshire in pursuit of Georgian silver. There would have to be an extraordinary meeting, convened for later on. On this unsatisfactory note they parted company.

Between one meeting and the next Beatrice Cray gave birth to a healthy boy, again with light English hair and dark Italian eyes. The child's father was torn between his pleasure at the birth and his grief that, at this very moment, the inheritance should be denied to the new Jacob Cray.

Jack was also dissatisfied, moody, and bitter; bound to remain in England meantime by reason of William's bail. At least William had not baulked at that; but he had made it politely clear that, owing to the further breach it would cause with his father-in-law, he could not offer hospitality. It was not in his or Maria's best interests, he went on to say; the existence of the letter he had already written Piet Herrema troubled him. He was unwilling for there to be a connection in the public mind between himself and the attempted overseas sale of the *croce*. Perhaps the detail could be overlooked; or, again, perhaps having now attained to the position of managing director of the House of Cray he need be answerable to no one. But that was after he had denied Jack houseroom.

Meantime, he examined the books; and at the extraordinary meeting would recommend the issuing of a number of ordinary shares on the market, to raise capital. Having done this, he went home to tea with his wife.

Maria was pensive. She had put on weight over the past years, and her plump white hands dispensed tea from her heavy tea-service gracefully enough. The flat had been furnished with chosen articles from Longhouses, pictures, chairs, beds. It seemed like home already, and William stretched his legs before the fire comfortably, drinking his tea. "Poor Papa," said his wife suddenly. "It was a great shock to him to lose his position. He had looked forward all his life to becoming the controlling power in Cray, and now there is nothing left for him but to retire."

"There is his son," William replied without thinking. Maria was silent and he bit his lip, conscious of his tactlessness. He rose from his place, set down the cup, and laid a hand on her shoulder and said, "Forgive me for that. It was thoughtless of me."

She looked up at him, this small slight hawk-nosed man who controlled all their destinies. Who would come after him? Annie's husband had not the brains. More than that Maria did not know; what went on in a boardroom was not a woman's business. She smiled at him to show that he was forgiven, took the cup he had set down, and poured him fresh tea. The hurt he had dealt her was thrust back in her mind, and in time forgotten.

Jack sat on the edge of his prison pallet, staring down at the coarse convict's uniform to which he had become almost accustomed. They had shaved his head close, because of lice. He was alone, and rather than feel the walls of the cell close in on him he was thankful for the solitude; it was his one place of partial privacy. Of late months he had none; the memory of them affected him still, like a man who has been stripped naked and exposed to the mockery of the world. They had pried publicly into every aspect of his life. The newspapers had been gratified; an illegitimate—they still made that assertion, which would once have enraged him, but now he was too weary—an illegitimate son of the late director of the House of Cray, that exclusive and fashionable store and arbiter of informed taste: the result of an unfortunate *liaison*, who had been given the chance to make good—that was how one reporter, more egregious than the rest, had phrased it—by being provided with a commission in the Army, and married to an heiress whom he had in due course deserted for another; like father like son, living in adulterous connection with the young woman he had conveniently seduced in India. Living on her inheritance, until, desperate for funds after deliberately sending in his papers, he had purloined perhaps the most valued article in his father's possession, the fabled Frankish Crucifix, whose presence had lent lustre to the House of Cray over the generations since its founding. Villains were fools, naturally, since any reputable dealer here or abroad would have known or at least heard of the ivory carving, which was unique. And far from taking the onus on himself this villain had tried to implicate Mr William Cosgood, a junior director in the store, by getting him to write a certificate of character—of character, m'lud!—to be shown to the most famous dealer in Amsterdam to facilitate the sale. The most famous carving, the most famous dealer; always do business at the top. But the business had redounded on Captain Cray's head when his uncle, Mr Jacob Cray, had rightly and understandably sent out a circular with a description of the missing *croce* to everyone in the trade both in England and in Europe, also, one believed, to the United States, but that had of course been without result.

The defence had been feeble. He himself could have spoken up better, had indeed tried to do so and been called to order and threatened with contempt. "If there had been a bit of writing to show, it would have been different," the fool who was representing him had told him already; but his father had been careful to put nothing in writing—except the letter he had sent and even that letter was burnt—and his father was dead. That they would not take his own word in the matter was evident; a married man who would seduce a young woman of good family was a rogue, untrustworthy and fit only for prison. And they had sentenced him to five years of that; and in five years what would Harriet have become, and he not with her?

That was the horror, the reason why he could no longer endure his life. Otherwise he might have put up with the humiliation of his daily round, the sight of other convicts with their various meannesses and crimes which they expiated—if one could call it expiation, this greyness, this negation, as though one trod a wheel without volition interminably—the foul food, the key grating in the door of the cell; the knowledge, which he found particularly appalling, that he could be watched at any time during the day or night through the square grille that gave on to the outer passage. It was like being in a cage for the benefit of spectators; worse, because they could come without being foreseen. He could do nothing to pass the time, the hours, the days; they would not give him writing materials and he could send and receive no letters. He had no means of knowing how Harriet was or in what way the news had been broken to her. If it had not—surely, surely that was not so!—she would think that he had deserted her on learning that she must become an invalid; and that was the worst awareness of all. It would come to him, unbearably, in the night, as he lay sleepless with his face turned away from the grille, turned towards the wall on which were men's initials and obscene messages, scratched in the paint as they had languished there. Could she believe, hearing nothing, that their love had been a sham, that he had stayed with her only for what it was worth to him, having shed the burden when it became heavy? There was even a possibility that her mother, who had never loved him for himself, would let Harriet persist in so mistaken a belief to be rid of the fact, after all an embarrassing one, that her only daughter had loved unsuitably and had defied convention to consummate that love.

Amsterdam, and the dead leaves on the canal, and Harriet in his furs with her cheeks coloured brightly by the wind. Long-houses, and the enchanted time with Harriet, Maria and William in the ice and snow . . .

William had betrayed him. William could, at the expense of some of his reputation for carefulness, have admitted that he wrote the letter to Herrema willingly, because he believed his, Jack's, statement about his father's free gift of the *croce*. But William had his career with Cray to think of. The judge had seen his embarrassment and had helped him over the difficult stile.

Jack moved wearily. To do William justice the truth might not have altered the verdict, the sentence. To have seen his embar-rassment and to let him go was all of a piece with the screen of respectability cast round everyone in the case except himself, the so-called bastard of Cray. And Uncle Jake, sitting unctuously in the courtroom, had not once met his eyes.

Lavinia had been in court also, her face veiled. This was balm to her, he knew, after what had no doubt been her own humiliation. She had sat in her stiff way throughout, showing no emotion for or against him. The players, the judge, the prosecution, the weak defence, his own impassioned evidence which they took to be the vehemence of a liar and a criminal, and now a bankrupt as well, had been theatre to Lavinia; second-rate theatre. The little while of ease for loving had cost him dear.

"Your father made no offer to employ you in the firm, Captain Cray?"

"No. He had kept the place for my uncle."

"But surely a lesser position, a departmental one, perhaps, or a salesman's? Even this was refused you? I suggest, m'lud, that there was doubt at this early stage of the suitability of the accused to hold a position of trust."

The defence had intervened, saying that was not relevant to the offence under consideration.

"M'lud, I was anxious to prove the dissatisfaction of the late Marcus Cray with his son's character and the unlikelihood that he would have made a gift of the most valued object in the store *after* he had further flouted convention, giving up the career for which he had been trained and causing great distress to his wife." The prosecution's lips shut tightly; even here it was not proper to mention Harriet by name, but everyone knew of the elopement; the papers were full of it.

He had struggled up then, oblivious of the restraining hand of the police. He could not remember now what he had shouted, but they had silenced him with that threat of contempt of court, and the inexorable hearing had proceeded, with Jake at last in the witness-box to give stolid evidence that he had always had doubts of the trustworthiness of his nephew and that his late brother had been brought to share those doubts by the young man's behaviour. That was partly why a commission in the Army had been thought of as likely to instil discipline into the boy, the spoilt boy, himself. He could do nothing to bring down the unassailable position in which Jake stood, the man who had succeeded by his brother's will to the place he now held, that place which should have been Jack's own. It should have been; there was some mystery. His mind could not take the weight of it; there was too much dragging at it already. He knew his father had loved him, and had not thought him unworthy. Yet to try to prove it to these avid-faced people needed facts he did not possess. His cause was lost from the beginning; when the judge pronounced sentence he had heard him dully, only thinking of the length of the years; five whole years. If it had been half that time there might have been hope.

He had appealed, of course. The time had passed in vain imagining, with the knowledge that, in any case, such money as he had left would go in legal expenses. There was no way out of the trap; were he to be set free it would be at best as Harriet's pensioner: Harriet, crippled and dying.

He looked down at his hands. Now that there was no hope he had already thought of ways of killing himself. But they had taken away everything he might have used, such as his belt, to hang with behind the door; there were no hooks or projections in the cell, though he might just have reached up to one of the bars on the single window. There was by now one other way, not pleasant.

Lavinia had visited him. He should have expected it, knowing her predilection for enjoying his suffering; and he was resolved that she should see none. He made himself distantly courteous, hardly looking at her where she sat on the other side of the grille that separated the prisoners from the world outside. She wore the same outfit she had worn in court; a becoming and expensive lilac coat and skirt, with a matching toque and half-veil. It gave her an appearance of cold competence; she might have been made of stone or plaster, except that when she saw his shaved head an expression passed across her face which he knew was unalloyed gloating. They talked of nothing in particular; he would as soon she had not come. Why she had done so was made evident at the end, when she had silently thrust a small narrow object through the grille, leaving her slender gloved hand lying there a moment, in case the guard at the door should look that way; a simple gesture, as though she left her hand lying near her husband's. A wife had the right to visit; Harriet would not.

After she had gone he looked at what she had brought. It was his service razor. He smiled; there was something almost classical in her action, like that of a Roman wife, inciting her errant husband to finish himself off in the approved manner.

For he would use the thing. The method itself had disgusted him, thinking of the pools of blood lying sticky and congealing afterwards in the cell; it was clean now, for he scrubbed it out daily. Someone else could do so, afterwards. He looked at the small square of sky beyond the bars; he had been fortunate in being given a cell which looked out on the exercise-yard, in the interior of the prison. They would find him when they came to let him out for the daily supervised walk, round and round the small yard. Once, not so long ago, the prisoners had been hooded so that they could not greet one another.

He bent his head and tried to pray; but the thoughts would not come. He had seldom taken time to think of God, and now there was none left; they would soon come and discover him. He asked for pity to be shown to Harriet and for her to die soon also: that way she could be with him, if such a thing were allowed in whatever after-life there might be.

He opened the razor; its gleaming surface was only a little affected by rust. He had last seen it in Simla, where he had left it in the bungalow in which they had shared their last leave together. He would have been touched if anyone other than Lavinia had kept it. Perhaps she had anticipated its potential, even then.

He had considered opening his wrists, but was afraid the vessels would close too soon. He had heard that when cutting the throat most made the mistake of severing the windpipe, which

304

did not bring death. The thing was to go for the vessels at the sides; the great jugular vein, which drained the brain's blood back to the heart: the carotid artery, which pumped it to the brain. He took the blade, and cut firmly in against the left side, then the right. It was hurtful but not so much as he had anticipated. He lay down on the pallet and let the blood begin to flow, massaging the place now and again with his fingers to give the seeping stuff more volume. It was dripping now; he began to feel faint. If only he could be dead before they came!

Man has only eight pints of blood. He had lost them before the warder came to release him for the exercise half-hour. His face was pale and peaceful, like a child's. There was nothing to be done; he was already dead. The warder straightened. There would be trouble for someone, probably himself. This kind of thing wasn't encouraged. Someone else could have the cell, perhaps Number 124 with the broken nose; they would have to clear up all that blood, scrub it out with carbolic. The exchange wouldn't be popular; the men didn't like a suicide, any more than they liked the morning a man was going to be hanged. He must make his report before seeing to the exercise file; he went out, locking the door. Jack lay alone and peaceful, the closed lips almost smiling. It had been the right answer.

"I should like to see the cathedral," said Susanna Pelosi. She had put on weight with the lack of her customary activity, and was bored. As usual she did not address herself to Mariana but to Angelo, who listened and nodded eagerly; he would have nodded if Susanna suggested going to Khartoum.

"We will go today," he said, "today."

"There is a cold wind," said Mariana. "You will catch a chill." She had no particular objection to an expedition to the cathedral except that she now objected to everything Susanna wanted, suggested, or did. She bitterly regretted bringing this young woman into her home, to turn her only son away from her. It was always Susanna wants this, Susanna that; never his mother.

"We will need money for the carriage," said Susanna.

"Susanna wants money," said Angelo.

Tight-lipped, Mariana counted out the coins of which she still held the purse-strings; that, and the directions for housekeeping, were left to her, or rather she kept them. She handed the coins to Angelo's hated wife and turned away.

305

After they had gone she let her hatred grow; she went about the household tasks absently, her eyes black with bitterness, her brain planning what must happen now; somehow, they must be rid of this young woman. It could be done if she herself were firm enough; there were persons in Milan, as everywhere, no doubt, who catered for this kind of thing. Alma Terranuova would surely know of someone. Mariana herself would say she wanted to kill rats. It was the thing to say; nothing was ever mentioned openly, but it could be done. It could be, and then Angelo would be her own again. She would turn it over in her mind, not hastening it; not today, not tomorrow. One must be careful, naturally. But the thing would be accomplished. She had determined on it.

Susanna and the driver helped Angelo out of the carriage at last and she guided him towards the steps of the many-spired, ornate cathedral, solid in its square. "Look, Angelo," she said, making him stop for breath. "It is beautiful, is it not? Look at the flower-beds. I am glad that we came. You are not cold? Soon we will be indoors."

No, he was not cold; she got him up the steps, stopping often to let him rest, and then when they were inside the building put him in a seat where he could see, and herself walked about; it was beautiful, ancient, ornate. She said a prayer before Our Lady's statue; she asked for help and patience. She had grown very fond of Angelo. He was gentle, kind, and lonely. The saints would help her. She rose from where she had been kneeling, brushing down her black skirts. They were made of taffeta, and not unbecoming; she had made Cousin Mariana take her to a dressmaker recently. One must be firm.

In the organ-loft, the organist started to practise an air from a motet by Pergolesi. The tune started faintly, with few pipes blowing, then grew strong and loud. Angelo waited rapt in his seat, hearing the music. He had not known he loved it so. Great chords burst against his brain, wakening him to himself as if by enchantment; he gaped in his seat, listening avidly, not even remembering Susanna as she walked about the cathedral by herself. All of his life he had loved to hear music, even if it were only an organ-grinder's; now, he was transported. Susanna must bring him here often, when they were going to play such magic. He would like to come to Mass here.

The great chords rolled on, filling the building with sound. Susanna looked back at Angelo to see that he was still quite comfortable; she would not leave him for too long. She saw in fact that he was trembling, and hastened back to be with him. His face was pale and his limbs twitched, as if he were in a convulsion; she knew an instant's alarm, but he did not look at her. The organ played on and finished with a mighty diapason, like the heart of God beating. Angelo gave a little cry and seized hold of her arm. Tears were running down his face. The organ faded into silence and the ordinary, mouse-like noises of the worshippers and sightseers could be heard again. "Do you want to stay, or shall we go back to the carriage now?" she whispered to him, and he turned to her smiling, his poor jutting jaw stilled, his eyes patient.

"I would like to go back now. Stay if you want to, Susanna." He delighted in the sound of her name, using it on every possible occasion. She smiled, shook her head and rose with him on her arm to go out; the organ was still silent, but as they emerged slowly it began to be played again in a small thin, piping tune. Angelo smiled and trembled. He would remember today always. Perhaps they could come back again soon, he and Susanna. He would like very much to come back.

When they returned to the square, the carriage had gone; no doubt the driver had found a better hire. She was disconcerted for a moment; it might be difficult to get another, with Angelo on her arm. She signalled frantically at passing vehicles, while the wind teased them, fluttering the ribbons on her hat, tugging at Angelo's hair. Presently an elegant private carriage drove by, and slowed. A young man leaned out. "May I assist you?" he said, and his quick grey glance took in Susanna, Angelo, and the situation.

She flushed; was it improper to accept such an invitation? She would be glad to get Angelo back to the house, away from the staring crowds. She smiled, nodded, and told the young man the name of the street; he leapt out, assisted her with Angelo, and saw them both safely esconced in the leather-lined, spotless black interior, with its delicate gold-banded paintwork. The carriage bowled off and the young man told them he was a lawyer, named Mario Fabrizio.

"It was kind of you to drive us, *signore*."

"Kind," echoed Angelo, and suddenly he said of his own accord, "Come in, and have wine."

Mario Fabrizio hesitated. He knew sympathy for the girl, so pretty, so wrongfully tied to this pathetic creature by the gold ring on her finger beneath her glove. Yet he had pity for Angelo too; one could not hate him. There must be a story attached; he was too cautious to expect to find it all out in one day.

"I will go now, for you are tired," he said gently to Angelo. Then, bowing to Susanna, "May I, Signora Pelosi, perhaps call during the week? I should like to do so, if you will permit it."

Susanna smiled and invited him; how pleasant to have somebody normal calling at the house, someone who was in touch with the world!

From behind an upstairs curtain Mariana watched, having heard the wheels of the carriage come. She saw them hand Angelo to the door and then the strange young man, who must be up to no good, bend over Susanna's gloved hand as if she were a queen. One would have to ask questions. She let the curtain fall into place, and went back into the room.

In London, William Cosgood was dealing with the problems of notoriety; a rush of customers of the wrong sort had come over the past weeks, mostly to stare at the rich upper-crust store which had been in the newspapers for one reason and another. Such goings-on were an excuse to take a trip into town, and see for oneself; but the goods on display were too dear and not everyone's taste, all those watery greens and yellows; they looked their fill, then moved on to Peter Robinson's, which they understood.

Jake in dudgeon having vacated his house, and gone off with Beatrice and the child to Italy, at least one was rid of that encumbrance; since the matter of Jack had come to a head, William had not been able to like his father-in-law very well. The trial had been expensive in more ways than one. Perhaps Luigi would help the couple in some way; it was doubtful if, even with Beatrice's dowry, there would be very much money. It would certainly be hard on the boy.

Jake and his wife and son had been escorted out of England by no less a person than Laxton, no longer in deep and obsequious mourning now that Luisa had been dead some years. He still, however, wore a black arm-band and an expression of decent grief. He seemed anxious to be helpful and Beatrice, surveying her husband's huddled form on the aft deck, turned to the little man with thankfulness. Her own feelings were a mixture of pity and shock; Jack's death had been dreadful, and of course one knew Jake had been, however inadvertently, to blame. Yet he himself seemed to bear no responsibility for the matter and was entirely taken up with his own dismissal by the shareholders. Beatrice felt her love and admiration for her husband dwindle; she would not take time yet to examine her feelings. Laxton talked interminably, amusingly; it helped the voyage to pass.

They had been lent a little house by Luigi meantime, until they could find one to rent. In fact it was the one where Hester Fenton had passed the unhappy years long ago, and it still held an aura of sadness, involving everything and everyone who entered. Beatrice tried to make it home-like by putting out a few of their things; but it was pointless to unpack too much. She took pleasure in the baby boy; he was quiet and amenable, and seemed healthy; but so had the others who had died. One waited and hoped, that was all.

One day a letter came. It was from William's secretary, stiffly written. Maria Cosgood was dead of cholera, and William himself too greatly stricken with grief to write.

"It is the judgment of God," said Jake. Beatrice stared at him. This man was a stranger who could speak so of his dead daughter; she did not know him or love him at all.

Susanna stood by the window, her back turned to Mario Fabrizio's freesias which he had sent yesterday and which were now in a vase, their tiny satin trumpets showing flame, mauve, white, pink, yellow, all emitting delicate scent. Mario himself stood again beside her; they had been playing spillikins when he had come. Angelo still sat farther back in the room, his eyes fixed on the flowers. Mariana had not come in; her ill-wishing could be sensed everywhere, like a miasma. One knew she was watching, perhaps listening at the keyhole. Mario was speaking in a low voice.

"You must believe me when I say that I am your friend, yours and Angelo's. It is advisable that you and he should be protected for both your sakes. I would gladly act as your lawyer if you will permit me."

She glanced at him, her long glance taking in his debonair good looks, the dark smooth hair, the smooth olive skin. "The marriage could be annulled," he murmured, "from what you have told me . . . or rather, not told me."

She flushed. "I am very fond of Angelo. He needs me now; I could not leave him."

"A young woman like you, with all your life ahead of you!"

There would be nowhere for her to go, she was thinking; her family would not receive her. As well stay here, despite the fact that she was beginning to be frightened. There was no reason for it that she could name; only a shadow, flitting always behind her, gone as soon as she turned her head.

He was still talking. Had she, had Angelo made a will? "It is a precaution," she was told. A precaution against what? He had the forms here, he was saying: he had brought them today, in case . . . "I can have them witnessed at the office," he told her. "It is a simple thing."

She watched him passively; she had begun already, during his visits, to lean on such help as he could give her. He sat down at the small table and carefully shifted the spillikins at which they had been playing and the flowers, then began to talk to Angelo, slowly and gently, giving him time to understand. The crisp rustle of the paper sounded presently in the room; Angelo nodded slowly, like a mandarin. "When I die," he said, "I hope to go to God."

"So you shall, I am certain, Angelo; but you would not want Susanna left penniless."

"No," Angelo replied, and showed his discoloured teeth. "Leave the money to Susanna." He looked at her and clapped his hands like a child. "Everything to Susanna."

"Your mother already has an annuity by the terms of your father's will, you say, and is unlikely to outlive you." It was fair to say all this to him, for he would understand, if it were put simply enough. Susanna stood and listened for the sound of Mariana at the door; but there was silence. Perhaps she had decided to stay upstairs.

The sound of the scratching quill came; Angelo had signed laboriously, his tongue protruding between his lips. Mario added the date and, without any demonstrable air of triumph, folded away the paper.

Susanna laughed. "I have nothing to leave," she said. If she had, she was thinking, it would be pleasant to leave something to Annina, to help her make a good marriage.

"You will have this," Mario said, and tapped the paper Angelo had signed. Presently he made her sit down and sign another. She knew that he thought of her as outliving Angelo. After that, she would be free.

A woman who had once been beautiful had visited them in the previous week. Time had drained Olympia Massini's flawless skin and deposited ugly brown rings about her eyes; she had long lost her figure, which these days resembled a sausage. It was difficult to recognise Luigi's first *bella amore* of long ago. She drank sweet coffee now, her little finger lifted, and ate a great many small sugared cakes from the confectioner's. Mariana said little; she and the woman had already come to an agreement. "It will cost you something," the creature said, when Mariana had made clear what she wanted.

"No doubt. How much will it cost?"

"Five hundred thousand lire."

"*Madre mia*! That is a great deal of money. I do not think—"

"If you are unwilling to pay, we can forget the matter. It contains certain risks for me; not everyone would undertake it."

"No, no, it can proceed," said Mariana hastily; she had no desire to let the woman go free now, gossiping no doubt about the town. If the thing were done, the *signora* would have to keep silent, for her own sake. "You are certain not to fail?" she asked, her flat gaze surveying the figure Olympia made; her life had not been successful, evidently; nothing would ever be traced to her. Olympia smiled on with closed lips, looking down into the grounds of her drained cup.

"I have never failed yet," she told Mariana, unsmiling.

Susanna was surprised when her mother-in-law accepted an invitation for them both to eat supper with Signora Strozzi, as Olympia now was. It was unlike Mariana to go anywhere; and Angelo had not been invited. "Alma will come to sit with him," said Mariana. "Our hostess is poor; two guests are enough."

So they set out, on the night in question; the house was near enough for them to walk. A humid heat hung over the city; Susanna longed for a refreshing gallop on horseback, out into the open country. Such a thing could never be suggested here. She was growing fat. Soon there would be nothing left of her as she used to be; the wife of Angelo was a different person from hoydenish Susanna Bondone, gentler no doubt, less active, less demanding, unfashionably dressed. Her family would laugh at her if they saw her now. "But Fabrizio does not seem to care," she told herself. She had deliberately refused to allow her mind to call the lawyer Mario. She was glad of his support, that was all. She had made Angelo say over and over again, "My lawyer is Mario Fabrizio." He could remember names.

They came to the house, which was unpretentious, with a curtain behind the door. There was a smell of stew with mushrooms in it. Olympia came and led them into a low-ceilinged room, containing a deal table and two benches. The stew bubbled on the stove, in an iron pot. It might have been a peasant's dwelling; there was nothing in it that was not essential, as if the owner could if required go quickly away, leaving no trace.

They sat down at the table and Olympia served them with stew and pasta, giving Mariana her plate first; then she turned her back and ladled out Susanna's, quickly shaking a dark dry powder into the mess and stirring it in with a finger, to mix it thoroughly. Her own food waited already in a dish on the stove; she served Susanna and then brought her own.

"We will say grace before meat," she said.

The pain did not start until after Susanna had come home with Mariana, till after she had gone to bed beside Angelo in the room they still shared. When it began she dragged herself out on to the landing, not to wake or disturb him. It was the most appalling agony she had ever felt in her life; a gripping, twisting horror, as though a hand squeezed at her intestines and wrung them like a sponge, pitilessly.

She tried to vomit; presently it came, and having voided it she crawled back into the room to try and sleep. It must have been the mushrooms; Elisabeth, her father's wife, always said one should never trust them. How wise . . . but the pain was here again, gripping, implacable. She had never imagined such pain.

Angelo was told next day to keep away from her; Mariana told him it was a fever he must not catch. On the second day, after Susanna had vomited continually for forty-eight hours, she called the doctor. Susanna was already past speech. "I am afraid of cholera," Mariana said. "No, she has eaten nothing."

She had cleared up the vomit and excrement. There was no

sign of what it could have been. The doctor looked at both women in sympathy; the younger was clearly dying. Good Signora Pelosi was a faithful member of the Church, and she would take comfort and would comfort her son. "You should send for the priest," he told her.

Susanna died on the evening of the second day. The funeral was not well attended on account of the cholera rumour. Angelo was not forced to come; he was bewildered, hurt; he had been told Susanna had left him.

One person who had attended the funeral went back with them to the house; he was uninvited; it was Mario. He stood and faced Mariana Pelosi, none of the ready sympathetic speeches always made to mourners passing his lips. His grey eyes sought the woman's flat ones; they were stern and accusing. "I must have a word with you," he said, "and I will see your son."

"Angelo can see no one," she told him. "Say what you have to say, and go. You are not welcome here; in future you need not come. But no doubt—" she smiled dreadfully, showing her few black teeth—"no doubt your reason for coming is no longer what it was." She did not, he was thinking, pretend any grief for Susanna; at least there was that.

"I will tell you what I came to say, which is that I believe you killed your daughter-in-law," he said softly. "If I cared to make trouble I could have her body examined for poison, which I believe she was given, probably in her food. Then you would be in grave trouble, *signora*. But I will not make that trouble, less for your sake than for your son's. Now I will see him, and in the future I will call to see him often, and you will permit that I do so whenever I choose."

All expression had fled from her eyes and face; it might have been a mask. "You may go upstairs," she said. She heard him go out of the room and the sound of his footsteps ascending. Suddenly she went to a mirror and beheld herself. There was no danger; she looked only like a woman who has received a great shock, and is in grief. She raised a hand to where there was a lump in her breast; it had come there lately, but she would not pay a doctor. She recalled herself to what she had been thinking previously and let her hand drop. One need only go on as usual.

313

Mario comforted Angelo and told him that Susanna was dead. "You did not think she would go and leave you? All her life was lived for you. Do you remember how she used to play with you, take you out in the carriage? She loved you very much, Angelo. Never forget her."

Angelo was sobbing. "I will never forget—never, never, never—"

Mario looked at the poor creature and a picture rose in his mind of Susanna's white fingers piling the spillikins; the two of them building castles, forever castles, in the pink and yellow sticks, always letting Angelo win in the end when they all fell down. Now all the castles had fallen; nobody would build them again.

Next time he called there was no one at home. They had gone into the country, a neighbour told him; nobody could say when they would be back.

26

Elisabeth and her husband Filippo had come to a calm agreement with one another as they grew older; she went her way, he his. They were however united in pride of their son, the clever and handsome Bimbo, so nicknamed because yet another Filippo in the family might cause confusion. As the boy grew older they began to discuss his future; of course it must be in the firm of Bondone. "He knows," said Elisabeth, who had grown tremendously stout, "the history of art as well as I know the classics," and this statement was not contested by her husband, who had grown wiser with the years. Bimbo also knew how to enjoy life; his presence in the house brought youth, friends, laughter. He was of course spoilt, and knew how to cozen his mother and, still more, his father; Filippo never ceased to be astonished at his own potency in having brought into the world so perfect a specimen. Bimbo's figure on horseback was like Apollo riding out, his curly hair stirred by the wind; they had had stables built on to the house where his favourite mare, Roxana, was kept, with a groom to polish her coat like satin and to feed her with grain. Bimbo was musical; his proud father had had one of the smaller rooms emptied to become a music-room, in which the pianoforte and violincello sat proudly, often used to entertain Bimbo's friends and, sometimes, by arrangement, his elders; though it was noted that Uncle Luigi fretted at having to sit still for so long as it took to perform the advanced pieces Bimbo had perfected. But the boy's chief interest was not music but life itself: pretty girls were observed to fall in love with him wherever he went, even if it were only to Rapallo with his parents for a holiday by the sea. As to that, nothing but the best would be good enough for Bimbo; his mother already cast her eyes over rich and prominent families with presentable daughters for him to consider. But the first thing was his career. Elisabeth had vainly accosted Luigi on the subject on several occasions, but had got no further; he could still snub her when he liked.

"You must go and talk to him," she said at last to Filippo. "It is time there was an agreement. He cannot spend the rest of his life dawdling about waiting for Bondone. You must be firm."

Filippo trembled a little; all his life he had been in awe of his brother, although it was true that none of Luigi's own children could hold a candle to his own son. Finally the day came, and when he reached the office he asked if they might talk privately for a quarter of an hour. He had already decided that this was preferable to settling the matter at the house; business was business. Luigi greeted him formally, pulled out a chair, and handed him a cigar. Filippo came straight to the point.

"My wife is worried," he began, "about our son's future."

"So?" Luigi inhaled his cheroot, blew out smoke carefully in a blue ring, and waited. Filippo grew somewhat red in the face.

"Luigi, the boy is eighteen. It is time that he was started on his career. We had thoughts that by now you would have offered to take him. His results at school have been excellent; his mathematics—"

"I have not offered because I have no intention of offering."

Filippo's colour deepened; the veins throbbed in his neck. "What is that you say? No intention? But we have always thought—"

"What you have thought is not my concern. I have grandsons of my own, for whom places must be kept; and I have promised poor Jake Cray a place for his son."

"That child! He will not be old enough for years! Your own nephew—" He bit back comments on the grandsons, who in his opinion were brainless. "I should not have to plead with my brother," he said. "Your own blood should come before a stranger's child. Why, who are the Crays but descendants of an Englishman who happened to marry Aunt Isotta? Why should you concern yourself with them and not—and not—" He choked; the blood was drumming in his head, alarmingly. Luigi was regarding the ceiling, his smoke-rings following one another in leisurely succession.

"You have spoilt your son," he said. "He is lax and untrustworthy. He would skimp his work and customers could not be sure of him, and neither could I."

"You dare—you dare—"

The air throbbed; suddenly Filippo fell forward. He lay still, his head on the table, the cigar smouldering ridiculously, loose on the wood where it would leave a scar. Luigi scraped back his chair and hurried to his brother. He lifted him in his arms.

"Filippo! Filippo!" But the little man gave no answer. They came in then, hearing the tumult; came in anxious, awed, silent, fearful. It was useless. The tears were already pouring down Luigi's face.

He did all he could to make reparation; it was as if he had promised the dead man everything he asked. He put Bimbo—he must call him Filippo now—in charge of framed drawings and etchings; he was knowledgeable enough and had good taste, and would attend to his work if he were supervised. The real problem was Elisabeth. She began to behave as if the store were hers and even gave orders to the staff when she came in, not waiting to see whether or not they ignored them. Also she was insufferably rude about Luigi's wife. It was a long time now since the young woman Elisabeth had once been had married Filippo because she loved his brother; whatever transmutation her feelings had undergone since then took revenge on Francesca. That lady endured a certain amount of calumny and then, one day when there was a witness present, said quietly, "If you do not withdraw that statement I will sue you for slander," and under orders from Luigi himself Elisabeth did withdraw it. But there was always dislike between her and the paragon who had taken over Luigi's life; Elisabeth herself felt she could have done it so much better.

In Milan, Mariana was still laying plans, and this time she had done it well; she would go back to her own people to find Angelo a wife who could look after him when she died. There was one girl in particular whom she had already thought of; a niece from the poorer branch of the family, one of several sisters, not beautiful nor by now very young, but plump, practical and obedient. She sent for the girl, whose name was Rachele, and put the question to her. There was no difficulty about acceptance; the family would be glad of the money.

Thereafter Angelo's life was purgatory. He was no longer taken for carriage rides after they returned to Milan. Nobody played spillikins with him, and he would pass the time in idly stirring the coloured sticks and watching them fall to the floor. Rachele scolded him for this; she was always scolding, and after Mamma became ill and took to her bed there seemed no limit to what Rachele would do to make him unhappy. Mamma had grown thin and yellow now, a bundle of bones; in the end she died. Angelo wept for Mamma as he had wept for Susanna; she had, after all, loved him after her fashion.

After the death of Mamma things changed for the worse; Rachele's family—how many of them there were, all poor, all greedy for food and wine and money!—would come to the house and eat and drink there, while Angelo sat silently in his place at the table. He said nothing, because nobody would pay any heed if he spoke; they thought, accordingly, that he did not understand, and would speak slightingly of him as if he were not there. It did not matter; he cared for none of them. Often his mind would remember Susanna and the days when he had been happy; tears would fill his eyes and the feasting relatives would scorn him and say that he was a poor idiot. He was not; he understood and he could remember.

Now and again he would be taken to church. He would kneel by the place where they had buried Susanna, saying his prayers, remembering always those for the dead, asking for peace for Susanna's soul and Mamma's. Perhaps soon they would all be together; Angelo himself knew that he must soon die. He felt ill, but did not tell Rachele; she would not care. Sometimes he would keep to his bed, and lie there alone, remembering.

At other times Mario the lawyer visited him; he was his friend, and would sit and chat to him and they would talk of Susanna. Mario had his will. Rachele knew this and had tried to get him to sign another, but he would not, and she had been cross and had stormed, but still Angelo would not; and Mario said he need not and that he, Fabrizio, would see that he was not forced. The will began to seem very important, and almost every day Rachele would remind him of it, but he would not yield; he closed his eyes and remembered Susanna and Mario. With them in his mind he no longer felt alone.

Susanna's younger sister Annina had been married while still very young to an employee of Bondone, well-born enough and able to pay the premium now customary on professional engagement; unfortunately he had turned out to be a philanderer, and Annina was often unhappy. She was a fair-haired, nervous young woman, lacking Susanna's joy in the power of her body, lacking her charm. There had been born two young daughters, who were with their mother when Fabrizio called to explain about the legacy; Annina listened, wept a little, and called the children to her. "It will be good for them both," she said. They were attractive children with a year between them, both dark-haired and dressed in pretty pastel-coloured linen smocks. The elder, Genoveva, smiled up at Fabrizio, already knowing how to attract the attention of a man; she would turn, he thought privately, into a little minx. He left Annina without too much regret; she in no way reminded him of her sister.

Vittorio, the children's father, came in late that night. On Annina's timidly informing him of the visit and the money, he was pleased, and kissed her hair; he was fond enough of her, but his opulent mistress demanded much of his attention. "It will give the girls a dowry," he agreed, and they went in to dinner, after which Vittorio went out again; she saw him go with bitterness. Surely on this night he could have stayed with her? But he would always put his own concerns first. She remembered their betrothal, and how she herself had run trustingly to him, shocking her stepmother who was accustomed to more formal behaviour on the part of a fiancée. Later, Annina had become less impulsive. Vittorio had used her, then abandoned her for one after the other woman; it was the way of the world. At least poor Susanna had not had to endure infidelity from Angelo. Annina crossed herself and said a prayer for her sister's soul. Uncle Luigi must be told of all of it; he visited them occasionally and they him, but lately he had not been well.

Illness in fact made Luigi angry; his body had always been perfect, obedient, glorious, except for his teeth which from the beginning had troubled him. Now he was in bed, lying ignominiously on his stomach; he had been operated on for an anal fistula, and the pain had been agonising; the first time it had not been a success, and there had been another operation, and a third. Between these painful occasions it had come to Luigi that he had heirs; he had sent for his two grandsons, even the younger who was still in petticoats, and had watched them playing about the room. They were handsome boys, better than one would have expected Luigini to get out of that strange silent wife, whose health was never good. He spoke to them occasionally; the elder boy, Luigi, was shy, but the second answered readily, his gold-tipped lashes modestly lowered to his cheeks. He was called

Giuffre. After they had gone Luigi began to plan their future; now that the money was to come to little Annina it might be advisable to marry the two elder boys to her two daughters, Genoveva for Luigi and Maria Luisa for Giuffre. It would be a pity to disperse the family fortune, and to allow the Milan branch of the business to fall into other hands.

He had been assiduous enough about the family. Immediately on his brother Filippo's sudden and regretted death he had sent for the widow and son, and had offered Bimbo his place in the firm, as atonement. The boy had done well enough; so well, in fact, that Luigi had lately bethought himself what more he could do for the younger branch of the family; it came to him that Bimbo must marry Annunziata, his own saucy blonde daughter by Stéphanie. The alternative was the precious Rosa-Maria, Hester's daughter, who should not be married to less than a nobleman. The rest were married already.

He had sent for Elisabeth and her son, and had told them; he could still feel hurt at their reception of the news. Bimbo had burst into tears, and his mother had flown into a rage and stated that she could trace her ancestors from the twelfth century, and was her only son now to marry a bastard? But Luigi had been firm; the young pair would suit each other.

The door opened and his wife Francesca came in, in her black gown, carrying sewing. She asked how he was; made his pillows comfortable, and stayed with him for an hour. He knew that she did so out of duty, not love; her ambition was to save his soul, with the help of priests; she cared nothing for his body. Marriage itself she had received coldly. Marriage! He had had less pleasure from it, all in all, than from his liaison with Stéphanie, or the long-ago romance with Hester Fenton. He thought of Hester sometimes and wondered if she prayed for him still. His love-children were exquisite; he did not regret their begetting. And though Francesca did not love him, she loved his children like a mother.

As for Luigini, the heir, what of him? He would not be capable of controlling Bondone Figli when his father died; it had been necessary to advance other men. Luigini was obedient, terrified—no doubt one had erred in severity with the early tutors, breaking the boy's spirit—and, like his mother, had no talents. It had only lately come to Luigi's notice that his son kept a mistress, a dumpy girl with bad breath, who no doubt made up in warmth what Luigini's wife lacked. Nevertheless the heirs existed; Luigini had done his duty there; there would be no such tragedy over the inheritance as there had been in England. Marcus Cray had been ill-advised not to acknowledge his brilliant eldest son.

The fistula wound stabbed and Luigi turned about on his pillows. Why should a man be humiliated as he grew old? He lacked teeth, lacked love; everything had gone with youth. Hester had loved him, and Filippo and their mother; and the rest? Teresa never; she had no love in her; Carla perhaps. Of her children, Susanna was dead and Annina afraid of him. It would not be long now till his own death, he thought; this degrading illness was the beginning of the end. Had he thought sufficiently of God? All his life he had gone through the prescribed outward motions of the Church's obedience, even to separating from Stéphanie each Easter before their inevitable coming together again in May. That had been like a flame. Now the fires had died and he lay here, an ageing wreck who had best make his peace with God.

He looked at Francesca suddenly; she was coolly drawing the thread through linen for some charity-garment. "Do you ever pray for me?" he asked her.

"Constantly," she replied unsmiling, the light glinting on the moving needle. He smiled a little. "That is good," he said, "continue in your prayers."

She had left him again when Jake Cray was announced, with his wife and son. They had come to enquire for his health; he would as soon not have seen them, for Jake was tedious and Beatrice difficult and domineering these days. He had done what he could to offer them hospitality when they first came out, defeated, from England with their baby boy. He was aware that Jake had expected to be offered a place in Bondone Figli by way of compensation, but Luigi had known the big stupid man would be a liability. "When your son is old enough I will consider him," he had said, not at that time visualising the probability that he himself would no longer, by then, be in a state to consider anything. But he had an affection for the dark-eyed, quiet, obedient child, and would leave instructions in his will accordingly. The trouble was to placate Elisabeth, who would expect the promotion for Bimbo.

Beatrice and Jake came in quietly, their clothes shabby and well worn. Luigi greeted them with the courtesy he seldom failed to summon. Little Jacob was with them and came carefully to the bedside to offer Luigi a box of fruit. "Put it on the table, *caro*," said the sick man, "it is the very thing for me." Afterwards he regretted not having told the child to help himself; no doubt grapes and oranges were rarities in that household. Why did not the Lupo del Pela relatives help? No doubt they had their own troubles. Jake had become very devout, disciplining himself for his former attachments to venery. Perhaps that was why Beatrice was pregnant again. "We hope it will be a little girl this time," she told him. "Jacob would like a sister."

They talked about nothing else notable, except that Cristina Cray was to return to Italy. "She was broken-hearted about Jack's death," said Beatrice clearly, and Luigi listened with a feeling of surprise at her cruelty: it was well known Jake was himself responsible for that suicide. He nodded and sought vainly for some other subject. Jake said nothing. He had the air of a man totally defeated who has withdrawn into himself; his hair was quite grey and his face wrinkled. Of the two, Luigi was thinking, perhaps Jack has won in the end. He remembered the gay, godlike boy for instants, then deliberately said aloud, "You may not have heard that the girl, his mistress, died very shortly after."

"Of a broken heart," said Beatrice. "It is possible."

She would spare her husband nothing. They left shortly, and Luigi settled himself to try to sleep.

In Milan, Angelo Pelosi was dying. The withered form on the bed seemed as if life had left it long ago, indeed had hardly dwelt there; this bag of thin bones had been thrown together by chance, by blind cruelty. His head was quite bald now and to keep the cold from it, they had put him in a knitted skull-cap; the fleshless nose jutted below, and the eyes were closed beneath papery lids of the texture of pressed dried flowers. His breathing hardly lifted the covers and it would be difficult to tell when it stopped.

There were not many in the room. Rachele was there, importantly. It could not be long now, she was thinking. She would be glad of her freedom. Perhaps, now there was some money, she would marry again. She was entitled to a widow's portion by law, however she might have failed in acquiring the whole.

The doctor hovered about the dying man, unwilling to leave.

322

Keeping Angelo alive had been like experimenting with some delicate exotic animal or reptile, and he still sought for ways of prolonging the experience, but could think of none; the patient was dying of senile decay at thirty-seven. At the other side of the bed a nurse sat; she had been sent for a month ago. On the near side knelt Mario Fabrizio, the lawyer, who during all these years had treated Angelo as a friend to be visited, to be kept from ultimate torment of the mind. His hair was thinning now and his face had grown heavier; he had the sleek air of success but was still a bachelor. His eyes were sombre as he watched Angelo die. It would not be long now; despite them all, he himself would stay till the end. Suddenly the sick man's eyes opened, fixing themselves upon him.

"Fabrizio." Oddly, he had never used the simpler Christian name. Mario reached out a hand and grasped the thin cold fingers.

"I am here, Angelo. I will not leave you." But the priest was waiting with the viaticum; whatever sins poor Angelo had to confess must be given absolution. Mario himself could not stay with him for that; but he would remain in the house.

"The will," breathed Angelo. "You have my will?"

"I have it safe, never fear."

Rachele bustled forward; she had never ceased in her attempts to force Angelo to sign a fresh will. "He wasn't of sound mind," she said in her loud voice. "He was influenced. Any existing will is invalid." The other lawyer whom she had tried to introduce had told her of that phrase; it sounded well.

Mario looked up at the plump high-coloured bully of a woman; it was a miracle that Angelo had kept any of his concerns his own. "His mind is as sound as mine or yours, *signora*," he told her. "He must take things slowly, that is all."

"Slowly! I've nursed him, coddled him for years. I ought to know he's an imbecile."

Mario ignored her and turned back to the bed. "Angelo, think for one moment, and then you shall be left in peace," he said softly. "It is about the money you are leaving, the Pelosi money. Your wife Rachele will receive her lawful portion. Would you like the rest to go to her also, or to Susanna's sister as the present will says?" He waited. The capped head turned with an effort, raising itself like a tortoise emerging from its shell. "Susanna," Angelo whispered. "I am going to Susanna and to God."

"And the will you have already signed contains your wishes?"

"Yes," he said on a long sigh. His head fell back on the pillows and he did not speak again. The priest made a sign for everyone to go out. Through the closed door afterwards his voice could be heard murmuring the prayers for those in danger of death. After a time of silence he opened the door. "It is done," he said, as Christ had said it at the end. The dead man lay peacefully, his face at rest. Mario Fabrizio made the sign of the cross. Why had Angelo lived at all? No one would ever know.

27

On her son's ninth birthday Beatrice Cray stretched her limited means and hired a carriage to take him and his little sister Louise into the mountains, first to visit the convent and later to romp in Nardini woods. She took a flat basket with cold food and watered wine. It was a fine day and, when they drove in at the pillared stone entrance, she thought at first that things had changed little here, unlike town.

She left the basket with the driver and, taking a child in each hand, pulled the rasper on the great door. They were expecting her and the porteress came without delay.

"*Madama*! You are welcome. And this is the little boy? A fine fellow." She led them along cool dark passages to the parlour, where they would be given almond biscuits and sweet wine while they waited for the Mother Superior. Presently the grille curtain was pulled back and she was with them, a nun in attendance behind her, a very old thin woman whom Beatrice did not know.

"This is Sister Assunta," the Superior said. "She was a pupil here when your husband's mother was at school." They knew all about family relationships in the convent, the Bondone, the Pelosi and Villaverde, the di Lupo del Pela. The Superior smiled at little Jacob, who was regarding her with robin-bright eyes. "How old are you, my child?" she asked.

"Nine years, *madama*." He had been brought up strictly, and made no attempt to show off as many children do. Louise was asked her age, and whether she said her rosary. She hid shyly behind her mother's skirts, her dark eyes peeping out; she was only six years old. "Answer when you are addressed," said Beatrice gently, and put her beside the grille. The Superior brought the other nun forward.

"I will leave Sister Assunta to speak to you of old days. It is good to see you, *signora*, and your children. We will pray for you in the chapel, and for your husband's soul."

Beatrice closed her eyes for instants; she had not yet recovered from Jake's death. Of late years they had grown close again despite everything, and when he had died at last she was both desolate and poor. Her dowry had not been soundly invested; no matter. A new voice sounded behind the grille, the voice of a very old woman.

"The *signora* will not remember me, for I was a pupil in the convent long, long before she was born," said Sister Assunta. "I am the oldest religious in the house. I remember Isotta Bondone well, oh, very well." She gave a little, almost youthful giggle. "She was naughty. She used to escape from among us in the drawing-class to go and meet her lover, the young Count Nardini. The whole school knew of it and said nothing. She was married shortly after. I remember her well, so pretty, and such a minx. They say she grew into a devoted wife."

Beatrice smiled and recalled the old secret she had suspected long ago, the day of her betrothal, when she had not gone in the boat with the rest and instead had found the portrait of Felice Nardini hanging in the great house with Cristina Cray regarding it. Truth took strange forms, yet triumphed in the end. Jake had been a true Cray. Their son was so also.

She talked for a time in her gentle way with the wrinkled erstwhile classmate of Isotta—what had her name been?—and then said farewell, laying the small glasses and the empty plate which had held the little biscuits on a side table. Jacob and Louise had eaten all the biscuits. That was not polite; some should have been left. She would speak to the children when she got them outside. For now, she left a message of goodwill to the Superior. "I should like to show the children the chapel," she said, on leaving. The public entry was separate; but it was better to ask.

They went into the chapel and knelt before the Blessed Sacrament, which was exposed. Behind a wrought-iron screen at the further end nuns prayed, one taking the other's place at intervals, all through the days and nights. The di Lupo del Pela endowment had been for perpetual adoration. Beatrice prayed for a little, then wandered round the memorials in front, quietly showing the children where the family used to kneel, and pointing to the tablet on the wall which commemorated Countess Ildefonsa. "She was your great-great-aunt by marriage," she murmured, and smiled at the complicated connection. Presently they went out into the sunlight and drove down to Nardini woods.

She had not asked if she might come today, and knew nothing

of what had happened to the house of late years. In fact it had been bought by a stockbroking syndicate, who used it occasionally for shooting. The pines were as always, dark and cool; the sun brought out their scent, and the cicadas rasped as they had always done; and there was the blue lake. Jacob laughed with pleasure and began to run towards it, followed by Louise who copied him in everything; Beatrice came on more slowly. By the time she reached the water's edge the children had been stopped by a man in a faded green jacket, perhaps a gamekeeper. "The grounds are not public, *signora*," he said coldly. "You must go."

"I am sorry," she said. "It is my son's birthday. I used to come here when I was a girl; it belonged to my cousin." She began to turn away, taking the two children with her. Behind them on the lake there bobbed a new, brightly painted and varnished boat, and the boathouse had been pulled down and rebuilt. Nothing was the same.

The gamekeeper pulled at his lip; this lady in black clothes was—well, she was a lady, and his employers were not here at present. "By all means look about, if you wish, *signora*," he said. "We have to stop most people, the world and his wife, you know the kind of thing; but God knows you're no trouble; the children are quiet. Happy birthday, lad. Look about before you go."

They thanked him and walked up to where the house stood, cleared now of its clambering roses; these had been taken away and the garden was an impersonal square of short foreign emerald grass, well tended. The shutters had been painted white and the front door replaced; it was shut, and she would not be able to go in and see whether the young Count's portrait still hung in its place. Perhaps it was as well; one could not go back in time. She took the children's hands and led them back to the carriage, and they drove away.

28

The last foregathering of the entire Bondone clan was for the double wedding in 1908 of Carla's granddaughters and Luigi's grandsons. Luigi himself, aged but not yet grey-haired, with his missing teeth giving his jaws the determination of a nutcracker, was the centre of attention, even outshining the two young brides; women in the modish S-shaped silhouette, elaborate flowered or feathered hats pinned to their heads, surrounded him, anxious for a word of approval from the famed connoisseur. But the talk hushed with the coming of the brides into church, shy and clad in white satin, simply; their mother's taste was good. Annina herself, watching Vittorio lead in his daughters, was unsure whether to laugh or weep; she would be losing her children, but at least they had made good marriages. Genoveva, her dark eyes demure, sailed up the aisle with a dignity notable despite her tiny height; Maria Luisa, who was taller, had less confidence. Their bridegrooms awaited them, young Luigi with a glint of avidity in his narrow dark eyes; he had long coveted Genoveva and had not been permitted to find out anything about women; he looked forward to tonight. Giuffre, his younger brother, likewise watched little Maria Luisa, who seemed to be in a difficult mood; her lips were pursed and she would not look at her bridegroom. But the vows were made without difficulty; neither bride would have had the courage necessary to defy Uncle Luigi, as their mother herself had lacked it. As for Vittorio, he was jubilant; rich bridegrooms for both his daughters, without the wearisome necessity of taking them about socially! He disliked responsibility and would devote his time henceforth to his mistress.

Afterwards there was a cold collation, with wine flowing. Genoveva fluttered about on the arm of her groom, roguishly parrying the sallies of the guests; she was already known for her repartee and her company was never dull. Maria Luisa was quieter; she was, in fact, frightened. Mamma had hinted to her that the duties of a wife were not always pleasurable, and she had a stubborn resolve not to let Giuffre have his way tonight; she had been bullied into the marriage. Genoveva likewise said little to her groom. She listened to the old woman, some connection named Signora Cristina, saying that she and her sister were almost all that were left of the House of Cray. That was in any case in England, and was not interesting. As well, there were two poor Cray relations; young Jacob, who was too serious to attract a girl, and Louise, who had been her sister's train-bearer. Louise was prettier than Genoveva and must not be permitted to steal the occasion; afterwards, when there was dancing, everyone applauded her and Jacob, saying how delightful it was to see a brother so devoted to his sister. Genoveva pouted a little and flounced her satin skirts in the waltz. After all it did not matter; she was the bride, and Louise Cray was too poor for anyone to want to marry her.

Afterwards they drove off, and Maria Luisa put into effect her resolve, causing young Giuffre to complain bitterly; next day she was persuaded as to her duty, and on the second night everything was as it should be. Perhaps the girl had had a premonition of what her marriage would be like; Giuffre had the Bondone temperament, and never in all their time together left her alone. She would die at twenty-four, having left one living child.

Genoveva's husband had meantime leapt into bed with her, so swiftly that old Luigi, who had been waiting at the door to give the pair his blessing, was turned back. Like his brother the young man had not been permitted to know women, and he concentrated all his affection and all his lust, which was considerable, on his wife. She endured it, as there was no option; but she liked best to escape from him and go to Signora Francesca and Uncle Luigi and make them laugh. The old pair loved her and encouraged her visits. Genoveva bore her husband two sons, one a year older than the other; the little boys were strong and normal, and Luigi had no worries about the future of Bondone Figli.

He had tried to keep his promise to the dying Jake Cray by taking his son into the business, but in fact Jacob had not the knack of pleasing customers; he was too shy. After two years of near-failure he asked to be released from his contract, and set out for England, which he had heard of from his father and mother. If there was a war, which would surely happen soon, he would enlist, and become a soldier. His English was good; he and his father had always spoken it together.

His sister Louise was to die of typhoid fever on her brother's first furlough, leaving their mother Beatrice disconsolate. After that Beatrice spent much of her time as a guest in the hill convent which had once sheltered Isotta; she found peace there. When she died, of long and agonising cancer, she left her few possessions divided between the convent and her son. There was one item the nuns were overjoyed to see again; the *croce*. No one enquired as to how or why Jake Cray had brought it abroad with him. The tumult by then in the world ensured that its whereabouts would be ignored, and it was put back in the place from which long ago Isotta had brought it at the bidding of Enrico Bondone.

The English firm of Cray did not fare well. After the death of William Cosgood—he did not live to be old and latterly spent more and more time alone at his beloved Longhouses—the management was given to Annie Cray's stupid husband Williamson, who held it till he died. Oddly, that was a time of prosperity, with an upsurge of young artists bringing in work which later would become famous. It was the last flare of a dying flame. The Williamson Smith couple's only son—there had been a long history of dead children—died of brain-fever before his twelfth birthday. His mother took no more joy in life and was in complete subjection to Sally, her domineering friend, until they quarrelled; afterwards another woman ruled her. The shares continued to show profit, and when Annie and her husband were dead at last there was some doubt about who should be asked to succeed as the head of the English branch, with its once-varied history of family control; but there were no Crays left in England. Young Jacob was suggested by a few, but his youth was against him, also the fact that he had been brought up as a foreigner—everyone was becoming consciously insular by then—and had not in any case shone during his time with Bondone Figli. So the inheritance went to Selina's son, George Røs. He promptly sold out his commission, modified his name and sailed for England, though he knew very few words of the language even yet. He was still not an appealing person although he had authority; it was an open secret that his wife had been locked up in an asylum in Sweden for many years. Ironically, Selina Røs herself had not lived to see the day when the House of Cray would be taken over; she had pinned all her hopes on the event and lived to be eighty-four, and then was found dead in her summer-house, a letter which she had been reading from her niece Elisabeth by her.

The war came, and brought tragedy to others besides Bondone Figli; but theirs was notable enough.

Genoveva had spent the first years of her marriage in giddy flirtation, avoiding her young husband when she could; she took no pleasure in his constant craving for her. She had had two miscarriages before her first son was born, and called Luigi; later there was another miscarriage, and whether it was due to the assiduous lovemaking of Genoveva's husband or to her own hectic way of life, nobody knew. Luigi and Francesca Bondone were too old to try to control her; she dazzled them, like a butterfly with bright wings.

With the war, however, Genoveva settled down; she began to help Francesca with Red Cross work, rolling bandages and knitting and packing comforts for the troops, consoling war widows, looking after soup-kitchens. Everyone noticed the change in her; and with young Luigi away with his regiment she took her rightful place as mistress of Bondone Figli, that old-established, almost unique firm.

Young Luigi came home on a brief leave. Some days later, Genoveva fell ill. The doctor diagnosed influenza, the new and dreaded scourge which had lately decimated more populations than the war. Genoveva did not recover.

They covered the body with flowers. But more deaths followed. In the shock which followed his young wife's death the bereaved husband had caught the infection. He died without regret; his life, he was heard to murmur on his deathbed, would have been useless without Genoveva.

Their children were left, too young to understand what had happened; they had their nurse, their governess. The double funeral took place amid scenes of such mourning that it might have been for the news from the front. Missing in the church was the dead man's father, Luigini as he was still called; old Luigi's only legitimate son. He had died suddenly of a fever and his plain and devoted mistress, whom he had recently married, was left a widow. No one else mourned him.

There were still the children; hardly had one begun to think of it when the elder boy, aged five, fell ill. He had been pretty and promising; and he died. One baby, one only, was left now to inherit, if he might, the glories of Bondone Figli. Old Luigi sent for him at last and took him in his arms. But the little boy cried for his nurse, a peasant woman who had saved him from death by taking him to her own cottage and keeping him warm, well fed and solitary. Old Luigi handed him back to the woman and sadly saw him go. He was mercifully not to know that in the child, his great-grandson, lay the seeds of death for Bondone. The last Luigi as a man would squander everything on yachting, women, pleasure, bringing bankruptcy and failure in the years before the Second World War.

But all that was still to come; and there was only Bimbo left to take charge now till the boy grew up; or else lame Bobo, Luigi and Stéphanie's bastard son. Bobo and Bimbo, baby-names, apt; in a way neither was adult, both had been spoiled, pampered, denied responsibility. Luigi knew he had lived too long.

The old man considered the dilemma in his clear mind. He knew well enough that his own prejudice had somewhat excluded Filippo's son even after Filippo's death. Yet there was good, even brilliance, in the young man, even though his forced marriage had been, predictably, a failure; in fact Bimbo seldom saw Annunziata except to give her a child a year, and kept his women and boys in Florence. As for Bobo, he was chaste enough, unnaturally so; nobody liked him except old Francesca, who doted. Her word as a rule carried some weight, but old Luigi knew that his bastard son was volatile, even weak; he might not have the ability and steadiness to carry on the firm without Bimbo, and the two loathed each other.

Luigi set his toothless jaws. Filippo's son must, after all, be left in charge of everything; he himself had done all he might and must soon die, full of grief. How much of beauty and good living had been lost in the war! The show-rooms, once so crowded, were empty now; a Red Cross committee of which Genoveva had been president occupied the office and, beelike, worked daily in the rooms to the subdued hum of talk. Nobody had time for pictures, pleasure, culture; there was only life and death. What would it be like when the war was over? Once he would have gone towards peace with an eager enquiring mind, a heart full of hope; but now he could only conserve, dully. Memories were everything; he remembered Carla more clearly than her grand-daughter now; but how dearly he had loved the pretty, giddy child Genoveva had been! She had almost renewed his youth;

now it was gone into darkness, she in her coffin, beside her husband who should have been his heir. "The young die, all the young, and the old live on," he mumbled aloud, and Francesca raised her grey head to hear what he was saying; it needed no reply and she fell silent. His mind wandered to consider Giuffre, the younger grandson, and his wife in Milan; there was trouble there too. They must deal with it themselves; he had no more strength left in him.

He had lately made his will again and had it read over; as he had foreseen, Francesca was not pleased. Her darling Bobo had relied on her when he was a little weak child with his leg in irons; was he to have nothing, to be forgotten? "You care nothing for me or him," she said bitterly. But Luigi pretended not to hear; his mind by now was made up.

It was the third winter of the war when Luigi died. He might have lived even longer, but gangrene had set in after a slight graze on his leg where he had caught it against some furniture. He died bravely, uncomplaining about the pain.

It seemed as if a world had come to an end, even with the war. Francesca hardly waited for the burial to take herself off as a *pensionnaire* to a convent. She was to live there many years, but longest of all was the life of the enclosed nun who had once been Hester Fenton. She lived into the thirties of the new century, and died at eighty-seven.

Bimbo meantime continued to administer the wartime fortunes of Bondone Figli with cynical, but sometimes brilliant, success. The shadow of Luigi lay on him a little, but he was never given credit for it. He would die in his fifties, in his mistress's bed; by that time, the youngest Luigi of all could look about him.

The war continued, with no sign of an early armistice as had been confidently forecast. Contracts for army equipment, boots, belts, shirts, were snapped up by those firms capable of undertaking them, and foremost among them was the House of Cray in London. They undercut everyone, cheated everyone. A fortune would be made out of shoddy manufacture for the men in the trenches, whose cardboard boots would disintegrate with wet weather.

The second Thursday of the month was always one of intense activity at the House of Cray, with carpet-sweepers and dusters in evidence from early morning. On this auspicious date Colonel

George Cray-Ross paid the store a visit, and if much of the preparation escaped him it did not escape the eagle eye of the managing director, or on a lesser level, the floor managers; God help the counter-girl who was late at her place or who had come without the prescribed clean collar and cuffs over her black dress, polished shoes, and tidy hair. The goods still for sale were laid out meticulously, and the special strip of carpet along which the Colonel would walk glowed triumphantly in the hush. All voices, when they were not completely silent, were at least lowered for the occasion.

The Colonel never kept them waiting. Sharp at ten o'clock it would be reported, by a kind of wordless telegraph, that his carriage once, and now his limousine, had approached at a dignified pace down the specially sanded street. The chauffeur sprang out, the Colonel followed, his small spare frame nipping smartly away from the opened door of the car. Left inside was his mistress, fat, thumbed and painted. The inspection began; few could meet the impersonal stare of those small hard brown eyes. Footwear, hardware, ladies' underwear, drapery, haberdashery, carpets, china, and last the paintings, now housed in a very small department, all passed beneath the gaze, latterly somewhat impatient for it was time for the Colonel's lunch. It was a matter of common knowledge that the Colonel did not care for paintings, knew nothing about them, and said so openly, and if he had his way—which he did not in all senses have—the department would be closed down as a waste of time. It did not make a steady profit from its very nature. Only the sentiment of certain of the older directors, and the general feeling of the shareholders that this branch was a very honourable one, having, as it were, been responsible for all the rest since the time of the first Marcus Cray, had saved it time and again. George Cray-Ross finished in the boardroom, where beneath the portrayed gaze of the elder and the younger Marcus, old Jacob, and Isotta in her flame-coloured bows, he would be regaled with brandy and a cigar. Then he went out, each departmental manager walking backwards before him in the same way as the nuns had done before the Mother Superior in an Italian convent long ago. The chauffeur waited at attention—he had been turned down for the army on medical grounds—the Colonel got in, the car started up and drove away along the sanded street, and staff and, no doubt, customers breathed once more and got on with their normal business.

Piccadilly was full of excited crowds; there had just been news of the German air weapon, the Zeppelin. A young man with dark eyes thrust his way between the blocks of jabbering excited people, and made his way towards the gilt Cray sign as it hung waving in the wind. He paused to look in the windows and a young woman handed him a white feather. Jacob said nothing; he was in fact on his way to the nearest recruiting-office, but before then hoped to buy a gift at Cray's for his sister Louise, who did not have many luxuries. He walked between the newly erected hoardings and heard the sound of machines humming in the shop; they were turning out army shirts in khaki. A young assistant—he noted that they were either girls or old men—came up and asked what he wanted. "A length of silk for my sister," he said, "in an apricot colour." That would suit Louise.

"We don't do that kind of thing any more. It's all army contracts now, shirts and boots and the like." The shopgirl stared at him; he was handsome, but a fellow in mufti was no good to her. She turned away and they parted, he to stare for a little time at all he would ever know of the House of Cray. He was not impressed; he could see they were making profit out of the contract by turning out cheap stuff; the boots would wear into holes during the first hour of the muddy march in Flanders.

"Are there any paintings?" he asked the empty air. But that department was now closed down, waiting for the armistice.

He gained the street again and found his way to the recruiting-office. He waited his turn and gave his name, age, qualifications if any; he could write, at least. He signed his name with a quiet flourish; Jacob Cray. It was an old name, of which he was proud. The recruiting-officer scanned it and then, by way of comment, said "Anything to do with them bleeders dahn the street? Proper lot o' sharks, they are."

The dark eyes of the last Cray heir looked back at him. "Nothing," said Jacob. "Nothing at all."